This book is dedicated to Margaret Hamilton—not the witch, but the programmer. Hamilton was NASA's lead software engineer for the Apollo project, and wrote the code that put us on the moon. She wrote a more complicated program than most of us will ever write, with more danger hanging on the outcome than most of us will ever have to deal with, and she did it with tools so primitive she may as well have been using magic. And it worked flawlessly.

Actually, you know what?
This book is dedicated to the witch, too.

"Binary is good for computers because it mimics the way a circuit works," said Marisa, "and computers are made of circuits. So: open and closed. On and off. One and zero. Once you know how it works, you can express anything in ones and zeroes—the entire world is really just a bunch of ones and zeroes, and . . ." She trailed off.

Ones and zeroes.

People who matter, and people who don't.

"You can choose which one you are," said Marisa. She looked at her little sister, staring at her intently—at her face, at her clothes, at her life. At all of their lives, all together. She spoke softly: "Are we going to be zeroes forever?"

"I think you're drunk," said Pati.

"I think I might be," said Marisa. "Because I'm seriously considering destroying a megacorp."

ALSO BY DAN WELLS

THE MIRADOR SERIES

BLUESCREEN

ACTIVE MEMORY

THE PARTIALS SEQUENCE

PARTIALS

ISOLATION
A digital novella

FRAGMENTS

RUINS

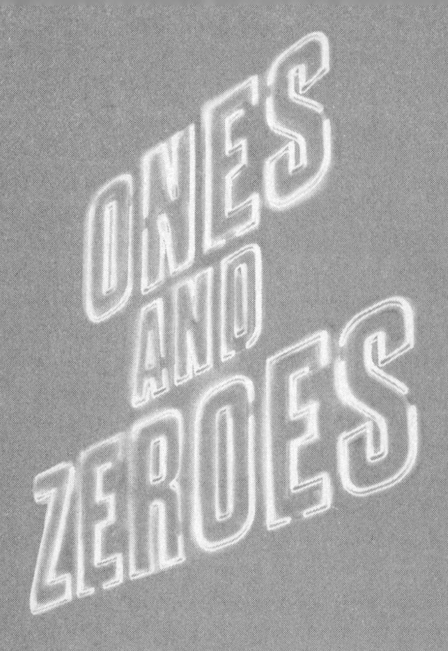

A MIRADOR NOVEL

DAN WELLS

BALZER + BRAY
An Imprint of HarperCollins*Publishers*

Balzer + Bray is an imprint of HarperCollins Publishers.

Ones and Zeroes

www.epicreads.com

Library of Congress Control Number: 2016949509
ISBN 978-0-06-234791-6

Typography by Torborg Davern
17 18 19 20 21 PC/LSCH 10 9 8 7 6 5 4 3 2 1
❖
First paperback edition, 2018

ONE

Mari, where are you? We're about to get swarmed!

Marisa Carneseca grimaced and blinked on the message. **I'll be there as soon as I can,** she sent. **Give me a minute.**

"A minute"? her father sent back. **Our livelihood is failing, with our home itself hanging in the balance, and you need "a minute"?**

Yes, Marisa sent back. **I'm almost done, and then I'll be right there.** She rolled her eyes, then immediately regretted it—the djinni interface could compensate for involuntary eye movement, but a dramatic gesture like an eye roll—and Marisa's eye roll had been as dramatic as she could make it—was as disastrous as a fumbled swipe on a touch screen. Apps and icons swirled across her vision, seeming to scatter to every corner of the swanky cafe she was sitting in. She blinked rapidly on each of them, bringing them back into place. The most important was the list of lunch orders: everyone who placed an order at the Solipsis Cafe left a digital trail, and she had camped on the cafe's network to route all of those orders through her djinni—a supercomputer implanted directly into her brain. Lunch orders ticked by, one every few seconds, on a list that her djinni projected directly onto her eye implants. The list seemed to float in the air in front of her, though of course no one else could see it.

Which was handy, because spying on someone else's network was very illegal.

Marisa found the conversation with her father and pulled it back into the center of her vision. An angry message flashed at the end of it, waiting for a response. **It's the lunch rush, morena,** he'd sent her. **We can't do this without you.**

I know it's lunch, she sent back. **Why do you think I'm here?**

Because . . . you don't want to help with lunch?

Marisa controlled her eye roll this time, instead closing her eyes and clenching her fist in frustration. It was so like her father to put ellipses in a message—she could practically hear his voice pausing in the middle the sentence.

She opened her eyes again and looked down at the cafe table in front of her, and the salad sitting on it. She already felt guilty for being here—her family really did need her for the lunch rush at San Juanito, their family restaurant—and now she felt even more guilty for buying a salad. She hadn't wanted to, but the cafe wouldn't let her stay otherwise. She looked at the wall beside her—right on the other side of it, barely three feet away, the Solipsis Cafe server sat on a desk, oblivious to her infiltration. A direct hack would have been too easy to detect, which was why she needed to be so close—she wasn't logged in to their network, she was literally just reading the wireless signals as they flew through it. She glanced at the order list again, hoping the one she needed would pop up before her father went apoplectic. Still nothing. At least her father hadn't looked up her location yet—

You're downtown? her father sent her. **You'll never make it back in time!**

Marisa looked at the ceiling, shaking her head. GPS locators were part of the parental controls her parents had enabled when they'd purchased her djinni in the first place—just like they had with all of her siblings. Marisa had circumvented most of the parental controls years ago, but she had to be careful about the really obvious ones, like location, where it was way too easy to be caught in a lie. And their punishment would be swift and merciless—they'd even turned her djinni off once, leaving her completely disconnected from everything. She shivered again at the memory of it. Someday she'd be able to pay for her own service plan, and then she could do whatever she wanted, but she was nowhere near being able to afford that now.

She could barely afford this salad.

Not only are you downtown, sent her father, **you're at the Solipsis Cafe!**

I know, she sent back.

Their salads cost ten yuan! We can't afford sixty-dollar lunches!

I know!

Did you use my account to pay for this?

Papi—

You come home right now, muchacha.

And waste this salad? she shot back. **It cost me sixty dollars!**

He didn't respond for a few seconds, and Marisa knew he was probably ranting out loud at whoever was close enough to hear him—her mother, certainly, and any of her siblings already roped into a shift at San Juanito. Which would be all of them, she thought, because only Problem Child Marisa would be terrible enough to run off during the lunch rush on a Saturday. She sneered at her uneaten salad, then speared a pepper with her fork and shoved it petulantly in her mouth. Her eyes went wide in surprise.

"Santa vaca, that's delicious," she said out loud, then immediately looked around to see if anyone had heard her. Most of the other diners were staring blankly into space, reading or watching things on their djinnis, but one man in a business suit eyed her strangely. Marisa turned back to her salad, wishing she could curl up and disappear.

Another message popped up in her djinni, from Sahara this time—Marisa's best friend and VR gaming teammate. **Where are you?**

Hell, Marisa sent back.

No, I already looked there, sent Sahara. She lived above the restaurant, renting the apartment from Marisa's parents, which made it easy for her to pop in and out. **Your dad's practically spitting nails.**

Careful, sent Marisa. **Pop in too often and he'll make you wait tables.**

Wouldn't be the first time he's tried, sent Sahara.

Your ID hasn't moved, sent Marisa's father. **Why aren't you moving? You're supposed to be on the train coming home RIGHT NOW. Or was I not clear?**

Marisa closed his message and looked back at the scrolling list of lunch orders. **I'm downtown,** she sent to Sahara. She took another bite of her salad. **This is the most expensive stakeout I've ever done, but holy crap is it delicious.**

Solipsis? asked Sahara.

Of course.

I've never eaten there.

A waiter nuli hovered nearby—basically just a watercooler with four rotor blades and a sensor. It pointed this sensor at Marisa's glass, decided she needed a refill, and dispensed a squirt of cold water before flying on to the next table.

I'm eating the roast pepper salad, sent Marisa, taking another bite. **The peppers are okay—honestly Dad's are better—but the salad dressing is amazing.**

How amazing can it be? sent Sahara. **It's salad dressing.**

Marisa picked up the little plastic cup the dressing had come in and dribbled more of it onto her vegetables. **It's like a baby koala saw its mother for the first time, and its tears of joy dripped down through a rainbow, and angels kissed every drop before laying them gently on my salad.**

That's the most unsanitary description of food I've ever heard, sent Sahara.

Trust me, sent Marisa, **eat here once and you'll want koala tears in everything you eat forever.**

Moving on, said Sahara. **You think you'll find him?**

Marisa said nothing, staring at the list of orders. "Him" in this case referred to Grendel, a hacker from the darkest corners of the net. He was a criminal, and a dangerous one, though Marisa's interest was more personal. She looked at her left arm—completely mechanical from the shoulder down. She'd lost it in a car accident when she was two years old, and the cause of that accident—they were virtually unheard of now that cars were self-driving—was only one of the unanswered questions about that day. The even bigger mystery was why she'd been in that particular car at all—the car of Zenaida de Maldonado, the wife of the biggest crime boss in Los Angeles. She'd had two of her sons and Marisa strapped in the back. Why had Marisa been there? Why had Zenaida turned off the autopilot? And when Zenaida died in that accident, why did her husband blame Marisa's father?

Marisa had never met anyone who claimed to know the truth about that day fifteen years ago—except Grendel. She and her friends had tangled with him a few months ago, and Marisa had been hunting him ever since, finally tracking him to an IP address. It was the only lead she had, and if she was going to follow it any further she needed to be here, right now, watching these lunch orders.

Another popped up. And another one.

But not the one she needed.

You gonna be ready for practice tonight? sent Sahara.

Should be, Marisa sent back absently. **If Papi doesn't cut off my Overworld privileges for missing work today.**

You're the heart of the team, sent Sahara, which wasn't

really true, but it was nice of her to say. Marisa smiled but never took her eyes off the order list. Another message flashed from her father, but she closed it without reading.

I want to try a new strategy tonight, sent Sahara. **Double Jungle. Keep you on the top, pretending to defend Anja, while she goes down to help Fang power through the sewers and hit the enemy vault, swift and fierce.**

I've read about some European teams trying that, wrote Marisa, **but they're always trying crazy—**

She stopped in mid-sentence, sending the message without thinking and focusing all her attention on the list of orders. One had just come in from KT Sigan.

I know it sounds crazy, sent Sahara, **but you never know what's going to work until you try it.**

I've got one, Marisa sent back. She blinked on the order and pulled up the details.

Nice, sent Sahara.

It didn't matter who the order had come from, only that it was an employee of KT Sigan. Sigan was one of the largest telecom companies in the world, providing internet service to millions of people around the world—including the IP address Marisa had linked to Grendel. If she could get inside their system, she could find out who he was, and where he was, not just online but in the real world. It would be the biggest break she'd had yet in her hunt for him. But hacking an international telecom was no simple matter, and dangerous to boot, so Marisa had started with the cafe: their cybersecurity was way lower, and if you were patient, you could get all kinds of information.

Such as the security code of a Sigan employee ordering lunch.

Marisa read the details of the order: it had come from someone named Pablo Nakamoto, who'd requested a chicken Caesar salad, and listed the delivery address as Port 9, on the third floor of the KT Sigan building. Somewhere in the back of the cafe's kitchen a chef was tossing together a salad, and filling up a little cup of salad dressing, and packing it all in a plastic box, and then a delivery nuli would zoom across the street and up to Port 9, where Pablo Nakamoto would take it and eat in his cubicle. Hidden behind the order was the good stuff: his financial information, which was encrypted, and the server path his request had followed to get here, which wasn't. Marisa followed this path backward to the source, finding not only his ID but the security code the server had used to process it. It was just a couple of numbers—a long string of ones and zeroes—but it was enough. Marisa could use it to log in to KT Sigan's system, masquerading as Nakamoto, and find everything she needed.

Another red icon popped up in her vision: her father was calling again.

Marisa clenched her teeth, staring at the security info, desperate to follow it . . . but saved the information to a note file and closed her cafe connection. The Sigan server would still be there later that night, but her family needed her now. She boxed up her salad, taking a last lick of the delectable dressing, and ran out the door.

TWO

Marisa collapsed on her bed, exhausted. For most of Marisa's life they'd lived in the apartment above their restaurant, where Sahara lived now, but a few years ago they'd managed to save enough money to buy a bigger house a mile or so away, and Marisa had gotten her own room for the first time in her life. Lying in that room now, bone tired from a long day waiting tables, she wondered how much longer she'd get to keep it. Both their home and their restaurant were in the Los Angeles neighborhood of Mirador, and Mirador was falling apart. Her family had done what they could—they'd cut expenses, they'd dropped luxuries—but it just wasn't enough anymore. A restaurant only made money if people paid to eat there, and day after day more people in Mirador were becoming too poor to go to restaurants. Power was free, for the most part—every building in the city was covered with solar trees—but essential utilities like water and internet were getting more expensive, and meanwhile everyone seemed to be losing their jobs to nulis. The only reason San Juanito had human waiters was because Marisa's parents had four kids they could use as free labor, and even then the restaurant was close to going under.

Marisa kicked off her shoes and rubbed her feet and calves, trying to massage the soreness out of them before she fell asleep. How much longer would they be able to keep this house? she wondered. How much longer would Marisa be in this room? She let go of her legs and fell back on the bed, staring at the ceiling. Bao, one of her closest friends, helped support his family by skimming microtransactions from tourists in Hollywood—the brave new world of high-tech pickpocketing. Was that Marisa's future? Her friend Anja, on the other hand, was the daughter of one of the richest men in LA. Marisa knew that *that* wasn't her future.

It was 2050. Los Angelenos had nearly limitless technology, and still most of them were struggling. Why wasn't the world more fair?

She watched the ceiling until it grew too blurry to see, and woke up to bright rays of sunlight stabbing through the gaps in her curtains.

"Wake up, Mari!" shouted her mother. "Church in an hour!"

Marisa squeezed her eyes shut and moved her shoulders in slow, painful patterns, trying to work out the kinks. It took her a minute to realize that it was already morning—the night had passed in a blink, and she didn't think she'd moved a millimeter from where she'd fallen the night before. Her legs were still dangling off the side of the bed, and as she moved them, needles of pain shot from knee to heel. She groaned, too tired to be angry, and rolled over on her side, curling into a fetal position.

Marisa's mother, Guadalupe, opened her door with a hurried flourish. "Come on, chulita, up and at 'em. Why are you wearing jeans? It's Sunday, mija, we need to go to church."

Marisa pushed herself to a sitting position, squinted against the light, and pointed at her San Juanito T-shirt with both hands.

"You fell asleep in your clothes!" said Guadalupe, bustling into the room and throwing open Marisa's closet. She was a large woman, with hair that hovered somewhere between blond and yellow. A laundry nuli rolled in after her, prowling for errant clothes, and Marisa wasn't able to lunge for her favorite shirt in time—the nuli grabbed it with a rubber-tipped claw and stuffed it into a basket for transport to the washing machine. Marisa groaned and fell back on the bed, covering her eyes with her arm. "I tell you this every week, Mari," her mother continued, sorting through the clothes in her closet, "but you don't have a single dress you can wear to church. Just because there's a band there doesn't make it a nightclub."

"I can wear the green one," said Marisa from under her arm.

"You can't wear the green one," said Guadalupe. "It goes halfway up your thighs. You can wear the blue one."

"I hate the blue one."

"Then stop spending your money on trashy dresses," said Guadalupe. "Nobody goes to church to look at your butt."

"I can think of three people off the top of my head," said Marisa.

"Sure," said Guadalupe, dropping the blue dress and a pair of black shoes on the bed. "But those aren't the kind of people you want looking at your butt. Now get up."

Marisa grumbled again, but she had to admit her mom had a point. Omar Maldonado, in particular, could stab himself to death with a wire hanger for all she cared. "What time is it?"

"You have a computer in your head," said Guadalupe, bustling back toward the hallway. "You'll figure it out. Now get in the shower fast before Pati gets there, or you won't have any hot water."

Marisa sighed in the sudden quiet, as her mom's blustering admonitions moved next door to her sister's room. She enjoyed the peace for a moment, contemplating for one glorious second the unspeakable joy of going back to sleep again, but then she rubbed her eyes, grabbed her dress, and headed for the shower. She made it there just two steps before Pati, and locked the door while the angry twelve-year-old rattled the handle.

"Let me in!" Pati whined. "I can pee while you shower."

"I'll be fast," called Marisa.

"Will you let me out first?" asked a male voice, and Marisa shrieked and spun around. Sandro, her sixteen-year-old brother, was combing his hair in the mirror—already showered and dressed. Because of course he was.

"Ugh," said Marisa, opening the door again. "Get out!"

"Thanks," said Sandro, smiling as he left.

"Thanks!" said Pati, and rushed in as Sandro walked out. Pati closed the door behind herself and started stripping down. "Morning, Mari, what's up?"

"For the love of . . ." Marisa shook her head, closing her eyes, then stepped into the shower and closed the curtain behind her.

"Can't I get a second of privacy?"

"You're wearing your clothes in the shower," Pati called out.

"I know," Marisa growled. "Just . . . don't follow me in *here*, or I'll upload every virus on the internet into your skull."

"I found a virus yesterday," said Pati cheerfully. "I tried to catch it, like you do, but I think I had my program set up wrong because the virus got into my active memory and I had to spend all afternoon cleaning out my djinni. And I need your help with my homework, because we're trying to learn binary and it doesn't make any sense—teacher said that two equals ten, and that two doesn't even exist, and it's the dumbest thing I've ever heard and I need you to explain it all to me—"

Marisa tuned her out, undressing and showering while the girl babbled on without hardly pausing for breath. When she turned off the water Pati was still going strong, extolling the virtues of some new antivirus package she'd just found online, and Marisa wrapped her towel around herself while they switched places. Pati's excited monologue continued from the shower stall, and Marisa stared at herself in the mirror—her hair was a twisted black bird's nest with fading red tips. Time to dye it again, or maybe try another color. Except that dye cost money, and she still had half a bottle of red. Red it was, then, but not this morning. She'd stay faded for another day. She dried herself and put her clothes on, sneering at the stupid blue dress, then retreated toward her bedroom to try to untangle her hair.

"Hey, Mari," said Gabi, her other little sister. Whereas Pati was a roiling singularity of energy, fourteen-year-old Gabi was practically a ghost—not because people ignored her, but because she tended to ignore everyone else. She drifted down the hallway with barely a wave, wearing a cream top and a black skirt with just enough bounce to look like a ballerina's. Gabi's ballet classes had been one of the more recent luxuries to face the budget chopping block, and ever since then she'd started looking for every opportunity to passive-aggressively remind the entire family what a tyrannical, life-destroying decision that had been. Now that Marisa looked a little more closely, she could swear that Gabi's entire outfit was a dance costume from one of last year's performances. Gabi went out of sight down the stairs, and Marisa went back to her room to find her makeup.

She didn't even think about the KT Sigan login information until her mother made another sweep of the house, dragging everyone downstairs to leave.

"Vámonos!" called Guadalupe, pushing everyone outside. Marisa ran the brush through her hair one last time before grabbing her shoes, hopping from one foot to the other as she tried to put them on in the middle of her mother's relentless drive toward the front door. She blinked open the notepad where she'd saved the security info, cursing herself for falling asleep so early last night, but before she could do anything with the data she was outside, blinking in the hot California sunlight, and her father was gathering them all with his loud, bombastic voice.

"Line up, Carnesecas!" he bellowed cheerfully. "Miran, qué lindos!"

Good morning, sent Sahara.

No time, Marisa sent back, sweeping the message away with a blink. **Church.**

"Late night?" asked Sandro, falling into step beside Marisa. The church was at least a mile away, and they couldn't afford an autocab, so they walked.

Ooh, sent Sahara. **Have fun.**

"No," said Marisa, trying to keep track of all her conversations at once. "I fell asleep as soon as we got home."

"Maybe there was a sedative in that pricey salad," said Sandro.

"Cállate," said Marisa. She focused on her Sigan security notes, hoping to use the walk for something productive, and almost immediately tripped on a broken slab of sidewalk. "Madre de—"

"Ay, qué fea," said her abuela, catching her right arm and steadying her before she fell. "That's a mouth, not a gutter." Guadalupe's mother had lived with them ever since the move to the larger house, and church was one of the only times she left it.

"I'm amazed she heard you," Sandro whispered.

Marisa waited for her abue to snap at Sandro for disrespect—they didn't call her la Bruja for nothing—but of course she only heard Marisa's breach of courtesy, not Sandro's. Of course. Marisa shook her head, considered trying to parse the data, but closed the notepad and blinked it away. She'd already scratched the toe of her shoe, and her abue was gripping her arm like a nuli with a broken claw. She'd have to resign herself to a morning with the family before she had a chance to break into Sigan's network. She leaned against her abuela's arm and sighed.

"Ay, abuelita," she said. "It's been one of those days."

"You've only been awake for an hour," said her abuela.

"One of those weeks, then," said Marisa. She looked at the

scratch on her shoe. "One of those lives, maybe."

"Why do you always wear the blue dress?" asked her abuela. "If I had your butt, I'd wear the green one."

Marisa smiled for the first time all morning. "I love you, Abue."

The seven of them made their way to church, already sweating in their stiff, uncomfortable clothes: Marisa, her siblings, her mother, her abuela, and at the head of them all her father, Carlo Magno Carneseca. The only one missing was her older brother, Chuy, but he was estranged from everyone in the family but Marisa herself, and even their relationship was strained. He'd left their home years ago, and now lived with his girlfriend and their year-old son. At times like this Marisa missed him even more than usual, but as long as Chuy insisted on running with a gang—La Sesenta, the most dangerous in Mirador—their father would never allow him back again. Chuy was probably too proud to come back anyway.

Men were idiots.

Is Omar going to be there? sent Sahara.

At church? asked Marisa. **Probably.**

If you slip the priest a few extra yuan will he damn him to hell?

Marisa smirked. **You think Omar needs help getting into hell?**

I just want to cover all my bases, sent Sahara.

Stop talking about Omar, Marisa sent back. **I'm going to church, I need to think reverent thoughts.**

What's up, my sexy bitches? sent Anja. Her message

popped up in the corner of Marisa's vision, automatically merging with Sahara's to create a single conversation.

Shh, Sahara chastised. **Marisa's trying to be reverent.**

Sorry, sent Anja. **What's up, my reverent bitches?**

I'm seriously going to just close this conversation and block you both, sent Marisa.

But then you'll miss my news, sent Anja. **It is both great and momentous.**

Aren't those the same thing? sent Marisa.

Marisa has news too, sent Sahara.

Yeah? sent Anja.

I found a Sigan security code, sent Marisa.

Toll, sent Anja. She and her father had moved here from Germany a year ago, and she used almost as much German as Marisa used Spanish. That word, Marisa knew, meant "cool," but that was pretty much the limit of Marisa's German. **What'd you find when you went in?**

I haven't yet, sent Marisa.

Then stop wasting time in church, sent Sahara. **Let's find Grendel!**

That's big news, sent Anja. **My news is bigger.**

Marisa laughed. **How am I possibly supposed to think about Jesus with you two chatbots babbling at me like this?**

Fine, then, sent Anja. **I'm calling a meeting. As soon as Fang and Jaya wake up, we shall convene our most sacred order of the Cherry Dogs.**

You want the team to meet in Overworld? asked Marisa.

So let it be coded, said Anja, **in the great central processor in the sky.**

She's either making fun of you, sent Sahara, **or this is really big news. She only talks churchy when it's serious.**

The seriousest, said Anja. **That's a stupid word, by the way.**

It's not a word, sent Sahara.

English is just stupid in general, sent Anja.

Blame Sahara, sent Marisa. **Yo soy Mexicana.**

"We're here," said Sandro, nudging Marisa subtly with his elbow. She refocused her eyes on the real world, and saw the big yellow church looming in front of them. Most of Mirador was right on the poverty line, if not well below it, but the Maldonados knew when to throw money at community projects, and the church they'd built was a massive tribute to both God and themselves, in relatively equal parts. Her eye caught a row of black autocars rolling up to the curb—two Dynasty Falcons, by the look of them, flanking a long, sleek Futura Sovereign. That could mean only one thing.

Gotta go, sent Marisa. **Don Francisco's here.** She blinked the conversation closed and glanced at her father—he liked to arrive early at church to avoid this exact situation, caught on the sidewalk at the same time as his nemesis. As much as Francisco Maldonado hated her father, Carlo Magno hated him back even more.

Marisa was dying to know why. She considered opening the Sigan information again, but held off.

"They look like they're here for a movie premiere," said Gabi.

Guadalupe bumped her firmly, universal sign language for "shut your mouth or I will shut it for you."

Sergio was the first one out of the cars, not the Sovereign but the Falcon in front of it. It was a nice car, but one built more for power than luxury, and in Mirador it served as the go-to vehicle for Maldonado's enforcers. Sergio was Don Francisco's eldest son, and he always wore his police officer dress uniform to church, either because it was the nicest thing he had or, Marisa assumed, because he just liked to underline his family's authority. *You know how you have to pay us protection money every month? Well, we're also the cops, so no one's going to stop us.* He helped his wife and kids out of the car, and led them in while the Sovereign's side door opened and Omar got out with a bounce in his step and a devilish grin. He was, in contrast, the youngest of the Maldonado children, just a year older than Marisa, and he couldn't have been more different from his brother. While Sergio *acted* like he owned the church, Omar *looked* like he owned it, while simultaneously looking like he didn't even care. He glanced quickly around the street, winked at Marisa, and then reached back into the door to help his sister, Franca. "La Princesa." Marisa stifled a sneer at the tall, gorgeous young woman, dressed in what Marisa assumed was the most ostentatious thing in her closet—a slim indigo dress, with a corset and shoulder pads of black leather. The pads were decorated with curls of polished sandstone, like little bits of barbed wire, as the final piece of pretension. In a fashion market where you could literally print any dress you wanted out of adaptable plastic, in any style and complexity, natural materials like leather and sandstone were the new way of conveying wealth.

"I want to punch her in the face," whispered Pati.

"I used to as well," whispered Marisa.

"What changed?" asked Pati.

Marisa couldn't tell her the truth—that Grendel, in his final act of horror before disappearing back into the darknet, had infected La Princesa's djinni with a virus that had controlled her mind. Marisa was pretty sure it was gone now. Pretty sure. Marisa had made it her quest to update Franca's antivirus software with everything it needed to close the gate that Grendel had opened—which was hard to do, considering how much La Princesa hated her. But enemies or not, no one deserved to be a living puppet.

"I'm the one who changed," Marisa whispered at last. "No one ever found happiness holding on to a grudge."

"Quiet," said Carlo Magno.

Marisa looked back at the car just in time to see Don Francisco himself step out, strong and solid, with a graying beard and fistful of bright metal rings on each hand. Omar and Franca were dressed to impress, but Don Francisco was in a simple black suit. He didn't have to work to impress anybody; the whole street knew who he was, and stopped to watch him. He offered La Princesa his arm, and they walked into church with Omar close behind.

"Let's go," said Guadalupe, once the Maldonados were out of sight. "Those hymns aren't going to sing themselves." She urged them forward, but none of them started walking until Marisa's father did. Marisa and Sandro helped their abuela, and Pati fiddled with her dress, as if suddenly aware of how shabby it was—it had been one of Gabi's, and before that one of Marisa's.

Marisa shot a final glance at the jet-black autocars, which

silently closed their own doors and drove themselves away. There was one more child in the Maldonado family, but he never came to church. Jacinto had been so badly injured in that mysterious car accident that he hadn't left the family compound in years.

Marisa touched her metal arm, and went inside.

THREE

Having to watch the Maldonados arrive in their pompous cars and ridiculous clothes destroyed any chance Marisa had of enjoying church; instead she spent the morning watching her parents' faces, and the back of Don Francisco's head. She rose and sat when her abuela did, and sang the hymns even more atonally than usual. It certainly didn't help that the church building was sweltering inside. The final prayer was like a call to freedom, and she rushed out into the fresh air—scalding, but fresh—as fast as she could. The walk home felt like a blessed escape; changing into a T-shirt and shorts was a profound liberation; and when she plugged herself into Overworld, every other physical sensation melted away, replaced by the crisp perfection of virtual reality. Nothing saved you from the horrors of the real world like escaping into a fake one.

The Cherry Dogs had their own private lobby, a constantly

shifting collage of all five girls' different decorating styles. A week ago Anja had replaced the entire floor with what looked like a window into a non-Euclidean abyss, but it gave the rest of them such vertigo that Sahara had sworn to change it; Marisa saw now that she already had, and the new floor was some kind of polished marble tile, like the lobby of a nice hotel. One wall was covered with floating monitors of various size and specialty, so the team could review the latest game developments together. Marisa's current game avatar was simple and utilitarian—a set of dark green army fatigues, with the flag on the shoulders replaced with the Cherry Dogs logo.

"Hey, Mari," said Fang, who was already waiting in the lobby. She was Chinese, and lived in Beijing, but the two of them had been playing together for years, and her English was perfect. Marisa felt a pang of embarrassment that her own Chinese hadn't improved nearly as much in the same amount of time, and greeted Fang in Mandarin to help make up for it.

"Nǐ hǎo."

Fang was wearing one of her typical avatars: a small figure in a tattered black cloak, her belt heavy with wickedly sharp knives and her face mostly obscured by a hood. Marisa had never met her in person, and had no idea what she looked like in real life. Fang smiled, a bit deviously, her mouth only barely visible in the shadow of her hood, and spoke again: "Nǐ juédé Anja zhèngzài chóuhuà zhège shíhòu?"

Marisa struggled the parse the sentence: something about Anja, obviously, and she was pretty sure she heard the word *plan*. She guessed at the possibilities: *Am I ready for Anja's plan? Do I know Anja's plan?* After a second she simply laughed and shook her head. "I'm sorry, I really suck at your language. This is why I'm failing all my classes."

"All your classes are in Chinese?"

"Fine," said Marisa. "This is why I'm failing *two* of my classes: Chinese and Business. I'm failing all the rest of them for completely unrelated reasons."

Fang smiled again, warmly this time. "Don't feel bad. I don't speak Spanish at all."

"But you could probably learn it in an afternoon," said Marisa. "It's stupidly easy."

"I could say the same about Chinese," said Fang. "Why else would it be the most commonly spoken language in the world?"

"Because there's more of you?"

"That's our secret plan for world domination," said Fang, looking back at the wall of viewscreens. "Unbridled procreation."

"Ooh," said Jaya, appearing in the lobby just in time to hear Fang's last two words. "Sounds fun—I'm in."

"Nǐ yǒu méiyǒu kàn dào láizì rìběn de jiéguǒ?" asked Fang.

"Hái méi," said Jaya. Jaya was from India, and spoke so many languages Marisa didn't even know them all. Worst of all, her English was even better than Mari's. "Hey, Mari, what's up?"

"Todo bien," said Marisa. "Y tú?"

"Todo bien," said Jaya with a smile. She was wearing an avatar that made her look like a hybrid human/plant, with soft green flesh under a flowing robe of flower petals. "I've got a date tonight with that hot guy from my office. Did I send you a pic?"

"Which one?" asked Marisa. "White shirt or maroon shirt?"

"Maroon shirt," said Jaya.

"Nice," said Marisa, remembering with a touch of envy the photo Jaya had sent a few days ago. The guy in the maroon shirt had been unfairly good-looking. "Touch his chest for me. Just, like, once, and then tell me about it."

Jaya laughed, and Fang rolled her eyes. "Is Anja going to get here soon?" asked Fang. "Or do I have to figure out how I can kill myself while sitting in the lobby?"

"Oh, come on," said Jaya, her voice practically rippling with laughter. "You don't have some boy somewhere?"

"Maybe she has a girl," said Sahara, appearing in the lobby with a flourish. She wore her standard avatar—an almost exact replica of herself, in a fancy, form-fitting dress. "Show a little imagination."

"Good point," said Jaya, and looked back at Fang. "Girl? Boy? Fluid?"

"Bored," said Fang. "Where's Anja?"

"And like a phantom she was among them," said Anja. She appeared in a cloud of pink smoke, like a genie from a cartoon lamp, but as the smoke cleared Marisa saw that her avatar was wildly technological—plates of sparkling armor, with little wings and jets poking out all over the place. She hovered in the center of the room for a moment, then landed dramatically. "I suppose you're wondering why I called you here today—whoa, who changed the floor?"

"Will you please just tell us your announcement?" asked Sahara.

"Fine," said Anja. "You ready for this? Are you all sitting down?"

"We're lying down," said Jaya, "plugged into a VR interface."

"I got us into a tournament," said Anja, her armor-plated face practically sparkling with excitement.

"I get us into the tournaments," said Sahara.

"Not this one," said Anja, shaking her head. "Imagine, if you will, a tournament so special you can't even get in without an invitation. So exclusive you can't get an invitation without knowing someone. And so high profile that you can't even know the right people without spending a grotesque amount of money."

"We don't have even a disgusting amount of money," said Marisa. "Grotesque is way out of our price range."

"And we don't do pay-to-play," said Sahara. "We've talked about this—anything we get into, we get into because of our skills in the game. No corrupt agents or organizers, and no gambling on ante prize pools."

"This is none of those things," said Anja, pointing at Sahara, and then pointing at Marisa with her other hand. "And we don't need any money, because the payment has already been made." She waved her hands in front of her, her fingers still pointing out. "By Abendroth."

Abendroth was the company her father worked for—one of the largest drone and nuli companies in the world. Marisa frowned. If Abendroth paid to get them into a tournament, that could only mean . . .

"Great Holy Hand Grenades," said Sahara. "You got us into Forward Motion."

Anja beamed.

"No way," said Fang.

"Whoa," said Jaya, "what's Forward Motion?"

"It's a charity event," said Marisa. "Like a . . . benefit concert, or something? I thought it was just for celebrity players, like Differential or Su-Yun Kho."

"That would be worth it all by itself," said Sahara. "Su-Yun Kho is my hero."

"Close," said Anja. "It's kind of like an ante pool, except the money you put in doesn't go to prizes, it goes to charity—specifically, in this case, to bulk up wireless networks in underprivileged areas. Giving starving little kids in Iowa or whatever a chance to get a real education, and for businesses to compete on an even footing. That kind of thing."

"So the ante is more of a donation," said Jaya. "That means they're all going to come from large corporations, like Abendroth."

"It also means publicity," said Sahara, and Marisa could hear the undercurrent of hunger in her voice. "Megacorps can give money to anyone, but if they're giving it to this tournament, it's because they want everyone to *see* them giving money. That's why they send teams and do a competition: so people will pay attention. There's going to be cameras everywhere, and reporters, and maybe even talent scouts—"

"No scouts," said Fang. "There are only two kinds of teams in a tourney like this: all-star superteams, pulled in to crush the competition, and spoiled rich kids who want to pretend they can play in the big leagues. Talent scouts don't care about either one."

"And we don't fit into either of those groups," said Marisa. "Are you sure we can join?"

"Of course we can," said Anja. "You've got your very own spoiled rich kid: me. I've spent a solid week talking my dad into sponsoring a team, and he finally broke down this morning when I made him breakfast in bed, served along with a link to an article detailing exactly the kind of visibility Sahara was talking about. Abendroth stands to gain a massive amount of goodwill in the corporate community, and we stand to gain a big giant spotlight in which to finally show off what the Cherry Dogs can do! Screw this minor-league garbage we've been playing in—a win here, or even a good performance, will get us the attention we need to push us right over the top and into a real league. We can go pro after something like this."

"No way," said Fang. "These charity events are a novelty—nobody important actually watches them."

"They'll be watching this one," said Sahara. Her avatar had the inert oddness of someone whose controller was looking at a separate data stream. "I found the article Anja mentioned—Forward Motion is going to be hosted this year by an internet service provider. Guess which one."

Marisa shot her a look. "Don't tell me."

"KT Sigan," said Sahara. "This is their pet project, and they control half the news feeds in this hemisphere—everyone is going to hear about this thing."

"Read the next part of the article!" said Anja, practically jumping up and down. "It's the best part of the whole thing!"

Sahara shook her head. "I . . . don't see anything exciting."

"The part about the network," said Anja, "read it read it read it!"

Sahara sighed. "Let's see. '"We have something special planned for this year's tournament," said KT Sigan president Kwon Dae.' Is that the right part?"

"Why would 'something special' not be the right part?" asked Fang.

"Because it's super boring," said Sahara.

"Just read it!" shouted Anja.

"Okay, okay. '"The entire tournament will be played on a closed network, on which we will use a randomized program to simulate the low bandwidth and frequent connectivity problems encountered by the millions of people around the world who don't have access to proper internet service. Not only will this help prevent cheating, keeping the tournament servers insulated against outside interference, it will also help shine a light on the often crippling data jams that are keeping so many regions underdeveloped. Once people see for themselves how those communities live, they'll be even more eager to help us create a positive change in the world."'" Sahara shook her head again. "They're just going to throttle the connection speed—that's not exciting."

"It is kind of insulting, though," said Jaya. "Slow internet is a legitimate problem in some places, I admit, but there's still, you know, world hunger. Disease epidemics. He's talking like a laggy video game is a world health crisis."

"Why does he mention cheating?" asked Fang. "No one's been able to cheat in a major Overworld tournament in, like, six years."

Marisa thought about the implications of a closed-network tournament, and suddenly the reason for Anja's excitement dawned on her. "Anja's right," she shouted, feeling a surge of joy run through her. She looked at Anja eagerly. "Is Abendroth paying for that bit, too?"

Anja nodded.

"Paying for what?" asked Sahara. "Can you just come out and tell us?"

"The tournament's being played on a closed network," said Marisa. "That means no one can connect remotely, which means—"

"We'll have to travel there in person," said Fang.

"Balle balle!" shouted Jaya. She looked at Marisa, then at Anja. "Abendroth's flying us to LA?"

"Yep, and putting you up in a hotel too," said Anja.

"Screw hotels," said Sahara, "you guys are staying with me!"

Jaya leaped at them both and smothered them in a hug. "I'm so excited!"

"This will be amazing," said Sahara. "All five of us, together on screen at the same time."

Of course Sahara was thinking about the publicity. Marisa smiled broadly, more excited at the prospect of getting everyone together than she'd been for the tournament itself. "Amazing is right," she said. "This is going to be the best."

"Ahem," said Fang. "How do you even know we all can make it?"

"I can!" said Jaya.

Anja looked at Fang. "Can you?"

Fang grinned. "Of course I can, but it's nice to be asked."

"The tournament starts next week, right?" asked Marisa.

"Yeah," said Sahara. "The opening ceremonies are on Monday."

"I can have Fang and Jaya here by Sunday morning," said Anja. "Los Angeles, get ready for the Cherry Dogs!"

FOUR

Pati screamed. "That's amazing!"

"I know," said Marisa, still grinning like a fool. "I can barely believe it."

"This is so cool," said Pati. "This is cool as sh—"

"Cuídate la boca," said Carlo Magno. "Ay, qué niña malcriada."

"Sorry, Papi," said Pati. "This is cool as . . . crap?"

"Just say it's cool," said Guadalupe.

"And get upstairs," said Carlo Magno. "You have school in the morning."

"Okay, Papi." Pati gave Marisa one last hug and a high-pitched squeal, and then bounded up the stairs to bed.

"This truly is wonderful," said Guadalupe. "You've been trying to get into a real tournament for so long."

"It isn't a real, *professional* tournament," said Marisa. "Just a charity thing."

"That means it's *better* than a real tournament," said Carlo Magno.

"It's definitely going to have a bigger audience than any of the minor-league stuff we've been trying to get into," said Marisa. She hesitated, then looked at her father. "Does that mean you'll watch?"

Carlo Magno sighed. "You know I can't get into that game."

"That's just because you don't understand it," said Marisa. She sat next to him on the couch, crossing her legs under her. "If you didn't understand soccer, you wouldn't enjoy that either."

"It's called football," said Carlo Magno. "Show some respect for your heritage."

Marisa hit him with a couch pillow. "Papi, don't tease me, this is important."

"Overworld is a game for the younger generation," said Carlo Magno. "I'm too old to watch it."

"You're forty-four," said Marisa. "eSports have been a thing since before you were born."

"You know he's never been a gamer," said Guadalupe. "Heaven knows I've tried to convert him."

"You have all these powers," he said, "and crazy costumes. Nobody in football dresses up like a pirate and shoots fireballs out of their hands."

"But imagine how awesome it would be if they *did*," said Marisa.

Carlo Magno laughed. "Fine," he said. "For you, mija, I'll watch it. But I don't promise to understand it."

"How can you not understand it?" shouted Pati from the stairs. "It's the greatest game ever!"

"To bed!" shouted Carlo Magno.

"I'll tuck her in," said Guadalupe, and shooed Pati back upstairs.

"I know you're supposed to blow up a vault," said Carlo Magno. "That's as far as I get."

"It's just like any other sport," said Marisa. "You have two teams of five, and each player—called an agent—has a position. Soccer has stuff like forwards, defenders, and goalies, and Overworld has General, Guard, Sniper, Spotter, and Jungler."

"Only one Jungler?" he asked. "Is there only one jungle?"

"Most of the time there's not any jungle at all," she said. "I don't know why they call it that—it's from some older game, I think. Anyway: like you said, each team has a vault, and you win by blowing up the other team's vault. But each vault is defended by turrets, which are too powerful for even the five players to take out by themselves, so each team also gets AI minions, which spawn every minute or so. They run across the map and attack the other team's agents and turrets. The General's job is to lead the minions and give them power buffs and that kind of stuff. She's the most important player on a team, so she has another player called a Guard whose whole job is to back her up."

"So you're the General," said Carlo Magno.

"Of course not," said Marisa, feeling herself blush. "Sahara's the General—she's the leader, and calls all the plays, and tells everyone what to do."

"But you'd be so good at that—"

"I would be a terrible General, Papi," said Marisa. "I don't come up with strategies. I just follow orders."

Carlo Magno raised his eyebrow suspiciously. "Are we talking about the same Marisa?"

"Papi, will you just let me explain the game?"

"Sí," he said. "So are you the Sniper, then? You'd be good at that, too."

"Anja's the Sniper, Papi. You said you'd let me talk."

"Sorry," he said. "Talk."

"Every game map is split into three levels, called lanes—there's the city, which is the main one with all the minions, then there's the sewers, which is where the Jungler goes—"

"It's not called the jungle?"

"It doesn't even look like a jungle."

"Does it look like a sewer?"

"Not . . . usually," she said. "Listen, will you quit getting hung up on the terminology so we can move on? Sports terms are just weird. Why is the goalie called a 'goalkeeper' if their whole job is to get rid of goals instead of keep them?"

"It's like a groundskeeper," said Carlo Magno. "They 'keep' the goal by, like, tending to it. Like a gardener."

"Well if they'd just call it a Gardener that would make so much more sense," said Marisa.

"This game has ruined you."

"Whatever, viejito," said Marisa. "So there's a city and a sewer. The third lane is called the roof, and that's where the Sniper and the Spotter play. I'm the Spotter—it's like the Guard, but for the Sniper."

"So you play backup to the backup?" said Carlo Magno, raising an eyebrow.

"It's an important position, Papi! And it's more variable than any other position—sometimes I spec for defense, sometimes for melee combat, and sometimes I'm like a second Sniper. I'm like a . . . swing position, who can do anything."

Carlo Magno beamed. "I knew my daughter was the most important one."

"Papi, you're impossible," she said, but inside she felt warm and happy.

"I assume," he said, "that 'spec' means 'build'? Or something like that?"

"It means 'specialize,'" she said. "This is where the fireballs come in. There are a ton of different ways to customize your character. At the start of each game you choose a role, like Flanker or Striker, and then two powersets, and each powerset has six different specialties and twelve different elements. So, like, Electricity Ranged has different powers than Electricity Defense, but they both obviously drain energy from the enemy."

"That's obvious?"

"They're electricity powers—what else would they do?"

He frowned. "Electrocute people?"

"Yeah, but that's, like, one power. There's seventy-two electricity powersets with two hundred and sixteen electricity powers; they can't all do the same thing."

"You said they all drain energy."

"In different ways," she said, scratching the back of her head. "Papi, you just need to watch a game. This isn't that hard to figure out."

"I'm trying," he said tersely. "I just . . . it's late. And you have school tomorrow too, just like Pati. Get some rest, and we can . . ." He grimaced. "Talk about this more tomorrow."

"You don't sound happy about that."

"If it's important to you, it's important to me."

Marisa looked at him for a long moment, then leaned forward to hug him. "I'm sorry I fight with you so much."

"What do you mean?" he asked. "We just had one of our friendliest conversations ever."

"I know," she said, "and we still snapped at each other."

He hugged her. "I love you, Mari. Even when I don't understand you."

"A ti también," she said, and then they both said in unison: "Which is most of the time."

Marisa laughed and hugged him back. "Te amo, Papi. I'll see you in the morning." She went upstairs, passing her mami on the way and giving her a hug and a kiss. "Te amo."

"Te amo, mija," she said. "Straight to sleep—no internet."

"I know, Mami," said Marisa, feeling only a little bad about lying. She had way too much to do to even think about going to sleep, and most of it was on the internet, but she wanted to wait until her family was asleep first. She went to her room and plugged into a "Speak Chinese" VR program her teacher had assigned her, instantly appearing on a street in Shanghai. It wasn't just a 3D movie, like the old days, but a full experience tied directly to the brain's sensory inputs—the VR program didn't just show you a picture and hope your optic nerves could interpret correctly; it literally told your brain exactly what to see, and what to hear and smell and feel, and then it did. She walked into a restaurant in the virtual Shanghai and ordered some food, practicing her pronunciation and some basic question grammar, but kept Olaya, the home computer, open in the corner of her vision. It monitored the family's positions, and as soon as everyone had retreated to their rooms, she unplugged from the Chinese program, locked her door, and sat down at her desk. She had three box computers, two tablets, her djinni, and a KT Sigan security code. Now was her chance to track down Grendel.

"Let's do this," she whispered.

Her security code came from that office worker, Pablo Nakamoto. She didn't need his passwords, and thank goodness she didn't need his biometric information; all she needed was the data string the Sigan network had assigned to him when he used their system to contact the Solipsis Cafe with his lunch order. Marisa woke up one of her box computers, routed her connection through a series of anonymous internet carrier stations, and then reached out to the Sigan network, looking not for the public facade but for the structure behind it, the moving parts that made the public stuff function. The Sigan server queried her own, the computer version of checking someone's passport at the border: Are you allowed to be here? She fed it Pablo Nakamoto's data string, the server accepted it, and she was in.

Columns of words and numbers cascaded down her screen—the internal filing system that kept the network organized. Marisa spread the display to two adjacent monitors, and fired up what she called her Goblins: little programs designed to perform menial tasks to aid in hacking. The first one, running on her primary box, would maintain a constant search for other users in the system, on the off chance that one of them was paying enough attention to notice her. She set her second Goblin on a more complicated task, and gave it a box computer all its own to do it: it made a quick copy of every directory Marisa visited, edited Marisa's presence out of it, and then redirected any other users in the system to the copy instead of the real directory; they could still find what they were looking for and perform any actions they wanted, but they wouldn't see anything she was doing. It was extremely unlikely that anyone would even care if they found her—she had a valid security code, after all—but it never hurt to be careful. With those two Goblins watching her back, Marisa tied in her two tablets and started a search on each of them: one looked for customer account information, and the other looked for the specific IP address she'd connected to Grendel. Then she sat back and waited, watching the hack unfold on her third large monitor.

She didn't use her djinni for any of it. If someone did notice her poking around, they wouldn't find any direct connection to her ID.

The search for the IP address kicked out a result every minute or so, and Marisa looked at each of them in turn, but none of them were helpful—lists of service data, records of packet transfers, and similar bits of junk that all boiled down to "this IP address is occasionally being used." None of them said anything about what the address was being used for, much less who was using it.

She looked at the other search, hoping to find the general archive of customer data, but what she found instead made her curse: "Mierda!" She immediately clamped a hand down over her mouth, her eyes wide, freezing in place and listening in case anyone had heard her. She looked back at the search results, seeing the bad news again: all of the customer data was hidden behind a permission wall. It wasn't enough to simply access the Sigan network; she needed to access the next layer down—the private, protected layer—in order to get into the good stuff. She growled again, but chided herself for ever getting her hopes up—of course the good data would have extra security, and she should have expected it. But she'd been so happy just to get in, she'd let herself believe she was closer to success than she really was.

Marisa read through the search results a third time, just in case the whole of reality decided to change itself to make her life easier, but it didn't. She was locked out. She let out a long, slow breath, considering her options. She couldn't reach the data she needed, but she could reach plenty of other data that might help her solve this new puzzle. Where was the breach in Sigan's digital fortifications? She glanced at her Goblins, confirming that no one was onto her yet, and then started looking through other aspects of the Sigan network.

She started in the customer service interface—that was where people on the outside spoke to people on the inside, which made it a common place to find vulnerabilities. After an hour of searching she couldn't find any holes, breaches, or anything else. Whoever had built the interface had been meticulous. She took a step back, tapping her metal fingers nervously on her desk, and then tried again, this time with the suite of tech support tools; just like the customer service department, the tech support department worked directly with customers, helping to troubleshoot problems with their internet service. Maybe she'd find a vulnerability there? After another fruitless hour, on the verge of quitting for the night and starting over with a new plan, she finally found it:

The Djinni Activity Log.

Internet service providers kept detailed records of all of your connection activity on a computer or tablet—provided you hadn't anonymized them, like Marisa had—but there was a whole world full of laws preventing them from collecting that kind of data from a djinni. Djinnis were too personal; that didn't make them private by any means, but it meant that a company like Sigan couldn't just passively pull your usage data without permission. Instead, each djinni kept its own records in the Djinni Activity Log, and when you called for tech support they downloaded the DAL to examine it. Marisa didn't know how other companies handled it, but Sigan's IT system was set up to pull a customer's DAL directly into the support server. Inside the specially secured layer of the network.

Marisa smiled.

"All I have to do is write a virus," she murmured, and blinked open Bowie, her current favorite coding program. She started sketching out the basics of the virus. "I hide this in the DAL, call Sigan for tech support, and when they download the log it will get inside and write me a fake security access profile. First I'll need it to replicate itself into another part of the system, though. . . ." She tapped feverishly on the screen, but after a moment remembered she was still logged in to Sigan's outer network; she exited, closed all her connections, and scrubbed a few of the pathways before diving back into the Bowie code. This could work. She could feel it.

Of course, she'd have to install the virus in her own head to make it work. Her experience with Grendel and the Bluescreen virus loomed large in her mind, warning her away, but . . . she was so close. It was a risk worth taking.

She pushed her fears away, and continued coding.

FIVE

"You want to install a virus in your own head?" asked Sahara, her voice echoing slightly in the Cherry Dog lobby. "That's insane."

"I think it's awesome," said Anja. "Play crazy."

"No," said Sahara firmly. They were lined up by the viewscreens, looking at a handful of powerset options. Sahara was dressed in her typical avatar—a black dress this time—and stood in front of the screens with her hands folded behind her back, like a general lecturing her troops. "Remember what happened the last time *you* had a virus in your djinni? Because I do."

"That was different," said Anja. "This is one Mari is writing herself—she can make sure it's safe."

"Exactly," said Marisa. "Thank you."

Fang shook her head; her avatar today was a zombie wolf, and putrescent saliva dripped from her teeth as she moved her head. "It's still kind of crazy."

"Maybe," said Jaya, glistening in an iridescent mermaid avatar. "I want to hear Marisa's side before I decide."

"It *is* crazy," said Marisa. "At least a little. But not because it'll hurt me. I'm a Sigan customer already, so I can call for tech support without raising any suspicions. And the virus is designed to attack the Sigan tech support system, not djinnis." She was dressed in a long green cloak, like a medieval archer, and she tapped her longbow against the floor as she talked. "As long as the virus is in my DAL, it's harmless."

"What does it do once they download it?" asked Anja. Her avatar was a red panda in a pirate outfit, and the feather in her hat bobbed adorably as she cocked her head to the side.

"It hides in a data log, writes me a security permission, then deletes itself," said Marisa. "After that it's not even a hack; I can just log in legally like any other tech support worker."

"Send it to me," said Jaya. She worked tech support for Johara, one of the only telecoms even bigger than Sigan. "I might be able to give you some pointers."

"You have no idea if Johara has the same vulnerability in their system that Sigan does," said Fang.

"All the more reason to check it out," said Jaya with a smile. "If I can plug up a hole like this in our system before anyone uses it against us, I'll be a hero. There's a huge bonus for that kind of thing."

"I'm the one who found it," said Marisa.

Jaya smiled broadly. "Obviously I'll split it with you, priya. Cherry Dogs forever."

"This is super heartwarming," said Sahara, "but we have

a tournament to prep for. Marisa is smart enough to play with viruses safely, and when she actually tries her attack we'll be there to help her, but right now we're looking at powersets. We need to figure out how to build our team. Forward Motion is using a Seoul Draft, and we haven't really done that before."

"I like Seoul Draft," said Fang. "It's a good system."

"What is it?" asked Marisa.

"It's really cool," said Fang. "Instead of going back and forth, we-pick-you-pick-we-pick-you-pick, it's all done in two waves. Both teams pick four of their players' powersets, all at once, and then we all reveal at the same time. Then we pick our fifth player's powers in the second wave."

"The Korean championships started using it last year," said Sahara. "Sigan's a Korean company, so I guess whatever executive is organizing the tournament is a fan of the home league."

"Ándale," said Marisa. "That changes everything."

"That's actually a great system," said Jaya. "The usual draft system typically ends up resulting in the same two or three strategies used in tournament play. Seoul Draft might encourage some riskier fringe strategies, since the rewards could be so much greater."

"Yeah, people might actually play the niche powersets," said Fang. "Nobody ever uses Air Defense, because it's too easy to end up with a match where it's useless. Now there might be times we want to play it in our second wave."

"This is awesome," said Anja. "I want to try Electricity Melee."

Sahara sighed. "Why on earth would we play a Sniper with a melee powerset?"

Fang laughed. "Here we go."

"Think about it," said Anja eagerly. "It would be impossible to react to. If they see a Melee Sniper in our first-wave reveal, it would throw them completely off their game. They'll have plans for their second wave, and how they'll react to us, but then we do something super weird that they haven't planned for and they'll fall apart. They'll make a suboptimal second-wave pick trying to second-guess us."

"More suboptimal than a Melee Sniper?" Sahara snapped.

"Hurting ourselves in order to hurt the enemy isn't a great plan," said Jaya.

"You always go for the craziest option," said Sahara. "I will not let you ruin this tournament for me."

"For *you*?" said Marisa. "Are we not a team anymore? Is this the Sahara Show now?"

"For *us*," Sahara hissed. "You know that's what I meant."

"Okay," said Jaya, inserting herself between Sahara and Marisa. "We're all pretty stressed out right now, with the tournament, and this Grendel thing with Sigan, and Marisa's family's restaurant starting to fall apart, and maybe we just need to take a step back for a minute and breathe."

"We don't have time for a step back," said Sahara. "We have time to act like the professionals we *claim* we want to be."

"You know who you sound like?" asked Marisa.

"Don't say it," said Fang.

Marisa set her jaw, staring Sahara in the face. "You sound like Zi."

"Wô cào," said Fang.

Sahara's eyes went wide, turning almost instantly into a terrifying scowl as she launched herself at Marisa, determined to tear her avatar's head off. Jaya and Anja stayed between them, struggling to pull them away from each other, but it wasn't until Fang's zombie wolf jumped in that they managed to pull them apart.

"What the hell is wrong with you!" shouted Fang. "If you don't want to get compared to Zi, *stop acting like Zi*."

"Who's Zi?" asked Anja, panting from exertion.

"And you," snarled Fang, pointing her muzzle at Marisa. "I know a 'Marisa's mad at her dad' tantrum when I see one. Keep your family arguments out of this lobby."

"I'm not mad at my dad," Marisa spat, but then she paused, thought for a moment, and sighed. "Okay, maybe I am."

"You're running yourself ragged trying to solve a mystery he could solve in one sentence if he was honest with you," said Jaya. "Of course you're mad at him."

"Will someone please tell me who Zi is?" asked Anja.

"You know her by a different name," said Sahara, taking a deep breath. "Yeoh Zi Chong was Nightmare."

"Wô cào indeed," said Anja. She stared at Sahara, then looked at Marisa. "Nightmare, as in, the psycho hose beast who used to lead the Cherry Dogs?"

"I have always led the Cherry Dogs," said Sahara coldly, "but Nightmare did her best to take over. She was our first Sniper, back when we formed the team: me and Marisa from LA, and Fang and Zi from Beijing. Our Guard was a girl named Jennifer Stashwick, and I don't remember where she was from, but that team only lasted a few months before Zi ran Jennifer off and we brought in Jaya."

"And if I'd known what I was getting into," said Jaya, "I never would have joined." She looked at the other girls and smiled. "So I guess I'm glad I *didn't* know what I was getting into, because you girls are my best friends."

"What happened to Jennifer?" asked Anja.

"I think you've actually met her," said Marisa, "at least online. She designs Overworld costumes."

"WinterFox Designs?" asked Anja.

Marisa nodded. "WinterFox was her call sign in the game."

"Zi was a bitch to everyone," said Sahara, "but she was terrible to Jennifer."

"Still not—" Marisa glanced over at Fang. "Still not as mean as she was to Fang."

"I just ignored her," said Fang.

"What'd she do to Fang?" asked Anja.

"Same stuff she did to everyone else," said Jaya, "just worse. Critiqued her, yelled at her, gossiped behind her back. No one was ever good enough for her."

"She wanted to go pro," said Fang. "She freaked out over every little mistake, and yelled and screamed if we didn't practice for ten hours a day, and when we did practice she spent half the time trying to call plays completely contrary to Sahara's. And we were better *players* because of it, I think, but we were a terrible *team*, and we hated every second of it."

"So you kicked her out?" asked Anja.

"I wish," said Marisa. "We were trying to figure out how to kick her out when she left on her own. She got poached by a Chinese team called Wu Squad, straight into the pros. She plays in the

Chinese leagues, which I don't really follow."

"I do," said Fang.

"So do I," said Sahara. "She's pretty successful."

"She's turned Wu Squad into exactly what she always wanted the Cherry Dogs to be," said Jaya. "Cutthroat and relentless. Joyless and precise. I don't want to go pro if that's what it takes to get there."

"And I know that," said Sahara. "And I don't want it either." She looked at each girl in turn, ending on Marisa. "I'm sorry I blew up like that. I was pushing myself too hard, and that meant I started pushing you. It's like Jaya said—you're my best friends in the world, and I don't want to lose that. But I . . . I don't want to lose this either. I believe in this team, and I know we can win this tournament, and if that means we have to buckle down and work a little harder, then I think that's totally worth it."

"Not if it changes who we are," said Anja.

"Do we even know who we are?" asked Sahara. "We're not Nightmare, but we're not . . . Melee Sniper, either. I wish I could get behind 'play crazy' as a slogan, because it's so amazingly marketable." She laughed, shaking her head. "But we have to temper that craziness with discipline, or every win we get is just random. If we want to be pros, we have to act like pros, and maybe once we get there we can play a little crazier, because that's a great way to throw off the pros we'll be playing against. But I just think . . . if we don't get our act together, if we keep using wild ideas as an excuse instead of as a careful and occasional strategy . . . I think 'play crazy' is pretty much indistinguishable from every other team that just doesn't play *well*."

The girls stayed silent a moment, thinking about her words. Marisa reached out for Sahara's hand and squeezed it, feeling comforted by the touch even in virtual reality. "You're right," she said. "I'm sorry for blowing up at you, and I'm sorry for playing sloppy."

"You haven't been playing sloppy," said Anja, but then she took Sahara's other hand. "I promise to take this more seriously. But I also think we can be crazy and smart at the same time. Play . . . smazy."

Sahara smiled. "That's not a real word."

"English is stupid," said Anja.

"Aw, hugs for everyone!" Jaya spread her mermaid arms wide and squeezed the three girls together into a clump. "Come on, Fang, team hug!"

"I don't hug," said Fang. She smiled with her zombie wolf teeth. "But I do kind of like you guys."

"Catch her!" shouted Jaya, letting go of the clump and leaping at Fang. "Catch her and hug her!" The four of them chased Fang around the lobby, eventually cornering her and smothering her in a dogpile.

"All right! All right!" Fang shouted. "I'm hugged! Get off of me."

They rolled away, sitting and lying in a circle on the floor, laughing with joy and the sweet release of tension. After a moment, Sahara started planning again.

"I've got a list of all the other teams in the tournament," she said. "There's a handful of spoiled rich kids, but most of the teams are a real threat. We're probably not going to win the whole thing, but we can impress the hell out of some pretty important people."

"Perfecto," said Marisa.

"How many teams are playing?" asked Fang.

"Sixteen," said Sahara. "All of them sponsored by multinational megacorps. Round one is spread over two days: four games Monday, four on Tuesday. The big teams will be getting all the press, but if we can make it through that first round we're golden: every match from then on is getting big budget promos, live commentators, the whole deal."

"Toll," said Anja.

Sahara nodded. "They haven't released the matchups yet, so we don't know which opposing teams to start studying, but I've found some replays we can watch of the prime teams."

Marisa sat up. "I'm up for some replays. Who've we got?"

"Ganika's hired the Saxon Violins to play for them," said Fang.

"Bunch of friggin' douchebags," said Anja, rolling her eyes.

"Saxon Violins is one of the best teams in North America," said Jaya. "Which is not saying much, let's be honest, but still. Ganika's not pulling any punches, are they?"

"When you're the world's largest djinni manufacturer, you don't have to pull punches," said Sahara. "The other interesting team is, fittingly enough, our own beloved KT Sigan."

"They sponsored the tournament," said Marisa. "They're running a team as well?"

"They hired most of Presto," said Sahara. "Last year's runner-up for the Korean National Championship."

"That explains the Seoul Draft," said Jaya. "If their own team's familiar with it, they'll have an advantage over the rest of the field. That's kind of dirty."

Anja frowned. "Why not hire the actual Korean champions? Why runner-up?"

"Plus, Presto broke up," said Fang. "They're not even a whole team anymore, so why bother with them?"

"That's why I said 'most of Presto,'" said Sahara. She started to smile, like she did when she had an exciting secret. "And that's why I said their team was interesting. They've got three members of Presto, the Guard from another Korean team called R4ina, and Kwon Chaewon."

Marisa waited for someone to remark on the name, but no one did. "I have no idea who that is," she said at last. Anja, Jaya, and Fang all shrugged and said the same.

"That's because she's not a pro," said Sahara, obviously relishing the chance to reveal whatever juicy bit of gossip she'd discovered. "Kwon Chaewon is the daughter of Kwon Dae."

"Dios mío," said Marisa, and then laughed out loud, her eyes wide in hilarious shock. "That's the CEO of KT Sigan. Chaewon's one of the spoiled rich kids!"

"Yep," said Sahara, and her eyes twinkled. "She's a spoiled rich kid who bought herself four pro-player friends. It's the best of both worlds!"

"That's the most pathetic thing I've ever heard," said Fang with a laugh. "Please tell me she made herself the General."

"Of course she did," said Sahara.

Fang and Anja burst into laughter, and Marisa couldn't help but join them. Even Sahara was chuckling.

"Wait," said Jaya. "She's riding the coattails of a champion-level team, pretending to be their leader, in a tournament which, let's remember, her father created and is hosting. He might have created it solely so she could play in it. That's taking 'spoiled rich kid' to a whole new level."

"I'm seriously dying over here," said Fang, between bouts of laughter.

Jaya was the only one not laughing. "Guys, I don't think it's that simple."

"Why not?" said Marisa.

"Because a girl who would put all this together just so she could pretend to be an Overworld pro is not a girl who's going to be content to lose. And her father owns the network we're going to be playing on." Her face was solemn. "I'll bet you right now, there's going to be some hardcore cheating."

"Either way," said Sahara, "we need to get practicing."

SIX

Marisa and Anja crouched on the top of a tree, peering across the leafy green jungle in front of them. Every Overworld map was functionally identical—the jungle canopy was laid out exactly like the warehouse roofs in the war-zone map, or the tops of the buildings in the medieval map, and the players could move across it in the same way, stepping on leaves and branches as if they were a solid platform. In this particular map the city was a loose collection of huts on the jungle floor, and the AI bots were guerrilla warriors. They were playing against a Korean team called Skull4ce—their name struck Marisa as hopelessly macho, but they'd been willing to try a Seoul Draft, so Sahara had accepted the challenge.

"Another wave down," said Sahara, her voice crackling over the comm, "but it was all bots. Haven't seen the enemy agents in a while."

"We haven't seen them either," said Marisa. "I'm going to

move out and check behind that big tree to the west."

"I'll cover you," said Anja. She was holding a long Arlechino sniper rifle, at least three times the length of her small red panda body.

"I don't see them in the sewers," said Fang.

"I've got the new shield," said Jaya. "Think it's safe to bring it out? I don't want to get sniped coming out of this cave."

"No," said Sahara, "stay there. If the whole team's missing, odds are good they're in the sewers, getting ready to blitz the vault."

"I'm telling you, they're not down here," said Fang.

"Head back to the base, Yīnyǐng," Sahara ordered. She insisted on using call signs instead of real names, thinking it helped put them in a professional mindset. Fang's call sign, Yīnyǐng, meant Shadow. "I'm going to try to take this turret as soon as the next wave of bots catches up to me."

"Go carefully, Yīnyǐng," said Marisa. Her call sign was the much less edgy Heartbeat. "You don't want to stumble into all five agents coming around a corner."

"Yes, I do," said Fang. "I bet I could take out two of them before they killed me."

"Go carefully," Sahara urged.

"No movement up here," said Anja. "Move out."

Marisa picked up her longbow and crept across the upper canopy, crouching low and staying in cover as much as possible. She came to the edge of a leafy platform and looked down at the mossy tracks and tree trunks below her; she could see a wave of bots moving forward, and the wireframe display in the corner of her vision showed Sahara's icon ahead of them, beckoning them forward to assault a turret. Were the agents lying in wait, planning to ambush her? Or were they really headed for the vault, like Sahara thought?

"I want to move forward and help Sahara with the turret," said Anja on the comm. Sahara had used her real name as her call sign, which seemed to Marisa like it missed the whole point, but that was Sahara for you. She lived her entire life online; keeping her name as visible as possible was part of her branding.

"No," said Sahara, "stay there."

"I'm sorry," said Anja, "who was that order directed at?"

"At you," said Sahara. She sounded frustrated, and Marisa rolled her eyes at Anja's teasing.

"Who, though?" asked Anja. "We're supposed to use call signs to be more professional."

Sahara grumbled over the comm. "I want you to maintain your position, Happy."

"That's not the whole call sign," said Anja. "Are we allowing nicknames now?"

Sahara sighed. "I want you to maintain your position, Happy-FluffySparkleTime. I also want you to die in a fire."

"Will do, Sahara," said Anja. Marisa smirked as they skirted the edge of the canopy.

"No dead drones in the sewers," said Fang. "I'm standing right under our vault, and there's nobody here. I'm literally turning around slowly in a pool of light, and no one's killing me."

Marisa readied her bow and stepped carefully through the leaves, sidling up to one of the gaps in the canopy. In the war-zone map this was a roof access stairway; here it was a collection of sloped branches and jury-rigged stairs leading down into a thick grove of trees. A large drone, in the shape of a massive silverback gorilla, crouched on the far side, munching on a banana as the game ran him through a series of idle animations. Marisa stayed back, barely peeking around the corner. If the drone saw her it would attack, and she wasn't equipped with a stealth suit to get away from it—

"Este cabrón," hissed Marisa, realization dawning on her in a sudden rush. "They're stealthed."

"The whole team?" asked Jaya.

"They're not built for it," said Sahara. "We saw their powersets—none of them have any stealth ability."

"That's why it's brilliant," said Marisa. "They showed us a team with zero stealth, so we didn't plan for it, and then they earned enough gold in the first half of the game to buy stealth suits from their vault, and now the whole damn team's invisible."

"That's stupid," said Fang. "They'll reveal themselves as soon as they attack—they spent a fortune on a trick they can only use once."

"No," said Sahara, "Heartbeat's right—this can totally work, because they caught us with our pants down. All they need to do is focus on one of us at a time and we're f—"

The canopy around Marisa erupted in a mass of gunfire and swirling blades, as all five enemy agents appeared out of nowhere to attack her at once. She tried to dodge out of the way, but there were too many; they broke through her armor in seconds, and her health a few seconds later.

"Heartbeat is down!" said the announcer voice. Marisa found

herself floating in blackness, and screamed at the sudden feeling of helplessness. She couldn't help her team or even talk to them until she respawned, and she'd gained enough levels so far in the match that her respawn timer was nearly thirty seconds long—more than enough for the stealthed Skull4ce agents to kill one or even two more Cherry Dogs.

"Quicksand!" shouted Sahara. "Sell everything you have and buy stealth goggles!"

"Got it!" answered Jaya.

"Happy, fall back!" shouted Sahara. "We need to regroup at the vault and let the towers protect us until we have the right gear to fight these idiots."

"Roger," said Anja.

"Falling back," said Fang.

"Yīnyǐng, you stay ahead," said Sahara. She sounded breathless, like she was running. "Rush their vault—don't attack it, just steal their credits. If they see their money start disappearing, they might send a few agents back to protect it."

"If they bought five stealth suits, they don't have any credits left," said Fang.

"Just do it!" shouted Sahara. "If you try a full attack, you'll get murdered by the turrets; this is the only way to split their focus—damn it!"

Marisa looked at the team display, seeing Sahara's health meter evaporate in seconds. A moment later Sahara appeared beside her in the waiting room, cursing horrifically.

"We should have survived that!" she shouted. "There's no way they should have been able to move that fast!"

"Where were you?" asked Marisa.

"Almost all the way back to the stupid cave," said Sahara. "They got you at the stairs, and then me at the cave, what, eight seconds later? Ten at the most? Nothing in their build says they can move that fast, and there's no way they could afford speed packs *and* stealth suits this early in the game."

Anja's health dropped by half in a sudden ambush, and crept steadily downward as the seconds ticked by. Marisa checked her own respawn timer: Six seconds left. Five. Four.

Marisa rematerialized in the vault just in time to see Anja limping past the turrets. Jaya was firing magic bolts into the forest at the retreating enemy.

"Only three agents," said Jaya. "Yīnyǐng split the team, just like Sahara said."

"Get out of there, Yīnyǐng," said Marisa. "They're coming for you, and their team moves crazy fast."

"They don't have any speed powers," said Fang.

"They used a slow power," said Anja, gasping in pain as she used a health pack. "That's the trick that makes this work."

"What slow power?" asked Marisa, trying to remember the Skull4ce build. "And how would one help them catch Sahara?"

"Their Spotter has Air Buff," said Anja. "I didn't think twice about it, because Spotters use that all the time for Wind Leap."

"Wind Leap doesn't boost your speed," said Marisa, "definitely not for the whole team—oh, holy crap, you're right. Feather Fall."

Anja nodded. "They killed you on the roof, then dropped into the city slow enough to survive the fall. They're not faster because they have a speed power, they're faster because they didn't take the stairs."

"I'm back," said Sahara, appearing behind them. "Yīnyǐng, you safe?"

"I got out just in time," said Fang. "Good call on the vault rush; that probably saved Anja's life."

"Maybe," said Sahara. "It's not going to help us win this match, though. In the time I was dead they dropped two turrets."

They bought stealth goggles and kept playing, but their team had already lost its momentum. Fifteen minutes later their vault exploded under enemy fire, and the announcer loudly trumpeted the Skull4ce win.

"It's okay," said Sahara in the team lobby, sounding more like she was trying to convince herself than anyone else. "This was a learning experience."

"I'll check some of the Korean forums," said Jaya. "If this is a common strategy over there, there's bound to be some good counterstrategies as well."

"You speak Korean, too?" asked Marisa. "Maybe you should just tell us what you *don't* speak."

"Finnish," said Jaya. "Trying to learn that one's like slamming your brain in a door."

"Whoa," said Anja. "Hold up."

"What's up?" asked Fang.

Anja looked shocked, which was rare. "Remember that spoiled rich girl we were all making fun of? Kwon Chaewon?"

"Daughter of the Sigan CEO," said Marisa. "What about her?"

"I just checked my messages," said Anja, "and she sent me an invitation."

"To what?" asked Sahara. "We're already registered for the tournament."

"It's an invitation to a dinner party. On the top floor of the Sigan building." Anja raised her eyebrows. "For all of us."

Fang frowned. "She knows who we are?"

"What night is it?" asked Sahara.

"Saturday," said Anja. "I'm forwarding it to you."

"Probably some kind of 'getting to know you' social before the tournament starts." Sahara's eyes gleamed, bright and eager. "This is going to be *amazing*."

"We won't even be in LA yet," said Jaya.

"I'll see if I can switch your flights," said Anja. "Maybe I can convince my father this is a key public appearance as representatives of Abendroth, I don't know."

"Don't worry about it," said Fang. "I'm not really a party person."

"But this is a *formal* party," said Sahara, reading from her own copy of the invitation. "Black ties, gowns—that's when you know it's a fancy party, when they say 'gowns' instead of 'dresses.' They're flying in a master chef from Korea. They're going to have ice sculptures of all the team logos!"

"Nothing you are saying is making this sound appealing," said Fang.

Marisa found the forwarded invitation in her own inbox, and blinked to open it. She skimmed through the details while the others tried to convince Fang, and her eyes struck on one detail that made her jaw drop.

"Girls," she said.

"They'll have champagne," said Sahara. "And no one will stop you from drinking it underage—it's a rich-people party, you can break any laws you want."

"We can hunt humans for sport," said Anja.

"Girls," said Marisa again, louder this time. "Did you see who's going to be there?"

"All the other teams," said Sahara. "Some of the local CEOs."

"Yeah," said Marisa, "but read to the end. The toastmaster is Su-Yun Kho."

The four other girls went instantly silent. Even Fang's mouth hung open.

"Su-Yun Kho?" asked Sahara. "As in, *the* Su-Yun Kho? The Su-Yun Kho who was the first female world champion of Overworld, and my first crush, and the greatest human being who ever lived?"

"I'm devoutly het," said Anja, "and I would still kiss her full on the mouth until I died of asphyxiation."

"I love Su-Yun Kho," said Jaya. "I have posters of her on my wall."

"I have the headjack cable she used in her second regional championship," said Fang, though she looked sheepish as she admitted it. "It . . . came with a certificate."

Marisa smiled. "Yeah," she said. "*That* Su-Yun Kho."

Fang closed her eyes and slumped against the wall. "I swore I'd die before I ever wore a dress, let alone a gown." She shook her head. "But this is totally worth dying for."

SEVEN

Marisa looked up as the waiter nuli approached. "One Solipsis Cafe roast pepper salad," she said. "Extra dressing." The nuli was Arora brand, and incredibly simple: little more than a digital screen with four small rotors, hanging in the air right at Marisa's eye level; the screen lit up with text confirming the order, and a speaker on the front spoke with an incongruously human-sounding voice:

"Will that be everything?"

It wasn't a real AI, at least not in the sense that it was self-aware—that kind of technology still didn't exist. Service nulis were fitted with a handful of prerecorded phrases most likely to come up in the course of their duties. If Anja had been there, she'd have started trying to stump it, probing the limits of its conversation tree just to watch it get flustered, but Marisa was on her own today. Which meant she barely had enough money for the salad, let alone anything else.

"Nothing else," she said. "Thanks."

"Would you like something to drink?"

She desperately wanted a Lift, but she needed every last cent for the train ride home. "Water's fine."

The nuli added a second line to its digital display: "Bottled Water—$9.45."

"Whoa," said Marisa, "just tap water, please—take that off there."

"The city of Los Angeles has designated today as a Red Drinking Day in this neighborhood," said the nuli's soft, feminine voice. "At Solipsis Cafe we care about our customers' health, which is why we have a policy never to—"

"Fine," said Marisa. It was just her luck that she'd be downtown on what was probably its one Red Drinking Day this month. "No water, just the salad. Nothing else." The water disappeared from the display, and the nuli floated away to the next customer. "And extra dressing!" Marisa shouted after it, but the charge for the salad had already appeared in her djinni display, and she just had to hope that extra dressing was part of it. She blinked on the charge icon, transferring funds from her account, and waited.

"The dressing's the best part," she grumbled.

She looked out the window at the giant KT Sigan building across the street. Was she really ready to do this? She'd better be—she'd just invested sixty dollars in a salad. She couldn't afford a second try. Marisa blinked open her Bowie coding program, reviewed her virus one last time, and then compiled it into a hidden executable and dumped it into her Djinni Activity Log. If everything worked the way it was supposed to, the Sigan tech support people would pull the log, and the virus would do the rest without being detected. If it didn't work the way it was supposed to . . . well, they'd catch her red-handed trying to plant a virus in an international megacorp's private files. The punishments for that were, to put it lightly, severe.

"I've got to find Grendel," she whispered. "This is the only way."

The woman at the next table shrieked in delight over something the man sitting with her said; they smiled at each other, cooing softly and touching hands, and Marisa rolled her eyes and looked away—being careful, this time, not to scatter her djinni's icons as she did so. It wasn't that she hated the idea of two people in love—it was the opposite. She loved being in love. She loved staring into someone's eyes and laughing at whatever random thing he said, as if it was the funniest thing anyone had ever said in the history of human interaction. Which was why it was so hard to watch it from the outside, flanked by a long trail of catastrophically failed relationships.

Lal had been the worst—it wasn't every day you fell for a guy who betrayed you as profoundly as he had—but the competition for second place was fierce. Maybe David? Maybe José? And she couldn't forget that cuate with the motorcycle, what was his name? Carlos? It served her right for dating a guy with her father's name—she should have known he'd drive her into a rage eventually. All she wanted was a simple, wonderful, storybook relationship. Was that so hard?

Or maybe just a boyfriend who didn't have a secret plan to destroy the entire city?

The couple at the next table launched a selfie nuli, and Marisa dropped her face into the palm of her hand. Now she'd be a side character in their life story forever: The Girl in the Background. If her salad hadn't come at that exact moment, gently deposited on her table by a delivery nuli, she might have packed up and gone home. Instead she opened the plastic box, saw not one but two little cups of salad dressing, and smiled.

"At least the waiter nuli loves me," she whispered. She opened one of the dressing cups and drizzled it out on the salad. "I love you too, little guy. Bring me three next time and I'll start picking out china patterns."

An icon popped up in her djinni: a text message from Pati. She sighed and blinked on it.

When can you help me learn binary? her little sister sent. **The assignment's due on Thursday, and that's a day and a half away. How do you say one and a half in binary? It doesn't make sense I HATE IT.**

Marisa smiled and sent a quick response: **I'll help you tonight.** She took a bite, savoring the incredible blend of flavors—she really needed to look up Solipsis online and see if they'd posted the recipe somewhere—and looked back out at the Sigan building. May as well get started. She followed the same steps any random Sigan customer would follow: she blinked open her djinni settings, found her net connection info, and blinked on the customer service number. It dialed, and she was in.

"Hello," said another automated voice. "Welcome to KT Sigan, the world's leading provider of networking and telecom services. How may we direct your call?" A menu scrolled across her vision, and she blinked on customer support. "Thank you," said the voice. "Please wait just a moment while we connect you with customer support."

She took another bite of salad, and had to swallow it in a rush when the support guy answered almost immediately. "Hi, Ms. Car-nessicka," he said, horribly mispronouncing her name. "My name is Pablo Nakamoto, and I'll be handling your call today."

Marisa had to bite down on her tongue to keep from laughing—this was the same guy she'd taken the security code from. Poor guy, she thought. If Sigan ever discovered the breach down the line, his name was going to be all over it.

"Please be aware that this call may be recorded for quality assurance purposes," said Pablo. "How can I help you today?"

"Hi," she said, trying to sound confident but naive. "I've been having some trouble with my connection. Could you take a look at it?" The other people in the cafe ignored her; most of them were having mumbled conversations on their djinnis as well. Only the loving couple was paying attention to the real world, and they were ignoring Marisa completely.

She shook her head and concentrated on her phone call.

"Of course," said Pablo, his voice obsequious and servile. "I'm very sorry to hear that you've been having trouble, and I'll do everything I can to fix it. Let me see here . . ." His voice trailed off as he did something on his end, reviewing what little data he had on her usage. None of it, she hoped, would be incriminating in itself—she was always careful to hide her more illicit internet activities from prying eyes. After a moment he spoke again. "I'm not seeing any significant losses of service or signal in the Mirador area," he said. "Could you tell me more specifically what trouble you've been having?"

"Every now and then certain websites get really slow," said Marisa, fabricating a story as she spoke. "Like, really slow, for no reason. I play Overworld all the time, with no problems, but sometimes it can't even handle Muffin Top, and I figure that can't be normal. You know Muffin Top? That game with all the little . . . muffin tops?" Social hacking was not her area of expertise; she needed to get him into the Djinni Activity Log and be done with it. "None of my friends or family have had the same issue, so I think it's got to be local to me, maybe something in my settings."

"I'm so sorry to hear that you've been having that problem, and I know how frustrating it can be," he said again. Marisa figured he must have been reading off a script. "What I'd like to do next is pull your Djinni Activity Log, which will show me exactly what's been going on with your signal. Is that okay?"

There it was. "That sounds great," she said. "Thanks for your help."

"Thank you," said Pablo. "That's very nice of you to say. I'll start the download now, and while I do I also want to let you know that KT Sigan is a true partner to every community that embraces our service." He continued with his "stall for time" speech while the download counter in Marisa's vision slowly counted out the percents. She hadn't realized her DAL would be so big, but she supposed it made sense—she was on her djinni, surfing the net, practically every waking minute.

What had she just permitted him to look at? The thought flashed through her mind, but if there was something to be worried about, it was already too late.

"There we go," said Pablo, as the DAL transfer completed. "Now, if you'll give me just a moment to analyze this data, I'll see if we can find the source of your troubles. Do you mind if I put you on hold?"

"Go ahead," said Marisa.

"Thank you," said Pablo. He put her on hold, and an hourglass icon appeared in the corner of her vision, surrounded by the words "Your call is important to us." She watched it for a moment, laughed, and then ended the call. When he eventually came back he'd probably just assume that she'd lost the connection. She took another bite of her salad and moved on to the next phase of the plan.

At this very moment, the virus was burrowing into the Sigan security center and fabricating a fake ID for Marisa to use to log in. She had no way of knowing when it was done; it wouldn't send her a message or an alert, it would simply do its job and delete itself. She needed to give it time, and while she waited she activated another program inside of her own djinni, hiding all of her identifying information and rendering her completely anonymous to anyone who tried to scan her, or her connection, digitally. Immediately another nuli swarmed her table, thinking she was a new customer and rushing to clear what was left on the table, but she waved it away. This reaction gave her courage: the stealth program was working. Now she activated the final piece of anonymity, connecting to the Solipsis Cafe Wi-Fi instead of linking to Sigan directly—that was why, in the end, she was doing this here instead of at home. If anyone did happen to find her inside the network, and got suspicious enough to actually trace the signal, they'd find the cafe instead of her, with no ID or GPS data to give her away. As far as they would know, it could be anyone here.

She took another few bites of salad, too nervous to really enjoy them, and then connected to Sigan's private network. She tried the fake ID the virus should have set up for her . . .

. . . Órale!

Marisa snapped her fingers, pointing at the ceiling with a triumphant whoop. A woman at another table glanced at her, but Marisa ignored her; a random shout from a girl on a djinni could mean almost anything. Just in case, she muttered, "One more turret to go," to give the impression that she was watching an Overworld match. Then she silently continued her hack.

She activated one of her Goblins—the one that copied the user list, deleted her presence from it, and redirected any other users to the cleaned-up copy. This would keep her completely invisible from any IT personnel who happened to be patrolling the network, just as an added security measure. Once that was done she started exploring the system, following the branching paths of files and folders, learning how everything fit together and where any secrets might be hidden. It looked like Sigan used Gamdog 4.1, a pretty common data shell for big corporations, and one that Marisa was at least passingly familiar with. That was a stroke of luck. She found the folder for the Overworld tournament in the "Corporate Events" section, and the fancy party Chaewon and Sigan were throwing; she glanced through the party's menu and some of the private emails, including a very strict order from Chaewon that one of the teams, called MotherBunny, was not to be invited or allowed in. Marisa wanted to read more, but she didn't know how much time she had. She moved on, promising herself she would come back later if there was time.

She found an entire subsection of the network full of business plans for the coming year, and another from the in-house creative department, filled with draft after draft of upcoming ads and banners and sensovids. One section had what she assumed were customer pricing discussions, and another held meeting notes about a plan for a global corporate reorganization. Marisa was floating through a treasure trove of data, enough to make herself immensely wealthy if she leaked some key bits of it to Sigan's competitors. She was more tempted than she cared to admit—she didn't mind breaking in to private networks, but it was usually only for fun, or to accomplish some other goal. Actually stealing anything, real corporate espionage stuff, was another thing entirely.

But then, so was her family losing their business and their home. Maybe she could justify it, just this once?

She shook her head. She was here for Grendel—that was her goal, and she had to keep her mind focused on that and not get distracted. Stealing data to get rich was something Omar would do; Marisa was only stealing data to finally learn the truth about her past. Her own family.

She clung to that slim philosophical distinction, and kept exploring the network.

What she needed were the client files: the lists of who bought telecom service from Sigan, and where they were located, and how she could find them. Once she could connect Grendel's IP address to a consistent physical location, it would only be a matter of time before she found him in real life; she could threaten him, she could dox him, or if he turned out to be close enough, she could even visit him in person, tearing the information out of him by hand. How much did he really know? Maybe a demonstration of skill would be enough: *I found you, I've passed your little hacker test, now tell me what I need to know.* Maybe she'd need more, but his location was the first step, and she searched the network for it as closely and carefully as possible.

As she explored the private network, she found references to the client database, but not the database itself. Where was it? She kept hunting, tracing every path in the network, every server connection . . . nothing. She growled in frustration, pounding the table, and glanced at the same woman who'd looked at her before. She was looking again. Marisa grumbled something else about an imaginary Overworld game, and looked back at the map of the network. The client files simply weren't there.

If all else fails, she told herself, *read the manual.* She went back to the IT section of the network and found the employee handbook, combing through it for some hint about where the client database might be hiding. Maybe they'd renamed it? That was a common enough security tactic, calling your core folders something nonstandard to help foil the more common viruses—if a virus was automated to attack the "client database," it would skip right by something called the "monkey swingset" without causing any damage. Maybe she'd already passed over the database without recognizing it? She found the client section of the handbook, read through it as quickly as she could, and swore again. The client database wasn't just renamed, and it wasn't just buried under a deeper layer of network security. This was worse.

It was airgapped.

The client database, along with the company's financial information, was completely disconnected from the rest of the network and the internet itself, 100 percent unreachable unless you physically entered the building, logged in to a specific workstation, and reached it from there.

"Toda la mierda en el mundo," Marisa muttered, and when the woman at the next table looked over, Marisa shot her a glare with every ounce of pent-up rage she was feeling. "My team *lost. Again!*" The woman looked away quickly.

Marisa didn't know what to do next. How was she supposed to find Grendel now? She looked around the cafe, half hoping some magical solution would materialize out of nowhere. She'd risked so much to get into the network, and for nothing. But, no, it wasn't past tense: she was *still* risking something. She looked back at her Goblin, checking to make sure that no one had found her in the user list.

Except . . . she wasn't in the user list.

Marisa frowned, staring at the djinni display. She knew she was logged in—she could see the network, she could move around in it—but the user list didn't *say* she was logged in. She wondered if maybe she was looking at the wrong copy of the user list, the one her Goblin was erasing her from, but no—she had both lists open, and she wasn't in either of them. The only way that would be possible was if she, too, was looking at a fake copy of the user list, being redirected by someone else. And the only way *that* was possible was if . . .

"There's a second Goblin," she whispered.

Somehow, against all odds, she was hacking into Sigan's private network at the same time as another hacker, and he must have been using the same copy-and-redirect tactic that she was.

What else was he doing?

Marisa stared at the user list, trying to figure out how to contact the other hacker. Her own plan was a bust, but maybe this new guy had something she could use? It was risky, but this whole thing was risky.

Maybe if she added a fake user to the list? Something like HeyICanSeeYou—something so obviously fake he couldn't help but notice it. But then, so would the IT department, and sooner or later they'd investigate it. Was it worth the trouble? She didn't even know what she'd say to the hacker if she got his attention—it wasn't like he was going to just offer his help out of the goodness of his heart. She refreshed the user list, trying to convince herself to create a fake username, and her jaw dropped open. The other hacker had already created one:

YoureNotSupposedToBeHere

Marisa shook her head, stunned, then smirked and added a fake username of her own:

NeitherAreYou

She refreshed again, hoping for a response. Nothing. She realized she was holding her breath, and forced herself to breathe. She clenched her fingers into a fist, and refreshed the list one more time.

The old fake name had been replaced by a new one:

GetOutNow

Marisa shook her head; she wasn't leaving without some answers, and she typed in a new name:

WhoAreYou

She refreshed the list, two, three, four times, desperate for an answer, and then there it was:

IJustTrashedTheirPaymentDatabaseGetOutNow

Almost instantly her Goblin beeped at her: someone was looking for her. She thought at first that the username conversation had attracted attention, and started to delete the fake names, but almost instantly she saw other alarms going off all through the system. She was logged in with full admin privileges, so she could see every alert, and whatever this other hacker had done had set all of them off. In seconds, the entire IT department started sweeping the system for anyone accessing the private servers. Marisa had been careful, but she wasn't ready for this—she hadn't bounced her signal, she hadn't brought in the extra Goblins; she was completely exposed. She had to get out now.

She cut her connection, jumped up from her table, and ran.

EIGHT

Marisa ran through the cafe and out the door into the scorching LA heat, stopping almost immediately as she got stuck in a giant crowd of people waiting at the corner. She took deep breaths, trying to force herself to calm down and blend in. Some of the people were in business suits or skirts, and some in street clothes that ran the spectrum from homeless rags to jeans and T-shirts to flashy constructions of see-through plastic and origami ruffles. More than a few glanced at her, probably wondering why she was running, but she knew they'd lose interest soon enough if she kept calm. She tried to look busy instead of terrified, and waited for the light to change. It didn't. She could turn and run the other way, but the fastest way out of downtown was the train, and that was just on the other side of the street.

The KT Sigan building loomed over her like a haunted mountain, full of probing eyes and eager claws. Her heart pounded in her chest, and it took all her concentration just to hold still.

The traffic speeding past her was like a river of steel and glass, hundreds of autocars driving by in perfect unison, and she had the sudden urge to simply ignore the lights and rush out into them, knowing they would swerve to avoid her. Autocars were networked into a swarm intelligence that had two inviolable directives: to get riders where they needed to go, and to keep pedestrians safe. If she jumped in front of one, it would move out of the way, faster than any human driver could have managed it, and simultaneously it would communicate her presence to all the other cars behind it, causing them to swerve or slow or even reroute to other streets. She'd studied the traffic SI a few months ago, after an incident with Anja running heedlessly onto a freeway, so she knew how it worked, and she knew that she'd probably be fine . . . probably. But as safe as the autocars were, there was always a chance of failure, and she of all people had a constant reminder of just how dangerous those failures could be. She rubbed her metal arm, and bit her tongue, and kept waiting for the light.

Across the street, the train station and the Sigan building shared opposite edges of a wide, tiled plaza, dotted here and there with planter boxes and carefully manicured trees. The Sigan main lobby was a three-story wall of sectioned glass, and Marisa watched as a stream of visitors and employees flowed in and out of the doors. Suddenly she gasped—a tiny, involuntary catch of her breath. A new man had joined the stream, a head taller than the others, the flow of people parting around him as he walked from the Sigan building straight toward Marisa. His eyes were covered with a solid, curved plate: a bionic vision implant that was used almost exclusively by special forces and private security. She couldn't see the rest of his body in the crowd, but he was dressed in black and moved with a terrifying sense of single-minded purpose. Some of the people in the plaza were meandering; others were rushing to work or to other appointments. This man was hunting.

Marisa opened a chat window to Sahara, and almost immediately closed it again. If this Sigan thug was coming for her, then the company was onto her, and they were closer than she'd dared to believe. If they caught her with a chat window open, actively discussing her crime, it could incriminate anyone she was chatting with as an accomplice. Better to stay solo, though it terrified her to be alone.

Did he already know who she was? What would he do if he caught her?

The traffic stopped, the light turned, and the crowd on both sides burst into the street like an avalanche, carrying her straight toward the visored guard. Should she try to turn and run? But no, she'd been at least that careful—the digital connection Sigan had used to trace her led only to the restaurant, not to Marisa herself. He was probably going there, and running now would only draw his attention. She took another deep breath, trying to control her heart rate, grateful that her bronze skin was dark enough to hide the flush that she could feel rising to her face.

The thug came closer, stalking firmly through the crowd: ten steps away, five steps, one step. She kept her eyes on the ground. He brushed past her in the middle of the street, their sleeves touching with an audible swish, and then he was gone, lost in the crowd behind her, and she kept her head down and walked up the short concrete stairs to the train platform.

She permitted herself a sigh of relief, clutching a railing as her knees shook from fear. She blinked up the train schedule: she had three minutes until the next train.

More waiting.

She watched as the Sigan thug went into the Solipsis Cafe, and her heart skipped a beat. She turned and started hurrying to the far end of the platform, nearly half a block from the cafe—trying to get as far as she could from the man. The train platform was elevated enough that she could see over the crowd, but the farther she walked, the less she could see through the windows of the cafe. What was he doing? She planted her feet firmly, not wanting to lose her balance, and activated one of her sense mods, an aftermarket app that Anja had programmed for their djinnis. It zoomed her vision forward, and she felt a moment of vertigo as the cafe flew toward her, magnified until it seemed to be just a few feet away from her. The image was distorted, especially around the edge, and she had to hold her head almost impossibly still, but she could see him: the thug was talking to the other customers, table by table.

It's okay, Marisa told herself. *Nobody was paying attention to me. They don't remember what I look like, they don't remember what I was wearing, they don't remember what I was eating, and the nulis will have cleaned it up already so he can't even get any DNA from it.*

She guessed that the thug was Asian, though with most of his face covered she couldn't tell for sure. He stopped at the table of the woman who'd kept looking at Marisa during the hack. Marisa caught her breath, not daring to breathe. She couldn't hear them, and she couldn't read their lips; she could only guess what they were saying from their body language. He said something and the woman shook her head. He said something else and she shook her head again. He stepped forward, stern and insistent. The woman scowled, shook her head, and looked away.

Marisa breathed again. Disaster averted.

The man turned to the lovey-dovey couple.

"Híjole," said Marisa, clenching her hands into nervous fists. "They took a picture of me."

Are you okay? sent Sahara. **Do you need anything?**

Marisa didn't answer. She glanced at her clock, and saw that the train was almost here. Just a few more seconds. The thug asked the couple a question, and they shook their heads. He asked again, and the woman behind him stood up, saying something with what looked like an angry face. "Thank you so much," Marisa mumbled. "Que dios te bendiga." The man ignored her and asked the couple another question. They looked at the woman, and then at him, and then at the woman . . .

. . . and then pulled out their selfie nuli, and showed him the photo.

"Damn it," said Marisa.

The thug studied the photo, looked up toward the train platform, and scanned the crowd until he seemed to be staring directly at her. His mouth hardened into a grim line, and he ran for the door.

Marisa shut off the sight magnification and the world snapped back into its normal resolution; she stumbled from the sudden shift, and then turned and ran, forgetting in her terror that she was already at the end of the platform. The railing loomed up like a barrier, trapping her, and she braced herself to vault it when suddenly the train roared around a corner and into the station, the wind of its passage whipping Marisa's hair around her face. She glanced behind her and saw the Sigan thug barely twenty meters away—impossibly close, moving impossibly fast. How had he reached her so quickly? She turned and ran toward the train, right as the doors opened; she pushed her way forward, dodging and weaving through the crowd, finding spaces in the crush of people that a man his size could never possibly fit through.

"StopAndSurrenderYourselfDontMakeMeChaseYou," yelled the man, amplifying his voice somehow so she could hear it clearly above the noise of the train and the passengers. Was his throat bionic too? Was that why his words seemed accelerated? Marisa didn't waste any more time wondering about it; she focused all her attention on getting away, and pushed out through the other side of the train to the far platform. She didn't know how much time she'd bought herself with the maneuver, but she plunged ahead, jumping over the railing and directly into the busy road beyond. The cars saw her coming, calculated her trajectory as she fell toward the street, and moved to miss her; she hit the ground in a patch of clear asphalt and bolted toward the sidewalk, not even slowing as she ran. The crowd parted in front of her, no one wanting to tangle with the crazy girl who'd jumped into the middle of traffic, when suddenly an arm caught her from behind, the grip as solid as steel, and yanked her to a painful halt.

"IdentifyYourselfImmediatelyIHaveJurisdictionInThisCity-ToEnforceCorporatePolicy."

"I don't know what you're talking about," Marisa said, trying to sound as innocent as she could. "I didn't do anything wrong."

"PlantingAVirusInAPrivateDatabaseIsACrimeUnderUSFederalProvisionNumberFourTwentySeven—" He stopped abruptly as something large and metal screamed through Marisa's field of vision, slamming into the thug and knocking him away. Marisa found herself falling as well, scraping her right hand on the rough cement of the sidewalk, people screaming all around her. As she struggled to reorient herself, she felt another hand—warm and human—take her by the arm.

"Sorry I'm late."

"What?" asked Marisa. She looked up, still reeling from the impact, and saw a young man on a motorcycle, his skin dark, his hair wild, his eyes covered by rough, weathered goggles. She'd never seen him before in her life.

He pulled again on her arm, gentle but insistent. "Mr. Park is more than eighty percent machine," said the young man, speaking quickly but calmly. He had an accent Marisa couldn't place; something European. "Even an impact from a motorcycle won't keep him down for long. We have to go."

Marisa looked at the thug who'd been chasing her, crumpled in a heap almost ten meters away. He groaned and moved one of his arms.

Another motorcycle roared up next to the first, its engine growling like a hungry predator. The blue-haired girl riding it scowled at Marisa, and growled her frustration in a sharp Chicano accent. "Grab her or leave her—I don't want to get boxed for some random chick on the street."

"Who are you?" demanded Marisa. "What's going on?"

The man he had called Mr. Park continued his recovery, sitting up and shaking his head. He didn't look like he was injured, just dazed, despite being thrown so far.

"Look, I'm the other ghost in the database," said the young man on the motorcycle, letting go of Marisa's arm and instead simply offering her his hand. His accent, she realized, was French, and now that she could see him properly, she found he was very good-looking. "Come with me now, or let him catch you. It's your choice."

Marisa looked at the bionic thug as he slowly clambered to his feet, and imagined what he would do to her if he got her back to the Sigan building. She made her decision, grabbed the young man's hand, and jumped up behind him on the motorcycle.

"Let's get out of here."

The blue-haired girl revved her bike with a wicked grin, and slammed it forward into Mr. Park, knocking him to the ground again. The young man followed her, both bikes bolting forward into the street, and Marisa felt her stomach drop away in the sudden burst of acceleration, left behind on the sidewalk as they wove in and out of traffic.

"Aytale!" shouted Marisa, gripped by terror as they whipped through tiny gaps between the speeding cars. "I hate human drivers."

"This is the only way for us to escape," he said. "I'm Alain, by the way."

"Why isn't the *bike* driving?" Marisa shouted over the rushing wind. "You'll kill us!"

"They could control an autopilot remotely," said Alain. He turned a sharp corner, leaning the bike at a terrifying angle, and Marisa shrieked. "If we let the bike drive, we'd never get away from him."

"From the guy you ran over?" asked Marisa. "Twice? I doubt he's going to catch up to us now."

"Look behind us," said Alain, and Marisa turned slowly, gripping him tightly with her arms and thighs. The road behind her was filled with speeding cars, and racing through the middle of them was Mr. Park, his arms and legs pumping, his mouth fixed in a furious snarl. Marisa spun back around, gripping Alain even tighter than before.

"He's still chasing us," she gasped. She glanced back again. "He's *gaining* on us!"

"We have a safe house we can hide in," said Alain, "but we have to get away from him first. Hey, Renata!"

The blue-haired girl braked her bike a bit, dropping back toward Alain and matching his speed. Her hoodie, Marisa realized, wasn't just colorful, it was animated—the fabric bore the bright image of a deep-space nebula, swirling and shifting like a real-time video. "Want me to take him out?"

"Good luck," said Alain. "Can you maybe buy us some time, though?"

Renata smirked at Marisa. "Hey, rich girl—ever seen a hand grenade?"

"We're in the middle of Los Angeles at rush hour!" shouted

Marisa. "Are you out of your mind?"

Renata smirked again and held up her left arm. Marisa saw that it was prosthetic, like her own, though the model was older, and the joints were grimy with dirt and oil. An old SuperYu, just like Marisa used to have. Renata pointed her arm backward and her hand launched off like a miniature rocket.

So maybe it wasn't *just like* her own after all.

Marisa twisted her head to watch in shocked fascination as the hand sailed back toward the running thug and grabbed him firmly on the arm.

"Three," said Renata, "two, one."

The hand exploded, hiding Mr. Park in a sudden burst of fire and light. Marisa shielded her eyes, and Renata cackled and revved her bike again, zooming back into the lead.

"Sorry about the pun," said Alain. "She's good at what she does, but she has a very special sense of humor."

Marisa looked backward again. In the clearing smoke she could see that the cars were all swerving around a specific spot in the road, and she assumed it must be the site of Mr. Park's mangled body. None of the cars looked damaged, though she could see through the windows that most of the people in them were just as scared as she was. She felt sick: she'd just watched a man die, abruptly, out of nowhere—

"Is he gone?" asked Alain.

"He just got blown up!" shouted Marisa. "Of course he's . . ." The ripple in the line of cars moved, first keeping pace with traffic, and then slowly speeding up. "Santa muerte," she said, "he's still coming! Who is this guy?"

"One of KT Sigan's primary security assets," said Alain, following Renata on another dizzying turn. They righted themselves again as he gunned the engine and rebuilt speed. "I wasn't expecting to have to deal with him today, but then I wasn't exactly expecting you, either."

"Is he human?"

"That depends on your definition," said Alain. "A 'human purity' group like the Foundation would call people like you and me abominations." He rapped his knuckles against his right leg, and it clanged metallically. Apparently he had a prosthetic as well. He shook his head. "Someone like Mr. Park, though . . . even the most liberal cybernetic activist would think twice about him."

"Because he's eighty percent machine?" asked Marisa, remembering the earlier warning.

"It's not the percentage," said Alain, "it's the parts. Mr. Park is overclocked."

Marisa's eyes went wide, and she found her arms wrapping involuntarily tighter around Alain's chest. She'd read about bionic overclocking, but she'd never actually seen it in the flesh, so to speak. It was expensive and illegal, mostly because it was very, very dangerous—outright deadly. Overclocking the human body worked the same way as overclocking a computer—speeding up the processor to make it faster and more powerful, which was safe enough if you kept it cool and didn't melt the circuits—except in this case, the circuits you were melting were your own neurons. Overclocked humans had better cognition, faster reflexes, and a host of superhuman abilities both mental and physical, but they lived, on average, only five years before the brain burned itself out completely.

"You could have told me he was overclocked when you first pulled up," said Marisa. "I would have gotten on this bike a whole lot faster."

"Most of his skeleton has been replaced by shock absorbers and internal armor," said Alain. "That's how he's still moving after everything we've done to him. And his endocrine system's been enhanced with an onboard suite of drug dispensers, which is *why* he's still moving. His bloodstream's probably half stimulant right now. According to a file I stole last month, most of his organs are synthetic, he can metabolize poison, he can recirculate his own oxygen supply for up to seven hours, and he can not only chew through metal, he can digest it when he's done." Alain smiled, just the barest hint at the corner of his mouth. "Which is why *we're* still moving."

"Who are you?" asked Marisa.

"Not now," said Alain. "Renata! Time to go off the grid."

"Hell yeah," Renata shouted back. She angled her bike to the side, swerved around a speeding truck, and turned down a smaller side road. Alain followed, and Marisa held on tight, squealing just a little as the motorcycle accelerated into the turn. Now that they were off the main road they had to dodge and swerve almost constantly, turning around corners and moving past pedestrians and dogs and other obstacles.

"He's still with us," said Marisa, glancing over her shoulder. "Barely half a block back and still gaining."

"I know," said Alain, talking through his teeth as he concentrated. "We know the terrain here better than he does—I'm hoping we can lose him."

The roads grew rougher as they raced through the city, and the buildings seemed to flash by in a high-speed strobe—quick images that came and went in an instant. Tall glass skyscrapers gave way to single-story storefronts, then run-down apartments, then a squalid neighborhood full of ramshackle houses and sagging warehouses and threadbare, dusty street mercados. Soon the roads were full of garbage and the walls were covered with graffiti, and the speeding iron river of autocars was replaced with handcarts and rickshaws and shirtless children running in the streets. Marisa blinked to open her GPS, and found that they were in a neighborhood called Kirkland, which her djinni was quick to indicate was currently under Red Drinking Day conditions—meaning the water there was effectively undrinkable. She blinked again to call up the history and found that Kirkland's water supply had been rated as Red for 647 days in a row. It didn't look like the city was even trying to clean it anymore. It didn't look like they were maintaining anything, either—the buildings were crumbling ruins, held together with cardboard and scraps. As the motorcycles spun around another corner, Marisa had to duck her head to keep clear of a protruding wall of corrugated tin.

This wasn't a neighborhood, it was a shantytown.

"We're losing our lead," said Renata. "Your plan sucks."

Mr. Park was closing the distance quickly now—he didn't know the area, but his robotic legs could handle the constant turns and swerves better than the motorcycles could. Alain jerked to the side to avoid a pile of dirt-crusted plastifoam bricks, nearly losing control of the bike, but Mr. Park simply jumped over it, shortening the gap even more. He was barely ten meters behind them now.

"I'm sorry," said Alain. "Losing him in here was our last trick."

"I told you not to pick up the girl!" shouted Renata.

"He's gonna catch us?" asked Marisa. She thought about Mr. Park chewing through metal, and shuddered.

"We have weapons," said Alain, "but the odds are against us. We'll try to hold them off while you hide—"

"Screw that," said Marisa. She scanned the road ahead and checked her GPS map. "You see that truck coming toward us?"

"The semitrailer?" asked Alain. "What about it?"

"We're going to hit him with it," said Marisa. "Renata, go straight toward that truck, and when it turns, follow it."

"I don't take orders from randos," snapped Renata.

"Do it," said Alain. "We don't have any better ideas." He glanced back at Marisa, and she was so close to his neck his hair brushed her face. "How do you know it'll turn?"

"Because if she heads straight for it it'll recalculate its route to avoid her," said Marisa. "That street on its left is the only other place it can go. Then as she keeps following it, it'll speed up to stay ahead of her. I've studied the traffic SI, so I know how it'll react."

"How does that help us?"

"Because we're going to get in front of it—turn here."

Alain swung his bike suddenly to the right, the tires squealing, and Mr. Park followed them barely five paces behind. Exactly like Marisa had hoped he would—he wanted her, not Renata. Renata kept going straight, and a moment later Alain nodded. "Renata just told me the truck turned, exactly like you said. What now?"

"Now we turn left," said Marisa, and leaned forward to make sure Alain could hear her. "I'm looking at the map on GPS, and estimating speed as well as I can. If I've timed it right, the truck will get to the next intersection the same time we do."

"And swerve to miss us," said Alain. "That's how the SI works."

"That's how the SI is *supposed* to work," said Marisa, "but nothing is perfect, and we're going to exploit a loophole. If an autocar gets into a situation where it can't avoid every obstacle on the road, it's programmed with very specific rules about which one of them to hit."

"It'll never choose a pedestrian over a motorcycle!" said Alain.

"No," said Marisa, watching the intersection rocket toward them. "But it'll always choose the larger pedestrian out of two."

They reached the intersection in a blur, and the truck loomed enormously in Marisa's peripheral vision. *Now or never*, she thought, and screamed as she let go of Alain and shoved herself backward off the motorcycle. Her senses seemed to slow as she hung in the air, the truck barely an arm's length away; Mr. Park was reaching toward her, his fingers just brushing the collar of her jacket, and then the SI made its choice and the truck swerved and rammed full force into the massive bionic thug. Marisa hit the ground with a jarring crash, her momentum still carrying her forward, tumbling and scraping across the asphalt until finally stopping in a pile of old containers and wispy plastic packing strips. She blinked a few times, almost surprised to be alive, and rolled painfully on her side to look back at the accident. The truck was stopped, and Mr. Park was underneath it, his legs splayed out like a frog under a shipping crate.

"Oh, hey," said Marisa weakly. "It worked." She tried to stand up, but her legs didn't want to move. "I'm going to pass out now."

She did.

NINE

The first thing Marisa saw when she woke up was the same scene: Mr. Park, under a truck, in the middle of the road. She jerked back in shock, only to realize that it was just an image, rippling softly on the folds of Renata's hoodie. The blue-haired girl smiled down at her, which was perhaps even more of a shock, and held the bottom hem of the hoodie with her hands, pulling it taut so the image was clearer.

"You like it? The hoodie has its own camera, so I can wear whatever image I want. This one was way too good not to use." She put her hand on Marisa's, gripping her gently. "I like you, random girl we picked up on the street. I like you a lot."

Marisa didn't know what to say. "Thanks?"

"She's awake!" Renata called over her shoulder. She looked back at Marisa with a beatific smile. "You need anything? You're doped all to hell on painkillers, and we've got sealant cream gooped onto all your major road rash areas—including your ass, but don't worry, I made Alain leave the room for that one. The whole time you've been unconscious, I promise that no one has rubbed your ass but me."

"That . . . doesn't actually make me feel better."

"Me quebras el corazón," said Renata, putting a hand to her chest. "Still, though, you're the Parkslayer, and that covers a multitude of sins. You hungry?"

Marisa looked around at the room they were in, finding it small and cramped—smaller than her bedroom at home, yet somehow filled not only with the bed she'd been lying on but a round kitchen table, two metal chairs, an electric stove, and some shelves that looked ready to fall right off the faded, filthy wall. The room had once been painted red, but the color was mostly gone now, peeling off and exposing large patches of brown. The combination made the room look organic and diseased.

Alain walked in, and Marisa got a better look at him now that they weren't on the run from a cybernetic nightmare. He was about her age, maybe a year or two older, with dark skin nearly the same color as his hair. His goggles were off now, exposing deep brown eyes, and she was struck again by how good-looking he was. Under his jacket he wore greasy mechanic's overalls, the pockets bulging with tools or spare parts or, for all she knew, weapons. The thought reminded her of their escape, and she looked back at Renata, seeing that she had both her hands back.

"What?" asked Renata.

Marisa searched for the words, couldn't find them, and instead just raised her hands, wiggling her fingers.

"Oh yeah," said Renata, matching the motion with her own completely not-blown-up hands. "I have a spare. This one doesn't blow up, though, and two of the fingers don't work very well." She picked up an assault rifle that was leaning in the corner, checking the chamber as she spoke. "Anyway, I'm going hunting. Any requests?"

Marisa shook her head, confused. Were there wild animals in this part of LA?

"Chinese," said Alain.

"Wait, *what*?" asked Marisa.

"Food," said Renata, grabbing a loaded magazine from the shelf by the stove. "Chill."

A loud gunshot sounded outside, and Marisa jumped. The movement aggravated her injuries from the crash earlier, which only increased her anxiety. Renata continued to prep her rifle. "Easy, Parkslayer, it's just the neighbors."

"We hunt nulis," said Alain. "Everyone in Kirkland does—or they steal from the people who do. When we're hungry, we look for food delivery nulis." He looked at Renata. "Actually, I think speed is more important than selection tonight. She needs to eat whatever we can find first."

"Got it," said Renata, and pulled her hood up over her head. She blinked, and the street scene on her hoodie changed to a dark blue-black camouflage. "Death to tyrants." She went outside, and closed the door softly behind her.

Marisa frowned when she saw the darkness through the closing door. "What time is it?" Before Alain could answer she blinked on her djinni, bringing up the clock display. "Ten forty-seven?"

she shouted. "My parents are going to kill me."

"I tried to send a message to whoever might be looking for you," said Alain, "but your ID says your name is Selena Gomez, and I feel pretty confident that that's a fake."

"Come on, now," said Marisa, blinking through the messages on her djinni to see who'd been trying to reach her. "You don't think I look like a fifty-eight-year-old Oscar-winning philanthropist? I'm offended." Five messages from her father, six from her mother, two from Sandro, two from Pati, and twenty-nine from Sahara. She even had a voice message from Bao. She sighed. "They probably think I'm dead." Either way, she'd be grounded for a month. She blinked on a few more programs, checking her djinni settings. "You're just lucky I'm still anonymized from the hack, or they'd have tracked my GPS and brought a half-dozen LAPD drones blasting down your door."

Alain shook his head. "I, um . . . took the liberty of scrambling your GPS signal, precisely to avoid that kind of thing." Her eyes flashed with anger, and he held out his hand, palm toward her in a calming gesture. "Just from the outside," he said, "no djinni hacking involved. Aside from the first aid, we haven't touched you."

Marisa remembered Renata's comments and grimaced. "I'm feeling a little violated from that as it is." She looked at Alain, suddenly aware all over again of how handsome he was, and how half-dressed she was, in a bed, alone with him. "Thank you," she said cautiously, "for not . . . for taking care of me."

Alain shrugged. "Obviously. I'm the one who got you into this mess, at least in part, so it's the least I can do. And I didn't mean for our daring rescue to end in you falling off a motorcycle—"

"I jumped off the motorcycle," said Marisa quickly. She smiled, just slightly. "Give me a little credit."

Alain smiled back. "And you probably saved our lives when you did it, so once again, I'm the one who should be thanking you."

"Just saving my own skin," she said, and looked at her scraped-up forearms. "In a way."

"Is there any digital damage?" he asked.

"From the crash?"

"From the hack," said Alain. "They got a virus into my djinni before I could jack out. You?"

Marisa frowned, and blinked up her control panel to start running diagnostics. "It . . . doesn't look like it," she said, reading the results as they came in. "All the root folders are clear, the firewall's still intact—"

"How's your connection speed?" asked Alain. "That's where the virus is hitting me; looks like it's trying to cut me off completely."

"That's horrible," said Marisa. She'd been forced to turn off her djinni a few months before, at the same time she was tangling with Grendel. It was, to put it mildly, unpleasant. She checked her diagnostic results, and shook her head. "Speeds are all normal. Looks like I'm clean, though I'll definitely run a deeper scan when I get home."

"Good," said Alain, "I'm glad you're safe." He watched her for a moment, then spoke again. "So what should I call you, if not Selena?"

"Heartbeat," said Marisa. Better to stick with her call sign until she knew if she could trust him or not. “And your name is Alain?”

“Alain Bensoussan,” he said, bowing slightly as he sat in the chair. “From the Free Republic of France.”

“The ‘Free Republic’?”

“One of the last nations left in the world not wholly owned by corporate interests.”

Marisa shook her head. “Only a handful of countries are wholly owned by corporations—”

“Do you really consider that a meaningful distinction?” he asked, interrupting her. His brow was furrowed now, his face intense. “Just because Haiti has been legally purchased and the US hasn’t, do you really think the US is any less of a corporate pawn?”

Marisa was taken aback by his intensity, and stumbled for an answer. “We’re still . . . we’re a sovereign nation.”

“Every meaningful decision your ‘nation’ makes is suggested, vetted, and approved by megacorps,” said Alain. “Your local governments are the same way. Just last year, Ganika changed LA’s zoning laws to allow themselves to purchase the land for their new plant, leaving neighborhoods like this one in shambles.”

“Everyone knows Ganika has a few seats on the city council,” said Marisa. “I’m not an idiot. But I’m just saying that we’re not . . .” She wasn’t prepared for a conversation about the separation of commerce and state. “Look, ninety percent of the country runs on the tech produced by a handful of companies. With megacorps that large, it’s inevitable that they’re going to control a certain corrupt segment of the government. But it’s not like they’ve rewritten the Constitution or whatever.”

Alain squinted at her. "You sure don't talk like a freedom fighter."

Marisa shrugged. "That's because I'm not one."

"In my experience, there are only two kinds of people who aren't," said Alain. "People who don't know the truth, and people who do know the truth but don't want to fight."

"So you're asking which I am," said Marisa, scowling at him. "Stupid or spineless?"

"That's not what I said."

"But it what's you meant," said Marisa.

"I . . . would never phrase it that way."

"Does that make it less insulting?"

Alain paused, then shook his head. "I'm sorry. I didn't mean to . . . I was hoping to recruit you."

"Recruit me? For what?"

"The war," said Alain. "The one underneath all that rationalizing you just offered me. The people against the megacorps. Ganika, Abendroth, KT Sigan—they're destroying the lives and livelihoods of people in this city, and all around the world, and we're doing what we can to stop them."

Marisa remembered Alain's final words inside the Sigan network: *I just trashed their payment database.* "You're a terrorist."

"I'm a revolutionary."

"Tell that to all the people whose lives you ruined with that Sigan hack you pulled," said Marisa. She hadn't been able to bring herself even to steal from Sigan, and this guy was trashing their systems without a thought for the people who depended on Sigan to communicate. "The people whose internet is going to be shot down until the payment systems are back online? The regular people who work at Sigan who are probably going to get fired for what you did?"

"I wouldn't expect a rich girl to understand," said Alain.

"Rich?" asked Marisa. "Are you kidding me? I'm barrio trash, one bad sales day from living on the street. In what possible world am I a rich girl?"

"In the one we just pulled you out of before coming here. Look, I didn't save you to argue with you about this. I saved you because your work on that hack was brilliant."

"Because I did the same thing you did?" asked Marisa.

"You keep twisting my meaning—"

"No," said Marisa, "you just keep meaning a bunch of really rude things, and don't like getting called on them. So here's the deal." She swung her legs over the side of the bed, no longer attracted to his arrogance and thus no longer shy in his presence. She might have still been curious about what he was trying to do back at Sigan, but his attitude had her blood boiling. "I'm going to save you the trouble of coming up with new ways to condescend to me and tell you that I'm not interested. I'm not a terrorist, I'm not a rich girl, I'm not amused, and I'm not staying here any longer." She stood up, putting a hand on the wall to steady herself from a sudden loss of balance. What kind of painkillers had they given her?

"This is not a safe neighborhood," said Alain.

"Yeah, I've met two of the residents already." Marisa looked down at her ripped, ragged jeans, and felt her backside with her hand—yeah, that was a lot of exposed skin. Not enough to raise any eyebrows in a dance club, but since the skin was just as ripped as the jeans, that changed the equation significantly. "You said you did some first aid—do I have any broken bones?" She couldn't feel any, but as drugged as she was, she didn't trust herself to feel much of anything.

"Just the road rash," said Alain.

"Good," said Marisa. "Do you have any pants?"

"I'll . . . get you some of mine." He stood up and moved to the next room. "I don't think any of Renata's will fit you."

Great, thought Marisa. *First he calls me stupid, then he calls me fat.* She took a few more steps, wobbling in the druggy haze, and looked into the room Alain had entered. It was the same size as the one she was in, but packed full of equipment: the two motorcycles, several box computers, and a dense stack of mismatched tools and greasy engineering equipment. She wasn't a motorcycle person, but these looked impressive—wide and heavy, possibly armored, with massive engines and low-slung seats that didn't sit above the wheels so much as between them. The wheels themselves were bizarre: they didn't have spokes or axles; they were more like metal and rubber rings that slid through a single connection point on the frame. The label on the back said *Suzuzaki*, but Marisa had never heard of it. She didn't see any other doors or rooms, and poked her head farther through the doorway, looking around at the corners.

"Where's the bathroom?" she asked.

Alain was rooting through a duffel bag. "It's outside. Do you need one?"

"Why is it outside?"

Alain shrugged, gesturing around at the tiny space. "Where would we put one in here?"

Marisa frowned. "How big is this place?"

"You've seen it all," said Alain, turning back to the duffel bag. "Two rooms, one door, no windows—though honestly we consider that last one a feature, not a bug. Extra privacy. Here you go." He stood up and turned toward her, holding out a pair of canvas cargo pants. "They'll be big, but we can cut up what's left of your old pants to make a cord and tie up the waist."

"You can't even offer me a belt?" asked Marisa.

"Look," said Alain, gesturing again at the tiny living space. "Where do you think you are? Where's the giant dresser full of free clothes that you seem to assume I have? I don't even have a bathroom, let alone enough belts to just give them away to people. Even giving you these pants means I'm down to two pairs, including the overalls I'm wearing, and buying a replacement will mean skipping at least one meal."

Marisa felt suddenly guilty but didn't want to admit it, so her words turned sour instead, shooting out like an accusation. "I thought you stole your food hunting nulis?"

"And you think ammunition is free, too?" asked Alain.

Marisa glowered, feeling stupid and furious but saying nothing.

"You think you're poor because you look up at the people above you and see how much more they have than you do," said Alain. "Try looking down sometime, at the people looking up at you, and see how much less they have. People whose neighborhoods were destroyed by corporate rezoning, or who lost their jobs to nulis, or who still have a job but pay so much for food and living space and everything else that they can't pull the ends close enough to make them all meet. You're not scared, Heartbeat, I'll grant you that." He held out the pants again. "But that might be because you don't have much of an idea what's really going on."

She tried to form a response, but her brain was such a jumble of anger and guilt that she couldn't get anything out. She took the pants mutely, and was saved from the awkward silence when the door burst open and Renata came in, the rifle in one hand and a cluster of white takeout boxes in the other.

"Find your own, güey!" Renata shouted back over her shoulder. Marisa heard an indistinct yell from somewhere in the street, and Renata lunged back out with a snarl. "Oh, verdad? Vente pa'ca y dime otra vez a la cara! Sale? Culo." She came in again, locking the door behind her and setting the boxes on the table with a flourish. "We're in luck: there was Chinese food in the second nuli I found."

Marisa looked at the white boxes warily. "You literally just . . . shot one down?"

"No—I shot two," said Renata with pride, and pulled a brick-sized bundle from the pocket of her hoodie. "The first had a waifu." She threw the bundle to Marisa, who caught it one-handed. The shipping label proclaimed the contents to be a TamaYama body pillow, size L, stain-resistant.

"Gross," said Marisa.

"Don't open it," said Renata. "We can trade that for something in the Hole tomorrow."

"The Hole is a secondhand market," said Alain, seeing the

look of discomfort on Marisa's face.

"That's good to know," she said.

"More like fifthhand," said Renata, clearing the rounds from her rifle before stowing it back in the corner. "Still, though, we can get something out of it. Enough bullets to replace the three it took me to hunt these nulis."

"Three?" asked Alain, and Marisa could see that slight smile creeping into the corner of his mouth again. "You only shot two nulis." His jokes were rare and dry, but he did seem to enjoy the occasional tease.

"This Chinese restaurant must have sprung for some kind of evasive tech," said Renata, sitting down. She unwrapped the first box and looked at the logo on the lid. "What is it, Noble House Chen? Well: I salute you, Noble House Chen, you were a worthy adversary." She opened the box and breathed deeply. "Egg foo yong. Guess that'll depend on how good the gravy is." She opened another box full of General Tso's mystery meat, saw that neither Alain nor Marisa was sitting, and nodded impatiently toward the seats. "What, you need a written invitation? Siéntense."

"Heartbeat is leaving," said Alain.

Renata glanced up from the final box, which held rice and chopsticks and a little sealed cup full of gravy. She looked at Alain, then at Marisa, then back at Alain again. "Is Heartbeat a code name or did your relationship go up a few levels while I was gone?"

"Code name," said Marisa. "Thanks for getting dinner, but I have to go."

Renata shook her head, breaking apart a pair of wooden chopsticks and rubbing them together to scrape off the splinters. "Even the mighty Parkslayer can't walk safely through Kirkland at night. Sit down, eat some food, and then I'll take you somewhere safe where you can catch a cab or something."

Marisa called up her clock again, imagining the yelling match she and her dad would have when she finally showed up, then sat down across from Renata. There were only two chairs, so Alain perched on the edge of the bed.

"For this food we are about to eat, we thank you Lord Cthulhu," said Renata, and held up her chopsticks in a salute. "Provecho." She poured the gravy over the egg foo yong, and dug in hungrily.

Marisa grabbed another pair of chopsticks and snapped them apart, looking at the food. The meal included four sets, and about four people's worth of food, and she couldn't help but wonder who was going to go hungry tonight so that she could eat. Somebody rich, like Anja? Somebody poor, like her own family? Or somebody completely destitute, a family who'd scraped together just enough money for a takeout meal on a special occasion? She imagined a single mother and three children, watching the skies for a delivery nuli that would never come. She put down the chopsticks.

"You need to eat," said Alain. They had no plates, so he and Renata were digging into the same box of food.

"I'm not hungry."

"Eat," said Alain again. "At least the rice. You need the nourishment after everything we went through today."

"I said I'm not hungry," Marisa snapped back, a little more harshly than she'd intended, but she didn't feel sorry for it.

"Then drink," said Alain, and reached under the bed with

his free hand. He pulled out a pack of colas, and handed her one.

"You're poor and starving but you drink soda?" asked Marisa.

"They don't have potable water in Kirkland," said Alain. "We have catch basins on the roof, but these days even the rain isn't very clean." He set down his chopsticks, opened the can of soda, and set it in front of her on the table. "It's not the healthiest, but it's better than the alternative, and it has plenty of sugar to keep your energy up. Please drink it before you crash."

"And while you're doing that," said Renata with her mouth full, "I want to know what's going on."

"*You* want to know what's going on?" asked Marisa.

"Who are you?" asked Renata. "Why are you in my house? I know how you got here, but I don't know why—Alain said you were inside the network when he trashed it, but that's pretty much it. Start with your name."

"My name is Heartbeat," said Marisa firmly, "and I don't like the balance of power here: I'm alone, I'm injured, and I'm not allowed to leave."

"Oh, you're *allowed* to leave," said Renata. "It would just be stupid."

"If you want my story, you tell me yours first," said Marisa. "What were you trying to do back there at KT Sigan?"

"Fair enough," said Alain. "If and only if you eat something first."

Marisa stared at them, trying to decide once and for all how angry, or how scared, she should really be. It was starting to feel like a kidnapping, but it had started as a rescue, and she was the one who'd made the choice to get on the bike. They'd been nice to her, they'd helped her, and, like Renata said, they weren't holding her captive. It was entirely possible that she was safe, and that they were good people. In spite of all the corporate sabotage and explosions.

Possible, she thought, but still very, very risky.

She grabbed the Coke, took a drink, and grimaced at the flavor. Too poor, apparently, to afford real Mexican Coke.

The thought made her feel guilty.

"Bon appétit," said Alain, pushing the box of rice toward her across the table. She dumped some of it in with the General Tso's, and he started talking while she ate. "KT Sigan isn't the largest telecom in the world, but it's the fastest growing, mostly because it's the most predatory. Their standard operating procedure is to move in to a new region, buy up all the hardware—fiber-optic cable, data towers, all of that—and then throttle the speeds of their network at the same time they increase prices on 'faster' internet service. The rich people with the most advanced djinnis are using fifty percent of the data, but they're only a small percentage of the customer base, and they don't care about their monthly bill. It's the rest of the customers who Sigan is asking to pay more than they can afford just to get a baseline usable connection. Bad connections means nulis get glitchy, autocars move more slowly, online retailers start losing work and missing payments. People can't hold down some jobs or apply for others; deliveries get missed; businesses start failing. Internet service is considered a natural resource by most people, and our society needs it every bit as much as it needs clean water—maybe more so, because there is no bottled alternative to pick up the slack." He jiggled his Coke bottle for emphasis. "Bad net connections mean bad neighborhoods, so concerned citizens try to pay for the good stuff they already couldn't afford. Then Sigan just moves in again with some subsidiary companies offering cheap loans and refinancing packages to help people maintain their overpriced connections."

"My parents are looking at one of those right now, trying not to lose our . . . house," said Marisa, stopping herself before saying *restaurant.* No sense giving up more information than she had to. "I had no idea the companies were connected."

"Almost guaranteed," said Alain. "They've done the same thing at home in Korea, in their big markets in China and Japan and India, and now they're moving into the Americas. Over the last two years they've purchased huge tracts of communications infrastructure in the US, Mexico, Brazil, and Argentina. An internet connection is the most valuable resource in the world right now, and they're cornering the market."

"All of this boring garbage," said Renata, "is Alain's inefficient way of telling you that they're evil, and they need to be destroyed."

"It's only boring if you don't understand it," said Alain.

"Which is his extremely efficient way of saying that people who don't agree with him are dumb," said Renata.

"He does have that habit," said Marisa.

"Here's what you need to know," said Renata. "Alain hates KT Sigan, he wants to take them down, and you stumbled onto the battlefield at a very dangerous time. Done."

"Your family stands to lose their house, you said," said Alain, looking at Marisa intently. "You're not the only ones, and you're definitely not the first. Sigan will bleed you dry, and then charge your neighbors to get rid of your corpse."

"Wait a minute," said Marisa, looking at Renata. "You said Alain hates them. You don't?"

Renata smiled wickedly. "I'm just in it for the money."

Marisa's eyebrows went up, and she looked at Alain. He took a slow breath, as if psyching himself up for something, and nodded. "I'm an idealist; Renata's a mercenary."

"Go ahead and say it," said Renata with a grin. "I'm hired muscle." She put a hand by her mouth theatrically and whispered to Marisa, "I love that phrase—I want it on my business cards."

"So wait," said Marisa, "you two aren't . . ."

Renata frowned, waiting for the second half of the sentence, then caught the meaning suddenly and guffawed, filling the room with laughter and flecks of gravy. "What? No me venga. Alain and me?" She laughed again. "You have got to be kidding me."

"But I just thought . . . ," said Marisa, gesturing around at the house. "I mean, I just assumed. There's only one bed."

"I sleep in a hammock in the workshop," said Alain, pointing to the back room.

"Okay, then," said Marisa, speaking slowly as she reorganized her mental assessment of the situation. "If you're hired muscle, who's paying you? Is there like an . . . army of you guys out there? Is this a whaddayacallit? A terrorist cell?"

"We're freedom fighters," said Alain, "and no, we're not a cell. Not in the way you're thinking."

"He has a network of contacts that supply us with stuff," said Renata. "Mostly weapons and equipment, which is why I have a spare cybernetic hand but I sleep on a used mattress in a Kirkland rathole."

"Her pay will come when Sigan falls," said Alain, and tapped his head—the universal symbol for "it's all in the djinni." "Every time we hurt them their stock price goes down, and the stock price of their competitors goes up. It's enough to keep us in business."

"Hitting their payment database probably made for a nice payday, then."

"Trashing their payment database was Plan C, at best," said Alain. "I was looking for their financial records—that's the only way to destroy them for good."

Marisa leaned forward but was careful not to look too interested. "How do the financials destroy them?" she asked. The financial records were surely behind the airgap, just like the client records. Did he have a way in? She wanted to keep him talking, to see if he spilled any info she could use.

"International trade violations," said Alain.

Marisa sat back, frowning. "Trade violations?" That was way more boring than she'd hoped it would be.

"I know it doesn't sound like much," said Alain, "but it's just like we were saying before—these megacorps are so big the law can't touch them." His voice was eager now, like he'd finally arrived at the core of his whole plan. "They're practically empires, and in most cases they're more powerful than actual empires. Two rebels in an LA slum can't bring down an empire—but if we can pit two empires against each other, the one with the bigger army wins."

"Who has the bigger army?" asked Marisa.

"Johara," said Alain. "The government looks the other way for almost everything a megacorp does—insider trading, unfair competition, predatory pricing, you name it—because the megacorps pay them off. It all comes down to money. But international trade laws are established and enforced by the megacorps themselves—they keep each other in check economically, because the alternative is unbridled competition. Outright war. If we can prove that one megacorp is actively undercutting another, in violation of their own agreements, the peace ends and the companies destroy each other."

"So you expose one, and damage two," said Marisa, nodding. It made sense now. "That's brilliant."

"If we can find and publish Sigan's full financial data, it will go beyond damage. Johara can use that data to hit Sigan where it hurts the most, carving them up like a roast duck."

"And leaving Johara stronger," said Marisa. "You're killing one monster but feeding another."

"We're hoping the fight will damage Johara enough to balance it out," said Alain.

"Hoping?"

"No plan is perfect," said Alain. "Whatever happens, we move on to Johara next. Eventually we'll break enough megacorps and monopolies to put power back in the hands of the people."

Marisa nodded again, and glanced at Renata. It sounded noble, but was it? She looked back at Alain. "Plus you'll get rich," she said. "So, bonus."

"I don't know how to convince you that I'm one of the good

guys," said Alain. "Sigan is a monster—all the megacorps are monsters. I slay them, and any money I make in the process goes straight into the next job." He looked around at the filthy hovel they lived in. "I'm obviously not doing this for the lifestyle."

"So why do you care so much?" asked Marisa. "Renata wants money, which I don't agree with, but at least I understand it."

"Gracias," said Renata.

"So what do you get out of it?" asked Marisa, fixing Alain with her glare. "I don't buy this altruistic freedom fighter stuff. Is it revenge? Did Sigan hurt someone close to you? Did they destroy the neighborhood you grew up in? Or maybe you're after the glory, blowing up databases and roaring around on your motorcycle trying to pick up chicks. Just to show that you can do it."

"Maybe," said Alain, and Marisa stopped short. She'd never expected him to admit it. He watched her for a moment before continuing. "Maybe I just need to prove that I matter—not to anyone else, but to myself."

"He must like you, Heartbeat," said Renata. "I've never heard this speech before."

"There are two kinds of people in the world," said Alain, "and please let me finish, because I know you think you know where this is going and I know you're going to think it's rude, but that's not what I'm trying to say. There are people who matter, and people who don't. There are people who act, and people who react; people who change things, and people who get changed. The most important thing in the entire world, in the entirety of human experience, is that you can choose which kind of person you are. I want to be the kind that makes a change."

Marisa stared at him for a long time, trying to decide what she thought of his answer. After a moment she asked another question. "So where does it all end for you? What does the world look like, after everything you've done to change it?"

"It looks kind," said Alain.

"I thought you were going to say 'fair,'" said Marisa.

"Fair is a dangerous word," said Alain. "There's too much baggage, and too much to undo; the only way to get 'fair' is to burn the whole thing down and start over, and no matter what you think of me I hope you don't think I want that."

"You want kindness," said Marisa, feeling for the first time as if something in this situation made sense. "You want the Kwon Chaewons of the world to look down and help out the children hunting wild nulis just to survive."

Alain smiled sadly. "Is that too much to ask?"

Marisa said nothing, and took another bite of the food.

"Now it's your turn," said Renata. "We told you our story, and now you tell us yours."

"Oh, me? I was just in there for fun," said Marisa, stirring her food. "Just a kiddie coder, joyriding their network for kicks." She shrugged. "I told you I'd trade my story for yours; I didn't say it'd be worth it."

TEN

Renata dropped Marisa off at a train station, by the platform for the Red Line, and Marisa watched her drive away and then walked through the crowd to the far side of the station, waiting for the Blue Line. Just to throw them off one last little bit.

While she waited for the train she composed several emails and voice messages, explaining to everyone where she'd been—or at least a version of it that wouldn't terrify any of them. Once she was on the train hurtling toward home she turned off her anonymizer and signed into her accounts again, sending out the pre-composed messages to Sahara, Sandro, and her mother. Her father she called directly.

"Marisa Jimena Carneseca Sanchez," her father growled, answering the call without even a hello. "Y donde estás?"

"Coming home," she said. "I'm sorry I didn't answer your calls."

"You turned off your GPS," said Carlo Magno. "You're not even supposed to be able to do that on the Ganika 7 djinnis. You get home right now."

"I told you I'm coming home," she said. "I'm on the train."

A message from Sahara popped up, but she ignored it, sending back a quick **can't talk right now** to quell any further interruptions. Arguing with her father required her full attention.

"It's nearly midnight," he said.

"I've been out past midnight before."

"Not on a school night."

"Technically I have," she said, and cut off his angry interruption with a hurried follow-up: "But I know that's not your point, and I'm sorry. I'm not trying to be bratty, I'm letting you know that I'm safe and I'm coming home."

"Your curfew is ten," said Carlo Magno.

"I know," she said, "and I'm sorry. I didn't mean to be out this late."

"So you accidentally stayed out two hours past curfew with your GPS turned off?"

Marisa squeezed her eyes shut, trying to decide if the truth would get her in more trouble than a disobedient lie. Was it even possible to tell him that she'd turned off her GPS for safety reasons without prompting more questions on the subject, and eventually explaining that she'd broken several laws and met some terrorists and blown something up and ran over a guy with a truck? Probably not.

"I was hanging out with some friends," she said. "And they live in kind of a scary part of town, and I was worried that someone creepy was going to scan my ID and try to find where I live."

"Mari, *I* can't even find you online, and we live in the same house."

"Because anonymity is important."

"Not from your parents."

"That was an . . . undesirable side effect," said Marisa. "I'm sorry."

"You should never turn your ID off."

"It's different for guys," she said. "You don't have to worry about some chango following you home."

"You shouldn't be hanging out with changos in the first place," he said.

"I know," she said, for what felt like the hundredth time in the conversation. "And I'm not going to hang out with them again, so don't worry."

"Good," he said with a sigh. "We almost called the cops, you know—not just the nuli responders, but the real police. Another ten minutes and I would have been talking to Sergio Maldicho Maldonado, begging him to help me find my baby girl."

"I'm fine," she said. "I can take care of myself. You need to learn that sooner or later—I'm going to college in a year, you know; I'm practically an adult."

"Oh mírale," he said, "my own daughter lecturing me on how to be a parent. You're the one who needs to learn some things, mija. You can't screw around forever."

"Do you remember college?" she asked. "I haven't even *begun* to screw around yet."

"This is the time to be saying that?" he asked. "I don't think you understand how much trouble you're really in."

"I'm almost there," she said, looking at the scrolling signs on the wall of the train. "Give me five minutes to walk home."

"Sandro's meeting you at the station," he said. "Vengan de prisa."

"Claro," she said, and blinked to end the call. She blinked again as the train slowed to a stop, asking her navigation program to find Sandro, and when the doors opened she stepped out to find a faintly glowing arrow superimposed on her vision, leading through the crowd to where her brother was standing. "Hey."

"Hey," said Sandro. "Have fun?"

"Not really," she said, falling in step with him as they turned to walk toward home. "Sorry to pull you away from your homework."

"I'm done for the night anyway," he said. "Eduardo fried a circuit in our ranger nuli, and we can't do anything else until we get a new part tomorrow."

"A ranger nuli?"

"For endangered animals," he said. "They use them in Africa all time, to follow elephants around and protect them from poachers."

"By shooting them?" asked Marisa.

Sandro smiled. "Well, *ours* doesn't shoot anybody, but I think I've figured out how to redirect the excess solar power into a stun gun."

"Be careful," she chided, "I've seen Mrs. Threlkeld throw a kid out of class for way less than proposing the plans for a hypothetical stun gun."

"Oh, you're giving me behavior advice?" he asked. "Hang on a sec, let me get the notepad app opened up so I can write this down."

She frowned. "So I'm out late," she said. "You don't have to be all Papi about it."

"What does your world look like?" he asked. "Once you don't have anyone forcing you to . . . brush your teeth, or not commit federal crimes, or whatever?"

She stared at him a moment, shocked by the similarity of that question to the one she'd just asked Alain. What should she answer? She looked down at the sidewalk they were walking on, and the street beside it; the weeds and the cracks and the garbage. How long until Mirador looked just Kirkland, too poor to take care of itself, and too broken to fix? Did she want to be rich? Her life to be easy? To be fair?

"My world looks kind," she said at last. "Or at least I want it to." It was the only word that felt right.

School night or not, half the house was still awake when Marisa and Sandro walked through the door; Marisa could hear her parents talking in the kitchen. "Welcome home, Marisa," said the house computer.

"Hey, Olaya," said Marisa. "Who's in bed?"

"Inez and Gabriela and Pati," said the computer. It was kind of a stickler for full names, but Pati hated "Patricia" and had somehow convinced it to use her nickname. One of these days Marisa would try to do the same for their grandma—nobody called Abue "Inez"; it was practically blasphemy.

"We're back," Sandro called into the kitchen, though Olaya

would already have told their parents they were home. He started up the stairs without waiting for a response. "Have fun."

Marisa wandered slowly toward the kitchen, dreading the encounter. These things always turned into a yelling match, and trying to explain the truth—that she was trying to learn the truth about her past—would make her father even angrier than the hacking. She took a deep breath and stepped into the doorway. Her parents were hunched over a tablet on the kitchen table, muttering softly. They were upset, but, she soon realized, not at her. Every couple of seconds one of them would reach out and tap or swipe the touch screen, and the two of them would stare at it, grimacing or clucking their tongues, before shaking their heads and tapping it again. Marisa watched them for a few minutes from the doorway, leaning against the side, not saying anything. There was only one thing that made them this quiet and concerned.

"Money?" she said softly.

"Technically," said her mother.

"The lack of it," said Carlo Magno.

Marisa felt her chest tighten. "How bad is it?"

Carlo Magno sighed and closed his eyes, rubbing them slowly with the palms of his hands. Guadalupe stared at the tablet a moment longer before looking up at Marisa with sad, tired eyes. "They raised the connection rates again. We just can't afford it anymore."

"KT Sigan?" asked Marisa, stepping forward. It was just like Alain said. "You've got to be kidding."

"I wish I could say I was surprised," Carlo Magno blurted

out, his anger erupting from deep inside of him like lava. "But what do we expect, when a company can swoop in and own the entire Mirador network—all the cables, all the repeaters, all the signal nodes—and push every other company out. Dios mio, I remember when I was a child and a connection to the internet was a luxury, something we used for shopping, or talking to our friends, or playing games. It made things easier. Now, it's just as necessary as electricity, or water. Nothing in this house or in the restaurant can run without it, and if we lose the restaurant we lose everything."

Marisa felt numb. "What are our options?" she asked.

"Sell the house," said Carlo Magno. "We could buy a few months if we move back into the apartment over the restaurant, but all our customers are in the same situation, and if they can't afford to stay customers, we'll just have to move again. Somewhere with cheaper service. Maybe all the way to Mexico—"

"She doesn't need to hear this," said Guadalupe.

"She's practically an adult," said Carlo Magno, throwing his hands in the air. "She told me herself."

"You don't need to hear this," said Guadalupe, looking at Marisa directly. "We'll find a way to make this work. Maybe Don Francisco can do something—"

"Never," said Carlo Magno, folding his arms sternly.

"He might," said Guadalupe. "He's a crook and a bastard—sorry for the language, Marisa—but he cares about Mirador. He protects us from the gangs—"

"Using protection money his thugs force us to pay," said Carlo Magno.

"But he does it," said Guadalupe. "His methods are questionable, but he's kept Mirador peaceful and livable while every neighborhood around us is descending into chaos. It's not in his interest for us to lose our home."

"He's a mobster," said Carlo Magno, dismissing the idea with a curt wave of his hand, "and Sigan is no better. They call it a price hike? I call it more protection money from more crooks."

It's happening exactly like Alain said it would, thought Marisa.

"Maybe we can refinance the restaurant," said Guadalupe. "The value of the house keeps dropping, but the restaurant is worth more than we paid for it—not much, but enough to squeak out another few dollars a month."

"Don't," said Marisa quickly. Her parents looked up at her in surprise.

"Why not?" asked Guadalupe.

"Don't talk to your mother that way," said Carlo Magno.

"In the next few days, maybe next week, we're going to get an offer to refinance," said Marisa. "Don't do it."

"But why not?" Guadalupe repeated. "I know it's frightening, chula, but we might have to—"

"Because it's exactly what they want us to do," said Marisa.

"Marisa?" said a sleepy voice behind her. Marisa turned and saw Pati, wearing shorts and one of Marisa's old T-shirts, bleary-eyed and holding a tablet.

"What are you doing up?" Guadalupe asked. "You're supposed to be asleep."

"Marisa promised she'd help me with my binary," said Pati.

"It's late," said Marisa.

"Just help her," said Guadalupe, rubbing her eyes. "She's been going on about this all week—help her and get it over with."

"It's after midnight," said Marisa.

"So come home earlier next time," said Carlo Magno, hunching back over the table.

"Blerg," said Marisa, looking at the ceiling. She sighed, trying to think of a way out of it, but she was too exhausted. "Fine," she said, taking the tablet from Pati's hand, "come on. If you're even awake enough to pay attention."

Pati followed her into the living room. "Whose pants are you wearing?"

"You're awake enough," said Marisa quickly, looking back over her shoulder. Had her parents heard that? She'd forgotten about the pants. Time to get this over with quickly and lock herself in her bedroom. She led Pati to the well-worn couch, fired up the tablet, and looked over the homework assignment. "Okay, this is pretty simple—they're just story problems, but you have to give the answers in binary instead of base ten."

"I know what it is," said Pati, "but binary is stupid."

"Binary is how computers think," said Marisa. "Everything we put into a computer gets turned into machine code—a bunch of ones and zeroes—and then the computer finds the answer, converts it back into human code, and gives it to us. You have to know binary so you can learn programming."

"I already know Artoo and Bowie and Piller," said Pati.

"You know Piller?"

"I know *some* Piller."

"Good for you," said Marisa. "I barely know any Piller. And

Bowie's not a language, it's an interface, but that's beside the point. Just trust me: binary's important, and you'll be glad you learned it."

"Uuuuuuuuuuuuuh," said Pati, sticking out her tongue and closing her eyes. "Fine." She opened her eyes and pointed at the tablet. "So in the first question Rodri has five sticks, and Selma has seven, and I need to tell this idiot robot how many sticks there are in total, and I said twelve and I was wrong. Please don't tell me that math is a lie, because I will burn this entire house to the ground."

"Robby the robot only speaks binary," said Marisa, pointing at the question. "So you have to convert the numbers. We use a base-ten number system, with only ten numerals."

"One through ten," said Pati. "I know this already."

"Ten's not a numeral," said Marisa. "It's a number made out of two numerals: zero and one. The ten numerals we use are zero through nine, and every number we want to make, we can make out of those."

"But binary only has ones and zeroes," said Pati. "Five and seven and twelve don't even exist in that number system."

"Sure they do; they just have different names. Binary and base ten are like English and Spanish—you can say all the same stuff, it just sounds different."

"Can't we just teach a computer base ten and . . . problem solved?" asked Pati.

"Binary is good for computers because it mimics the way a circuit works," said Marisa, "and computers are made of circuits. So: open and closed. On and off. One and zero. Once you know how it works, you can express anything in ones and zeroes—the entire world is really just a bunch of ones and zeroes, and . . ." She trailed off.

Ones and zeroes.

People who matter, and people who don't.

"You can choose which one you are," said Marisa.

"What?" asked Pati.

"It's not just that you *can* choose," said Marisa, "it's that you *have to* choose. And if you don't choose, the world chooses for you, and it will always choose zero."

"What are you talking about?" asked Pati.

Marisa looked at her little sister, staring at her intently—at her face, at her clothes, at her life. At all of their lives, all together. She spoke softly: "Are we going to be zeroes forever?"

"I think you're drunk," said Pati.

"I think I might be," said Marisa. "Because I'm seriously considering destroying a megacorp."

ELEVEN

"Good practice today," said Sahara. She was trying out a new avatar, an armored suit with imposing spikes and curves, colored in a palette of greens and blues. She took her helmet off in the team lobby and shook out her avatar's hair—an exact copy of herself, as always. "Jaya, that was some of the best healing you've ever done, and I'm not just saying that. Anja, you were on point, and Fang, you were a coldhearted mistress of death."

"Xiè xie," said Fang. Her avatar looked like a ghost, the opacity scaled down as far as the game would allow.

"Marisa," said Sahara. She paused, trying to form her thoughts, or possibly trying to find a polite way of saying what she needed to say.

Marisa, dressed in her old black stealth suit, smiled weakly. "Sorry."

"Your head wasn't in this today," said Sahara.

"I know," said Marisa, "and I'm sorry. I've been kind of distracted."

"This is a big deal," said Sahara. "I know that you're still looking for Grendel, and you know that I'll help you any way I can—if you'd invited me to help you yesterday I might have been able to do something then. But the tournament is next week. Five days away, and we're not even close to ready—"

"It's not that," said Marisa. "I mean, it's not *all* that—Grendel's definitely a part of it—but right now it's . . ." She puffed out her cheeks, trying to find the courage to bring it up. "It's . . . I've been thinking about the party, and the fact that we have two extra invitations."

"Don't remind me," said Jaya. Her avatar today was an elf sorceress, her elegant dress hanging down in long, flowing lines. She threw her arm over her eyes in exaggerated despair, and the giant sleeve hid almost her entire body.

"I did my best," said Anja, though her featureless gray avatar didn't seem to move or even react as she spoke. "I begged, I pleaded, I even offered to start selling my clothes, but the earlier flights were completely sold out. And my dad will do almost anything for me, but he won't reassign the company jet."

Fang snarled, angry all over again. "What's the point of a company jet if you're not going to let your daughter pick up her friends in it?"

"It's not my fault!" said Anja.

"Be fair," said Jaya. "Her dad *is* flying us out for the

tournament, just not early enough to go to the party."

"The party is the part with Su-Yun Kho," said Fang. "Screw the tournament."

"The tournament is a big deal," said Sahara. "This is our chance to impress the right people and get invited to a real league. We do this right and we can go pro—"

"I want to bring somebody to the party," said Marisa, interrupting them all. They'd already had this argument four times, and she wasn't going to sit through it all over again. Her friends looked at her in silent surprise, and she put on the biggest smile she could. "Two somebodies, actually."

"Who?" asked Sahara.

"We're not even cold in the ground and she's already giving away our spots," said Fang.

Jaya frowned. "Is this about a boy?" She smiled. "Of course it's about a boy." Her smile turned angry. "It better be about a boy."

"Easy, there," said Anja, "you're going to hurt yourself."

"I have too many emotions!" shouted Jaya. "Mari, just tell us!"

"Bao," said Sahara, trying to guess. "And . . . I don't know. That boy from a couple of weeks ago? With the hair?"

"Ooh," said Anja, "I liked the boy with the hair."

"Just let her talk!" shouted Fang.

They calmed themselves and looked at Marisa expectantly. She swallowed.

"Not Bao," she said slowly, measuring each word as it came out, "and not the hair guy. I want to bring . . ." She paused again, mustering her courage, and then spat it out as fast she could: "The people I met yesterday." She smiled again, though she felt more terrified than happy.

"The terrorists?" asked Sahara.

"They're revolutionaries," said Marisa.

"They're criminals," said Jaya.

"So are we," said Marisa. "You broke into Zhang last month, and Anja tries to hack into Kwan, like, every week. Every single one of us is a hacker with multiple security violations."

"But we don't *destroy* anything," said Jaya. "I was looking for patch data for a laundry nuli—those people from yesterday broke into Sigan's network and trashed their payment system. Who knows what they've got planned next?"

"They want to bring the whole company down," said Marisa. The girls gasped, and Marisa took a deep breath. "And I want us to help them."

"Now you're talking crazy," said Sahara.

"I like it," said Anja.

"Careful," said Fang. "When Anja agrees with you, you know you're on the wrong side of the asylum wall."

"We're not terrorists," said Jaya.

"Revolutionaries," Marisa corrected her.

"A revolution from what?" asked Sahara. "They're a telecom company, not a dystopian regime."

"Define 'dystopian regime,'" said Marisa. "I spent all night reading up on Sigan—not just what they say they're doing, but what they actually do, and what happens when they're done. They've been taking advantage of eroded communication laws for over twenty-five years; they don't just throttle speeds, they throttle information. Because they control who connects to who, and how, and where. Everything they're doing to Mirador right now they've done to other cities and neighborhoods all over the world. They cut out competition, hike their prices, throttle their speeds, and worse. Communities lose money, which means they lose businesses, which means they lose jobs, which means they lose more money, and it never ends."

"That doesn't mean you destroy the company," said Jaya. "You just find another provider. That's what capitalism is all about. Come to Johara; we have plenty of service in LA."

"Sigan owns all the hardware in Mirador now," Marisa snapped. The other girls fell quiet, and Marisa looked at the floor, too emotional to dare meet anyone's eyes. "I heard my parents talking last night—we're going to lose our house, maybe the restaurant. We might have to move."

"I'm . . . sorry," said Anja. "You know I'd do anything I can to help—"

"I'm not asking for money," said Marisa.

"You're asking for revenge," said Sahara. Her voice was cold. "That's not who we are."

"Hurting Sigan won't keep another company from coming in and doing the same thing," said Jaya.

"I'm not worried about that right now," said Marisa. "I'm worried about my home, and my neighbors, and how everyone who has the power to do anything is just turning a blind eye. Look: I need to break into Sigan's network anyway, because it's the only way to find Grendel, and I can't use the same trick that got me in the last time. The database is airgapped, which means we have to get inside the building to access it, and this party is inside the building. It's our only chance."

"You say that as if it actually makes sense," said Sahara.

"I want us to mean something," said Marisa. She looked at Sahara. "Sigan is doing something horrible, and no one is stopping it. We might be able to."

"I want us to mean something too," said Sahara. "I know I keep saying this, but the Forward Motion tournament can be the difference between obscurity and celebrity—and celebrity matters. It can take us from a bunch of nobodies to a bunch of somebodies; if we can hit the pro circuit here, that's not just fame, that's money. That's influence. You can support your family without becoming a terro—" She corrected herself. "A 'revolutionary.' Mari, you almost got black-vanned by a security thug just for looking around in their network; if they catch you actually sabotaging their system, who knows what they'll do to you."

"So help me," said Marisa. "We can do this."

"It's not worth the risk," said Jaya.

"I don't know," said Fang. "Mari might have a point."

Marisa looked at her in relief, then at the whole group. "That's two of you who support me, and two who think I'm crazy."

"I still think you're crazy," said Anja. "That's why I support you."

Marisa shook her head. "Let me at least tell you my plan."

"Yes," said Sahara, "definitely tell us the plan. But it had better be amazing."

The four girls looked at her, waiting, and Marisa nodded.

"Okay. The man I met yesterday is named Alain Bensoussan, and most of this plan is one he already worked out: find Sigan's financial records, expose some international trade violations, and let Johara destroy them for us."

"This doesn't sound nearly as awesome as I'd hoped," said Anja.

"I know trade violations aren't sexy," said Marisa, "but they're effective."

"Johara was accused of some trade violations last year in Nigeria," said Jaya. "A local telecom called AirWave took over half our business there before we finally stabilized."

Marisa nodded. "The government won't step in, but another megacorp can do it for us if we give them enough ammunition."

"So if Alain and Renata already have a plan," asked Fang, "why do we have to do anything?"

"Because they can't execute their plan without getting inside the building," said Marisa. "If we give them your tickets, we can hack a hard-line workstation while we're at the party."

Anja giggled with delight. "This just got awesome again."

"Even if we can get to a workstation," said Jaya, "how are we going to log in?"

"Sigan uses Gamdog 4.1 for their file system," said Marisa. "Gamdog 4.1 has an overflow vulnerability we can use to bypass the login; I read about it on Lemnisca.te. They're relying on the airgap to provide most of the security, as they expect the most dangerous hacks to come from outside the system." She looked at Jaya intently. "This plan will work."

"So now I have a whole new question," said Fang. "If we can

do it all ourselves, what do we need Alain and Renata for?"

"Alain knows what we're looking for," said Marisa. "We get him in, he does the job, boom."

"It's still too dangerous," said Jaya. "It's scary enough if they catch you online—how are you going to get away if they catch in person?"

"If they catch *him*, you mean," said Sahara. "He'll be the one doing the hacking, so worst-case scenario, we tell everyone we're not a part of it—that we barely know him." She looked at Marisa. "Which is true."

"Agreed," said Marisa, though she felt guilty for saying it. Alain had rescued her.

"Is there any chance Sigan will recognize you?" Jaya asked. "You barely got away from them yesterday—maybe it's not smart to waltz right into their headquarters."

"If they knew who I was, they'd have come to my house by now," said Marisa. "The hack was done through an anonymous ID, and the only person who saw my face has been broken down for spare parts by now."

"See, that doesn't make me feel better," said Jaya.

"I will not let this ruin the party," Sahara insisted. "Robin Hooding a megacorp is all well and good, but this tournament means more—to all of us—than revenge. We have to remember that."

Marisa looked at her expectantly. "Does that mean . . . ?"

"Yes," Sahara sighed. "You've sold me on the hack, and on bringing in Alain and Renata."

"Yes!" Marisa shouted, pumping her fist.

"But they're on their own," said Sahara firmly. "And if they do anything that could compromise the rest of us, I'm going to sell them out in a nanosecond."

Anja smiled. "I love it when you guys do crazy stuff."

"Not in real life," said Jaya.

"But are you with us, Jaya?" asked Fang. "I'm in, but I don't want to do this without everybody agreeing."

"She won't even be there," said Anja. "Both of you will be on planes during the party, somewhere over the Pacific."

Sahara shook her head. "Fang's right, though—this could ruin all of us if even one of us gets caught, so we all have to agree." She looked at Jaya. "Plus we might need some help from the outside, monitoring the security system or . . . I don't know. But we won't do it without you."

"Oh, you're definitely not doing it without me," said Jaya. "I'm not going to fly all the way there just to visit you in prison."

"So are you in?" asked Marisa.

Jaya grimaced, trapped in hesitation. Finally she nodded. "I'm in," she said, "but I reserve the right to call this off the moment anything starts to go sideways."

"Agreed," said Sahara. "So: the first step is to figure out the layout of the building."

"That's the second step," said Anja. "This is a live infiltration, so our first step is to talk to someone who specializes in live infiltrations."

Marisa nodded. "We need to talk to Bao."

TWELVE

Bao Behar leaned against a light post on a Hollywood street corner, staring at Marisa and Anja with raised eyebrows. "This is a joke, right?"

Marisa shook her head. "Nope."

"You're recording me for a segment on Sahara's show," said Bao, "like a big prank thing, right?" He looked around at the crowd of tourists gawking at Mann's Chinese Theater. "You've hired some people to act like FBI agents and hide in the crowd, and as soon as I say yes we'll all get fake arrested and I'll freak out and Sahara will get like a million extra downloads or something. It's the only explanation."

"This is as real as it gets," said Anja. "That's why Sahara's not here, because she doesn't want her nulis to record this conversation. The nulis will also be our alibi during the party, because we'll have video proof that none of us left the room."

"I know it sounds ridiculous," said Marisa, "but we're really doing it, and we really need your help."

Bao squinted in the bright LA sun. His mother and stepfamily—his stepfather and twin sisters—were Chinese, but Bao was half Russian, born in a slum in Novosibirsk. His father abandoned him and his mother when Bao was only two, and they'd survived on the street for nine years before coming to America. Every now and then Marisa thought she could see a hint of that desperate street-rat lifestyle still lurking behind his eyes. "You're going to destroy an international megacorp," he said dryly. His voice dripped with disbelief.

"We're going to wound it," said Marisa. "Maybe scare it out of the country, best case. That's still worth it."

"The worst case is that you all get caught, including me as an accomplice." His phone buzzed in his pocket, and he pulled it out to look at it—Bao was one of the only people Marisa had ever met who didn't have a djinni, communicating solely through exterior devices. It struck her as unimaginably primitive, but he refused to do it any other way. He read something on the phone's screen, then held it up for them to see. "I'm at capacity for this corner: one hundred dollars. You know what one hundred dollars will buy? Like, one and a half of your fancy salads."

"Will everyone please let go of the salad thing?" sighed Marisa.

Bao started walking, and the two girls walked beside him. "This is where I am in life," he said. "This is what I do. My stepdad can't work, and my mom has to take care of him, so I support them and my sisters doing this: skimming micropayments from tourists' djinnis. Everyone who shopped at that gift shop for the last couple of hours paid, on average, about twenty-five cents more than they thought, and all of that extra was collected through this phone onto a dummy account. I have to keep the amounts small so that nobody notices, and I have to keep moving so that anybody who does notice won't find me. And if I do that in enough places, day after day and week after week, my family can eat and pay the rent."

"I know it's hard," said Anja.

"I'm not telling you that it's hard," said Bao, "I'm telling you that I'm busy. My sisters help—and thanks to Mari hacking their IDs, they help a lot—but they spend most of their time in school and that's where they belong. I'd rather they have a real life." He waved the phone. "I'm out here doing this so they can stay in school, and if I stop coming out here because I'm in jail, my family will starve—or my sisters will have to drop out to start skimming full time, which I'd say is just as bad."

"We can play the stock market," said Marisa. Anja and Bao both shot her confused looks, and she hurried to explain. "That's how Alain is financing his operation—we could do the same."

"Who's Alain?" asked Bao.

"He's the criminal we're working with," said Anja.

"Revolutionary," said Marisa.

"Please," said Bao, stopping at the street corner. "He may have convinced you, but there's not enough handsome in the world for him to sell *me* that line."

"There's a girl, too," said Anja.

"She's kind of scary, though," said Marisa.

"Hey," said Bao, "I like scary." Marisa tried to read his

expression, but his sunglasses made it impossible.

"Besides," said Anja, "I've never even met them."

Bao snorted. "You're doing this with people you've never even met?"

"I've met them," said Marisa, "but I haven't introduced the others because we don't even know if they'll agree to our plan. We wanted to talk to you first to see if it was even possible."

The light changed, and they started across the street. "Let's see," said Bao, tapping the screen of his phone. "The KT Sigan building has eighty-two floors, helipad on the top, balcony garden on the seventy-seventh—"

"How do you know all this?" asked Marisa, craning her neck to get a look at his phone. "What are you reading?"

"Personal notes," said Bao. "There is a reason you're coming to me for advice."

"So you've infiltrated Sigan before?" asked Anja.

"No, but I like to know my options. I've got notes on most of the major office buildings downtown, just in case. Most of it you can find online if you take the time, so I just . . . took the time."

"You're my hero," said Marisa. "What else can you tell us about the building?"

"The elevators don't go all the way to the parking garage," said Bao. "They upgraded the main elevators about fifteen years ago, but the underground stuff they couldn't replace for some reason. Building codes or something. So the garage elevators are the old style that only go up and down."

"Will that help us or hurt us?" asked Marisa.

"Probably won't affect you at all," said Bao. "I'm just telling you what I know."

"What about breaking in?" asked Anja. "Alain will have to slip away from the party, find a workstation, and have access for at least ten minutes, maybe as long as half an hour, to find and download everything he needs."

"We assume," said Marisa.

"Well," said Bao, stopping on the sidewalk and staring at his phone. "It's not *impossible.* I know that I could do it a lot more easily than any of you could, because the building has scanners all over the place."

"They track where everyone is inside the building?" asked Marisa.

"Most big office buildings do," said Bao. "But they're not tracking you, they're tracking your djinni. Someone without one could move through the building almost undetected."

"Maybe we need you to come with us, then," said Anja.

"Maybe you need to forget the whole thing," said Bao. "This is super dangerous."

"But it's important," said Marisa. "You live in Mirador, too—Sigan is squeezing all of us. You can't run your skimming scam if you can't afford to be on the network. Then what options will your family have?"

Bao nodded, but grudgingly.

"I'm not any happier about it than you are," said Marisa. "I told you—we're losing our house, maybe the restaurant as well. We're all losing something. This is our chance to fight back."

"Maybe," said Bao, closing his eyes. He let out a long, slow sigh. "I have to admit, the more I think about breaking in to this place, the more . . . intrigued I am by the challenge." He opened his eyes and grinned.

"There's the Bao we know," said Marisa.

"But I need more info," said Bao. "A job like this needs factory precision."

"Then let's go get it," said Marisa, and blinked on her djinni to call an autocab.

"What," said Bao, "right now?"

"I'll cover your next couple of hours of work," said Anja.

"I don't want your money—"

"Too late," said Anja. "Just transferred the funds." Bao's phone buzzed, and Anja laughed. "Did you just skim twenty-five cents from me sending you money?"

Bao grinned, looking at the phone. "Twenty-*six* cents." He put the phone away. "Looks like you just hired me. Let's go meet some cybercriminals."

An autocab rolled up, and Anja paid it while Marisa linked to its navigator and fed it the address in Kirkland.

"Los Angeles County has declared a Red Drinking Day for the Kirkland area today," said the autocab. "Would you like to stop along the way for a clean beverage? There are thirty-seven cafes along our route."

"No ads," said Anja, and paid an extra fee to shut them off. The interior of the cab was like a miniature train car: too low to stand in, but with two benches facing each other across a central aisle. It was like a little room on wheels. The cab pulled out into traffic, seamlessly joining the endless stream of cars, and Marisa leaned back on the bench.

"So what should we expect?" asked Bao. "I've never met a wanted criminal before."

"I find that hard to believe," said Anja.

"I've never met any who brand themselves as revolutionaries," said Bao. "They sound intense."

"Intense is a good word," said Marisa. "Alain Bensoussan is . . . driven. And idealistic in the sense that ideals are what's driving him. But he's kind of funny, too; I mean, it's not like he's a joyless scold or anything."

"Calm down," said Anja, "you're not writing him a Valentine's card."

"And the girl?" asked Bao.

"Scary," Marisa repeated. "He's the brains, she's the muscle. Her name's Renata."

"Last name?" asked Bao, pulling out his phone.

"What is it with you two?" asked Anja. "This is corporate espionage, not a dating service."

"I want to look them up," said Bao, tapping on his phone. "Assuming those are real names, I'm sure I can find out a bit more about them."

"I didn't get her full name," said Marisa. "And I didn't risk scanning their IDs."

"Alain Bensoussan has no criminal record," said Bao, reading from his screen. "French national, immigrated to LA a couple of months ago. Is this him?" He held up the phone, and Marisa nodded at Alain's familiar face.

"Girl, he's hot," said Anja. "You didn't tell me he was hot."

"I didn't really notice," said Marisa, hoping her face didn't give her away.

"That is a bald-faced lie," said Anja. "You rode on the back of a motorcycle with this guy—you noticed."

"You can't see someone's face when you're behind them on a motorcycle," said Marisa.

"That's because your legs are wrapped around him," said Anja, grinning wickedly.

Bao laughed. "If that's how you ride motorcycles, I think you're doing it wrong."

"All I know is," said Anja, "if that guy sat in my lap on a rumbling motorcycle, I would make sure not to leave without a very clear sense of how hot he was."

"So he's hot," said Marisa, eager to change the subject. "Fine. That's pretty much his least important characteristic on this mission."

"Yes," said Anja, stabbing the air with her finger. "Let's call this a mission. Wait: Mission or job? Which sounds better?" Her eyes went wide. "Or quest. Can we call this a quest?"

Bao smiled. "I've never planned a robbery with a four-year-old before. This should be fun."

"Please," said Anja, "I'm seventeen. That makes me at least four four-year-olds."

"Have you guys ever been to Kirkland?" asked Marisa.

"Never," said Anja. "Is it as run-down as they say?"

"Just look out the window," said Marisa.

The autocab pulled off the main highway and wove down

into Kirkland, and Marisa noted again the slow, subtle shift as the giant city turned slowly into a slum. Men and women in ragged clothes walked past them on the street, pushing carts full of junk; children played in patches of shade; solemn gangsters with dark, darting eyes stood on the street corners and watched the cab roll by. The three friends watched in silence, until at last the autocab pulled to a stop in front of a low cinder-block shack.

"You have arrived at your destination," said the cab. "Thank you for choosing Gonzalez Transport."

"You're sure this is the right place?" asked Bao.

"I wasn't here during the day," said Marisa, putting her hand on the cab door but not yet opening it. "I recorded the GPS coordinates, though. The shape is right at least."

"Let's go, then," said Anja, and triggered the button to open the cab. The door slid open, letting in a furnace-like blast of hot air from the dusty street. Marisa climbed out, glanced at the other pedestrians, who were staring at her, and stood in front of the door. After a moment she shrugged her shoulders and knocked.

"Quién es?" shouted Renata from inside.

"Heartbeat!" Marisa called back. She heard a faint click and some rapid muttering, and then the door flew open.

"Parkslayer!" shouted Renata. She was dressed in an oily tank top, her hands covered in black dust, but she threw her arms around Marisa anyway and smeared her with both. "And you brought friends! Hi, friends." She pulled a thick black handgun from her waistband, its modified barrel hinting at some kind of special ammunition. "My name's Renata, and if you tell anyone that, I'll kill you. Come on in!"

Bao shot Marisa a grim look, but followed the girls inside the little shack. The autocab drove away, and Renata closed the door behind them.

"I didn't expect to see you back again," said Alain. He was also in a tank top—the shack was sweltering—and he and Renata were working on something intricate and messy on the old kitchen table.

"We're making bullets," said Renata, sitting down. "Want to help?"

"Yes," said Marisa, "but not with the bullets."

Alain hadn't taken his eyes off of her. "Marisa Carneseca," he said. "Is that your real ID?"

"I'm not using the anonymizer today," said Marisa. "This is the real me, and these are my real friends."

"I'm Anja," said Anja.

Bao waved. "I'm Bao. Nice to meet you both. Is the bullet thing like a hobby, or do you intend to actually kill people with them?"

"If you love something," said Renata, "shoot it out of the barrel of a gun."

"I think I got a card like that once for my birthday," said Bao.

Alain wiped his hands on his overalls. "You said you want to help us. With what?"

"With this, first of all," said Marisa, and pulled from her bag the pair of pants she'd borrowed. "Folded but not washed. The nuli can't do anything unless they're chipped, and then the house would know we had an extra pair of pants, and then my parents would know, and it would be a whole thing." She handed him the folded pants. "Thanks for letting me borrow them."

Alain took them. "You're welcome. Now: What else are you planning to help with?"

"With your Sigan hack," said Marisa. She steeled her courage and said it. "We want to help you take them down."

Alain shook his head. "This isn't a clubhouse."

"I know that," said Marisa.

"We're not running a fantasy camp for rebellious teens," Alain continued. "I'm glad that something has made you care, but you're not warriors."

"I agree with him," said Bao. "Let's call that cab back."

"You tried to recruit me before," said Marisa.

"That was before," said Alain. He picked up a bullet casing and clamped it in a vise, ready to fill with gunpowder.

Marisa stepped forward, covering the casing with her hand. "The plan you told me didn't involve shooting anyone."

"Plan A never does," said Alain. "The bullets are for Plan B."

"You start shooting at literally the first setback?" asked Bao.

"There's a better way," said Marisa. "We can get you into the database."

"You're a great hacker," said Alain, "but it's airgapped. No one can get into it."

"We can," said Marisa.

Alain paused, setting down his tools and looking up. "Okay, I'll bite. How are three rich kids going to get us into a hard-line workstation?"

"The way that only rich kids can," said Marisa. "We're going to take you to a party."

Renata stopped working and looked up, her eyes gleaming. "Now I'm intrigued, Parkslayer. What party?"

"Anja and I are on an Overworld team," said Marisa. Alain shook his head dismissively, and she waved her hands to keep his attention. "No, listen. Our team's been invited to the Forward Motion charity tournament next week, and there's an opening gala this Saturday night, in the Sigan building. Any other day of the year you couldn't get past the lobby without six forms of ID, but on Saturday, we're the honored guests."

Alain considered this a moment. "What's your plan?"

"It starts with Bao," said Anja. "He doesn't have a djinni. He'll be able to move through the building without being detected."

"Maybe," said Alain. "If they're having a gala, though, they'll have plenty of human security as well."

"The invitation says to come to the main doors by the plaza," said Anja. "They'll do a standard ID check and security screening there."

"And they'll pay extra attention to the guy with no djinni," said Renata. "Since I assume they'll be scanning everyone at the door."

"I can fake a djinni ID if I need to," said Bao, holding up his phone. "And I can probably slip past any guards."

"The building will be passively scanning all night," said Alain. "If you turn off your fake ID, it'll know, and they'll go on high alert."

Bao nodded. "So I'll keep it on, and leave it in the party somewhere."

"And then what?" asked Renata. "You'll just walk out of the

room, find a hard line, and log in?"

"More of a sneak than a walk," said Bao, "but yes. We'll get a new tablet for the hack, completely clean of any identifying information, and prep it in advance."

"That's my job," said Anja, wiggling her eyebrows.

Marisa looked directly at Alain. "We'll go in with you, me, Anja, Bao, and Sahara—she's our other friend, and the leader of our Overworld team. Bao fakes the ID, we get inside and head up to the eightieth floor for the party; Bao slips away, finds a hard-line workstation, and plugs in the tablet. We can use a buffer overflow to log us in, the tablet Wi-Fi will bridge the airgap directly to your djinni, and then you can just . . . look through the whole database and find whatever financial data you need."

Renata chuckled. "You lied to us, Parkslayer." She fixed Marisa with her glare. "You're way more than just a kiddie coder joyriding someone's network."

"I'm looking for some info behind the airgap as well," said Marisa. "I'll connect to the tablet just like Alain. We get what we want, you get what you want, and Sigan gets what they deserve."

Alain looked at each of them in turn. "It's risky," he said, and then paused. "But it's doable."

"Maybe," said Bao. "I still need some details from you."

Alain nodded. "What?"

"Timeline," said Bao. "ID scans aside, I figure I'll have maybe twenty minutes away from the party before a human guard notices I'm physically absent. Thirty tops. Can you get what you need in that time?"

"I can," said Marisa.

"I can't," said Alain. "First: I can't get rid of the virus Sigan uploaded into my djinni during the last hack, and it's slowing me down. My connection speed is pretty antique right now."

"You want me to look at it?" asked Marisa. "Anja and I have pretty hardcore antivirus setups, most of which we built ourselves. We might be able to do something your software can't."

"Thank you," said Alain, "but I don't like other people tinkering around in my head. I think I've found a solution, but even if I'm working at full speed again, this is not going to be a fast job. We're either downloading petabytes of data, which will take hours over Wi-Fi, or we're searching for a very specific folder—maybe even a specific file—and then downloading that. That's going to take way more than twenty minutes."

"How much more?" said Bao.

"An hour?" said Alain. "Maybe two? How long does the gala last?"

"From eight p.m. until two or three in the morning," said Anja. "So we have time, we just can't have Bao missing for more than a few minutes of it."

"He could leave the tablet and then go back for it later," said Marisa. "Ten minutes at the beginning, and ten more right before we leave."

"That means I'll have to sneak through security twice," said Bao, "which doubles the chance that security will notice and the mission's a bust."

"*Yes*," said Anja, her eyes slitted. "Call it a mission again."

"What if we never go back for the tablet?" asked Marisa. "We can pull all our data over the Wi-Fi, and you only have to sneak away once to set it up."

"I don't like leaving evidence behind when I steal from all-powerful megacorps," said Bao.

Marisa shrugged. "We could rig it to . . . explode or something, I don't know."

"We'll never get explosives past the security scan," said Alain.

"Then we could just brick it," said Marisa. "Set it up to wipe itself clean when we're done with the transfer."

"Unless it literally melts itself, it'll still have traceable data on it," said Anja.

"Not to mention physical evidence," said Renata. "Even if everyone who handles that tablet wears gloves, it'll still collect some fallen skin cells, maybe bits of hair—any one piece would be more than enough for a DNA test to connect it straight back to us."

"Come on," said Marisa. "There's got to be a way to make this work."

"I . . . ," said Bao. He paused, just for a moment, then shook his head. "No. There's no way."

"Bao," said Marisa. She knew him too well: he'd definitely thought of a way to do it.

"It's impossible," Bao insisted. "You have to have somebody who can get into the building, and then out of the party, with everyone seeing them but also not noticing they're gone. It's impossible."

"Bao . . . ," said Anja.

"No," said Bao, but he looked away from them as he said it.

Marisa nodded, staring at him as she talked her way through the puzzle. "Someone who can fabricate a djinni ID, just like Bao can, but who Bao doesn't want to endanger—" Her eyes went wide as she realized the answer. "Santa vaca."

"No," said Bao again, but this time he looked straight at her. "You can't use them."

"Use who?" asked Alain.

"Bao's sisters," said Marisa. "They're perfect for the job."

"Not a chance in hell," said Bao.

"What makes them so perfect?" asked Renata.

"They're twins," said Marisa. "Perfectly identical." She looked at Bao. "And thanks to a hack I did for them two years ago, they only have one ID between them. They share it back and forth. They can do all kinds of tricks with it—including having one of them at the party, and one at the hard line, without anyone ever knowing."

"We won't even need a tablet," said Anja. "They have djinnis, so they can hook in directly." She looked at Renata. "Less evidence, less chance of getting caught."

"Will this work?" asked Alain. He looked at Bao. "Can they do it?"

"It'll definitely work," said Bao. "And they definitely have the skills to pull it off." He looked at Marisa. "But if anything happens to them . . ." He leaned forward, enunciating clearly. "Nothing can happen to them."

"I have some devices we can use to help cover your tracks," said Alain. "In case anything goes wrong."

Marisa raised an eyebrow. "How do you get all these 'devices' if you're living in monastic poverty?"

"He's got contacts," said Renata. "Never tells me who they are."

"She's a mercenary," said Alain.

"You still haven't answered my question," said Bao.

"You didn't ask a question," said Alain, "you just demanded something."

"Then I'll demand it again," said Bao. "Nothing can happen to my sisters."

"You have my word," said Alain, standing up. He offered his hand, and after a moment Bao shook it.

"Perfecto," said Marisa. "Now let's get to work."

THIRTEEN

Marisa wore the green dress, and it was perfect.

"I think it fits you better now than when you bought it," said Sahara.

The two girls were in Sahara's apartment, finishing the last little touches to their makeup and clothes. Sahara was wearing a dark gray dress with long, puffy sleeves; the waist, bust, shoulders, and cuffs were all decorated with nested arcs of stiff fabric, and the hollows between them were lit with hidden LEDs, so that instead of shadows the gaps were glowing with a rich yellow light. She wore a hat of the same material, with a few lights of its own, though the hat was empty in the middle and Sahara's natural hair poked up through the ring. More like a crown, thought Marisa. Maybe a tiara. Whatever it was, it looked amazing, and Sahara, of course, had designed it herself.

As always, Sahara was accompanied by Cameron and

Camilla—her two camera nulis that followed her everywhere, recording her life and streaming it live to an eager audience of reality addicts. Marisa blinked on the djinni icon that connected her to Sahara's feed, and suddenly she was looking at herself, a nuli's-eye view projected into the center of her vision. She turned around, watching herself in the video for a full 360-degree view. The top half of the dress seemed to wrap around her, forming a diamond shape at the waist and opening up in a wide semicircle just above her bust, framing her collarbones and shoulders and neck inside of a dark green collar that complemented her brown skin perfectly. The bottom half of the dress went about halfway down her thighs, hugging her legs and butt tightly. Marisa smiled.

"I wish I had your curves," said Sahara. "Look at that."

"Does it look okay?" asked Marisa.

"It looks amazing," said Sahara. "Are you kidding me? If I looked like that, I'd quit this life of crime and be a model."

"You're gorgeous," said Marisa. "And the dress you made is perfect—"

A text message from Sahara popped up in Marisa's djinni, and she blinked on it to open it. **Oh, I know,** sent Sahara. She used text messages when she didn't want to say something over the video feed. **Humility's one thing, but let's be honest: we look hot as hell.**

Another message popped up from Pati: **Your dress looks amazing!**

Marisa smiled and thanked her. **You're watching Sahara's feed?**

Of course! I'M SO JEALOUS YOU GET TO GO TO THIS PARTY!!!

Marisa started texting a response, but another message popped up and distracted her. This one was from Jin Lee, Bao's sister: **Anja's here. We'll pick you up in a few minutes.**

Marisa looked at Sahara. "Anja and Jin are on their way." She was careful not to mention Jun, Jin's twin sister, who was coming in a separate cab—if evidence of the deception showed up anywhere on Sahara's video feed, they'd essentially be streaming their entire crime live for all to see. Pati wasn't the only one watching; Sahara's vidcast was popular enough that she was sometimes recognized on the street. For tonight, as far as they were concerned, only one sister existed.

Sahara looked in the mirror one last time, touching up her lipstick and then blotting it on a tissue. "Done. Ready to wow some rich boys?"

"Always," said Marisa. She grabbed her tiny handbag and opened the door, stepping out onto the narrow landing at the top of the stairs; the camera nulis followed, one behind and another zooming forward to get a better angle as the two girls walked down the stairs. The one in front was Cameron: Sahara had stuck a tiny top hat on one of them, and a hair bow on the other, to help tell which was which. When they reached the sidewalk Marisa opened the side door and went into the restaurant.

"Mira, qué lindas," said Marisa's mami. She was smiling from ear to ear. "You look beautiful! Both of you!" She tapped a nearby customer on the shoulder. "Look at my beautiful daughter!"

"I thought you didn't like that dress," said Gabi, passing by with a tray full of steaming plates of food.

"I don't like it for church," said Guadalupe, though Gabi hadn't waited around for a response. Their mother looked back at Marisa. "This is a party, and Marisita's going to knock them dead."

"Qué bárbaras," said Carlo Magno, stepping in from the kitchen. He wiped his hands on a towel and then threw it over his shoulder. "My own daughter, showing more leg than a swim team."

Marisa smirked. "It's 2050, Papi. Women can wear whatever they want."

"Oh, mija's a woman now?" He looked at Guadalupe. "She can wear whatever she wants, she's a woman." He looked back at Marisa. "When did you turn twenty-one and not tell me?"

Marisa raised her eyebrows. "You expect me to believe you'll start leaving me alone when I'm twenty-one?"

"Of course not," said Carlo Magno, "but you could at least wait that long before you start pushing every boundary you see."

"They look fine," said one of the customers. He was an old man named Beto, and a regular in the restaurant. "Déjales, Carlo." He blinked, and Carlo Magno slapped him on the shoulder.

"Delete that photo, Beto."

"I wasn't taking a photo, I was just blinking!"

Carlo Magno fell into an argument with him, and Marisa turned back to her mother. "Wish us luck."

"All the luck in the world," said Guadalupe. She didn't know about the hack, but the party itself was just as nerve-wracking, if not more, and Marisa was grateful to hear it. Computer systems were something Marisa understood. Fancy galas with the super wealthy, well . . . she was a bit more out of her element.

"Cab's here," said Sahara, looking out the window.

"Te amo," Marisa told her mother, hugging her gingerly so she didn't mess up her dress or her hair.

"Te amo," said Guadalupe. "Buena suerte."

Marisa followed Sahara to the door, calling back over her shoulder as she went. "Te amo, Papi!"

"Te amo, mija!"

She stepped outside, and the restaurant billboard pinged her djinni with a request, probably a coupon urging her to come back soon; Marisa's djinni automatically deleted it, as she'd told it to do with all of the ads that storefronts tried to send her.

It was only seven thirty, and still bright outside. She hurried down the two clean steps to the sidewalk, where an autocab waited at the curb with the door already open. Sahara climbed in, sitting next to Jin, and the nulis floated in after her, clinging to the charging stations on the ceiling. Marisa sat by Anja, and leaned close to hug her, but yelped and scooted back when something sharp jabbed her in the leg.

"Qué traes!"

The cab closed its doors and rolled away, and Anja grinned, sticking her leg out straight into the space between the benches. "New tights," she said. "You like them?" Her legs were covered in what looked like fishnet chain mail, gleaming in the light and covered with sharp metal spines.

"That's insane," said Marisa.

"I love it," said Sahara. "And I love the hair."

Anja was wearing a sleeveless dress, black and covered with slim rubber panels that looked almost like body armor; her arms were wrapped with a series of thick leather bands, latched with heavy buckles and studded with silver spikes. Most shockingly, she'd shaved the left half of her head.

"I can't decide which is weirder," said Marisa. "The hair or the legs."

"Neither," said Anja, rubbing her hand on the bald side. It was smooth as an egg, while the other side was still nearly two feet long. "I look badass."

"Totally," said Sahara.

"But . . ." Marisa was very proud of her own hair, long and dark brown and perfectly wavy, with the tips dyed carefully red, and she was always surprised when other people didn't feel the same about their own hair. "Just because you like it now doesn't mean you'll like it forever, right? You can cut it off on a whim, but it's way harder to grow it back."

"What is the point of changing something if you can just undo it later?" asked Anja.

"I like it," said Jin.

"Oh my gosh," said Marisa, looking at Jin with wide eyes. "I'm so sorry I didn't say hello!" She leaned across the gap and put a hand on Jin's knee. "How are you?"

"Fine," said Jin. "Scared."

"Don't be," said Sahara, giving her a maternal smile. She was almost certainly sending Jin a text message as well, reminding her to be careful what she said in front of the nulis. "This is a very big party, with a very exclusive guest list, but they're all just people, and they're all just looking to have a good time. Right?"

Jin nodded. At sixteen years old, she and her twin were just a year younger than Marisa and the others, but in many ways they were far more experienced at this kind of deception. Ever since Marisa had helped them fake the ID on their djinnis, they'd used the shared identity to con all sorts of people: street sellers and shop owners and even restaurants and movie theaters.

"You'll be great," said Marisa, and then, for the benefit of the cameras: "Thanks for coming with us when our teammates couldn't make it."

"Of course," said Jin, and almost magically her nervous fidgeting was replaced with sunny confidence. Whatever their other skills might be, Jin and Jun were exquisite actors. Tonight, of course, they were dressed identically: a red dress with a slim, sleeveless top, all in traditional Chinese style, changing at the waist into a flowing Korean chima skirt. That might help to impress Chaewon and the other Koreans at the party, but more important than the style was the freedom of movement: instead of the tight dresses Marisa and Sahara were wearing, Jin's wide skirt would let her sneak around and, in a pinch, run at full speed. She was even wearing flats instead of heels, just in case. In her hand Jin clutched a cute faux-leather bag, containing a special item Alain had procured: an electromagnetic grenade called a TED. If the worst-case scenario came true and Jin got caught, she could trigger it and wipe the workstation, erasing all the evidence of what they'd been doing. Adorably, the TED was hidden inside of a teddy bear.

They were ready.

The cab wove carefully through the city, bringing them closer and closer to the Sigan building. Marisa held up her compact mirror and checked her makeup again.

"We get to meet Su-Yun Kho," said Anja. She sounded as nervous as Marisa felt.

"Just don't fangirl all over her," said Sahara. "Let's try to look professional."

"Watch," said Anja, glancing at Marisa. "She's going to fangirl way more than either of us."

"I used to watch Kho's games all the time," said Jin. "I still have one of her trading cards."

The cab pulled up to the curb, and the nulis swirled out of the door to get good footage of the girls as they stepped onto the sidewalk.

"You're early," said Alain. His French accent rolled off his tongue like liquid charm. He stood up from a nearby bench, dressed in a tuxedo Anja had bought him for the evening. He looked hot—like, so much hotter than Marisa had been expecting. His hair was still spiky and wild, but it made such a perfect contrast to the clean lines of the tuxedo that he looked more at home here than he did in his slumdog workshop.

"I didn't recognize you," she said. "You do clean up well."

"I don't know how to take that," said Alain, and the corner of his mouth crept up into that subtle smile. "You sound more surprised than I'd hoped."

Marisa raised her eyebrow. "Hoped?"

A message popped up in Marisa's djinni, from her sister Pati: **Santa vaca, he's dreamy.**

You're still watching Sahara's feed? she sent back.

I wouldn't miss this for anything!

"You must be Alain," said Sahara, stepping forward and elegantly offering her hand.

Alain took it gently, and nodded. "And you must be Sahara."

"Marisa's told me all about this exciting new boyfriend of hers," said Sahara, using the backstory they'd invented as part of the deception. Marisa blushed. "She's a lucky girl."

"Not as lucky as I am," said Alain, and offered Marisa his arm. "Shall we?"

Marisa tucked her hand in the crook of his elbow, finding a satisfyingly strong bicep as she did. She smiled. "Absolutely."

Other people were arriving at the same time, scattered groups of Overworld players and coaches dressed like Hollywood royalty and streaming across the plaza toward the doors of the building. Marisa blinked back to Sahara's feed, watching her group out of the corner of her eye as they walked toward the building. They looked . . . out of place. This was a charity tournament for the super wealthy, and most of the other contestants came by that wealth naturally. They carried themselves differently, like they belonged there. Like Anja did. Marisa and the others were interlopers, and everything about them seemed to scream it. She took a breath, her heart fluttering, then straightened her back and held her head high. She was just psyching herself out. She could fake it with the best of them.

You look great, sent Bao, the message bouncing in the corner of her vision.

Where are you? she sent back.

Across the street with Alain's bike, he sent back. He was part of their getaway plan, if things went poorly. **Jun's with me, and Renata's on another street with the other motorcycle. As soon as you get back outside, we can get you out of here in seconds.**

Marisa grinned to herself. **Can you even drive a motorcycle?**

They don't drive themselves?

Marisa almost snorted; Bao knew exactly how the motorcycle worked, but he never passed up the chance for a joke. **You're the worst getaway plan ever,** she joked back.

"Is everything okay?" asked Alain.

"I'm fine," she said quickly. She couldn't talk about Bao with Cameron filming her every word, so she talked about Pati instead. "My sister's watching the feed, and keeps texting me."

"What's she saying?"

"She thinks you're hot." Marisa glanced at Alain as they reached the door.

"Say thank you from me," said Alain, holding the door open. "And tell her the feeling is mutual."

"You've never seen my sister," said Marisa.

"But I've seen you," said Alain. "I'm extrapolating."

Marisa felt her stomach flip over, and hoped Alain didn't notice.

The lobby of the KT Sigan building was three stories tall, with the back wall adorned by the stylized Hankul symbol that was the company logo. Security guards stood around the periphery of the room, watching the partygoers idly, but the majority of the actual security was being performed by the building itself: Wi-Fi scanners read their IDs and checked them against the guest list; chemical sniffers passively probed them for weapons and explosives. Alain had assured them that the TED would go completely undetected, but Marisa couldn't help but hold her breath. Would there be an alarm? A swarm of security nulis descending on Jin with tasers? Or maybe just a silent call to the human guards? They moved forward through the crowd, waiting nervously, but nothing happened. The TEDs hadn't been detected. Marisa breathed again, shaking her head, and gripped Alain's arm more tightly in silent thanks.

"Told you," he murmured.

As the crowd moved forward, the security guards began herding them up the stairs, to where the express elevators were waiting to take them eighty floors up. Marisa found herself walking next to a slim Japanese girl in a blue dress, inlaid with pearlescent flakes of seashell. Another Overworld player, just famous enough that Marisa knew her face but couldn't quite place her name. The girl turned her nose up at Marisa and murmured to her friend in Japanese; the other girl laughed. Marisa looked away.

"There's Saxon Violins," said Sahara, nodding toward a group of five tall, blond white boys laughing loudly in the center of the room. They were at least a head taller than most of the other guests, and stood in the flow of foot traffic like boulders in a river, letting everyone else move around them.

"What a bunch of douchebags," said Anja.

"We're on camera," said Jin, pointing at Cameron and Camilla.

Anja laughed. "You think I won't say it to their faces? Let's go right now." She grabbed Jin's hand, ready to drag her across the lobby, but Sahara shook her head.

Anja sighed, then caught Cameron's attention and pointed straight into the lens. "Saxon Violins are a bunch of entitled dude-bros, and I don't care who hears me say it." She flipped the camera off with her other hand, and Marisa shook her head.

Sahara led them to an escalator, where the girls in the tightest dresses were risking their heels to avoid trying to navigate the stairs. They rode to the top and waited by the elevators, where a smiling attendant was sorting people into the six main elevators.

"Welcome to the Forward Motion opening gala," said the woman. She was dressed like a flight attendant, with a peaked cap perched on the side of her head. She bowed, and then looked at Sahara, her eyes flicking almost imperceptibly over the data her djinni was feeding her. "Ms. Cowan, I see your entire party is here. Are you ready to go upstairs?"

"We are," said Sahara, bowing back just like they'd been taught in school. "Thank you."

"Number four, please," said the attendant, and turned to the next group. Marisa and the others looked for the numbers, and walked to elevator four. They seemed to have it to themselves. The other groups watched them from the sides of their eyes, everyone sizing up everyone else, and when their elevator finally came Marisa sighed in relief. They stepped inside, and the doors closed.

"Do they all have to stare at us?" Marisa asked.

"It's because we're so friggin' gorgeous," said Anja.

There were no buttons in the elevator; it went where the building told it to go. Marisa thought she could feel it moving, but it was so smooth she couldn't be sure.

"I need to tell you that my connection speed is very poor," said Alain.

"Is it because of the—" Marisa stopped herself, and resent the message as a private text. **Is it because of the virus?**

Alain paused, waiting while his crippled djinni downloaded the text, then nodded and sent one back. **Yes. I won't be able to search the database.**

Jin sent a message: **I'll still be connecting to Marisa. Can you find the files instead of him?**

If he tells me what to look for, sent Marisa. She didn't like that plan—it gave her less time to search for Grendel.

The elevator opened, and they stepped out onto the eightieth floor. Marisa gasped at the sight of it: beyond the small elevator alcove, the entire floor seemed to consist of a single hall, the high ceilings dripping with chandeliers, the walls covered with an alternating pattern of loose drapes and flat fabric screens. The screens lit up with a series of images, some of them scenes from Overworld games, others glamour shots of the players at the gala. Marisa didn't remember anyone requesting glamour shots from them, and wondered if Sigan had found them on their own . . . or if the Cherry Dogs would be left out of the rotation.

The hall was filled with round tables and chairs, and in the center a long black buffet was practically overflowing with tiny bowls of various sizes and shapes, each filled with bite-sized morsels of a different food: grilled abalone, pickled water radish, spicy beef in red bean jelly, pan-fried gingko berries, and hundreds more. Marisa could smell it from across the room, and it made her mouth water.

"I don't see her," said Jin.

"Yu-Sun Kho?" asked Sahara.

"Yeah." Jin scanned the room intently, looking at every face, but Kho wasn't there. She sighed. "I was looking forward to meeting her."

Marisa sent her a message: **I'm so sorry.**

Jun will tell me all about her, sent Jin. She smiled, but her smile was sad. **I guess this is it.**

You're the best, sent Sahara.

I'm jealous, sent Anja. **I hate these parties. You get the fun job.**

Jin smiled again, then said loudly: "I need to touch up my makeup. I'll see you in a minute." She walked toward the end of the hall, holding her bag tightly, searching the room one last time for a glimpse of Su-Yun Kho. She turned a corner, and a moment later her ID disappeared from Marisa's group chat window. A few seconds later it reappeared.

Hey, girls. It was the same ID, now switched from Jin to Jun.

All clear, sent Sahara. **Come on in.**

Be careful, sent Bao. **And the rest of you take care of her. Of both of them.**

Always, sent Marisa.

"Time to mingle," said Sahara. Jin would be making her way down through the fire stairs by now, ignored by the building because she had no ID to scan, and it would be at least half an hour before she found a workstation to log in to. Would she be okay? Marisa took a deep breath, determined to look as normal as possible while her stomach was tied in nervous knots.

"Spread out," said Anja, eyeing a group of boys near the side wall. "Talk to people. We may as well enjoy ourselves."

"I think that's Sila Terzi," said Sahara, pointing to a group standing by one of the tables. "She's the Guard for Canavar—that must be the whole team."

"Who are they playing for?" asked Marisa.

"I'm not sure," said Sahara. "I want to say . . . Tandon? But that's an Indian company; Canavar's Turkish."

"Eagle, then," said Anja. "Come on, let's go say hi." She dragged Sahara toward them, but Marisa looked at the food again.

"Hungry?" she asked Alain.

"Starving," he said. "But I'm not really familiar with this kind of food."

"It's called Hanjeongsik," said Marisa, pleased that she could remember the word. "We learned about it in International Relations at school." She started walking toward the buffet table, and Alain stayed close by her side.

"I never had that subject," he said.

"Typical," said Marisa.

"Why do you say that?"

She turned to look at him. "Well, that's the whole stereotype, right? I mean, you know what people say about France?"

"That it's a glorious country with a rich history?"

"That you think you're better than everyone," said Marisa.

"Maybe fifty years ago," said Alain. They reached the table, and he picked up a small porcelain plate and a pair of metal chopsticks. "Things have changed. We're insular, but only because we fight to preserve our culture."

Marisa picked up a plate and chopsticks of her own, surveying the vast array of food choices. "You don't see how that makes you seem standoffish?"

"I don't know that word."

"That you stand off from the rest of the world," said Marisa. She took a piece of what looked like a pancake, and topped it with some sautéed squash and mushrooms. "That you keep yourselves separate."

"Look at me," he said, and spread his arms slightly. "I have a French tongue, an Algerian body, an Indian brain implant, and a Chinese leg. And I'm fighting for American freedom. Of course they teach International Relations in French schools—but I didn't go to school."

Marisa cringed, mentally kicking herself for jumping on his comment in such a rude way. She'd only meant to tease him a bit, but Alain was so serious all the time he was practically unteasable. She looked at his face, at his strong chin and cheekbones, and said the only thing she could think of.

"You have a French tongue?"

"Was I using that phrase wrong? I mean I speak the French tongue."

"Do they teach classes in that, too?"

Alain stared at her a moment, and then that subtle smile crept onto his face. "Are you asking for private lessons?"

Another voice blared in Marisa's ear: "You're Heartbeat,

right?" She turned and saw a group of five people, four boys and a short teenage girl, staring at her with their arms folded. The white boy in the middle spoke again. "From the Cherry Dogs?"

Marisa nodded, caught by surprise. "Yeah." She reminded herself to smile, and moved her chopsticks to her left hand so she could hold out her right to shake. None of them took it.

"We've watched your games," said one of the boys. Marisa recognized them from the net; they were a pretty successful team called Your Mom. The boy who'd spoken was Esteban Diamante, from Mexico. "You're better than I expected," he said, "but you're not going to win."

Marisa raised her eyebrows. "Excuse me?"

"We loved the drone launch you did," said a black boy standing in the back. Juan Moreno, from Aruba. "It was clever. You could probably do pretty well in exhibition games."

Marisa turned squarely toward them, planting her feet solidly on the floor. "But not in real ones, you mean."

"My name is Alain," said Alain, stepping in and holding out his hand. They didn't take it, either, but instead of dropping it like Marisa had, he pushed it forward, advancing toward them, until finally the white boy shook his hand.

"I'm Ethan Sproat," he said. "Sproatagonist. General of Your Mom."

"Excuse me?" asked Alain.

"That's the name of a team," said Marisa. "You guys are playing for NovoGen, right?"

"Your Mom is playing for NovoGen," said the short girl. Maija-Liisa Nomura.

"That's what I just said," said Marisa.

"That's what Your Mom just said," said Nomura.

Marisa struggled to control her anger.

"Obviously anything can happen," said Diamante, "but the numbers don't lie. The semifinals will come down to us, MotherBunny, World2gether, and Saxon Violins."

"Bunch of douchebags," said Sproatagonist.

"You don't think the Cherry Dogs have a shot?" asked Marisa.

"I don't think the Cherry Dogs have a prayer," said the fifth player. Javier Mixco, if Marisa remembered his name correctly.

"We don't want to be enemies," said Moreno, "but we're not really here to make friends, either."

"I never would have guessed," said Alain.

"The final game is probably us and MotherBunny," said Diamante. "Maybe us and Saxon Violins, depending on how the bracket works out."

"That's a bet I'll take," said Marisa. She thought their own chances were weak, at best, but couldn't resist a sudden bit of grandstanding. "I say the Cherry Dogs are going to win the whole tournament."

"Your Mom is going to win the whole tournament," said the girl.

"That's . . . not an insult," said Marisa.

"No," said Sproatagonist. "It's a fact." He gave a thumbs-up, and smiled with incongruous cheer. "See you around; enjoy the party." The five of them turned and walked away, and Marisa watched them go with her mouth hanging open.

"What on earth was that?" asked Alain.

"I think that was trash talk?" said Marisa. "I honestly don't . . ." She frowned and turned back to him. "I honestly don't know if I'm offended or confused."

"I'm confused by this entire thing," said Alain, looking around at the party. "Is this typical of Overworld? Huge parties like this?"

"Never," said Marisa, looking back at the buffet and adding a plum to her plate. "Most tournaments are completely online—we're only meeting in person now because that girl wants to throw herself a party." She pointed with her chopsticks at one of the screens on the side wall, currently showing a fifteen-foot photo of Kwon Chaewon. She looked so meticulously cute Marisa wanted to throw something at her.

Alain glanced at the photo, but looked back at the food quickly. He picked up a short rib and some bamboo shoots in a persimmon dressing. "Who's she?"

"Daughter of the Sigan CEO," said Marisa. "Everything we're doing tonight, and as far as I can tell the entire tournament, is her personal fantasy: she wants to play with the pros, win a tourney, and meet some celebrities, so she bought her way into it."

"So did you," said Alain.

"Chaewon is—wait," she said. "We're doing this so that we can . . . well, to help you, for one thing."

"And to play with the pros and meet some celebrities," said Alain. "I'm not saying it's bad."

"You're equating me with Kwon Chaewon," said Marisa. "That's the same thing."

"I'm not trying to insult you," said Alain.

"You don't have to try," said Marisa, "you're just naturally gifted." They'd been flirting barely two minutes earlier—what happened? She'd never seen anyone walk the line between appealing and infuriating like he did.

Sahara and Anja returned, and Marisa knew by the scowl on Sahara's face that something had gone wrong. She put her hand on Sahara's arm.

"What wrong?"

"She's here," said Sahara.

Marisa frowned, confused. "Not . . . you're not talking about Su-Yun Kho."

"Not her," said Anja, and pointed toward the front of the room. "*Her.*"

Marisa looked up, at an elevated stage with a handful of camera nulis buzzing around it like flies. A small group of people was standing near it, and she recognized Chaewon. Was that who Sahara was mad about? But she'd known Chaewon would be here. It must be the person next to her. . . .

"Mierda," said Marisa.

The tall Chinese girl next to Chaewon looked over and saw Marisa at the same time Marisa saw her. The girl smiled, though there was no kindness behind it, and walked straight toward her through the crowd. Her dress was sky blue and almost shockingly unadorned; her long black hair was curled up into a bun, topped with some artful wooden twigs and a tiny blue bird. It moved its beak, and Marisa realized it was animatronic. Because of course it was. She shook her head, trying not to swear again, and then the girl arrived at their group and smiled again, with all the warmth of a crocodile.

"Nǐ hǎo, Sahara." The girl dipped her head just slightly, the barest hint of a bow. "Marisa."

"Zi," said Sahara, her face plastered with a broad, fake smile. "So good to see you."

"I was so surprised to find your names on the tournament list," said Zi. "I didn't think you'd quite reached that level yet, but then I saw that a major Abendroth executive had a daughter on your team, and it all made sense." She nodded toward Anja. "Anja Litz, I presume?"

Anja put one chain-clad leg forward, and reached out to shake with her arm covered in leather belts and buckles. Her predatory grin was absolutely genuine. "Call me HappyFluffySparkleTime. Are you who I think you are?"

"Yeoh Zi Chong," said Zi, shaking Anja's hand. "Call me Nightmare."

FOURTEEN

Sahara looked at Zi with thinly veiled hatred. "It's been a while. Still playing Overworld?"

Marisa kept her face blank. Sahara knew full well that Zi had stayed in the game, following her successes with mounting disgust and no small amount of late-night gossip sessions, consoling themselves with ice cream Marisa had stolen from the freezer at San Juanito.

"A bit," said Zi, her voice innocent. "And you've managed to keep the Cherry Dogs together?"

That frigid little bitch, thought Marisa.

"We have," said Sahara. "It's nice to have an event like this to catch up with all our old friends from the pro scene."

"It is," said Zi, and her smile showed that she knew exactly how much of Sahara's statement had been an exaggeration. Marisa wanted to slap her. Zi turned to Alain and bowed her head. "You must be Alain."

"It's nice to meet you," said Alain politely, but Marisa's mind was racing. How did Zi know who he was? Almost instantly a message from Sahara popped up in her djinni:

Does she have access to the guest list?

It's the only place his name is connected to ours, Marisa sent back.

That only makes sense if she's—damn it.

I just looked at the tournament list, sent Anja. **She's on World2gether. That's Chaewon's team.**

Sahara kept her voice mild and diplomatic. "I noticed you're playing for KT Sigan. I guess that explains why so many of the teams here are rating them so highly."

"I think we have an excellent chance," said Zi, lowering her eyes in false humility.

"I think Your Mom has an excellent chance," said Marisa. Zi looked at her, a moment of shocked confusion giving way to an understanding glare. She'd clearly already met the same team the rest of them had. Marisa smiled. No wonder that Nomura girl said that all the time; it was super fun.

"It's too bad the rest of your team wasn't able to make it in time for the party," said Zi, her voice icy. "I was looking forward to seeing Wong Fang again. She is still on the team, right? It's so nice of the rest of you to let her play."

"She's one of the highest-rated Junglers in non-league play," said Marisa, trying to keep her voice from bristling with rage.

Zi only smiled. "Ah, yes, the good old days of non-league play.

Don't worry, you'll make it someday."

Sahara started to speak, and Marisa was terrified it was going to be some very bad words, but Anja cut her off before she could say more than the *F* sound. "So you were the old Sniper, huh? Still playing the same position?"

"I would never claim to be an expert at it," said Zi, lowering her eyes again. "Though I do have one of the top ten PK records in the Greater Asian Region. League play, of course."

"What's PK?" asked Alain.

"Player Kill," said Marisa.

Zi glanced at him, then back at Marisa. "Not a player or a fan, then. Just arm candy?" She tilted her head slightly to the side. "I never took you for the kind to use a rental."

Fancy party or not, Marisa was ready to punch Zi right in the face, but was saved from the scandal when Jun arrived, stepping out of the crowd like magic.

"I'm back," said Jun. "You would not believe the girl I was listening to in the restroom—she broke up with her boyfriend on a djinni call, right there in the next stall. I had to stay until I heard it all; it was like the greatest reality show ever." She looked at Zi. "Oh, I'm sorry, you were talking to someone." She bowed. "I'm Jin Lee."

"Of course you are," said Zi. She shot a glance at Sahara. "This one's yours?"

"She's a friend," said Sahara. "Though I can understand if you're unfamiliar with the term."

Zi raised an eyebrow. "Well. This was a fairly civil conversation a moment ago. I guess some people can't let go of old baggage."

Anja smiled. "How did you know that's what they called you?"

Zi turned and walked away.

Marisa let out a long, slow breath. "I can't believe Nightmare's playing in the tournament."

"And on Chaewon's team," said Sahara. "You realize what this means, right?"

"We have to crush them," said Anja.

"Only if we get lucky with the bracket," said Marisa. "You've seen what we're up against—these are some of the best players in the world. Remember, we're just here to show off what we can do, and impress some networks."

"We were," said Sahara. "Now I'm here for blood."

"Her bird's still here," said Alain, pointing at the table next to them. Zi's tiny bird-shaped nuli cocked its head at them, stretched its wings, and flew away. "Twenty yuan says it was listening to us."

"Then be careful what you say out loud," said Sahara. "We don't know how many more of those things are floating around."

A group message appeared from someone labeled [empty]: **I'm in position.** It was Jin.

"Find a table," said Marisa. "We can cover the fact that we're not talking better if we're sitting down and eating."

Alain led her to a nearby table, half the seats already taken by a group of Brazilian girls. Marisa tried to make small talk, but all they gave her was a sidelong glance before turning back to their own high-speed conversation. Marisa was already tired of being offended, so she adjusted her collar and pretended not to notice.

"This isn't bad," said Alain, sampling the short rib he'd put on his plate. "I can't even remember the last time I had beef."

Marisa nodded. "This sort of crowd, they probably have it every day."

Sahara, Jun, and Anja joined them, their tiny plates brimming with codfish gills and pickled mushrooms and crown daisies and all kinds of exotic delicacies. Jun sent a group message: **Sorry that took so long. The building had already registered my ID when Jin came in, but hadn't checked her out when she turned it off. They made me wait at the elevators while they tried to figure out how I got out of the building; I told them I'd gone back out for tampons.**

And they believed you? sent Sahara.

Eventually.

Anja smiled, the only outward sign that any conversation was taking place. **This is the best. We should break into megacorp galas more often.**

Marisa shot a quick glance at Alain, wondering how long it would take his crippled djinni connection to download all the messages. She turned back to her food, took a bite of the plum—it was far more tart than she'd been expecting—and sent a private message to [empty].

You're alone?

The building doesn't even know I'm here, Jin answered. **This place is spooky in the dark. We're lucky no one's working late, though.**

Chaewon might have ordered everyone out of the upper floors for the party, sent Marisa. **Machinzote. Where are you?**

Seventy-five, sent Jin. **Nice round number. The plaque**

on the door said I'm in accounting, so any of these computers should work.

Find one with two cables, sent Marisa. **One's always power, but a second one will mean it's wired in to the air-gapped network.**

Already on it, sent Jin.

"I don't see anyone from MotherBunny," said Sahara.

"Maybe Chaewon didn't invite them," said Anja. Marisa let them talk, tuning them out and sending a message to Alain.

What should I be looking for?

It seemed to take ages for him to receive her message and reply: **It has to be something Johara can use against them—sales data is good, and international sales data is the best.** She waited, and several long seconds later another message trickled through: **You'll have to cross-reference their sales records with usage data to see what's actionable and what's not.**

Marisa chuckled, and sent a short reply: **You make corporate espionage sound so boring.** She waited, and when Alain laughed she knew he'd seen the message.

"It is boring," he said out loud. "But it works."

I'm in, sent Jin. **Took me a bit to find a workstation with an extra cable slot, but I'm connected and your buffer overflow worked perfectly. I have full access.**

Perfecto, sent Marisa. **Will the cable reach far enough for you to hide under the desk?**

I'll try, sent Jin. Marisa waited while she repositioned herself. **Yeah, it reaches. I have to crane my neck a little, though—these base-of-the-skull data ports are great**

for VR gaming, but they're in a terrible place for covert cyber-infiltrations.

You should file a complaint on their website, sent Marisa, smiling at the absurdity of it. **You're doing great, though. Ready to link up?**

Here it comes, sent Jin, and a moment later Marisa got a connection request from a network labeled Guest017. Jin was essentially using her own head as a router, running a private network with only two users: Marisa, and a Wi-Fi bridge into the airgapped Sigan network. The network connection initialized, and then Marisa was in—everything she'd been looking for, right at her fingertips. She couldn't stop the smile from spreading across her face.

"Merde!" said Alain. Marisa didn't even have time to look up before he put one arm around her shoulders and used his other arm to turn her chin. His face was almost touching hers, like he was about to kiss her, but instead he whispered softly, his lips practically brushing her cheek. "He's here."

"Who?"

"Mr. Park," Alain whispered.

FIFTEEN

Marisa felt herself go cold, all the blood draining from her extremities. "I thought Park was dead."

"Or at least too injured to show up tonight," whispered Alain. "Apparently he's better armored than we thought."

"You're sure it's him?"

"I have a facial recognition app," said Alain, "just in case anybody who knows me shows up. I've got it running in the background, and my djinni just spotted him."

"Diablos," muttered Marisa. She leaned into him now, putting her arms around him. Mr. Park couldn't see their faces if they pressed them together.

"Hey, guys, get a room," said Anja.

Marisa sent a group message. **The security guy who chased us the other day is here.**

Get out of there, sent Bao.

He hasn't seen us yet, sent Marisa. **He would have come for us already if he knew we were here.**

Should I abort? asked Jin.

Yes, sent Bao.

No, sent Sahara. **Tell me what he looks like.**

Look for a tall Korean guy with a metal faceplate, sent Marisa.

Got him, sent Anja. **Up by the front. Wow, he's scary-looking.**

Marisa and Alain broke their embrace and turned toward the back of the room, keeping their faces hidden from Park and everyone on the stage. **He's a monster,** sent Marisa. **We do not want him to see us.**

Want me to distract him? asked Jun.

No, sent Bao.

No, Sahara agreed. **We need him out of the room, and that means the best distraction will be downstairs.**

On it, sent Bao. **I can buzz this motorcycle right past the front doors.**

It won't be enough, sent Marisa. **If we want Park to leave the party, you've gotta cause a bigger scene than that.**

You want me to drive through the glass doors? asked Bao.

And get shot? asked Marisa.

Better me than Jin and Jun, sent Bao.

Can Renata do it? asked Sahara. **That's her whole job.**

She's not answering my calls, sent Bao.

Alain was growing more nervous. **Whatever you're planning, do it quickly.**

We could try to hack their security system, sent Marisa.

Not from inside their own building, sent Sahara. **We'd be way too obvious. Where are Fang and Jaya?**

Somewhere over the Pacific Ocean, sent Anja. **I'm pinging Jaya now.**

Marisa took a nervous bite of her food, trying to look nonchalant with a hired killer just a few meters away.

"What's our exit strategy?" Alain whispered. "If we have to abort and leave early, how do we get out?"

"We didn't really think about that," said Marisa.

"You're kidding."

"How were we supposed to know Park was still alive?" asked Marisa.

"You can never know everything that might go wrong," said Alain. "That's why you plan an exit strategy. That's the first rule of mission planning: don't go in until you know how to get back out again."

"Well, great," said Marisa. "Now we know."

"Come with me to the restrooms," said Alain. "It will buy us time."

Go, sent Sahara. **We'll think of something.**

The speech hadn't started yet, and most of the crowd was still standing, milling around and sampling the food and talking to each other. Marisa stood and, to make it look good, took Alain's hand, dragging him toward the back of the hall, where the restrooms were tucked into a hidden alcove. She recognized a few people as she went, and smiled politely, but none of them acknowledged her.

"I feel like I'm invisible," said Alain.

"I wish," said Marisa.

I'm here, sent Jaya. **What's wrong? I knew this was a bad idea.**

Mr. Park is here, sent Marisa. **We need you to pull him downstairs.**

Jaya hesitated before responding. **I'll see what I can do.**

Marisa and Alain reached the alcove in the back, and Marisa shivered nervously. "Okay. Keep watch while I focus on the database."

He nodded, and Marisa looked back at her djinni, blinking on the Guest017 network connection. It expanded to fill her vision, blotting out the real world completely, and she scrolled through lists of folders, looking for the ones she needed. "International Finance" looked like a good place to start, so she blinked on it, only to watch her display fill up with even more folders, organized in a system she could only barely comprehend. She knew most computer systems backward and forward, but accounting was like a completely different language.

"I need a file tree," she muttered. Gamdog 4.1 was easy enough to navigate, if you knew what you were looking for, but just roaming around and exploring it was maddening. "How am I supposed to know where anything is?"

"Welcome," said an amplified voice, "to the first annual Forward Motion Overworld Tournament Charity Gala!" The buzz of conversation in the main hall was replaced by loud applause. "We have a very special presentation prepared for you. Please find a seat, and give just a moment of your attention to the screens around the room." A few seconds later the hall filled with thunderous music, and Marisa imagined they were showing some kind of Overworld gameplay video to get the crowd pumped up. She desperately wanted to be in there, watching it, but kept her attention on the filing system.

She was really starting to hate this filing system.

I can't get in, sent Jaya. **Their security's too tight, and all the holes Marisa went through before have been patched up.**

They're starting a presentation, and want everyone to be here for it, sent Sahara. **Mari won't be able to stay in the bathroom forever—we need Park gone.**

Crashing the front door is still our best plan, sent Bao. **What if Jaya grabs some nulis to do it for us?**

That . . . might work, sent Sahara. **What's nearby?**

There's like fifteen restaurants here, sent Bao, **they've got to have delivery nulis.**

On it, sent Jaya.

Marisa blinked around in the database some more, hoping one of the folder chains would turn up useful information. She shook her head in frustration. No wonder Alain had said it would take a few hours at least.

The music ended, and the crowd in the main hall cheered.

Are you ready yet, Jaya? sent Sahara. **The intro's done, and they're going to start talking any second.**

Working on it, sent Jaya.

Work faster! sent Sahara.

"Please put your hands together," said the amplified voice, "for our wonderful hostess this evening: Kwon Chaewon!"

More applause, though this time it was polite instead of passionate.

Marisa found the International Finance section of the database, and blinked it open. More folders.

"Thank you," said Chaewon. Her voice was accented, but only barely. "It's wonderful to see so many of you here tonight. This tournament means so much to me, as I'm sure it does to all of you. Internet connectivity is a basic human necessity—it's how we communicate, it's how we work, it's how most people *find* work—and yet there are parts of the world where this fundamental need is unavailable. Even here in Los Angeles, one of the greatest cities in the world, entire neighborhoods have no way for workers to connect to their jobs, for students to connect to their schools, for children to connect to their parents and families. We are the lucky ones. We use the internet for recreation, for hanging out, for shopping at high-end stores and websites. By participating in this tournament, you're doing your part for those who use the internet just to survive."

More applause. Marisa found a folder titled "Yearly Expenses." That was only outgoing money—where were the records of money coming in?

She makes me want to choke myself, sent Anja.

Someone's coming toward you, Marisa, sent Jun. **Guy in a suit. Not Park.**

Jaya . . . , sent Sahara. Jaya didn't respond.

"We have an incredible treat for you tonight," said Chaewon. "I remember when I was just a little girl in Seoul, watching Overworld tournaments and dreaming of one day winning the world championships—but of course that was impossible. No woman had ever won a world championship, and only a handful had ever won regionals. But then, in 2039, everything changed."

"We have company," Alain whispered, and half a second later Marisa heard footsteps coming toward them. She blinked away the database display and the alcove reappeared; Alain was standing close by, and she stepped toward him, taking his arm like a girl in love, hoping they could sell the story of two people hiding in the back room to make out. A Korean man in a suit stepped toward them, stopping just a meter away. His smile was professional and emotionless.

"The presentation is starting," said the man. He gestured toward the main hall, where Chaewon was talking about Su-Yun Kho's legacy of Overworld victories. "Please join us—we'd hate for you to miss the special guest."

Marisa's mind raced, trying to find some way of stalling. She slid closer to Alain, until she was practically hanging on him. "Sorry," she purred, "we were distracted." She flashed the man a mischievous smile, but he didn't react.

"Please," he said. "Ms. Kwon would like everyone present."

Marisa took a step forward, and Alain came with her.

Do something, sent Marisa. **We're coming back in.**

The man stepped behind them, herding them silently toward the main hall. They couldn't turn back without fighting him.

Jaya! sent Sahara. **Where are you?**

I'm going for the door, sent Bao. **If I get caught—**

Got it! sent Jaya.

Marisa and Alain stepped around the corner into the hall, and Marisa looked up at Mr. Park . . .

. . . right as Mr. Park looked down at the floor.

I flew a delivery nuli right through the front door, sent Jaya. **Friendly Burger. Took me forever to hack the guidance system.**

The door's completely shattered, sent Bao. **Security guards are running everywhere.**

Park's reacting, sent Sahara. **Not leaving, though.**

Mr. Park started to look up again, and Marisa turned around to face the man behind her. "Is it true?" she asked, trying to act silly and naive. "Is Su-Yun Kho really here?"

"If you'll take a seat, you'll find out," said the man, calm and impatient as ever.

Park's leaving, sent Sahara.

"She's my hero," continued Marisa, stalling for time as Mr. Park walked out of the room. "I have her posters on my wall; I have her limited edition Overworld avatar; I have a dancing Su-Yun Kho emoji in my djinni display right now that lights up every time she shows up in the news—"

He's gone, sent Anja.

"I'm so excited!" said Marisa. "We'll go sit down now."

"Thank you," said the man.

Marisa and Alain made their way back to the table the Cherry Dogs were sharing with the Brazilian team, and sat down quietly as Chaewon finished her introduction.

"That was the day the world changed," said Chaewon. Marisa and her friends had been trash-talking her for so long, Marisa had half expected some kind of hollow plastic nuli, annoying to look at and devoid of human feelings. Instead she looked approachable and friendly, with a round face and bright eyes and a straight-lipped smirk. She wore a dress that somehow looked simultaneously like overalls and an evening gown, playful and elegant at the same time. She looked genuinely nice, and Marisa wondered if she wasn't just some spoiled rich kid after all. "That was the day," Chaewon continued, "that Su-Yun Kho, and her team 2Seven2, won the world championship. In the eleven years since, Overworld has become a beacon for equality, a sport where anyone, regardless of gender, nationality, or any other factor, can be a winner. For that, on top of everything else, we owe her an incredible debt of gratitude. Ladies and gentlemen, please welcome Su-Yun Kho."

Chaewon stepped back, gesturing to the side of the stage, and the room erupted in shouts and cheers and clapping as Su-Yun Kho appeared on the stage. She waved, smiling at the crowd, wearing auburn hair and a pixelated minidress: green and yellow, white and black, with here and there a splash of red to give it texture. The crowd kept cheering, some of them calling out Su-Yun's catchphrase from her days as an active player:

"Naeil!"

"Naeil!"

"Naeil, naega dangsin-eul dasi igil geos-ida!"

"What does that mean?" asked Alain.

"Quiet," said Marisa, blinking back tears. "That's Su-Yun Kho!"

"This is the greatest thing that's ever happened to me," said Jun.

What's going on? sent Jin. **Did you get caught? Did you get away? Is Su-Yun there? She is, isn't she?** She paused, and a moment later sent another message: **I hate you all.**

Marisa blinked, starting a recording of everything she saw. **Our heads are networked together, Jin; patch in and watch.**

Thanks, sent Jin.

Su-Yun tried to quiet the crowd, but they kept cheering, and she laughed. Soon the claps and shouts became more rhythmic, eventually coalescing into a chant: "Su-Yun! Su-Yun!" Marisa clapped and chanted with the rest of them, feeling like she fit in for the first time since they'd arrived at the party. Alain was clapping as well, but deliberately out of sync with the rest of them, and Marisa laughed.

"Okay," said Su-Yun, "okay. Thank you. That's enough, thank you." The crowd quieted, and she started her speech. "Thank you so much for having me here today, and thank you to Chaewon for that incredible introduction. I'm honestly kind of embarrassed now—I'm just a person who was pretty good at games. You guys are the real heroes. You're doing an incredible thing for the people in underprivileged communities, and now it's my turn to give you a round of applause." She started clapping, and the crowd exploded in another round of cheers and clapping of their own.

How's the search going? asked Bao.

Su-Yun Kho is talking, sent Marisa. **Want to watch?**

Do you have time to watch? sent Bao. **Mr. Park's not going to be down here forever.**

"Crap," Marisa muttered. Su-Yun finally quieted the crowd again, and started talking about her own childhood in one of Seoul's most destitute neighborhoods. Marisa desperately wanted to listen, but Bao was right. She blinked on the database icon to open it again, and once more her vision filled with an endless series of files and folders and super-exciting financial information. She sighed, and continued her search for Mexico's yearly sales data.

Raise your head, sent Jun.

Marisa was confused. **What?**

You're staring at the table, sent Jun.

Sorry, sent Marisa. **I'm not actually looking through my eyes right now.** The database display was being fed from her djinni directly into her optic nerves—they weren't *actually* blocking her vision, just her perception of it, so Jin could still watch Su-Yun's presentation through Marisa's eyes. Marisa straightened, and whispered to Alain: "Make sure my head is pointed at her, and nudge me if I should ever applaud or laugh or anything."

"Nudge for applause, poke for laughter," said Alain, and Marisa imagined the sly smile that was almost certainly on his face as he said it. Yet another thing she'd rather be looking at than the database.

She found the folder marked "Mexican Yearly Sales," and a minute later the subfolder for 2049's sales data—2050 must be stored somewhere else, because the year wasn't done yet. Did that mean this was older data? How had she wandered into an archive? No matter—if there were infractions to be found, she could still find them here. She started sifting through it, looking for something juicy, then remembered Alain's suggestion of just downloading it all and studying it later. She started the slow process of copying it all across the Wi-Fi connection, and then just to be on the safe side she grabbed nine more folders, to give her all of the last ten years. Normally a bunch of spreadsheets wouldn't take that long to download, but the size of this database gave a whole new definition to "a bunch of spreadsheets." She'd known KT Sigan was huge, but wow. "Megacorp" was right.

Alain poked her, and she applauded, and he immediately grabbed her hands in his own.

"Poke means laugh," he whispered. She gasped, mortified by the thought of herself clapping like an idiot, and everyone else staring at her. She laughed, and he squeezed her hands—not a gentle reassurance, but a firm "shut up, you're making it worse." "Too late," he said, "you missed the moment."

"What did I just laugh at?"

"Her mother had to work three jobs to afford their school clothes."

"Can you please murder me?" Marisa whispered. "Right now. Everyone in the room will forgive you."

"Just be quiet and work," whispered Alain. "I'll guide you better next time."

Marisa nodded and refocused on the database. Now that she had the data on how much money Sigan earned, she needed to find the data for how much they paid in taxes and international tariffs—the discrepancies between those two sets of numbers would be the thing that destroyed the company. But where did they store their tax information? And how could she find her way there from here in the sales archive?

Alain poked her, and Marisa heard laughter, so she laughed and hoped it sounded natural. She really wished she could be listening to Su-Yun.

Is Park still down in the lobby? sent Jaya.

Yes, sent Bao. **With about ten security guards.**

Marisa gave up on trying to find the files unassisted, and opened a search window. A simple search would be ridiculous—with so much data to search through, it would take hours—so instead she started writing a simple script that would narrow the search and speed it up, cutting out the obvious dead ends and going straight for the stuff she needed. Or at least she hoped it would.

Park's heading back for the elevator, sent Bao.

I'm not done, sent Marisa.

Jaya, sent Sahara, **do you still have control of that nuli?**

It's trashed, sent Jaya. **They're not designed to go through plate glass.**

But can you do anything with it? sent Sahara. **Wiggle the fins, spin the rotors . . . activate the ads on the speaker, I don't know. Anything to buy Mari more time.**

I'll try, sent Jaya. Marisa kept coding her search function, trying to go as fast as she could without screwing it up.

Something just got their attention, sent Bao.

I didn't think that was going to work, sent Jaya.

Did Park stay? sent Sahara.

No, sent Bao. **He's gone.**

Alain nudged Marisa with his elbow, then started cheering loudly, and Marisa clapped with him. "This is the end," said Alain, leaning in close and lifting her arm. After just half a second she realized that he was pulling her to her feet: Su-Yun Kho had finished, and this was her standing ovation. She blinked away the database and stood up, clapping and shouting with the others. She'd missed the entire thing—her hero was right there, and she'd missed it. The audience started chanting the catchphrase again—"Naeil, naega dangsin-eul dasi igil geos-ida!"—and Marisa chanted it with them.

"I like her," said Alain. "She's not a trust fund rat like the rest of the room."

"That's good," said Marisa. "If you didn't like her, this would be a very short relationship."

"There's a relationship?" asked Alain.

"I mean our . . . alliance," said Marisa, suddenly flustered. "Whatever this is."

"So what are they chanting?" he asked.

"Something she said after her first big win in a national tournament," said Marisa. "Her team beat the reigning champions, and their captain told her she got lucky and her plays were inconsistent and her strategy was garbage. A vidcaster was recording the whole thing, and asked if she had a response, so she looked this jerk square in the face and said: 'Tomorrow I'll beat you again.'"

"Cool," said Alain.

We don't have a lot of time, sent Sahara. She was still clapping wildly, and no one watching her would even guess she was sending messages. **We don't know if Park is coming back up**

here, or if he's headed somewhere else in the building.

He might be going to a security office, sent Jun.

Or to me, sent Jin.

There's no way he knows you're even there, sent Marisa.

If he comes back here I can distract him, sent Anja. I've got an awesome idea.

That makes me very worried, sent Sahara.

I don't know what else I can do, sent Jaya.

Find us another way out, sent Marisa. We can't use the elevators if he's standing right by them, and if he's chasing us we won't have time to walk down eighty flights of stairs.

We can't just leave, sent Sahara. That's going to look incredibly suspicious.

You could say you just came for Su-Yun Kho, sent Bao.

We could, sent Sahara. That's super rude, but it's at least believable.

People don't get arrested for being rude, sent Marisa.

You haven't seen me distract anyone yet, sent Anja.

Alain and I will go back to the restrooms, sent Marisa. No one has to leave if we can stay hidden.

Someone will come looking for you again, sent Sahara. And there's really only one way to explain why you're hiding with a boy in the restroom.

Marisa smiled. If I have to make out with a guy in order for our plan to work, that's a sacrifice I'm willing to make.

Whatever you do, do it quickly, sent Bao. If Park's heading back toward you he'll be there any second.

Su-Yun left the stage, and the applause was finally starting to die down, so Marisa grabbed Alain's hand and inclined her head toward the back of the room. He nodded and went with her. Was everyone watching them? What were they whispering to each other? She leaned close to Alain. "If someone comes back to look for us, our only cover story is that we can't keep our hands off each other. So, you know . . . get ready."

"I've been getting ready for that since we met."

Marisa stumbled. "Don't say things like that."

"Why not?"

"Well . . . are you serious? You can't say things like that unless you're serious."

Alain looked at her. "Do you want me to be serious?"

"I . . ." The team at the nearest table stood up, headed for more food, and Marisa used it as an excuse to stop walking. "I'm trying to write a program, okay? I don't need to be thinking about your lips the whole time."

"Then don't," said Alain. "The mission is more important."

"Careful," Marisa muttered, "you never know what weird little robot birds might be listening." She looked at him, at his rich, dark skin and his full lips, and his broad shoulders under his perfectly fitted tuxedo. How could he move so quickly from flirting to business? It was giving her whiplash.

If only they weren't here on a mission. . . .

But they were. And she had to focus on it. The sales data was still downloading, and her search program was almost ready. All she needed was two more minutes of peace, and she could get everything they came here for—

"You two seem awfully anxious to get back in the alcove," said a cheerful voice in front of them, and Marisa looked up to find their path blocked.

By Kwon Chaewon herself, and her entire team.

SIXTEEN

Chaewon smiled, but the girls flanking her made her look like a mob boss: Zi on her left, a tall white girl on her right, and two more Asian girls behind them. Chaewon's dress was even more improbably perfect up close, and in fact the entire team were some of the best-dressed girls at the gala. The white girl was wearing a peach-colored dress and hat faintly reminiscent of an old southern belle, with a vest and gloves of delicate white lace. Even in the dimmed lights of the party Marisa could see deliberate flaws in the lacework—signs that it had been made by hand instead of printed. These girls would give even Franca Maldonado a run for her money.

Nightmare's bird nuli, Marisa noticed, was sitting harmlessly in her hair. Unless she had more than one?

Marisa forced herself to smile. "Ms. Kwon! It's a delight to meet you. This evening has been wonderful so far, and we can't thank you enough for the invitation."

"Thank you so much for coming," said Chaewon brightly. "We're just doing what we can to make the world a better place." She smiled, and looked at Alain. "I saw on our RSVP list that you were marked as a plus one, not a player. It's so nice to have you with us tonight."

Don't say anything rude, Marisa thought.

Alain bowed slightly. "It's always a pleasure to talk to a fellow philanthropist. So few people are concerned about anyone but themselves these days." He gestured around at the party. "Did you arrange all of this yourself?"

"Down to the last speck of glitter," said Chaewon. "Did you like the short rib?"

Marisa frowned slightly. *Did she watch us eat? How closely were they watching us—and why?* She had to force herself not to glance nervously at the elevator—obviously Sahara would warn her if Park came back, but Marisa's entire body was on edge, and she felt like she needed to *do* something. Looking, pointless as it was, would be doing something.

What about Sahara's nulis? Marisa faked a small, polite cough, using the movement to mask a blink and call up Sahara's video feed. The image appeared in a corner of her vision, and she let out a small sigh of relief—one of the nulis was camped on a wall, staring at the elevator, giving Marisa a perfect view of it. No Mr. Park yet.

"The rib was delicious," said Alain, "though I can't help but wonder how much something like that costs, and how that money could have been put to better use if the Forward Motion tournament had—"

"I'm sorry," said Marisa, jumping in as soon she realized what he was saying. "He's very passionate about his charity work."

The tall white girl pursed her lips. "I can only imagine."

"The food was mostly donated," said Chaewon, never missing a beat or dropping her smile. "Most of the top-shelf caterers in LA owe my father a favor, so I called them in. What charity work do you do, Alain?"

"It's mostly freelance, on the ground—" said Alain, but Marisa cut him off again, fearing the worst.

"He's being modest," she said, gripping Alain's arm tighter than she needed to and hoping he got the message.

"Not at all," smiled Chaewon. Marisa didn't even know it was possible to *smile* a sentence, but there it was. "It doesn't matter how much money we raise for new cables if there's nobody out there to lay them, right?"

Marisa's eyes widened. Somehow, despite the angelic smile and positive tone, that entire comment had felt like a slap.

"Ms. Kwon," said Sahara, stepping up next to Marisa. Anja came with her, grinning like a cat as it tried to decide the best way of eating a mouse. "I want to thank you personally for hosting this event."

"Of course," said Chaewon. "And thank you, Ms. Cowan, so much for being a part of it! It's great that the younger kids in the audience have a group of amateurs to look up to. They can't all be world champions, but they can be you." Her smile was so warm,

Marisa wanted to hug her and punch her at the same time.

A movement on the nuli feed caught her attention: the elevator opened, and Mr. Park stepped into the room.

Code Red, sent Jun.

I'll cover you, sent Anja. **Keep your faces turned away from him, and get to the elevator while I hold his attention.**

How are you going to hold his attention? sent Sahara.

By doing exactly what we're all wishing we could do, sent Anja. She stepped forward, covered in straps and buckles and spikes, and planted herself in front of Chaewon.

Don't hit her! thought Marisa.

Anja flipped her half-shaved hair and spoke so loudly Marisa wondered if she had an amplifier patch on her jaw: "It's too bad those kids you're talking about don't have as much money as you do, or they could all just buy their way onto a championship team."

The entire gala fell silent, everyone turning to look at them.

Chaewon's smile disappeared, slowly fading as they watched, and Marisa couldn't help but feel a pang of deep concern, as if Anja had just kicked a kitten. But her smile didn't turn into hurt or sadness; it turned into nothing: Chaewon's face became completely inert, with no expression at all, as if she weren't a human but a VR character whose connection had dropped. It was one of the most unsettling things Marisa had ever seen.

"This is my party," said Chaewon. Her voice was flat—no emotion, just stating a fact.

"I'm so sorry!" said Anja, her voice echoing through the hall. "I thought this was a party for everyone."

Move, sent Sahara, the message bouncing in Marisa's vision to get her attention. **Park's coming.**

Marisa glanced at the nuli feed: the camera was following Park as he crossed toward them from the elevator. Marisa grabbed Alain's arm and pulled him to the side, keeping their backs to Park. Would their movement attract his attention? Would he follow them?

Zi stepped forward, planting herself between Chaewon and Anja. "Nothing wrong with a little trash talk, right?"

"Nothing at all," said Anja. "So let me go bigger: Chaewon's pathetic little all-stars team is the most selfish cry for attention since she dropped out of her mother's—"

"What the hell?" said Sahara.

"I can see what you bring to the team," said Zi. "You've got more guts than Sahara ever did."

"We don't need to do this," said Sahara.

"See?" said Zi.

Chaewon was still just staring, like a broken doll.

"This got scary," said Alain as they moved away. "Is Anja always like that?"

"More often than we'd like," said Marisa. "All we needed was a distraction, not a . . . howling catfight." They moved into the alcove, out of sight of the rest of the hall, and Marisa gripped his arm for balance as she focused on the nuli feed. Zi and Anja were practically nose to nose, but a guard stepped between them, holding out his hands in a placating motion.

What's going on in there? sent Bao.

Anja's trying to get us thrown out a window, said Marisa. **That's not what I had in mind when I asked for an exit.** She could still hear Anja yelling in the main hall. She switched her target from Chaewon to Zi, and eventually from Zi to the security guard—to whoever she could yell at the most, it seemed.

I'm going to kill her, sent Sahara.

She helped Alain and me escape, sent Marisa. **That's better than nothing. Do you see Park?**

He's gone, sent Sahara. **I programmed Cameron to find him and follow him, but he lost the target and came back to me. It doesn't make sense.**

I think the mission's a bust, sent Marisa.

You think? Sahara's message dripped with frustration. **We need a way out. Jaya, have you found anything?**

That building's a fortress, sent Jaya. **I've got one idea, but I'll need help.**

We're a little busy, sent Sahara. **Find Fang—she'll be on a plane, like you. Wake her up and get us out of here.**

Marisa nudged Alain. "We have to hide—let's duck in there." She moved to the door to the fire stairs—the same door Jin had used earlier when she'd run down to the seventy-fifth floor—but Alain stepped in front her, blocking her way.

"The restroom's safer," he said. "The building will know if we go into a stairwell."

Marisa nodded. Of course the building was reading their locations—that's why they needed Jin for the mission, because she could turn off her ID—

"That's it," she said suddenly. "He can drop his ID."

"What?" asked Alain.

"Mr. Park can drop his ID," said Marisa. "Just like I did in the cafe, and Jin did when we got here. The nuli lost him because it was fixed on his ID, and then that ID disappeared, so it went back to Sahara."

"Then we have to go *now*," said Alain. The last remnants of his flirtatious attitude disappeared, and he became as focused as a laser. "The only reason for Park to disappear like that is if he perceived a threat—maybe it was the nuli downstairs, or Sahara's nuli followed him too closely and he got suspicious. Whatever it was, he's onto us, and inside of this building we're completely at his mercy."

Marisa looked up, dread gnawing at her stomach, and traced her eyes along the line where the wall met the ceiling. She found it in the corner: a tiny black tube, just barely protruding from the wall. A security camera.

She turned her face away, but it was too late. Every camera in the building had seen them, had been watching them for an hour, and now Park was reviewing all of that footage with his overclocked brain.

"Run," she whispered.

Alain turned and shoved open the stairway door. Marisa kicked off her high heels and ran after him, rushing down the cold metal stairs in liner socks. **We're screwed,** she sent to the group. **Get out! Park knows we're here and he knows who we are.**

Where are we supposed to go? sent Jun. **We're on the eightieth floor!**

I'm working on it! sent Jaya.

Why'd you wait so long to wake me up? sent Fang. **You know I love breaking into stuff.**

Just break us out! sent Sahara.

Marisa heard the door above them open, and shouted to Alain, "He's in the stairwell!"

"It's us!" Sahara shouted back. Marisa heard her voice echo through the stairwell, followed by a tiny explosion, like a firecracker. "He's right behind us," shouted Sahara, "but I used Camilla to fuse the lock." Footsteps thundered down the stairs. "That'll slow him down."

"Not enough," said Alain.

A new message appeared: **HOLY COW!**

Marisa looked at the sender: it was Pati. **Are you watching this?** she sent back.

Everyone's watching, sent Pati. **Why are you all running?**

Turn it off, sent Marisa, and blocked her, to keep any new messages from popping up and blocking her vision.

Another message popped up from her mother: **What are you doing?!**

I'll explain later, sent Marisa, and then blocked the whole family just in case.

Alain and Marisa reached a landing, with "78" painted on the wall in large gray letters.

"We're only on the seventy-eighth floor," she called back. "We can't run the whole way down." She hesitated for half a second, and then ran to the next flight of stairs anyway—until they had a better plan, running was all they could do.

"We can't go for the elevator," yelled Sahara. "They have full control of it—it'd be like locking ourselves in a prison cell."

"Unless Jaya takes it over," yelled Anja.

Sahara's yell turned angry. "Thank you, by the way, for freaking out on Chaewon like that. I wouldn't be surprised if she kicks us out of the tournament."

"She wouldn't dare," said Anja. "It would look like she was afraid of us. Besides, you know the other teams loved it."

Can you hack the elevator? Marisa sent to Jaya.

I've gotten you a faster exit, sent Jaya, **but you're not going to like it.**

Anja's going to love it, sent Fang.

I hate it already, sent Sahara.

Marisa reached the seventy-seventh floor, and heard another crash far above them.

"SurrenderYourselvesToOurCustodyAndYouWillNotBe-Harmed!" Mr. Park's voice was unmistakable, amplified and accelerated and terrifying. His footsteps echoed through the stairwell, gaining on them impossibly fast.

Whatever it is, do it, sent Marisa.

Go to the seventy-fifth floor, sent Jaya. **Take a right outside the stairwell, then the third left.**

"Follow me," Marisa shouted. They clattered down the stairs, Park getting closer with every step, and when they reached the seventy-fifth floor she threw the door open and jumped through. Alain was right behind her, and they didn't even dare to breathe while they held the door for Sahara and the others. How far back were they? Park's footsteps seemed to drown out all the other noise in the stairwell, and Marisa worried that maybe he'd already caught up to them, incapacitated them, and moved on. Should she run? Park was too fast—they couldn't wait any longer.

Marisa bounced on her toes, too terrified to think, and suddenly Jin came around the corner, leaping down the stairs, followed closely by Anja and the camera nulis, with Sahara bringing up the rear.

"Close it!" Sahara shouted, and dove through the open door just as Mr. Park came barreling around the corner behind them. Marisa and Alain slammed the door closed, and Cameron zapped the doorknob with a bolt of electricity. Park slammed into it almost instantly, but the door held. "It's the taser," said Sahara, panting as she climbed back to her knees. "If you burn out the full charge, it can melt a door lock." Marisa helped her up, and they started running again. "That means I only had enough juice for two doors, though, so I'm out of tricks."

"Where's Jaya taking us?" asked Anja.

"Another elevator?" said Marisa. "I don't know."

"You're putting a lot of trust in this person," said Alain.

"We're putting a lot in you, too," said Sahara. "You'd better be worth it."

They ran past offices and cubicles, reaching the third hallway just as the door behind them burst open, and Mr. Park came after them with ferocious speed and a quiet, unnerving calm. They raced around the corner and sprinted forward with everything they had.

Where next? sent Marisa.

Straight forward, sent Jaya. **If you're where you're supposed to be, there's a big double door just ahead of you.**

I see it, sent Marisa. **It's glass.**

Go through it, sent Jaya.

No! sent Bao. **You're on the seventy-fifth floor—that's the balcony garden! It's a dead end!**

"StopWhereYouAreIAmLicensedToUseForce," said Mr. Park. He was already at the turn, just a few steps behind them. They leaped forward, reaching for the door, but Mr. Park grabbed Alain by the neck and jerked him back—

—and then dropped to the floor, twitching and unconscious.

"Híjole!" said Marisa.

Jin stepped out from behind a corner. "Jaya led me here," she said, and held up the TEDdy Bear. "I used this—it's the only weapon I had."

"It buzzed my djinni pretty hard," said Alain, wobbling on his feet. He grabbed Marisa for support. "But Mr. Park has an almost fully digital brain—he'll be down for a while."

"Cool," said Anja.

Mr. Park groaned.

"Not as long as we need," said Sahara. "He's already rebooting. Let's see what's out here."

She opened the glass door, and they stepped out into the dimly lit garden. Night had fallen, and wind whipped around them, tousling their hair and chilling Marisa to the bone. She shivered and rubbed her arms. Beyond the edge of the balcony other skyscrapers reared up, glittering monoliths surrounded by the endless stretch of the city below. They walked toward the railing, but stepped back in surprise as a swarm of heavy nulis rose up before them.

"Defense drones?" asked Sahara.

Delivery nulis, sent Fang.

I know it's not ideal, sent Jaya, **but it's our only option.**

"You . . ." Marisa's jaw fell open. "You don't mean . . ."

"Oh, hell yes!" shouted Anja. "There's six of them—one each. They have good handholds, and they're rated to carry loads twice as heavy as any of us."

Mr. Park rolled over, groaning again.

"You've gotta be kidding me," said Sahara.

You'll be fine, sent Fang. **Kids in Beijing ride nulis all the time—it's like a new sport.**

"We're not—" said Sahara, but Mr. Park planted his arms on the floor and rose up, slowly regaining more control of his body. She looked back at the nulis, her jaw set and determined. "Fine, we are."

"Woo!" shouted Anja, and pulled her nuli closer; it dropped toward the floor and she jumped on its back, gripping the frame tightly. It was barely big enough to hold her. "Mr. Wizard, get me out of here!" The nuli rose up, and hovered out past the railing, and Anja screamed with joy and adrenaline as it dropped away, slow and controlled, taking her down to the street.

"You're next," said Sahara, motioning for Jin and Jun. Mr. Park rolled his neck in a circle, stretching his reinforced muscles. "Grab one—we don't have time to be scared."

"You're underestimating how good I am at being scared," said Marisa.

"Just get on," said Sahara. She helped Jin and Jun each up onto a nuli, and then climbed on to the back of her own. Her camera nulis, tiny in comparison, hovered around her. "This is going to play great on the feed, isn't it?" She laughed, too scared to do anything else. "See you at the bottom." They moved toward the open air, and Marisa reached for one of the last two nulis. She pulled it toward her, when suddenly it shook in her hand, breaking apart as if something had struck it.

Sahara's head snapped toward her. "What was—"

"I don't know—"

A gunshot echoed through the air, and Marisa's eyes went wide.

"Someone's shooting!" shouted Alain.

Marisa looked toward Mr. Park, but he was still on his knees, his eyes blank as his brain finished its reboot cycle.

A tree next to Alain exploded, and the sound of another gunshot wafted toward them across the empty air.

Jaya, we've got a sniper, sent Marisa. **Get them out of here now!**

Jin's and Jun's nulis dropped out of sight, far faster than Anja's but still controlled. Sahara started the same descent, but yelped as her nuli crumbled beneath her, shattered by a third bullet. She plunged out of sight with a terrified scream. Marisa ran to the railing with a scream of her own—the shards of broken nuli plummeted toward the ground, seventy-five stories below, and Sahara tumbled with them.

"No!" screamed Marisa.

"You have to go!" shouted Alain. "Take the last nuli!"

Another bullet pinged off the railing nearby, but Marisa ignored it, keeping her eyes on Sahara. What could she do? How could she save her? Her best friend was going to die, and there was nothing she could—

"SurrenderYourselvesImmediately," said Mr. Park, rising slowly to his feet.

"Take the nuli and go!" shouted Alain. "I can get out of this—you can't—"

"Neither of us is getting out of this," said Marisa fiercely. "I'm not leaving you."

Alain grabbed her by the arms, and after a moment of hesitation, he kissed her. "Make yourself matter," he said.

And then he threw her off the building.

The wind roared around her, drowning out her screams as she tumbled through the night sky. Lights from the street and the other buildings bounced off the windows beside her, blurring into a single neon whirlwind until she didn't know what was up or down or anything else. She screamed again, her entire life compressing to a single moment, a single burst of fear and helplessness, and then something touched her ankle, and the world stopped spinning.

Gotcha, sent Fang.

Marisa looked up and saw the last delivery nuli, its rubber claw clamped tightly around her leg.

She struggled to catch her breath. **How'd you do that?**

I'm amazing, sent Fang.

Marisa looked down—they were still falling, but more slowly, and she could see Sahara tumbling below her. **Catch up to Sahara,** she sent. **We can still get her!**

The nuli dropped faster, and Marisa sent Sahara a message: **We're coming for you.**

I've got Cameron, sent Sahara. **If I can grab Camilla with**

my other hand they might be able to slow me enough to land safely.

They're too small, sent Marisa. She was catching up—but the ground was catching up faster. "We're not going to make it," she muttered. **Fang,** she sent, **come on!**

This is as fast as it goes!

Marisa could see cars now, and other nulis, and people staring up and pointing. Ten floors left. Eight. Sahara was so close now Marisa could almost touch her—almost, but not quite. Six floors left. Sahara lunged for Marisa's hand, Cameron's tiny rotors straining against her mass, but their hands missed. Four floors. Three. Marisa screamed, and Sahara lunged again—

—and missed Marisa's hand—

—and grabbed Camilla.

"Pull up!" Marisa shouted.

All three nulis angled their rotors, trying to move up, draining every last ounce of their batteries. Marisa lunged one final time and caught Sahara's arm, heaving up with all her strength, and inch by inch their downward motion became lateral, pulling them into an almost-horizontal flight path, flying over trees and cars and shocked pedestrians. A semitrailer roared toward them, and Sahara lifted her knees to her chin, avoiding the truck by inches. They dipped lower, still hurtling through the night air, and Marisa watched as the crowd screamed and dove out of the way. The nulis were nearly out of juice, and they were still going to crash—

And then Bao was there, spreading his arms wide, and broke their fall with his body. The three of them tumbled across the sidewalk, banging and bruising and grunting in pain, but soon enough they stopped. And they breathed.

They were alive.

Anja ran up to them, her face as white as the moon. "Everyone okay?"

"I think so," said Bao.

"Holy crap," said Sahara.

"Yeah," said Marisa. She sat up, looking back at the massive skyscraper they'd just fallen from. "We're alive," she said. "We're alive."

SEVENTEEN

"We need to hurry," said Bao, pulling Marisa to her feet. "The motorcycle's over here."

Everyone okay? sent Jaya.

We landed safely, sent Marisa. **Alain got caught.**

"Where's Renata?" asked Sahara. "We can't all fit on one bike."

"I still can't find her," said Bao.

I'm so jealous of you guys, sent Fang. **Seventy-five stories? You're my new heroes.**

Not now, Fang, sent Marisa. **Hey, Renata, you around?**

"This way," said Bao, and led them down an alley toward the waiting motorcycle. It was big, but it wouldn't hold all six of them.

Marisa sent a message to Alain, hoping his connection was still strong enough to receive messages. **Where are you? Did they catch you?** She was still processing the last few minutes—he had thrown her off a skyscraper—but she'd deal with that later. And kick him in the junk while she was at it. For now, all she wanted was to make sure he was safe.

"I'm calling an autocab," said Anja.

"They'll track it," said Bao.

"They already know who we are," said Anja. "It's not like we used fake names at the gala."

"We can't even go home, then," said Jin. She looked even worse than Marisa felt.

Alain hadn't written her back yet. "I can't get a message through to Alain," Marisa said. "His djinni was crippled as it was—maybe that TED killed it?"

"He didn't come down on a nuli?" asked Sahara.

"They shot it," said Marisa. "He . . . insisted that I take the last one."

"Then they got him," said Bao.

"Cab's here," said Anja. "Come on—our only hope is to make it to my father's house: they won't dare touch us there." They followed her down the alley to another street, where an autocab was waiting. "Sigan might mess with us, but they're not gonna mess with the CFO of Abendroth."

Marisa sent another message to Alain, asking if he'd been caught, and then wrote another note to Renata: **Are you here? Did they get you too?**

"Where do you think Renata is?" asked Bao, helping Jun into the cab.

"She's not responding to anything," said Marisa. "She hasn't been all night."

"You think they set us up?" asked Bao.

Marisa frowned. "What do you mean?"

"The entire job went south," said Bao, "and suddenly we can't find either of them. This could have been a setup from the beginning."

"We got away, and Alain didn't," said Anja. "It's as simple as that. I can't see how any of this would benefit them, or Sigan."

"Maybe they weren't working with Sigan," said Bao. "Maybe they were playing both us and Sigan against each other, to get something they wanted."

"If he wasn't working with Sigan, then he's a prisoner right now," said Marisa. "I'm telling you, they're on our side."

Either way, you have to go, sent Jaya. **However this shakes out, it's not going to matter now.**

"Fine," said Marisa, but gave one last, long look at the street around them before climbing into the cab.

"I think I know how to get Sigan off our backs," said Sahara, settling onto the bench. She held up the two camera nulis, now virtually dead after spending all their battery life trying to keep Sahara airborne. "We have that entire chase recorded—it already streamed, live, for everyone to see."

"That's not going to save us," said Marisa. "That's going to pound a few more nails into our coffins."

They all found seats, and the doors closed. "Would you like to stop for a snack on the way home?" asked the cab, pulling away from the curb. "Our route will take us past four tapas restaurants and more than one hundred and fifty—"

"No ads," said Anja, blinking to pay the extra fee. "And there's an extra fifty in it for you if you get us there fast."

"I am not permitted to break any traffic laws," said the cab, "but I assure you that Gutiérrez Taxi Company is always—"

"Fine, shut up," said Anja, "just drive and stop talking."

Sahara opened a voice call to Fang and Jaya, so they could participate in the conversation. "My nulis aren't recording anymore," she said, wiggling Cameron's inert plastic housing, "so we can talk freely. We were using the video feed as an alibi, to prove we weren't doing anything wrong, but now I think we can use it the opposite way: we publicize it. We spread that eighty-story dive all over the internet, and tell people it was part of a publicity stunt Sigan helped organize."

"No one will believe that," said Marisa.

"Sigan will deny it," said Bao.

"They can't," said Sahara. "They have no proof that we hacked them, but we have proof that they took Alain prisoner—and even though megacorps are allowed to capture criminals, they're not allowed to hold them. Federal law requires them to turn over any corporate prisoners to the police for processing."

"So they have to agree with our story," said Anja, catching on to the idea, "or they admit that they're illegally holding someone captive. It's their only way out."

"Or they could turn Alain over to the police," said Fang. "They might surprise us by doing the right thing."

"The police can't hold him without evidence," said Bao, "which, like Sahara said, they don't have. If they turn him over, they lose their chance to question him. That's why these megacorps never deal with the government when they can get away with it—and why people like Mr. Park exist in the first place." He looked at Sahara. "I think it's worth a shot."

"The video is all out there anyway," said Marisa. "We can't keep it secret. Spinning it like this is our only chance."

"Then I'll start editing something together," said Sahara. "We'll say it's an augmented reality game or something—a publicity stunt to help advertise Forward Motion." She leaned back against the bench, zoning out as her vision focused on her djinni instead of the real world.

"Now the rest of us have a different job," said Marisa. She remembered the kiss at the edge of the railing. "We've got to find Alain."

"That's easy," said Bao. "He's in a KT Sigan security office, handcuffed to an interrogation table."

"We can hack Sigan's internal system and try to find him on a camera," said Anja.

"No good," said Jaya. "I already tried hacking in, when you were still at the party, and it's tighter than a drum in there."

"Another telecom, then?" asked Anja. "If you know who he uses for djinni service, you could get into the satellite system and try to pinpoint his GPS. If it's Johara, Jaya might even be able to do it legally."

"That assumes his djinni's still connected," said Marisa. "His connection was down to a trickle at the end there, and I bet that TED blast finished it off. Even when he reboots, he'll stay offline."

"It's at least worth a try," said Jaya. "I've already logged in to my work computer remotely, and run a simple search. Both Alain and Renata are Johara customers."

"I love you," said Marisa. "Can you find where they are?"

"GPS data is hard to get," said Jaya, "but I'll get to work on it."

"I'm trying to connect to Renata's ID," said Anja. "She's got herself firewalled like you wouldn't believe. I can't even get a request through, let alone an actual connection. I can't pull any GPS data."

"But you've found her, right?" asked Fang. "I mean, you're on her front step, you just can't get in the door."

"Sure," said Anja, "but that doesn't tell me anything about her real-world location."

"But it'll tell you about her virtual location," said Fang, "including any other networks she's connected to. If she's linked in to a building's Wi-Fi, or a cafe or something, you should be able to see it."

"Okay," said Anja, and blinked again, her eyes darting back and forth as she maneuvered her way through the connections. "I've got one, but it's weird. It's like a . . . a Wi-Fi connection to a single chip. It's tiny, whatever it is. Something called Wee-Bey?"

"That's a clothing company," said Bao. "They made my camera hat."

"Her hoodie!" shouted Marisa. "Renata's wearing a camera hoodie, just like Bao's hat—she can take pictures with it and display them. She used it when Park got hit by a truck."

"If it has a camera, I should be able to get into it," said Anja. "Then we could at least see what she's looking at. What do you want to bet she still has the hoodie on factory settings?"

"I'll find the password," said Marisa, and blinked over to

Lemnisca.te. Hackers loved sharing information with each other, both to enable future hacks and to brag about their brilliance. She searched for Wee-Bey, and sure enough there was an entire thread that listed the factory passwords for Wi-Fi clothing. She copied it and sent it to Anja. "There you go."

"Got it," said Anja. She blinked again, entered the password, and then a slow grin spread across her face. "I'm in. I can see everything her shirt sees."

"That's not a sentence you hear every day," said Bao.

"I can't see much," said Anja. "Looks like she's in a small, dark room somewhere."

"Do you think they already captured her?" asked Jin.

"We need a tablet," said Anja, refocusing her eyes on the inside of the cab. "I want to project this so you can all see it."

"I've got my phone," said Bao.

"No," said Anja, "something bigger."

"Some of these cabs have screens built in," said Jun.

"Of course!" said Anja. A screen was like a tablet with no computer attached—just a monitor, so people could link it to their djinnis and share information on a central display. Anja blinked again, and the side window lit up with a dark, blurry image. Marisa saw what looked like a hand, casting an angled shadow; the rest was black.

"Definitely a small space," said Bao, squinting at the image. "That angle shows the shadow crossing a corner from one wall to the next. The light source is above her."

Marisa leaned forward. "But is she captured or hiding?"

"Patch me in," said Fang. Marisa blinked, setting her eyes to stream, and shared the connection with Fang just like she had with Jin at the gala.

"She's moving," said Jun. "Maybe . . . climbing up something?"

"No," said Bao. "She's not climbing up a wall, she's crawling on a floor. The camera's on her shirt, so we're getting a tilted perspective. Can we get sound?"

"Video only," said Anja. "The shirt doesn't have a mic or a speaker."

"What is she crawling through?" asked Fang.

Bao smiled. "You see the rivets there? That's an air duct."

"Could she . . . ?" Marisa began. Her heart sped up. "Do you think she's in the Sigan building? Is she already trying to rescue Alain?"

The shadows kept moving, until finally the source of the light came into view: a vent in the duct. Renata peered through the vent, and then she pushed herself up and started prying it loose. The shadows jumbled together and Marisa lost track of what was happening, until at last Renata dropped down through the ceiling into the room below, and stood up.

She was standing in front of Alain.

"Yes!" shouted Marisa. She punched the air. "Go Renata! Get him out of there!"

Alain stood up and started talking, though they couldn't hear what he was saying. His wrists were chained to the table in front of him.

"I hate being right," said Bao.

"Argh!" said Fang. "Why don't those hoodies have audio?"

"Try a lip-reading app," said Marisa. "Accessibility companies use them all the time for people with hearing problems who can't afford cybernetics."

"I'll look," said Anja.

They watched the conversation raptly, trying to work out what Renata and Alain were saying. The video quality was excellent, though of course the camera moved every time Renata did . . .

. . . and suddenly it occurred to Marisa that Renata wasn't moving nearly as much as she should have been. Why wasn't she cutting the chain on the cuffs? Why wasn't she checking over her shoulder for noises at the door?

"Hurry," muttered Fang.

"Got one," said Anja. "Give it a sec to install."

A moment later the autocab's voice blared through the vehicle: "—certain the girls got away?"

"What?" asked Marisa.

"It's the lip-reader," said Anja. "It's already patched in to the cab's screen, so I think it just borrowed the voice as well. That's Alain we're listening to."

They couldn't hear the answer, though Alain was obviously listening to one. Renata's face was out of the frame, and a lip-reading app couldn't read lips it couldn't see. Alain started talking again, and the cab's voice followed a split second later: "That's good. Are you in contact with them now?" Pause. "Can you send Marisa a message?"

Anja looked at Marisa and raised her eyebrows, a huge grin on her face. "Guess we know what his priorities are."

"Shut up," said Marisa, though she couldn't hold back her own smile. It made her feel warm to hear him say her name.

"Tell her I'm sorry I pushed her," said the cab's voice, "but it was the only way to save her. I knew the nuli could grab her, and Park got me barely two seconds later." There was another pause, then he nodded. "Thank you. What did she say?" Another pause. "Well, I guess I deserved that. I did throw her off a building."

"Wait," said Marisa. "She didn't send me a message."

"Apparently she told him that she did," said Anja. "And that you responded."

"She's lying," said Bao, already a step ahead of them. "Something's very wrong here."

"Why would she lie to Alain?" asked Jun. "They're partners."

"No, she's a mercenary," said Bao. "He told us himself."

"Maldita muchacha," said Marisa. She looked at Alain on the screen. "Do you think she tipped off Park that we were there?" She stopped suddenly, wide-eyed, the possibilities spinning out further. "Do you think she was the sniper who knocked out our nulis on the roof? She's a crack shot at hunting drones."

"She's been playing us this whole time," said Bao, smacking the side of the cab. He gestured to the screen, where Alain was listening intently to whatever Renata was saying. "Who knows what crazy lie she's telling him right now?"

"This is still just speculation," said Marisa, though she only half-believed her own protests. "We know she's lying, but we don't know why. I can't imagine she's working with Sigan—she's had every opportunity to turn us in, and never has."

"You're sticking up for her?" asked Fang.

Marisa threw her hands in the air. "Maybe she has a good reason—"

"That's an interesting idea," said Alain. "Are you sure it'll work?" Pause. "Honestly, very few of my contacts will be helpful in breaking me out of here—I don't know why you're so keen on talking to them."

"*That's* her plan," said Anja. "She's trying to get to his criminal contacts—either to work with them or to sell them out to Sigan for extra cash. They probably all have bounties on their heads."

"If Sigan can figure out who his contacts are, they can dismantle the entire resistance movement," said Bao. "They could try to interrogate him, but how much easier would it be to just trick him into giving them up? So they pay off someone he already trusts."

"Fine," said Marisa. "So let's say she's a traitor. She sold him out, and she's probably the one who shot at us. How do we warn him?"

"I've already told you we can't hack into the building," said Jaya. "There's no way to get a message in there."

"Girl, *please*," said Anja. "I'm hacked into a shirt with a digital display."

Marisa's jaw dropped. "Holy crap."

Anja blinked. "The controls are pretty simple, probably the same basic interface Bao uses on his hat. You want photos or video?"

On the screen, Alain shook his head, and the cab's voice spoke just barely out of sync with his mouth. "SkullBuddy is an arms dealer—he's not going to help."

"What is it with boys and skulls?" asked Jun.

"We need to hurry," said Bao.

"Can we do text?" asked Marisa.

"In a wide selection of fonts and colors," said Anja with a grin, her eyes focused on her djinni. "Ooh! I can make them blink."

"No blinking," said Marisa. "If anything moves, Renata's going to notice it."

"She'll probably also notice that Alain is suddenly reading her shirt," said Bao.

"I'm going to put the words right across her boobs," said Anja. "She won't notice anything out of the ordinary. What do we want to say?"

Marisa thought through it, composing the conversation in her mind. No matter what they wrote on the shirt, Alain's first impulse would be to ask Renata about it. So the first message had to be a warning. "Okay: take a picture of me." She looked directly at Anja, and put her finger in front of her lips in a "Shh" gesture.

Anja blinked. "Got it."

"Send him that photo with the words 'Renata is lying to you.'"

Anja's pupils darted back and forth, and she blinked. "Done."

They watched the screen. Alain listened to Renata, then his eyes dropped down to the shirt as the message caught his eye. He stared at it, dumbstruck.

"Come on, don't just stare at it," Marisa murmured.

Renata's hand moved at the edge of the screen, and Alain looked back up at her face.

Bao smirked. "'Eyes up here, buddy.'"

"Okay," said Marisa. "Next message: 'We think she's working

with Sigan. She sold us out, and now she wants your contacts.'"

"Done," said Anja, and spoke out loud as she wrote the next sentence: "Say . . . the word . . . elephant . . . if you . . . understand."

"What?" asked Marisa.

"We have to know!" said Anja.

"But how's he going to say 'elephant'?"

"It's not that hard," said Anja. "You just said it."

"But it's hard to work it into the conversation—"

"Let's talk about the elephant in the room," said the cab's voice. Alain tapped his fingers on the table. "I'm being held on the seventy-ninth floor of the tallest building in Los Angeles, in an armored interrogation room."

"Whoa," said Bao. "Is he talking to us?"

"While pretending to talk to her," said Marisa. "He's feeding us information."

"How . . . can we get . . . you out?" said Anja, writing a new message on the shirt.

The cab's cheerful voice continued. "The only way you're getting me out of here is if the higher-ups decide to move me."

"Somebody record this," said Bao.

"Already recording," said Marisa and Anja in unison.

"You'll have to deal with Mr. Park," said the cab's voice. Alain gestured with his hands as he spoke. "But you'll have a window while I'm out of the room."

"What does he expect us to do?" asked Fang. "We're not a special ops team."

"How . . . do we stop . . . Park?" wrote Anja.

"We're not going back in there," said Bao. "You barely got out the first time."

"He saved my life," said Marisa.

"He threw you off a skyscraper," said Bao. "*Fang* saved your life."

"He's one of us," said Marisa. She thought about the last words he'd said to her: *Make yourself matter.* She nodded, still staring at the screen. "We have to get him out."

"There's no way—" said Bao, but the cab's voice cut him off.

"I know," said the cab. "I know you don't have the equipment. So I'm going to—I know, that's what I'm doing. I'm going to give you one of my contacts. He'll be able to help."

Alain looked abruptly to the side, and a moment later Renata did the same. The camera showed the edge of the doorframe.

"They hear someone coming," said Marisa.

Renata looked back at Alain, and only then did he start speaking. "His name is C-Gull. He can help get me out of here." Pause. "I don't know his ID; he takes messages through an old handheld phone, which he keeps stashed somewhere remote. That way no one can track him directly. The number is 9780062347163." He held up his hand as he finished the number: his pinkie and pointer fingers raised, and the other fingers down.

"What's that?" asked Fang.

"My abuela does that sometimes," said Marisa. "It's like a heavy metal thing."

"Alain just threw the horns?" asked Anja.

"I'm more surprised that Marisa's grandma throws the horns," said Bao.

"I just tried the number," said Fang. "It doesn't work."

"He gave us a fake number?" said Bao. "Why would he do that?"

"Maybe he just screwed it up," said Anja. "Please . . . repeat . . . the number."

Alain looked directly at the hidden camera. "There are people who matter, and people who don't," said the cab. "There are ones, and there are zeroes."

The image moved as Renata stepped up onto the table and climbed back up into the vent in the ceiling.

"Wait!" shouted Marisa. "We're not done!"

The image went dark.

"Wow," said Bao. "That was anticlimactic. A fake number? We're back to square one."

"I think it was a clue," said Jaya. "He didn't give us a fake number—he gave *Renata* a fake number. That last little speech must have been a clue to help us track him down."

"He talked about ones and zeroes," said Fang. "Maybe it's some kind of binary transposition of that number he gave us."

"That's a ton of possibilities," said Bao. "This could take forever."

"I'm on it," said Fang. "This plane doesn't land for six more hours: What else am I going to do?"

"I'm finished," said Sahara, finally rejoining the conversation. "I edited the footage of our skyscraper dive, got some good angles on it, and made it look awesome. I posted it everywhere I can think of, with the story about us and Sigan planning the whole thing together as a Forward Motion publicity stunt."

"We're almost to my house," said Anja, glancing out the window. "I guess we'll see if anyone's there to murder us."

The screen on the window flashed white, and the cab spoke again: "Ababababurbebaburbeebun."

"What on earth?" asked Sahara.

"It's a lip-reading app," said Marisa, looking at the screen. "Renata just dropped out of the vent, and she's—este cabrón!" She slammed the wall with her fist. "That's Park." Mr. Park was standing in front of Renata, centered in the image from the hoodie's camera.

"She's definitely working for Sigan," said Bao.

"Zubububububerk," said the cab.

"He's talking too fast for the app to translate him," said Anja.

"He did that in the building, too," said Jun.

"He's overclocked," said Marisa. "So in addition to being an unstoppable killing machine, his brain moves ten times faster than ours."

Anja's eyes went wide. "Overclocking is *punk rock.* It burns out your brain in, like, seven years."

"Five," said Marisa.

"It's also super illegal," said Jaya.

Bao leaned back heavily, putting his hand over his face. "I can't believe we let ourselves get involved in this."

"It's okay," said Marisa. "Sahara's little ruse is going to get us off the hook, for the time being at least, so all we have to do is rescue Alain."

The cab slowed. Marisa looked out the window and saw

Anja's house. "Gracias a dios," she sighed. The lights were on, and the streets were empty.

"Looks like we're safe," said Sahara.

"But for how long?" asked Bao.

"Okay," said Marisa. "Let's figure this out. We know what Sigan wants from him, right? They want his underworld contacts. All the arms dealers and freedom fighters and who knows what else that he works with—and since they're not exactly subject to the law, they can go to any lengths they want to get it out of him. Their trick with Renata didn't work, so now what? They'll . . . I don't know, download his djinni storage?"

"If he's smart, he's wiped the memory," said Anja.

"Then all they have left is to beat it out of him," said Marisa. "They'll interrogate him, they'll torture him, they'll break him any way they can, and when they're done he'll just disappear. Nobody knows they have him, so they can do whatever they want."

"We have to contact this C-Gull person and hope he can help," said Jaya."

"Dababibiburgurgurdle," said the cab.

"I could listen to that all day," said Anja. She jerked upright suddenly, staring at the screen. "Scheiße, that's Chaewon."

They all looked back at the screen, and there was Kwon Chaewon, still in her party dress, looking as cheerful and chipper as ever.

"Are you Renata?" she asked, then smiled and nodded. "Thank you so much for your help." Another pause. "The fee is contingent, of course. Were you able to get the information we need?"

"I hate them both," Sahara mumbled.

"What about the girls he was with?" asked Chaewon. "I need to know if this was all a plan to ruin my tournament."

"'Her' tournament," said Anja. "Because of course it is."

Chaewon's eyes practically sparkled with joy. "That's too bad, but it doesn't matter. They've already put out a story about how this was all a stunt, planned with our help, and we're going to go along with it. It's the only way we can keep Alain here without involving the police." She turned to Park. "Mr. Park, get something out of him that my father can use to end this little crusade against the company. By any means necessary."

"See?" said Marisa. "They're going to beat him."

"Hbd?" said Park.

"That's up to you," said Chaewon, smiling like a beauty queen. "The police don't know we have him, so it doesn't matter what condition you leave him in. And the walls of that room are quite soundproof."

"Something is very wrong with her," said Bao.

Renata must have said something, because Chaewon looked back at her suddenly. "Please don't talk to me. You can go away now."

Renata didn't move, and a moment later Chaewon's serene smile faltered for the first time.

"Of course there will be consequences," said Chaewon. "For starters, they're out of the tournament."

"No," said Sahara.

"We'll spin it as part of the so-called publicity stunt," continued Chaewon. "If the stunt was the only reason they were invited into the tournament, well, now the stunt is over. The Cherry Dogs will not be playing."

She turned and walked away, and Mr. Park led Renata to an elevator.

Marisa fell back, closing her eyes.

"So it worked," said Bao. "They saw our story, and they're running with it—no charges filed, no overclocked thugs coming to carry us away in the night."

"That's *wonderful*," Jin insisted.

"Weren't you listening?" said Sahara, her eyes like fire. "We got kicked out of the tournament!"

"Are you serious?" asked Jun. "*You're not going to jail*, Sahara, or into a secret cell like Alain. I'd say that's a win."

"Yeah," said Sahara, looking out at the darkness. "We're real winners."

EIGHTEEN

Marisa curled up in an overstuffed leather chair in Anja's living room, wrapping herself in a blanket and sipping a bottle of Lift to stay awake. The rest of her friends were scattered around the room in similar states of exhaustion and shock, silently staring at the wall or blinking on their djinnis as they tried to recover from the disaster the evening had become. They'd failed in their mission, and been kicked out of the tournament to boot. One ally had betrayed them, and the other was being held in an impenetrable high-rise prison. They couldn't even go to the police without admitting to a long list of cybercrimes.

Marisa took another sip of Lift, feeling the carbonation crackle in the back of her throat. Only one thing left to do: she braced herself, and unblocked her parents from sending her messages.

The flood of incoming messages wasn't nearly as bad as she'd expected: five or six from her mami, two from her papi, and ten or so from Pati. She read the first couple from her mother, but they were all just variations of the same basic theme: **What's going on? Are you okay? Unblock me right now!** Marisa closed the rest without reading them and started a voice call. Guadalupe picked up on the first ring.

"Marisa! How are you! Are you okay!"

"Yes, Mami," said Marisa. She spoke softly, so she wouldn't bother the others. "We're at Anja's house, healthy and safe."

"We've been tracking your djinni's GPS," said Guadalupe. "Your father's practically tearing his hair out."

"That's why I called you instead of him," said Marisa.

"He's not mad, he's worried." Marisa's mother sighed. "Corazón, do you honestly think we'd be angry before we were concerned about you? We love you, and we want you to be safe no matter what happens."

Marisa felt a tear roll down her cheek. "Gracias."

"Te amo," said Guadalupe. "Now, for the love of all that's holy, will you please tell me what happened tonight? Did Sigan really hire you for a publicity stunt?"

Marisa nodded to herself. Her parents had heard the story already; news traveled fast, she thought, but then she supposed they'd probably been actively looking for news about it. She hated lying to her mother, but it was for the best. "Yeah," she said. "Not really hired; we didn't get paid—it was publicity for us, too. To help spread the word about the Cherry Dogs."

"Were you safe?" asked Guadalupe. "It looked so real—"

"We were tied to nulis hidden just out of frame," said Marisa, digging deeper into the lie. "We were totally super-amazingly safe." She thought back to that sickening feeling of plummeting through the air, unsupported and certain she was about to die. "Totally safe."

"You should have told us," said Guadalupe. "Sigan should have told us—how do they justify asking a bunch of teenagers to do something like that without even once contacting their parents? At least tell me they're not making you do any more stunts, because you are one hundred percent prohibited from anything like that ever again."

Marisa felt a twinge of despair, and closed her eyes. "No more," she said softly, and told her the same lie Chaewon had told Renata: "We were never really in the tournament; it was all just part of the stunt."

"Really?" asked Guadalupe. "This article doesn't say anything about that."

"Just wait," sighed Marisa. "It will."

Guadalupe read the article aloud: "'A prepared statement from the Forward Motion Foundation states, "The Cherry Dogs are delightful daredevils both in the game and out. We're delighted to have them as a part of Forward Motion, and we look forward to matches just as thrilling as this nuli dive."'"

Marisa sat bolt upright. "What?"

"It sounds like you're still in the tournament to me," said Guadalupe.

"We're still in the tournament," said Marisa loudly, waving her hands to get her friends' attention. "Everybody search it—look up every article about the nuli dive!" Sahara and the others stared at her, frozen in mid-movement, eyes wide from shock, then collapsed in their chairs and began blinking rapidly, searching for any scrap of news they could find.

"What are you talking about?" asked Guadalupe. "Wasn't this part of the plan all along?"

"Of course it was, Mami, I love you, I'm sleeping at Anja's house tonight, bye." She blinked to end the call, and scrambled to start a news search of her own.

"Great Holy Hand Grenades," said Sahara.

"Is it true?" asked Marisa. She found a link and blinked on it.

"I think I found it," said Jin.

"They call us 'delightful daredevils,'" said Anja. "Is that a compliment or are we being patronized?"

Marisa read an article about the press release, and then the press release itself, and then watched a news clip where an anchor-woman recounted the whole story and showed some of the dive. She shook her head. "Is this real?"

"How are we still in the tournament?" asked Anja. "I called Chaewon's father a cut-rate ladyboy prostitute, and that wasn't even the worst of it."

"It's real," said Sahara. Marisa looked at her, and saw her friend sitting stock-still, her eyes unfocused. Her jaw was hanging open.

"What did you find?" asked Marisa.

"I got an email," said Sahara. Her eyes refocused on Marisa's face. "From Nightmare."

Marisa frowned, and stood up to walk toward her. Her body still ached from the crash landing, but she didn't even care. "What does it say?"

Anja and the others crowded around Sahara as well, and

Sahara read out loud: "'I couldn't care less about you, or your team, or this idiotic tournament. The whole thing's a joke. I didn't come here to win, and I didn't come to play paid BFF with some rich báichī—I came here to beat you, and I can't do that unless you play. I don't have a lot of strings to pull, but I pulled them, and Chaewon is mad as hell, but you're back in the tournament. Don't mess this up again.'"

Marisa was speechless.

"Wow," said Bao. "Score one for old grudges, I guess?"

"How's this even possible?" asked Jun.

"Zi's one of the best Snipers in the Asian leagues," said Sahara. "I guess she has pull."

"And Chaewon can only do so much," said Anja. "Based on the search results we all just ran, that nuli dive was huge news. The tournament's probably overjoyed to have us on the roster."

"So . . ." Marisa shook her head. "So what do we do now?"

Sahara nodded, and straightened in her chair. She was back in leadership mode, and her eyes practically shone with determination. "We go to sleep, we pick up Fang and Jaya from the airport, and we practice like crazy women. The brackets go up tomorrow, so we'll know exactly what we're up against."

The Los Angeles airport was larger than some cities; it had seven terminals, 329 gates, and more shops and restaurants than Mirador did. Marisa, Anja, and Sahara took a cab to one of the international terminals and waited in a little cafe for their friends to emerge from customs.

"How are we going to recognize them?" asked Anja. "You've never met them, right?"

"Never in person," said Sahara. She had only one nuli today: one of Cameron's rotors had been damaged when Sahara grabbed it in the fall, so only Camilla, newly recharged, was hovering over them filming.

"I did a videoconference with Jaya once," said Marisa. "I can't remember why. Djinni calls are so much easier."

"They'll recognize us, at least," said Sahara. "They watch the vidcast all the time."

It was nearly six a.m. when passengers started trickling out of the doors and into the arrivals area, clutching their bags, eyes red from the overnight flight. Marisa sat up straighter, wishing she'd thought to put some makeup on—early morning or not, this was going to be her first time meeting two of her best friends in real life. She wanted to make a good impression. Even her clothes were a disaster, since all she had to wear were Anja's clothes, and she was at least two sizes larger than her stick-thin friend. She shrugged. Judging by the state of the people coming through the customs door, Jaya was bound to look as disheveled as she was.

That's when a tall, long-legged Indian woman stepped out of the doors, dressed in vibrant orange and blue and looking almost impossibly elegant. Her trousers and blouse were both loose, swishing around her like a dress, and even her long hair looked brushed and lustrous. On her forehead was a large blue panel, like a diamond or a gem, which contrasted gorgeously against her light brown skin.

"Of course," Marisa mumbled.

Jaya looked around, then saw them and squealed, running toward them with her arms stretched out for a hug. Her suitcase followed, a little rolling nuli programmed to follow close behind its owner. Marisa's fatigue seemed to melt away, and she couldn't help but smile and jump to her feet, Anja and Sahara close behind. They wrapped each other in a tangled hug, the overeager suitcase bumping into their legs like a puppy.

"It's so good to see you!" said Jaya. Now that they were closer, Marisa could see that Jaya must have touched up her makeup right before the plane landed, as she looked impeccably sophisticated. She also was, Marisa couldn't help but notice, visibly older than the other girls. The three Cherry Dogs who lived in LA were all seventeen, and while Marisa had known that Jaya was twenty-two, she'd never really thought about it. Confronted with the difference in person, it suddenly felt like a gulf between them.

Jaya, for her part, didn't seem to notice or care. "Sahara!" she shouted. "You're every bit as classy in person as you are on the vidcast. Classier!" She opened her eyes wide, and clamped her hand over her mouth. "Unless that's an insult! I didn't mean it as one! You look wonderful on the vidcast as well!"

"Thanks," said Sahara, smiling broadly. "You look incredible, too. How can you possibly look so good after a red-eye flight over the Pacific Ocean?"

"And across the international date line," said Jaya, nodding solemnly. "It's Sunday again, right?" She laughed. "I've traveled into the past!" She turned to Anja. "Your hair looks so much wilder in person! I love it!"

Anja wiggled her eyebrows, rubbing her half-bald head with one hand. "Did you have a good flight?" she asked. "Pacific flights are so much better than Atlantic ones."

"This is my first one," said Jaya, "but it seemed fine to me. I'll need to thank your father for the millionth time when I see him. It was definitely smoother than those little planes we have that jump around from city to city."

"Does India have hypertubes?" asked Sahara. "That's how I first came here from Boston, and they're great. It's like riding in an elevator."

"We do," said Jaya. "I think I like planes better, though—they're more exciting." She looked at Marisa and smiled warmly. "What do you prefer?"

"I've actually never left LA," said Marisa. She shrugged. "So, cabs I guess."

"Honestly?" said Sahara. "The best local travel is Omar's car—but only if Omar's not in it." They all laughed.

"So," said Jaya. "I'm in town for a week, and we can only spend so much of that time playing Overworld. What are we going to do? I'm ready to party!"

"Parties will be partied," said Marisa. "Starting with a party in my restaurant. Have you ever had Mexican food?"

"I have," said Jaya, pointing at her emphatically, "and it was terrible."

Marisa raised an eyebrow. "Where'd you have it?"

"Chennai," said Jaya, looking guilty. "So I assume it was not the most authentic Mexican food in the world?"

"Oh, honey," said Sahara, "you have no idea. And San

Juanito's the best in LA."

"We pay her to say that," said Marisa with a laugh. "Five bucks off her rent for every customer she brings in."

"After the restaurant we'll take you to see a little of Mirador," said Anja. "The lovely warehouse district, and the many five-star drug dens."

"It's not that bad," said Marisa.

"And with our drugs duly purchased," said Anja, sweeping on with her plans without responding to Marisa, "we shall put on our finest dresses, show off our finest legs, and go to the finest nightclubs in LA, there to shake our finest assets at some—let's face it—relatively midrange boys."

Jaya laughed. "Not the finest boys? Where are they?"

"They're all at home," said Anja, "trashing government websites and leaking corporate secrets." She shook her head dramatically. "Definitely not in the clubs, but, you know: love the one you're with."

Marisa laughed, and then Jaya's suitcase bumped her legs again and she stepped aside to let it past. As she did she saw a little girl, almost lost inside of a large, shapeless hoodie, watching them from across the hall. Probably a beggar, she thought, and felt suddenly uncomfortable to be wearing Anja's expensive clothes.

"Where's Fang?" asked Anja.

"Her plane landed about the same time Jaya's did," said Sahara, glancing at the giant arrivals display on the wall nearby. "She should be here by now."

"The customs line is ridiculous," said Jaya. "My plane and hers, and at least one or two others. Maybe she's still in there."

They turned and looked around at the crowd, and Marisa's eyes fell on the girl in the hoodie again. She peered closer this time, and saw that the girl probably wasn't a street rat like she'd thought—her shoes were nice enough, and she had a backpack and a small suitcase with a long handle. She just stood like someone who didn't belong there, her shoulders hunched, her face hidden, her chin tucked low like she was trying to curl in on herself and disappear. She acted like she didn't want anyone to see her, which made it all the more strange that she was standing in the middle of the hall, staring at them so conspicuously.

She raised her head to meet Marisa's gaze, just enough to let a little light fall on her face. She was definitely Chinese.

"Híjole," said Marisa, and called out to the girl. "Fang?"

The girl hesitated for a moment, before finally raising her hand and waving shyly.

"Sac!" cried Jaya, and ran to her. Fang winced, seeming to shrink even farther into her hoodie, and endured the round of hugs the rest of the Cherry Dogs subjected her to.

"I'm so sorry I didn't recognize you sooner," said Marisa, wrapping the girl in her arms. Fang was fifteen, two years younger than Marisa, and much shorter than she'd expected. Now that she could see her face inside the hoodie, she looked younger as well.

"It's okay," said Fang. Her voice, at least, was instantly familiar.

"Why didn't you come introduce yourself?" asked Sahara.

Fang grimaced, and Marisa could see that she was searching for the words. Fang spoke perfect English—if she was looking for words it was because she was shy, or embarrassed, or simply uncomfortable. Marisa jumped in to help her, putting her arm around her shoulders: "The question is, why weren't we paying better attention? She's our guest, and we're going to treat her like a queen." She grabbed the handle of Fang's long suitcase. "Are we ready?"

"Ready for a nap," said Sahara. "You're probably both exhausted, right? Let's get back to my place—I've got a couch and an air mattress already set up." She pointed toward one end of the long hallway. "Train's that way."

"I thought we were treating them like queens!" said Anja. She faced the front door, leading out to the pick-up/drop-off area, and spread her arms wide. "Gentlemen, your finest autocab for my friends here. We shall spare no expense!"

They shrugged and followed her—if she was paying, a cab was always preferable. They got the largest one they could find, the interior of which was almost the size of Marisa's bedroom; its door opened smoothly, and they piled in with all their luggage. Jaya deactivated her suitcase's auto-follow routine with a blink of her eyes, and Marisa helped her lift it into the storage area on the inside wall. Not only was it larger than Fang's little roller bag, it was nearly twice as heavy.

"Qué pasó?" grunted Marisa. "What have you got in here?"

"I'm here for a week!" said Jaya. "That's, what, fifteen different outfits?"

Marisa lifted Fang's bag into the cab. "What about you?"

Fang shrugged. "I brought some clothes." Her voice was almost too soft to hear.

"Is everything okay?" asked Marisa.

"Was I . . . not supposed to bring clothes?"

"No," said Marisa, "what I mean is, you seem really quiet. Are you tired?" Fang was usually a crackling ball of energy and motion, trash-talking with the best of them.

"Yeah," said Fang. "Just tired."

Marisa nodded but wasn't sure she believed it.

They settled down in the autocab, and Anja gave it the address. "Would you like some breakfast?" asked the cab. "There are more than one hundred coffee shops along our route—"

"Oh, for Cthulhu's sake!" shouted Anja. "Will you please shut up! And tell all the other cabs to stop offering us deals every time we get in one!"

"Would you like to take advantage of our special no-ad extended pass?" asked the cab. "Save on ad-free rides, every ride you take. You can order it by the week, month, or year."

"Give me the year, please," groaned Anja, slumped so far down in her seat she was practically lying on the floor.

"I didn't know that was even an option," said Sahara, and looked directly into Camilla's recording lens. "You heard it here first."

"Oh my gosh," said Jaya, "I didn't even realize it! I'm finally on the show, aren't I!" She waved at the camera, then wrapped her arm around Fang and leaned in close, their cheeks almost touching, and waved again. Fang smiled, but only for a second.

Sahara grinned. "All five Cherry Dogs, together in the real world for the first time. Cherry Dogs forever!"

The other girls—all except Fang—raised their hands triumphantly and shouted it back: "Cherry Dogs forever!"

"Woo!" shouted Marisa. The cab merged out of the airport access road and onto the freeway, speeding up just suddenly enough that Marisa reached out for the cab's wall. She looked around the cab and couldn't help but smile. "This is the best. You girls are literally the *best*."

"Tell me about the forehead thingy," said Anja, pointing at the gem on Jaya's head. "It's changing colors." Marisa noted with surprise that the pale blue had turned bright yellow.

"It's because I'm excited," said Jaya. "It's a mood panel—it changes with my neural patterns. Yellow is excited, blue is happy, violet is really happy, and brown is nervous. Green is pretty average."

"What's red?" asked Marisa.

Jaya laughed. "If you ever see it red, offer me chocolate and back away slowly."

"That's brilliant," said Sahara. "I've never seen one of those before—are they big in India?"

"Not necessarily," said Jaya, "but you see them around. I got mine about six years ago, when I was struggling with some emotional stuff. I thought I was just moody, and I figured my parents would be able to navigate my hormones a little better if I just had a sign on my forehead that told them what I was feeling." She laughed. "So I got one installed. It didn't really help, but I think it's pretty, so I've left it in. The really valuable implant is this one." She leaned forward, pulling up her sleeve to expose her upper left arm. She had a small metal console embedded in her skin, just below the shoulder, about the size of a tube of lipstick. A pair of lights sat at one end of it, one green and one blue, and at the other end was a small button. Between them was a small glass window, revealing some kind of readout that Marisa didn't know how to interpret.

"This one's not for fashion," said Sahara.

"Pure utility," said Jaya. She pushed the button and the console clicked open, revealing a little space in her arm with an off-white cartridge about two inches long. Jaya popped it open and held it up. "Turned out everything I was dealing with was related to depression. This helps regulate my brain chemistry so I don't go all death and despair anymore." She kissed it and popped it back into place, closing the console with another soft click. "Way better than the pills I used to take, since it can monitor and adjust medication levels on the fly. I don't know what I'd do without it."

"That's awesome," said Marisa.

"Back to the forehead thing," said Anja. "Is it religious?"

"You can't just ask that," said Marisa.

"Why not?" asked Anja. "I'm curious."

"It's not religious," said Jaya. "It's *super* not—my grandma still has a fit every time she sees it. It's not a bindi, and I can't really wear a bindi with the panel in the way, so it's kind of a whole thing."

"I thought bindis were mostly just a cultural thing," said Sahara. "Not really religious anymore."

"That depends on who you talk to," said Jaya.

"Does that mean you're not really religious, either?" asked Sahara. "Marisa's a pretty devout Christian, and Anja doesn't care one way or the other, so it'll be nice to have another atheist on the team."

"I'm very religious," said Anja. "Don't impugn my faith."

Sahara's jaw fell open, and she stared at Anja for a moment. "You're kidding."

"I've never seen you do anything religious," said Marisa. "Except mock it, I guess."

"I'm a devout Simulationist," said Anja. "My entire life is dedicated to my faith."

"I've never heard of that," said Jaya.

"Because she's making it up," said Marisa.

"Consider the facts," said Anja, smiling as she leaned forward. "In your opinion, is it possible to create a full simulation of the universe, indistinguishable from the real world?"

"Computer theory suggests that it is," said Jaya. "Virtual reality games like Overworld are already pretty close."

"Exactly," said Anja. "And we're closer to it now than we were ten, twenty, fifty years ago. And it's not hard to imagine that with another ten, twenty, even a hundred years, we'll get there. It might take a while, but it's a completely believable, feasible technology."

"Sure," said Marisa. "So does a 'Simulationist' look at that technology as, like, saving the world or something?"

"Fact two," said Anja, ignoring the question. "If even one such simulation exists—indistinguishable from reality—then we have a fifty-fifty chance of being in it. Just one simulation. If even two such simulations exist, we are more likely to be in a simulated world than in a real one."

"That's ridiculous," said Sahara.

"It is scientifically sound," said Anja.

"So you think we live in a simulation," said Marisa. She could barely believe what she was hearing. "You honestly believe that."

Anja held up her finger, as if speaking words of inviolate wisdom. "Consider this: every mammal on the entire planet, regardless of mass or bladder size, takes an average of twenty seconds to pee. Every single one. What's more likely: that this is some amazing biological coincidence, or that some programmer somewhere got lazy and just reused some animation code?"

"There's no way that's true," said Marisa.

"Time yourself," said Anja.

"I can't believe you're basing your religion around how long it takes to pee," said Sahara.

"This is fantastic," said Jaya. She was smiling from ear to ear. "So that's what a Simulationist believes, but what does one do? How does it guide your life?"

Anja shrugged and lay back against the bench. "The only possible reasons to simulate a world are to study it or to play with it, right? I mean, those are the only reasons we ever do it. And since I'm pretty sure we're not a game, we're probably in a study, which means somebody is watching."

Marisa laughed. "So God's a scientist, and we're all unwitting subjects in some massive experiment?"

"I don't know who made it," said Anja. "Call it God if you want. The one and only thing we know about this being is that it's watching us, right?" A wide, wicked grin spread across her face. "I'm just trying to get its attention. I'm trying to be so unfathomably unpredictable that the big Lab Technician in the Sky can't help but notice the anomaly and take a closer look."

"And . . . then what?" asked Marisa. "He pulls you out of his little rat maze and you live forever in paradise?"

"Maybe," said Anja. "Or maybe all we can do is ruin his simulation. I'm happy either way—who does that blowhole think he is, anyway?"

Jaya laughed, and Sahara stared at Anja with a look of strained patience. After a moment of glaring she rolled her head back to Jaya. "Welcome to Los Angeles," she said. "Where weirdness is apparently a religion now."

"I'll be atheist with you," said Fang. All four other girls looked at her in surprise, and she shrank back into her seat. "I mean, if you want."

"Thank you, Fang," said Sahara. "I'm glad I'm not the only sane person in this autocab."

"I've never understood atheism," said Jaya. "I mean, I'm not really a practicing Hindu, despite my family's constant preaching, but I believe in it, you know? Like, I know what it says about the world, and what I should be doing to get all the rewards, or whatever."

"But you're not doing them?" asked Sahara.

Jaya shrugged. "Not really."

"That's what *I* don't understand," said Sahara. "If I believed that there really was a purpose to this world, and to us in it—some big, guiding hand behind it all—I'd follow it to the letter. I'd build my entire life around it, because why wouldn't you? Why would you believe something is true and then ignore it?"

"You believe math is true," said Jaya. "But you're not a mathematician."

"So what *do* you want?" asked Marisa. She looked at Sahara closely. "Just . . . to be famous? More eyeballs on the vidcast, more wins for the team? You spend so much energy trying to master all of these little systems, but . . . what does that get you?"

Sahara looked back calmly. "It gets me another system to master." She looked at Marisa a moment, then rolled her shoulders, working out some of the stiffness. "Honestly, though? What do I want right now? I want to save your restaurant. I want to get Alain out of that room he's locked in. I want to wipe that smug look off of Kwon Chaewon's face, and Nightmare, and . . . Leggy McSupermodel or whatever that white girl's name was. I want to bring them all down."

"Yes," said Anja.

"I want to win," said Fang.

"The first-place prize is ten thousand yuan," said Sahara. "That would get San Juanito back on its feet."

"But you've seen the other teams," Jaya said. "With the exception of Chaewon, we're the only amateurs there. Hooray for self-confidence and all, but honestly? Our only plausible shot at the final is if Anja's magic alien scientist suddenly notices us and decides to mess with the simulation a little."

"You never know," said Anja. "At least, you never know until you paint yourself blue and go streaking through a supermarket."

"We can win," said Sahara firmly. "We can do more than win—we can dominate. The tournament's being held in the Jeon

Convention Center, right?"

"Yeah," said Marisa. "So?"

"So that's connected to the Sigan building," said Sahara. "That's how they're doing the little 'fake lag spikes' thing they're planning, by running it all on Sigan's own closed network. But that's also our big chance, because getting into one building means we can get into the other." She grinned. "We're not just going to win the tournament; we're going to rescue Alain."

NINETEEN

The taxi dropped them off at the restaurant, though it, like most places in Mirador, was closed Sunday morning. Marisa kissed Fang and Jaya good-bye and left them in Sahara's capable hands, knowing that if she didn't show up in time for church, her parents' acceptance of the night's activities would come crashing down in an avalanche of punishments. Her house was only about a half mile away, so she took her bag containing the scuffed remnants of her green dress—a nuli-borne crash landing was not good for your clothing, it turned out—and walked.

The sun was already beating down, even at eight a.m., though Marisa knew it would get worse as the day wore on. Sometimes she wondered why anyone ever bothered to live in the real world at all, when VR was so much simpler—plus you could fly. She laughed to herself, thinking of Anja's lecture in the cab. Maybe they were already in VR, and just didn't realize it. She hoped not.

If whoever was running the world had the power to let her fly, and wasn't doing it, she was going to be pissed.

And what about Fang's odd behavior? She'd known Fang for years—longer than Jaya or Anja or even Bao. Fang had always been a bright spot in Marisa's life, irreverent but loyal, mouthy but kind, tirelessly dedicated to the Cherry Dogs and to anything else their little group of friends got caught up in. Was she really just tired from the flight, or had something happened?

It occurred to Marisa that as much as Fang supported her, she'd never done much to support Fang. She'd never had to bail Fang out of a botched criminal escapade, like Fang had done for her last night. She'd never even helped Fang decide what to wear on a date, which she'd done for all the other girls—even Jaya, who lived on the other side of the world from her. Had she not been a true enough friend? She sent Fang a quick message as she walked, being careful not to trip on any cracks in the sidewalk:

I just wanted to say again how awesome it is to see you in person. You've been one of my best friends for such a long time. We can talk more when I get back from church, but please remember that you can always talk to me about anything. I'm here for you.

That would have to do for now. She walked the last few blocks to her house, Olaya automatically unlocking the front door as she approached. Pati came barreling down the stairs like a thunderbolt, and her mami soon after, hugging her and kissing her and telling her she looked like she hadn't slept a wink, and what on earth happened to her shoulders, did she really get that banged up in the fall? The house smelled like eggs and frijoles and hot flour tortillas fresh off the stove, and Marisa returned their hugs and answered their questions while she slowly worked her way to the kitchen for some breakfast. Her abuela was hunched over the stove like always, in a blue nightdress and a pair of foam sandals, picking up hot tortillas with her bare hands and flipping them over on the hot black comal. Her father was sitting at the table, his arms crossed and his eyes flicking through the morning news on his djinni. He looked up at Marisa, opened his arms for a hug, and gave her a peck on the cheek when she leaned down to embrace him.

"Te amo, chiquita," he said.

"Te amo, Papi."

"Eat," said her abuela, pulling a plate from the cupboard and covering it with eggs and beans and tortillas. "You're skin and bones—boys like a little more booty to hold on to."

"Are boys holding on to your booty, Marisa?" asked her father, still looking at his news feeds.

"Ay, Papi, no," said Marisa. She washed her hands, then spooned chile all over her eggs. "Besides, Abue, I'm not skin and bones. I'm bigger than any of the other girls on the team."

"Then they need to eat, too," said her abuela.

The food was delicious, and the shower was cold, and Marisa wore her blue dress and walked to church in the scorching heat, watching wavy mirages rise up from the asphalt on the road. Omar Maldonado winked at her, like he always did at church, though this time he managed to corner her as she slipped out for a bathroom break, smiling so widely she thought his head would split open.

"I saw the dive," said Omar. His smile became more of a smirk. "How much of that story was real, about the publicity stunt and Sigan being in on the whole thing?"

Marisa looked at him, her mouth closed tight, trying to decide how much he actually knew and how much he was simply guessing. Better to assume the worst with Omar, but that didn't mean she had to confirm it for him.

"We were completely safe," she said, folding her arms. "We'd been practicing the stunt for weeks."

"Sure you were," he said, leaning against the wall. "What were you really doing at that party? Trying to steal something?"

"What makes you think we were trying to steal anything?"

"You had the twins with you: Jin and Jen, or whatever their names are. Wearing identical clothes." He shrugged. "I know a con when I see one."

"I need to use the restroom," she said firmly, and pushed past him. He stepped aside too late, their arms brushing as she opened the door. She closed it behind herself, and found a stall to pee in.

Twenty seconds exactly.

"Welcome to San Juanito!" said her father, opening the doors of the restaurant and ushering the girls inside. "Sit wherever you want! It's not like we're going to get any other customers."

"Not much of a lunch rush on Sunday?" asked Jaya.

"Not much of an anything," said Guadalupe. "Who can afford to eat out anymore?" She saw Anja and shrieked. "Ay, este niña malcriada. How could you do that to your hair?"

"With a razor," said Anja.

"I was thinking of doing the same thing with mine," said Sandro, and smiled when Guadalupe threw up her hands and stormed toward the kitchen.

Marisa held the door while her friends filed in, and frowned as a piece of plastifoam garbage went tumbling down the gutter in a low gust of wind. She thought about the filthy streets of Kirkland, and feared that Mirador would soon be the same.

"This is my favorite table," said Sahara, leading them to a large round booth in the corner. The Cherry Dogs sat down, and Marisa's family took the next table over. The center of each table held a touch-screen menu, and Sahara looked at the other girls. "Do you guys like spicy food?"

"Please," said Jaya. "I'm from *India*."

"Spicy's okay," said Fang.

"Perfect," said Sahara. "How about chocolate?"

"Also delicious," said Jaya, "though I assume we're not eating them together." She laughed, but Sahara shook her head, and then it was Marisa's turn to laugh as a look of horror crossed Jaya's face. "What? You eat spicy chocolate?"

"It's called mole," said Sahara, "and I had that same reaction when they first told me about it, but trust me. It's like the greatest thing ever. Is chicken okay?"

"I'm vegetarian," said Jaya.

"We have tofu," said Carlo Magno, and started toward the kitchen. "Gabi, come help me get drinks. Horchata for everyone!"

Gabi glowered at him, and Marisa jumped up quickly to save her sister the trouble. "I can do it, Gabi, don't worry." She followed her papi into the kitchen and pulled ice-cold jugs of horchata out of the giant industrial fridge. She counted everyone in her head—eleven people, plus one more if Bao showed up—and set out a plastic glass for each. She sent Bao a quick message while she filled the glasses with ice and poured out the smooth, silky drink, and then carried them back into the dining room on a large tray.

"I'm impressed," said Jaya. "I'd drop that entire thing if I tried that."

"Years of practice," said Marisa, handing out the drinks. "My parents don't like using nuli waiters—they think a personal touch 'adds value to the dining experience.'"

"What do you say?" asked Jaya.

"I say better a nuli than me," said Marisa, "but here I am." She gave everyone a plastic straw, and peeled the paper covering off of hers as she sat down.

"What's this?" asked Jaya.

"It's called horchata," said Sahara. "It's like rice milk and vanilla and cinnamon."

Jaya took a sip, and grimaced in shock. "Aree!" she shouted. "That's sweet!"

"Tell me about it," said Anja. "Friggin' Americans."

"It's like bubble tea," said Fang.

"Kind of," said Marisa. She was just glad Fang was talking.

"The mole's going to take a while," said Sahara, and blinked to send her nulis to the far side of the room—they'd record a nice wide shot of the group, but they wouldn't pick up any audio. With that taken care of, she looked at the group solemnly. "That gives us time to talk about C-Gull."

"Why are you talking about seagulls?" asked Pati.

"Mind your own business," said Marisa, shooing her back to her own table. She looked at her friends. "What do we know so far?"

"Fang tried the numbers," said Sahara.

Fang nodded. "The number Alain gave us had two zeroes and one one. That's eight total variations if we assume that some of those numbers are supposed to be transposed." She looked down, as if suddenly embarrassed that she had talked too much. "None of them work."

"Then it has to be something else," said Marisa. "He clearly tried to give us some sign so we could make sense of the fake number. This is our only lead—it's got to work somehow."

The bell on the front door rang, and they looked up to see Bao come in. "Sorry I'm late."

"Hi, Bao," said Pati, grinning like a maniac. Her crush couldn't be less subtle. He waved politely and sat down in the booth next to Marisa. She pushed his glass of horchata toward him.

"I did some internet searches for the name C-Gull," said Anja. "Looks like he's an underground arms dealer, but I couldn't find any way of contacting him."

"I asked around with some people I know," said Bao. "Same thing."

"Why would he give us the name of an arms dealer?" asked Sahara. "He specifically told Renata that an arms dealer wouldn't be any help."

"Maybe this isn't about arms dealing," said Jaya. "Maybe

C-Gull has . . . other skills."

"He was probably lying to Renata," said Bao.

"What about that hand signal?" asked Fang.

Sahara held up her hand with the pointer finger and pinkie finger extended. She looked at it, turning her hand around. "What could this possibly mean?"

"Maybe he was just trying to look cool," said Bao.

"He doesn't have to try to look cool," said Marisa.

"Maybe it's a code," said Anja. She made the same symbol with her hand, studying it. "Let's assume he gave us the real number, but with one or two digits changed to throw off Renata. This symbol could be a way of telling us what the right digits are." She looked at it again. "Maybe it's an eleven?"

"How could 'eleven' help?" asked Jaya.

"Who's got the video?" asked Sahara.

"I'll play it on the table," said Marisa, and blinked on her djinni to access the restaurant's computer system. She found their table, linked to the touch screen, and played the video.

"I don't know his ID," said Alain. The lip-reader data was still there, though this time the words came out through the restaurant computer's voice, which was modeled on Carlo Magno's. "He takes messages through an old handheld phone, which he keeps stashed somewhere remote. That way no one can track him directly. The number is 9780062347163."

"He flashes the hand signal right at the end," said Sahara, pointing at the screen. "Right on the 'one.' I'm betting that's important. Maybe we replace that one-six with a one-one?"

"I think the two lowered fingers have to mean something,"

said Anja. "If he just wanted to show us two ones, he'd hold up his first two fingers, but he didn't. This is more like . . . one zero zero one."

"That's four digits," said Sahara. "If the replacement sequence starts on the one, we'd be replacing three digits with four—it'd be too long."

"I just tried it," said Fang. "Doesn't work."

"Try the last four digits," said Jaya. "Change 7163 to 1001."

Fang blinked, waited, and shook her head. "No good."

"Ha!" Marisa shouted. She looked up at the group. "It's binary."

"How?" asked Bao.

Marisa made the symbol with her hand. "One finger up, two fingers down, one finger up—that's 1001, just like you said, but just to make extra sure Renata couldn't crack the code he gave it to us in binary. He even said it at the end: 'There are ones and there are zeroes.' Convert 1001 from binary to base ten and you get seventeen, so if we just replace this one-six with a one-seven, it might work—"

"It's ringing," said Fang.

The whole table fell quiet.

"It's a voicemail," said Fang.

"C-Gull's voicemail?" Bao asked.

"I can't tell," said Fang. "The message is generic. What should I say?"

"Tell him . . . we're friends of Alain Bensoussan," said Sahara. "Tell him Alain's been captured, and it's vital that we speak to him as soon as possible."

Fang nodded, waited for the beep, and then relayed the message. She sounded far more confident on the message than she had since she'd arrived. When she finished, she blinked to close the call.

"Wow," said Anja.

"Good job, Marisa," said Bao. "I never would have figured that out."

"Now we wait," said Sahara, "and hope that was really C-Gull's number." She tapped her fingers on the table, and nobody made a sound. "I really hate this part."

"How long will it take?" asked Marisa.

"Alain said he only checks it sometimes," said Bao. "It could be tonight; it could be days."

"It's not like we have forever," said Anja. "The tournament starts tomorrow—what if we go out in the first round? That's our only access to the building."

"The mole will be out in a bit," said Guadalupe, bustling up to the table with another wide tray, loaded up with bowls and baskets. She began setting them down on the tables with practiced efficiency. "Homemade chips, homemade salsa, homemade guacamole, and our house specialty: chiles con queso. Also homemade."

"The brackets are posted," said Fang.

"Who are we playing?" asked Sahara.

"Thunderbolts," said Fang, reading the list. "They're an Indian team, playing for Johara, and very good."

"I love them," said Jaya, but then she frowned. "If we beat them, do you think I'll get fired?"

"Whoa," said Anja, her eyes moving as she scanned the brackets on her djinni. "There's a bye."

"Someone gets a bye in the first round?" asked Marisa. "Please don't tell me it's Chaewon's team. I'm going to punch her."

"How is there a bye?" asked Sahara. "There were sixteen teams exactly."

"Somebody dropped out," said Anja. Her eyes refocused on the group. "The Saxon Violins."

"What a bunch of douchebags," said Bao.

"Why'd they drop out?" asked Marisa.

"Personal injury," said Sahara, looking up the data for herself. "Apparently their General, Donny Chu, broke his wrist and arm at their hotel last night."

"He was probably drunk," said Jaya.

"So?" asked Anja. "You don't need either of those to play a VR game."

"I'm going to call them," said Sahara. "The Saxon Violins are douchebags, but they're excellent players—probably the best team in the tournament, after World2gether and maybe MotherBunny. Don't you find it suspicious that Chaewon's only real competition just voluntarily dropped out? I'll patch it through a speaker so you can hear." She blinked, and they heard a ringing sound coming from a speaker in Sahara's purse.

"Hello," said a cheerful voice on the other end. "Thank you for calling the LA Downtown Marriott; how may I help you today?"

"I need to talk to Donny Chu," said Sahara.

"Do you know the room number?" asked the clerk. She sounded suspicious; now that everyone had a djinni, no one called the front desk unless they didn't know the person they were trying to reach personally. They probably had a policy against these kinds of calls to help protect their celebrity guests.

"Tell him Sahara Cowan wants to talk to him," said Sahara. "He'll take the call."

"Just one moment," said the clerk, and the speaker started playing tepid hold music.

"How do you know he'll want to talk to you?" asked Bao.

"Because he lurks in my chatroom all the time," said Sahara.

"Hey," said a male voice on the speaker. "Is this really Sahara?"

"It is," said Sahara. "I was wondering if you—"

"Dude, we watched your nuli dive like a hundred times! That was the balls, girl, like, the total balls."

Anja mimed strangling herself.

"Thanks," said Sahara. "Donny, I was wondering if you could tell me—"

"So I've always wondered," said Donny, ignoring her, "if you film your whole life, why don't you ever film yourself in the shower? Like, your subscriber numbers would go through the stratosphere."

Sahara ignored the question. "I'm trying to find out—"

"And you're a lesbian, too, right?"

Sahara sighed. "Yeah, so?"

"Why don't you ever film that? Our whole team would be, like, paying sponsors—"

"Listen, you walking sphincter," said Sahara. "There's no way you would ever back out of this tournament, injury or not, and we already think Chaewon's trying to fix the results, so shut up and tell me the truth: Did they pay you off?"

"Like hell they did," said Donny. "There's no way we would ever lose for money. What do you think we are?"

"Then what's going on?" asked Sahara.

"Sweet!" said Donny. "I'm watching your vidcast of you calling us while I'm talking to you—that's trippy. Are you all listening right now? Hey, girl in the red shirt, you busy later? I've got a broken arm but the rest of me works just fine."

Each of the girls looked down, not remembering which color shirt she'd put on that morning. Marisa sighed when she saw that it was her, and put her hand over the camera lens.

"If not money, then what?" asked Sahara. "An injury shouldn't keep you from playing, so what did they do? Did they threaten you? Is this whole broken arm story just a cover?"

There was a moment of silence. "It's really broken," he said at last. All the bravado was gone from his voice.

Sahara glanced at Marisa, and swallowed. The tone of the conversation had changed abruptly, and Marisa had a sinking feeling she knew the reason why.

"Did . . . they break it?" Sahara asked.

"You can't tell anyone," said Donny.

"You *have* to tell someone," said Sahara. "This is illegal."

"Do you know how connected Kwon Chaewon is?" asked Donny. "We bow out of this now and she owes us a favor, but if we talk we don't play in another major tournament for the rest of our lives. She can do that, you know."

"She doesn't run the world," said Sahara.

"Maybe I just don't want any more bones broken," said

Donny. "Dude snapped my wrist with his bare hands—do you have any idea how much that hurts?"

"Who did?" asked Sahara.

"Huge dude," said Donny. "One of those military eye-plates that covers his whole face—no eyes or forehead, just solid metal."

"Park," said Marisa.

"Thanks," said Sahara. She hesitated a moment. "I'm sorry about what happened to you."

Donny's sneering voice came back. "Then howsabout a little sympathy show for an injured ma—"

Sahara blinked, and ended the call.

"So," said Anja. "Chaewon's a cheater, a kidnapper, a torturer . . . and now an extortionist."

"Saxon Violins were up against MotherBunny," said Fang. "Now they have a bye."

"No way she lets a team that good have a bye," said Sahara. "Watch—this time tomorrow they'll have 'voluntarily' dropped out too."

"This burns me up," said Marisa. "This tournament doesn't even matter—not for her. We'd at least get some notoriety out of it, and that ten thousand yuan could save my family, but Chaewon already has all of that and more. What does she even get out of this?"

"She gets a trophy," said Jaya.

"If she wants one this bad, she could just buy one," said Marisa. "Why drag the rest of us through this? And why spend so much time and energy on something so . . ." She struggled for words that wouldn't get her grounded by her parents. "So *pinchingly* pointless."

"You made that word sound way harsher than it has any right to be," said Bao.

"You should have heard the word I was *going* to use," said Marisa.

"Some people are just spoiled brats," said Jaya. "You have to let it go."

"I can't," said Marisa. "KT Sigan is taking away everything I have, making Chaewon's family unconscionably rich, and all she's using that money for is winning a fake tournament." She shook her head. "I can't just let it go."

"So let's do something about it," said Sahara. "People with power don't get to win just because they have power. We've stopped other people, and we can stop her. Rescuing Alain is our top priority, but you know what? As long as we're there, we might as well beat Chaewon, find Grendel, and—what the hell?—destroy Sigan too while we're at it."

"I want to kiss you," said Anja.

"We don't have a plan," said Jaya.

"Or even enough info to make one," said Bao.

Sahara shook her head. "Not yet, but we will. Look at the bracket: we don't play until day two, so we have all of today and tomorrow to come up with something brilliant."

"And if we can't come up with anything?" asked Marisa.

"Then we hope C-Gull has something amazing," said Sahara. "Because we'll need it."

TWENTY

The Forward Motion tournament began on Monday, and the whole world seemed to pause and take notice. As part of its mission to raise awareness for those with low or no internet connectivity, the entire tourney was being played on a private server in a carefully controlled environment, complete with artificial lag spikes and fabricated speed issues. The richest players in the world, and everyone watching them, would get a taste of what the vast world of underprivileged people had to go through every day. Bao and the Cherry Dogs joined a crowd of eager fans in the convention center, watching and cheering from their nosebleed seats while, far below in the center of the arena, the head of the Forward Motion Foundation got up to speak. His image was projected on two giant screens.

"Opening ceremonies are so boring," said Anja. "Seriously. Has anyone ever been to a good opening ceremony? Why don't they just start the actual event? Wouldn't literally everyone watching prefer that?" Nobody answered, and she shrugged. "Shut up," she yelled at the screen, and threw a corn chip. A boy sitting in front of them turned around to glare at her, and she shouted back, "What, you want to start something?" The boy rolled his eyes and looked away.

Marisa glanced at Fang, sitting quietly on the end of the row. They'd spent the night practicing, and in the game Fang had been her usual chipper self again, but now she was back to being quiet and closed-off.

"That's Su-Yun Kho!" squealed Jaya. They all looked up, and even Fang leaned forward eagerly.

"I can't believe you got to meet her," said Jaya.

"I was hacking the whole time," said Marisa. "I barely saw her at all."

"But you were closer than we are now," said Jaya.

"We're in the same room," said Fang. "This totally counts."

"This is my cue to go," said Bao, and stood up. "I'll explore the building and report back—if there's any way into the Sigan high rise, I'll find it."

"Good luck," said Marisa, and looked back at the screens. "Now we just have to figure out how to stay in this tournament long enough to matter."

Su-Yun Kho gave more or less the same speech she'd given at the gala, and then the ceremony ended and the tournament began. The first round was eight games, with four scheduled for Monday and the remaining four on Tuesday—including the Cherry Dogs' first game, and MotherBunny's bye. Today's two games were being played simultaneously, though only one was considered a showcase: Chaewon's team World2gether, versus the Brazilian team Rocinha Pipa, playing for the energy company Brazucar. Camera nulis buzzed around each team as Su-Yun introduced them, and they ran onto the stage waving to the crowd.

"We get to be onstage with Su-Yun Kho?" asked Fang. "She's going to say my name? Like, with her mouth?"

"Are you okay?" asked Sahara.

"Shut up," said Anja. "She's going to say my name, too. Don't cheapen this for us."

The stage had been set up with rows of VR chairs, and each team moved to their own row and started plugging in. Marisa recognized a boy she'd seen at the gala, and now that she wasn't preoccupied with a doomed data heist, she could look at him more closely. "João Acosta," she said, reading his name off the screen.

"What about him?" asked Sahara.

"He's gorgeous," said Marisa.

Sahara cocked her head to the side, considering him. "I don't see it."

"Are you kidding me?"

"He looks like every other guy you drool over."

"I'm not drooling."

"Who's drooling?" asked Anja.

"Marisa," said Sahara. "That dude, the Spotter."

Anja studied him for a moment, as he sat down in the reclining chair and plugged the cable into his headjack. "I don't see it."

"I'm surrounded by blind women," said Marisa. "Fine, then: more for me."

"You already have Alain," said Anja. "Save some for the rest of us."

"Is Alain as juicy in real life as he looked on the vidcast?" asked Jaya.

"More," said Sahara.

"You don't even like boys," said Marisa.

"I can still appreciate them aesthetically," said Sahara. "I can think a painting is beautiful without wanting to make out with it."

"Quiet," said Fang, "they're starting."

The match was being played in the pirate version of the map—a series of sailing ships, all jumbled together and connected with cargo nets, gangplanks, and grappling hooks. The roof was made of sails and crow's nests; the sewers were cargo holds and tunnels, filled with bilge rats the size of wild dogs. Marisa held her breath, waiting for the match to start and the first wave of pirate-shaped minions to go swarming across the screen, but instead it went to a waiting screen displaying all ten players' avatars: World2gether on the top, and Rocinha Pipa on the bottom. A clock in the middle of the screen began a two-minute countdown.

"I forgot," said Marisa. "The Seoul Draft."

"This is where it gets interesting," said Sahara.

The boy in front of them turned around again. "Are you going to talk through the whole match?"

"What?" said Marisa. "You're not?"

All five girls watched the screen intently, waiting to see what powersets the players chose. Chaewon, using the call sign Mago, was playing as the team's General, with Nightmare as the Sniper.

Their Guard was named Chaeg, their Spotter was Makendro, and their Jungler was Bubba. Marisa frowned. "Which one's Bubba?"

"The white girl," said Fang.

"Leggy McSupermodel?" asked Marisa. She looked at the screen, where the camera was slowly panning across the players lying still in their chairs. Bubba was almost six feet tall, dressed in super-short cutoff jeans and a sleeveless red flannel shirt rolled up to show her toned abs. "She's going all-in on the Southern redneck thing, isn't she?"

"I wish we could see what powersets they're considering," said Anja.

"They have to keep them secret until they lock them in," said Jaya.

"There it is," said Sahara. The waiting screen showed the first round of picks, and it was all pretty standard stuff: not just standard, but safe to the point of boring. Marisa didn't understand why these pros had chosen such lackluster powersets until she saw Chaewon's selections.

"An Electricity Striker with self-buffs for damage," said Marisa. She glanced at Sahara. "I thought she was playing General? That's a long-range Sniper build."

"Maybe they're trying something new," said Jaya, though she didn't sound hopeful.

"Not with those other powersets," said Sahara. She peered at the screen, reading the info a second time, then laughed. "Holy crap. Chaewon's trying to solo the match—she's not supporting her minions, she's not supporting her team, she's just pumping out damage and relying on her Guard to keep her alive. That is total noob crap for a General, and she's doing it in an international tournament."

"She wants to be the hero," said Anja. "Kill everything herself."

"I wish we were playing against them," said Fang. "We'd destroy them." Her voice held a hint of the old fiery Fang Marisa knew from online, but then she fell quiet again.

"They saved Nightmare for the second wave," said Sahara. "Fifty bucks says she plays standard Sniper build, no frills, using whatever elemental powerset targets the Rocinha Pipa's biggest weakness. That means . . ." The girls looked at the Rocinha Pipa powersets, and Sahara clicked her tongue while she read them. "Nightmare's going to go with . . . water-based Striker with ice-based control powers. She'll freeze the enemy in place and wear her down."

"I guess we'll see," said Marisa. She was still getting the hang of Seoul Draft, but she always trusted Sahara to read a metagame.

"There it is," said Fang, as the second-wave picks popped up. "Water-based Striker with ice-based control." She flopped her head back, clenching her hands into fists. "Tā mā de, Sahara! They're going to lose before we even get a chance to beat them!"

"Wait," said the boy in front of them. His friends turned around this time as well. "Are you playing in the tournament? Wait—are you the Cherry Dogs?"

"In the flesh," said Sahara with a smile.

Anja threw another chip at him. "Shut up, we're trying to watch."

"Analysis," said Jaya.

"Rocinha Pipa's got an awesome team," said Sahara. "Their General and their Guard will do great in the center, supporting the minions, and all three of their other positions are built for hunting and killing players. The World2gether Guard is going to spend half the game waiting to respawn, and Chaewon's going to spend it blind and running away. They don't stand a chance."

Ten minutes into the game, they realized the truth.

The first lag spike hit during a Rocinha raid on a World2gether turret—a pirate's cannon, firing heavy iron cannonballs into the Rocinha minions. All five agents were gathered in one place, pouring damage into the turret while World2gether raced to respond in time, when suddenly the lag hit, and the game seemed to freeze—behind the scenes, deep in the game server, numbers were still flying and calculations were still being made, but on the screens and in the VR no one could see them, because the graphics were broken. It was only for a second, but it was enough for a dodge to be fumbled, for a power to be activated just barely too late, for the tides of the raid to turn. When the graphics snapped back into place, the Rocinha Pipa Sniper was dead, brought down by the turret, which had already chosen a new target and was blasting away at their Guard. She scrambled to heal herself, which meant she wasn't healing her team, which meant that when World2gether arrived in a flurry of attacks they were able to take down a second Rocinha Pipa agent. Rocinha retreated, and World2gether pressed their advantage.

"Lucky," said Jaya.

"Was it?" asked Anja.

The commentators launched into a long spiel about how this

kind of connectivity issue was exactly what Forward Motion was trying to call attention to. The Cherry Dogs ignored them, frowning suspiciously at the screen.

"Let's figure this out," said Marisa. "What would it take for Chaewon to fake a lag spike like that?"

"You think they're cheating?" asked the boy in front of them.

Fang ignored the question: "They'd need full control over the server, the connections, and the play environment. Which they have."

"They'd also need a way to hide it," said Sahara. "Even running the tournament themselves, they can't be too obvious."

"How do you hide fake lag that only helps one team?" asked Jaya.

"By hitting both teams," said Anja.

"Let's keep a chart," said Sahara, blinking to open a spreadsheet. "We'll time them, we'll time the gaps between them, and we'll mark each one for who it 'helps.'"

"Keeping in mind that they might not 'help' anybody," said Marisa. "They might just be random."

"They might be," said Sahara.

They weren't.

By the time World2gether won the match, at sixty-two minutes thirty-three seconds, there had been exactly fifteen lag spikes major enough to disrupt play, and eight more minor ones that just caused little screen jumps. Of those fifteen, three happened at completely innocuous times, and twelve affected the outcomes of fights, with five hurting Rocinha and seven hurting World2gether. It looked balanced, but the lag spikes that hurt World2gether were all in minor fights against single agents or neutral monsters—one spike robbed Nightmare of a perfect sniper shot, and another got Bubba eaten by a sea monster. The lag spikes that hurt Rocinha, on the other hand, were mostly in team fights, resulting in multiple deaths and significant swings in the balance of power. There was nothing overt, no hard evidence of any actual cheating. And yet World2gether won, and the lag spikes were definitely a factor.

"Check the other games," said Jaya. "How was their lag?"

"I was watching the other one on my djinni," said Fang. "Canavar versus Hailztorm. The lag looked just as bad, though I wasn't able to watch both games and keep records at the same time."

"I'm amazed you were able to watch both at all," said Marisa.

"Sorry," said Fang.

"It wasn't an insult," said Marisa.

Fang didn't answer.

"Whoa," she said.

Marisa looked over. "What? Something in the tournament?"

"I just got a message," said Fang. She looked up at them, and her eyes practically shone with excitement. "From . . ." She stopped, looked at the boy who kept eavesdropping on them, and sent a message instead: **From C-Gull.**

"Hot damn," said Anja.

"Send it to us," said Marisa.

Fang nodded, and a moment later the message popped up in Marisa's eyeline:

I only negotiate in person. Meet me Wednesday night in a bar called Lowball, by the pier in Santa Monica. Sit in

the third booth on the left. I will contact you.

That's it? sent Sahara.

Fang nodded.

Meeting in public is smart, sent Sahara. **If Sigan is tracking our IDs, all they'll know is that we're out at a bar. They won't be able to connect us to anyone specific.**

Marisa blinked to open a search, and found images of Lowball. Immediately she wrinkled her nose. **That place is a dump.**

We're meeting a black market arms dealer, sent Anja. **Where did you expect it to be?**

No, seriously, sent Marisa, and sent everyone the link as well. **This is an absolute dive. Look at the photos—we'd be the only ones in the bar who aren't black market arms dealers, or worse.**

So we give him a different place, sent Anja. **Somewhere we can blend in.** She blinked and searched. **Perfect. There's a pretty posh dance club, like, half a block away from Lowball.**

Posh? sent Jaya. **That close to a dive?**

That's Santa Monica for you, sent Marisa. **Fang, tell him we'll meet him there instead.**

It's called Daze, sent Anja.

"I don't," said Fang out loud. She looked intensely uncomfortable. "I don't want to go to a dance club."

"It's perfect," said Sahara. "We go clubbing all the time, and if we happen to meet some random dude in one, no one will suspect anything."

"Plus we know we can get in," said Anja. "Five hot girls in

tight dresses? The bouncer will wave us right through the front door."

"What are you talking about?" asked the boy in front of them. "Are you going dancing?"

"Shut up!" said Anja. "We're delightful daredevils, we can go dancing if we want to!"

"Can I come?"

Anja jumped to her feet and spread her arms wide, looking over him like she was ready to tear his throat out with her teeth. "Ask me that again, blowhole!"

The boy went pale, and moved to another row.

Try to get him to meet us sooner than Wednesday, sent Sahara. **We need to move as fast as possible if we're going to rescue Alain.**

Fang said nothing, but took a breath and sat still, staring into her djinni. After a moment she nodded. "Okay, I sent the message."

Marisa sighed. "Now we just have to wait again—"

Got a message back, sent Fang. **All it says is "Daze, Wednesday." He'll meet you there, I guess.**

You're not coming? sent Marisa.

I hate dancing.

Bao slid into the chair on the end of their row, moving so silently Marisa hadn't even seen him approach. "Bad news," he whispered. "Well, not really bad, just not awesome."

"What did you find?" asked Marisa.

"I found a way in from the convention center to the high rise, but it's a maintenance tunnel. Give me some time to work out a janitor costume and I can get in pretty easy, but getting the rest of you in will be difficult. To say the least."

"We can't use our contestant status to . . . I don't know, fake a tour of the building? Or something?"

Bao gestured at their row of seats, almost at the back of the arena. "Your contestant status didn't even get you good seats to your own tournament."

Marisa nodded, and sank lower in her chair. "So. Rescuing Alain, finding Grendel, and bringing down an evil megacorp all hinge on us staying in the tournament long enough for the one person without any hacking skills to get inside the building and . . . what?"

"Win a fencing match, drop a cutting one-liner, and swing away on a chandelier," said Bao. "Isn't that usually how these things go?"

TWENTY-ONE

The next morning the Cherry Dogs ran through the streets of LA, racing to get to the tournament on time. They'd stayed up practicing as long as they'd dared, testing different Seoul Draft strategies until Sahara finally forced them to log off and go to sleep. Marisa didn't feel like they'd gotten enough of either—practice or sleep—but they were here. They had their chance.

All they had to do now was win.

The tournament was being held at a large conference center attached to the Sigan building, and they dodged through crowds of eager onlookers to reach the front door.

"The line's back there," said a guard, pointing at the massive crowd behind them. "Doors don't open for another ten minutes."

"We're competitors," said Sahara, far less out of breath than Marisa was. "The Cherry Dogs; check your list."

"The . . ." The guard blinked, scanning their IDs and then

reading something off his djinni. “You’re late,” he said.

“The train was delayed,” said Sahara.

“The competitor entrance is on the other side,” he said, gesturing down the length of the building, but Anja cut him off.

“You already said we were late!” she shouted. “Just let us in!”

“I’m sending a message to your handlers,” said the guard, opening the door. “Turn right when you get inside, and look for someone in a red jacket.”

“Thank you!” said Marisa, as Sahara shoved everyone through the door. They sprinted down the hall, and saw a woman in a red jacket beckoning them to the far end. Marisa was completely out of breath by the time they reached her.

“You’re late,” the woman snapped.

“Train,” Marisa gasped.

“Follow me.” They followed the woman through another short hallway, and into a waiting room where a swarm of makeup artists were frantically dabbing powder on the faces of the other five teams. The woman called out to the nearest makeup tech, “These five too, as quick as you can.”

“I don’t wear makeup,” Fang mumbled.

“It’s for the stage,” said Sahara. Her eyes were fierce and eager. “The lights will wash us out, so we need makeup to look normal.”

“I don’t need makeup to look normal,” said Fang, even softer than before.

“It’s just a stage thing,” said Sahara with a snarl. “Get over it!”

“This is it,” said Jaya. “We’re really here. This is really happening.”

“Unless Chaewon stops it,” said Marisa.

The makeup tech came and started working on their faces, using a biomimetic powder that adapted its own color to match their different skin tones. Fang let her work, but obviously didn't enjoy it.

Three people in red jackets started guiding the players out into a waiting area behind the stage. The one who'd met them first came back. "You five stay at the end of the line, and wait for the signal from the stage manager."

"Is there a problem?" asked Marisa.

"Only if you don't do what I tell you," said the woman, and moved on to wrangle more of the crowd. The girls got into the back of the line, and stood in the dark behind a curtain while the crowd filed into their seats. Exactly on time, a booming voice announced the beginning of the event, and introduced Su-Yun Kho. The conference center erupted in applause.

"I think I'm going to pee myself," said Marisa.

"Is everyone ready for some Overworld?" shouted Su-Yun. The crowd went wild, and she introduced the day's bracket, with each team running out from behind the curtain as their names were read. "For our first match today, we have the Pixel Pwnies playing for ZooMorrow, and Rick Stranger and Stranger's Rangers playing for Vision Mobile."

"That is a crazy long name," said Anja. "Is that a reference to something I'm supposed to know?"

"Nothing I recognize," said Marisa.

Anja shrugged. "Americans are weird."

"For our second match," said Su-Yun, "the mighty Cereal Killers, playing for Du/Lin Energy, and the up-and-coming Get

Rekt Nerd, playing for Zhang."

"Get Rekt Nerd aren't up and coming," said Fang. "They're the best team in Nigeria, which pretty much makes them the best team in Africa."

"It's a joke," said Marisa.

They shuffled closer to the curtain as each team ran out onto the stage. Soon it was only them and the Thunderbolts.

"Wait a minute," said Sahara. "There should be another team here. Aren't there four matches today?"

"For our third match," said Su-Yun Kho, "I have some very bad news. MotherBunny, who were supposed to have a bye, have made the decision to excuse themselves from the tournament for personal reasons."

"Tā mā de," said Fang.

"'Personal reasons,'" said Anja. "Getting your legs broken by a paramilitary thug is a 'personal reason,' apparently."

"There's no way Su-Yun knows about that," said Sahara. "She wouldn't be a part of this if she knew."

"But now!" said Su-Yun. "Our final match of the day! Please allow me to introduce the Thunderbolts, playing for Johara!" The Thunderbolts ran through the curtain, one of the youngest teams at the tournament, and one of the only all-male teams as well. Marisa couldn't see what was happening, so she blinked into her streaming app and connected to the vidcast feed. Su-Yun put her arm around KneeCap, the Thunderbolt General. "Are you ready?"

"Y-yes," said the boy, obviously too nervous to think with Su-Yun's arm around his shoulder.

"You know who you're playing against, right?" The expression on Su-Yun's face was impish, delighting in dragging out the announcement.

"Um, yeah," said the boy.

"How many of you saw that video from Saturday night?" asked Su-Yun. "The team that jumped off the seventy-fifth floor of this very building, and rode some nulis all the way down?" The crowd roared in approval, and Sahara clenched her fist in victory.

"Yes!" she said.

"Are you ready," said Su-Yun, "for the craziest team in the tournament: the unpredictable Cherry Dogs!"

Sahara frowned at the sudden label of "craziest," but the stage manager hissed at them to go, and Sahara pasted on a smile and led the way through the curtain, striding across the stage like she owned it. The lights were bright, and the crowd was screaming, and Marisa felt like her heart was going to explode from excitement.

Su-Yun bowed to Sahara, then took her by the hand and pulled her closer to the floating microphone nuli. "This is Sahara Cowan, the Cherry Dog General. Tell me, Sahara: Whose idea was that insane dive? Yours?"

"That was all KT Sigan," said Sahara, shining her perfect beauty-queen smile on the audience. "We can't thank them enough for their dedication to this cause, and when they contacted us about this incredible stunt we couldn't help but say yes."

"I love you," said Fang, and then immediately turned bright red, her eyes wide open in horror.

"I don't think she meant to say that out loud," whispered Anja.

"Okay!" said Su-Yun, glancing at Fang uncertainly and then

looking back at the audience. "Well. Sahara—all the Cherry Dogs—all the players we have today: Are you ready to rock this thing?"

"Bring it on," said Sahara.

"Let's play some Overworld!" shouted Su-Yun, and the crowd roared, and the red jacket brigade started pointing the players toward their VR chairs. Marisa followed her team, trying to stay calm, and couldn't help but notice one face on the far side of the stage, staring at them with unmasked hatred: Chaewon. Marisa avoided eye contact, but Anja waved at her cheerfully.

"We're up against Get Rekt Nerd," Sahara whispered, picking up the cable for her VR chair. "That sucks."

"We're playing the Thunderbolts," said Marisa.

"I mean for the vidcasts," said Sahara. "Our game and theirs are streaming at the same time, and then the two American teams will be later by themselves. We want people to watch us."

"We're the famous nuli dive team," said Jaya. "Who's not going to watch us?"

"You want to stay famous?" asked Anja. "Play crazy." She plugged her cable into the back of her neck, and sat down in the reclined VR chair. Her eyes were already zoned out, but she thrust one fist defiantly in the air. "Cherry Dogs forever!"

"She's right," said Sahara. "We have to win, but we have to win flashy."

"What's our strategy?" asked Marisa.

"Log in first," said Sahara. "Sigan's probably monitoring everything we say in-game, but at least the Thunderbolts won't hear us."

Marisa slid the cable into the back of her neck, and settled in the VR chair. It was so much nicer than the ones she'd used in gaming cafes, and of course miles ahead of her bed, where she lay down when she played at home.

A message popped up from Bao: **Good luck. I'm watching from a sports bar down the street.**

Thanks, sent Marisa. **We'll need it.**

You'll destroy them, sent Bao.

Marisa smiled, and blinked, and entered Overworld.

"All right," said Sahara, standing in their team lobby. "Everyone's here." Even on the private server, they had access to their own game accounts, mirrored from the Overworld network, which meant they had their own lobby and their personalized collection of avatars and costumes. Marisa chose an old one from her library, a kind of schoolgirl uniform with a pleated miniskirt. She didn't wear it often, but against an all-male team it couldn't hurt to offer a little extra distraction. It looked like the others had chosen the same strategy: Sahara wore the thigh-high slit version of her classic tight red dress, Jaya was in a flowing, diaphanous gown that showed plenty of cleavage, and Anja had gone all in with an avatar that looked like a dark blue bodysuit, with all the feminine curves but none of the exterior features that would make it into actual nudity.

"Oh come on," said Fang, who was wearing her favorite "ragged assassin" costume. "What are we, the T&A Team now?"

"Every little bit helps," said Sahara. "We only have a moment before the countdown starts, so we need to plan quickly: I say we go for a double Sniper build on the roof, with Jaya and me heavy on the crowd control."

"I like it," said Anja. "Mari, let's take Flankers, so we can stay mobile and concentrate our fire."

"Ándale," said Marisa.

"No," said Fang. "You want to concentrate fire, and you want to surprise the other team? Let's use the Feather Fall build."

"What?" asked Sahara. "You mean that gimmicky stealth build we played against last week?"

"Exactly," said Fang. "They don't know us, and they probably don't know Seoul Draft. Even if they ran across the Feather Fall trick while practicing, like we did, they won't be expecting it from this weirdo American team that came out of nowhere."

"If they've run across it at all, we're dead," said Jaya. "If they see the trick coming, it's too easy to stop."

"It's worth the risk," said Anja. "They're a good team, and we're tired and undertrained. It's not as if we have a better shot with a more traditional loadout."

Sahara considered for a moment, interrupted by a five-second countdown: the first phase of the draft was about to start. "Okay," she said, "we'll try it. This only works if they don't bring any anti-stealth, so—" The timer finished counting down, and suddenly their team lobby disappeared, replaced by the powerset selection lobby. Another timer appeared in the corner, counting down from two minutes. "Heartbeat, wait for wave two," said Sahara quickly, switching over to call signs. "If we get lucky and their first-phase picks have no anti-stealth, Heartbeat will spec as a Spotter with Air Buff; if they do bring Stealth, Heartbeat goes for ranged damage and we play double Sniper."

"Got it," said Marisa. The girls picked their powersets, finishing just before the timer ended, and they looked at the display to see what the Thunderbolts had chosen.

"Double Tank," said Fang. "Their General and their Guard both have huge defense."

"But nobody has stealth detection," said Sahara. She smiled hungrily. "We can do it. Heartbeat, take Air Buff and . . . Ice Control. We can't kill their center line, but we can freeze them in place and kill everyone else. Fan out and play normal, and move on my signal."

Marisa chose her powersets, and when the timer finished they saw that the enemy Sniper's powersets were just standard stuff, with no surprises. They waited for the final countdown while the map loaded, and then suddenly it appeared around them: dark metal walls, pipes on the ceiling, and bright red lights that flashed in the shadows. It was the Research Lab—the same layout as every other map, as always, but themed to look like a secret government laboratory, swarming with escaped, plague-ridden zombies. Anja started running, her blue skin flashing purple in the warning lights, and Marisa followed—down the hall, up the stairs, and onto the roof, where they got to work immediately killing zombies and racking up cash. Marisa, as the Spotter, kept her eye out for the enemy, and soon enough saw them on the far side of a wide ravine—it was a street in the medieval city map, and a tree-lined path in the forest map, but here it was a jagged hole blasted into the laboratory, exposing the main hall below. Sahara and Jaya were already down there, leading their AI minions and trading casual shots with the enemy agents—nothing serious, just probing their defenses, watching to see how they would react. Far below them, in the sewer level, Fang would be prowling through the darkened substructure killing zombies and hunting the enemy Jungler.

The Thunderbolts played aggressively, pushing hard against the Cherry Dog turrets, and leading charges against their defenses. They even made an early run against the vault, trying to steal their money, but Fang attacked from behind and almost killed one before he trapped her in a patch of sticky webbing and made his escape. By about eight minutes into the match they'd managed to gain slightly more ground than normal, with only a handful of lag issues, but then Anja killed a superzombie and raised the last bit of money they needed for their stealth kits.

"Everyone grab a kit," said Sahara, her voice crackling over the in-game radio. "Be discreet about it, so they don't know what you bought, and then Yīnyǐng, you go and sit on their vault—don't attack, stay invisible, and watch their total. As soon as it drops low, right after they spend it all on something big and expensive, you give the word and the rest of us will go dark and race to the roof. That'll give us as much time as possible before they can buy some stealth goggles and fight back."

"I'm on it," said Fang. They bought their stealth kits and went back to game as normal, still playing as nonconfrontationally as possible, waiting for Fang's signal.

"Their Guard just came back to shop," said Fang. "Get ready."

"Everyone hide and go dark," said Sahara. "Gather on the roof."

Anja and Marisa hid behind a ventilation shaft, stealthed, and then ran out the other side. The enemy Sniper and Spotter didn't notice them at all. Soon Sahara and Jaya joined them, and they moved into position. The Thunderbolts were just starting to look like they'd noticed the Cherry Dogs were gone.

"The vault is drained," said Fang.

"Yīnyǐng, wait in the city for our second ambush," said Sahara. "Everyone else: attack!"

The four of them dropped stealth and blitzed the enemy Sniper, using their four-to-one advantage to drop him almost instantly. The Spotter got a few hits in before realizing exactly how badly he was outnumbered, and then tried to run, but Marisa slowed him down with a freeze ray and they finished him off.

"The rest of their team is freaking out," said Fang. "They're running back to the nexus—looks like they've figured it out."

"Gather close," said Marisa, and then hit her team with the Feather Fall buff. They all jumped down through the ravine in the ceiling, letting the Thunderbolts run and focusing instead on the turrets, dropping two while the other team regrouped.

"That was good," said Sahara. "Think we can get one more ambush?"

"We need to hit them close to home," said Fang. "Stop them from farming any more gold, so they can't buy anti-stealth goggles."

"Don't waste time, Yīnyǐng," said Sahara. "If we spend all our time stopping them from earning gold, we're not earning gold either. We do another ambush."

"Fine," said Fang, but Marisa could tell she wasn't happy about it. They dropped back into stealth and set another ambush, but only dropped two enemy agents this time. The Thunderbolts recovered quickly, and within minutes the Cherry Dogs were on their back feet again.

"Great," said Sahara. "We had one trick and we blew it—now we're stuck with subpar powersets in a straight-up fight."

"I told you we needed to stop them from buying new gear," said Fang.

"And I told you to stop complaining and do your job," said Sahara.

Marisa opened a private channel to Fang: "I'm glad we finally have the old in-your-face Fang back again, but you need to be in Sahara's face a little less."

"She's making bad calls," said Fang.

"Just fight the Thunderbolts instead of each other," said Marisa. "We have a—oh crap." It was her turn to be ambushed, and the enemy attacked her viciously. She managed to keep Anja alive, but died in a sudden burst of lag that slowed her connection to an agonizing crawl. She didn't even see herself die—one minute the game froze, and the next she was floating helplessly in black space, waiting to respawn.

They were going to lose; she could feel it. They needed a better strategy.

A thought occurred to Marisa: if the whole tournament was being played on private Sigan hardware, closed off to any internet connection, that meant that whoever was messing with the lag speed was directly connected to the same hardware. Could she find him? She blinked out of the VR interface and into her djinni's file manager, looking for the local file system. She found it . . .

. . . it was Gamdog 4.1.

Marisa frowned, and looked more closely. The security was strong, but did the buffer overflow still work? She tried it, and got in.

"Santa vaca," she breathed. "We're inside the airgap."

"Heartbeat!" yelled Sahara, and Marisa snapped to attention, blinking back into Overworld to find herself still floating in the blackness of death.

"I'm still dead?" she said. "Why haven't I respawned by now?"

"You did," snarled Sahara. "And then you stood there like a blowhole and got killed again when they raided our nexus!"

"Oh my gosh," said Marisa, putting her hand over her mouth in shock. "I'm so sorry."

"What in the hell were you doing!"

Marisa shook her head. "I was—"

"It doesn't matter," said Fang. Marisa saw that she and Anja were also dead, which meant Jaya was out there all by herself. "We're going to lose in about ten seconds—they're trashing our vault."

"I'll respawn in five seconds," said Marisa. "Maybe I can—"

"No, you can't—" shouted Sahara, but then Marisa reappeared in the base, right next to the vault. She started firing immediately, and then took stock of the situation. Jaya was almost dead, but they were ignoring her and pouring damage into the vault, eager for the win. All five Thunderbolts were there, at various levels of health. Marisa looked at her powerset: her holds wouldn't do any good, because they were already where they wanted to be anyway. She had a single target freeze, but that was useless against five targets. Stupid Feather Fall, of course, was an absolute waste. She picked the one power she thought might help, and blasted them all with a chilling wind to slow them down. It was a channeled spell, which meant she couldn't do anything else while she was casting it: just stand there exposed. She'd be dead in seconds. All they had to do was turn and kill her.

They didn't.

The Thunderbolts' damage output dropped as their attacks slowed, but they stayed focused on the vault—it was almost dead, and then they'd win. Jaya kept hammering on them with her magic blasts, but they ignored her and fought stiffly through the chill, beating on the vault with everything they had. Its hit points fell to triple digits. Jaya killed their Jungler; the vault had 500 hit points left. Marisa kept her chill going, but she was going to run out of energy soon. Fang respawned, and joined in with Jaya. They killed the Thunderbolt Sniper. The vault fell to 99 hit points. They killed the Spotter. Sahara respawned, and they killed the Thunderbolt General. Anja respawned. The vault dropped to 10 hit points. Marisa ran out of energy, and her spell fizzled to a stop.

The last of the Thunderbolts died.

The vault had two hit points left.

"What?" asked Anja.

"Run!" screamed Sahara. "Hit their vault before they respawn!"

The five of them tore across the map, ignoring the minions and the zombies and everything else. The Thunderbolt turrets were already down, so they swept into the enemy base like a storm and attacked the vault with everything they had. The Jungler respawned, and Sahara shouted for everyone to take him down.

"Don't make the mistake they did!" she shouted. "Drop each one as soon as he comes back! And don't let any of them escape!"

The Thunderbolts were better practiced, and better equipped. The Cherry Dogs were poorly specced and barely alive. But as long as they camped on the vault, killing each enemy agent as he appeared, they outnumbered them five to one. It took another three minutes, with barely a moment to take a breath, but they kept the enemy down and attacked the vault when they could, and finally it exploded. The minions started dancing, and the computer's announcer voice boomed across the laboratory:

"Cherry Dogs win! Cherry Dogs win!"

Marisa stared at her hands, still gripping the stupid sniper rifle she'd been using to attack the enemies three feet in front of her.

"How on earth did that just happen?" asked Jaya.

Sahara simply stood there with her mouth open.

"Wake up," said Anja. "We have adoring fans to celebrate in front of."

Marisa blinked out of the map and into the lobby, then blinked again to exit the game. She didn't even look at her stats. She opened her eyes slowly, shocked by the brightness of the real world's lights, and then remembered she was on a stage. The thunder that seemed to echo through her ears was cheers and applause. She sat up, unplugged the cable from her headjack, and looked out. The whole audience was on its feet, and the roar almost made her dizzy. Anja stepped toward the crowd and raised her hands triumphantly, roaring back.

"That was one of the most nail-biting wins I've ever seen," said a voice behind Marisa, and she turned to see Su-Yun Kho smiling and clapping her hands. "But it was also the luckiest win I've ever seen, so don't get cocky, because you're never going to be that lucky again. Now: if you don't want to be branded as bitches for the rest of your tournament career, get over there and shake hands with the Thunderbolts."

"Cherry Dogs forever!" shouted Anja.

Marisa walked to the Thunderbolts, still sitting in stunned shock in their VR chairs, and hugged every one of them.

TWENTY-TWO

"'A stunning upset and a classy show of sportsmanship,'" said Sahara, reading the article out loud for the seventh time. "'The Cherry Dogs have made a resounding entrance to the international stage.' I could read this all day."

"You have read it all day," said Marisa, reaching past her to grab a brush from Sahara's bathroom counter. "Now start looking hot or we're not going to get into this club. And C-Gull doesn't seem like the kind of person who gives rain checks."

"We could set up an automated routine to read it for us," said Jaya, carefully applying bright blue eye shadow in the mirror.

"I can read it for you," said Fang softly, standing just outside the doorway in her oversized hoodie. "I don't have anything else to do."

"You need to get dressed," said Jaya.

Fang looked at the floor. "I'm not going."

"Come on," said Marisa, "it'll be fun."

"You could wear one of my dresses," said Sahara.

Fang walked away, mumbling, "You're like five feet taller than me."

Marisa sighed, and pushed past Sahara to go into the living room to talk with Fang directly. "She wasn't trying to offend you," she said softly.

"I wasn't offended," said Fang.

"Then why are you acting so . . . downtrodden all the time?" asked Marisa. "I've been trying to figure you out ever since you got here, and I have no idea, so I'm just going to ask. Are we being mean? Are we not including you? Are we overwhelming you with . . . something? With Mexican food? What's wrong?"

Fang kept her head down. "Nothing's wrong."

"Then why are you being so quiet?" Marisa demanded.

"Because I'm quiet," said Fang.

"You were back to your old self again in the match today," said Marisa. "I thought we had you back, but now you're clamming up again, and you won't come with us tonight, and I just don't understand."

"Then think about it for two seconds," said Fang, her voice growing annoyed. "Do I look like the kind of person who likes to go to dance clubs? Who likes"—she searched for the right word—"people?"

"Is this because of Zi?"

Fang frowned. "Why would it be because of Zi?"

"Because she was so mean to you?"

"Oh," said Fang, "so now I'm a coward."

"That's not what I meant."

"It's what you said."

"Look," said Marisa. "This is a secret meeting, but we're going to stick out if we don't look like we're having fun. And clubs, my dear, are *fun*. Have you ever been to a club before?"

"Why would I ever go to a club?"

"Because . . . they're fun," said Marisa. "Because you get to let your hair down, and lose some inhibitions, and dance around and move your body—"

"I hate dancing," said Fang. "Everyone just, what, jumps around? In unison?"

"It's not choreographed," said Marisa.

"But everyone's still doing the same thing," said Fang, "at the same time, in the same way. It makes me angry just thinking about it."

Marisa sighed. "We're not trying to make you angry—"

"Then stop telling me how to have fun!" shouted Fang. Marisa's eyes went wide, and Sahara and Jaya leaned through the bathroom door to look. It was the loudest Fang had been since she'd gotten to LA. She looked at the floor, saying nothing.

"I'm sorry," said Marisa. "I just want you to . . . come out of your shell."

"I like my shell," Fang snapped.

Marisa nodded. "Okay. You're right. You don't have to tell me anything, and you don't have to go to the club. I'm sorry for trying to . . . drag you around."

"I'll patch in through a djinni call," said Fang. "I want to be there for the meeting, I just don't want to be *there* there for the meeting. You know?"

"Anja's outside with an autocab," said Sahara. "Ready to go?"

"Let me finish my hair," said Marisa. She dragged the brush through her hair one final time, then looked at Cameron and Camilla. "And you, Pati, are going to make sure Mami doesn't see the vidcast."

A message from Pati popped up in Marisa's djinni: no text, just an image of a thumbs-up.

"How did you know she was watching?" asked Jaya.

"She's always watching," said Marisa, and set down the brush. "Let's do this."

Sahara spun on her heel, showing off her dress. "How do I look?"

"Amazing," said Marisa. It was another of Sahara's own designs—a brown base almost the exact color of her skin, overlaid with a pale white thicket of fabric in the shape of crooked aspen branches, growing denser as they climbed up toward her neck. Her bust and upper arms were covered with actual twigs and tendrils, and underneath them it was almost impossible to tell where the fabric ended and her skin began.

"You make the rest of us look terrible," said Jaya.

"That's Sahara's specialty," said Marisa. "You look great too, though."

"Thanks," said Jaya. She was wearing a dark red dress made of folded diagonal layers, covered with rich golden embroidery. "You're not bad yourself."

"It's Sahara's," said Marisa, looking down at the black vinyl panels and the giant, asymmetrical collar flaps. It was at least one size too small for her, but the interlocking panels did a tolerable job of hiding it. "I've wanted to try it on ever since she got it, so I guess that's one good thing to come out of losing my own best dress BASE jumping."

Te ves chidissima, sent Pati.

"Anja's going crazy out there," said Sahara. "Come on."

"See ya, Fang," said Marisa, waving as they walked out the door.

"I'm right here," said Fang, initiating the call, her voice piping out through the speaker in Marisa's purse. Marisa laughed. Maybe Fang would feel more comfortable interacting with them online.

Anja was waiting in the autocab, wearing what looked like a navy-blue military jacket, with matching booty shorts and thigh-high boots, all of it accented with a wine-colored bustle of thick, ruffled taffeta.

"Epic!" said Anja, helping Sahara into the cab. "This is going to be awesome. And check it out . . ." She held one finger in the air, listening, but Marisa didn't hear anything. She shook her head.

"What?"

"Nothing," said Anja. "No ads! That ad-free membership thingy is the best yuan I ever spent." The cab waited for everyone to get settled, then pulled away and started the drive to Santa Monica. "Can we talk about how amazing that game was yesterday?" asked Anja. "I'll start: it was amazing."

"We've been talking about it all day," said Fang.

"Hi, Fang," said Anja, and laughed when she realized where

the voice was coming from. "Some girls keep a dog in their purse; Mari keeps Overworld's best Jungler."

"It was amazing," said Sahara, "but it was sloppy."

"We won," said Anja.

"No," said Sahara, "they lost. There's a big difference. If they hadn't gotten greedy trying to kill our vault, we would have lost everything. We play Canavar tomorrow, and we can't rely on them making the same bad decisions."

"You're absolutely right," said Marisa.

Sahara looked at Marisa pointedly. "The other thing we can't do is disappear for fifty-two seconds in the middle of the match, getting ganked at the spawn point while you pick your nose."

Marisa's mood plummeted as she remembered her massive mistake. "I'm sorry."

"You want to tell us what that was about?" asked Sahara. Her voice was firm and angry, and Marisa couldn't blame her. Disappearing like that was a terrible thing to do.

Marisa was careful not to look at the camera nulis. "I thought I saw a rhinoceros."

"You saw a what?" asked Sahara. "Oh." She shook her head, taken by surprise, and then blinked. "Rhinoceros" was the code word for "I'm about to say something that can't go out on the public video feed." Now that the nuli dive video had made them famous, Sahara's viewership was bigger than ever, and they'd started taking extra precautions. "Speakers are off," said Sahara, "and the cameras are pointing at Anja and Jaya."

"We'll dance," said Anja, and started to wriggle in her seat to some music only she could hear.

Marisa looked at Sahara. "The tournament's being played inside of the Sigan airgap."

Sahara's eyes went wide. "You're kidding."

"I blinked out to look at the server, thinking maybe I could find whoever was controlling the lag spikes, but I found the entire system—the same exact system I was in at the gala."

"It's part of their setup," said Sahara, nodding as she thought about it. "We're playing in a closed network, so they can simulate connection issues and make sure nobody cheats."

"Except Chaewon," said Jaya.

"This means we have hard-line access to the private database," said Marisa. "We didn't think we could help Alain because we couldn't access the top level of their security, but now we can. Every time we're logged in to the game, we can hack into Sigan."

"There's no way they'd just leave themselves open like that," said Anja, still dancing for the camera. "I'm trying to be vague in case someone's reading my lips."

"She's right," said Sahara. "They wouldn't give sixteen teams full of total strangers that kind of access."

"Maybe they thought we wouldn't find it," said Marisa.

"Maybe it's booby-trapped," said Fang.

"I already tried it," said Marisa. "I used the buffer overflow and got in just fine—they didn't protect it at all."

"Then they don't know it's there," said Jaya.

Sahara hesitated a moment, thinking it through, and then laughed out loud. "Chaewon, you gorgeous little brat!" She looked at Marisa, practically bubbling over with excitement. "Sigan doesn't know about the hole! Chaewon must have been so desperate to cheat she made a hole the company doesn't know about—Sigan is evil, but even they're not petty enough to rig a silly little tournament like this. The other megacorps playing against them would take it as a huge insult. So: Chaewon put a back door into the game server to allow her accomplice, probably a worker somewhere in the company, to get in and mess with the lag manually. Think about it: she's the only one with the motive and the access to do it. And Mari found the back door." Sahara smiled, and pointed at Marisa. "You're amazing."

Marisa beamed.

"This could be our ticket to getting Alain out," said Fang. "How, though?"

"The pieces are coming together," said Marisa. "Bao can get in physically, and now we can get in digitally." Her face fell. "But access isn't enough. We need something more."

"We'll see what C-Gull has to offer," said Sahara. "Alain seems to think he can help, and back door or not, we need all the help we can get."

"We're almost there," said Anja. "Now everyone start dancing with me before I punch you!"

Sahara turned the nulis' microphones back on, and blinked into the cab's music system to pick a song—a Taylor Swift dance song from her comeback album in 2048. All four girls started dancing in their seats and singing along at the top of their lungs. Marisa imagined Fang rolling her eyes, and smiled.

The cab rolled up to the Daze dance club about thirty minutes later, and even Anja was astonished at how easily they got in. The line was long, but the bouncer recognized them from the nuli dive video and jumped them right to the front of it. Once they were inside, they were immediately disoriented: no two surfaces in the room were perpendicular to each other, including the floor, and the walls and ceiling were covered with bright, spherical lanterns in various shades of pink and blue and purple, which only added to the chaos. Marisa felt dizzy, but Anja pulled her through the maze of oddly shaped tables and platforms to the actual dance floor, which was comfortingly stable. An Aidoru band was playing, and the girls, already energized from their karaoke in the cab, started bouncing to the music.

Shouldn't you be looking for C-Gull? sent Fang.

"You don't have to send a message," said Marisa, "just talk. No one can hear you anyway."

Don't talk, send a message, sent Fang. **It's too loud; no one can hear you.**

Marisa smirked at herself, and shot a message back. **It's still early; it'll take him forever to get through that line outside.**

Better safe than sorry, sent Fang.

"Blah," said Marisa. She touched Sahara's arm and leaned close. "I'm going to go claim the booth and wait for C-Gull."

"Good idea," said Sahara. "He said 'third on the left.' I'm going to keep dancing for a while; it plays great on the feed."

Marisa nodded and worked her way back through the tables, trying to figure out which booth would be the "third on the left." She started at the entry, counted two tables, and moved past a tall purple pillar that seemed to change shape every time she looked away from it. Beyond the pillar were two tables that might both lay claim to the title of "third on the left," and after a moment's hesitation she decided to simply pick the emptier of the two. She slid onto one of the couches, nodding at the touchy-feely couple on the far side, and tapped out a drink order on the table's touch screen. Water, because she couldn't afford anything else. She sat back to wait for the waiter nuli to bring it, and sent a message to the other girls.

There's a couple here trying to make out at the table. If enough of us show up and start talking really loud they'll probably look for somewhere more private, and we can have it to ourselves.

On my way, sent Anja, though she and Jaya didn't arrive until a few minutes later, when the booming dance song transitioned into something a little more slow-paced.

"Woo!" Jaya flopped down on the bench with an exhausted laugh. "I love this place! Are all American clubs like this?"

"Most of them don't give you vertigo," said Marisa, "but yeah, pretty much." It was slightly easier to hear over here, away from the dance floor, and Anja leaned down to shout at Marisa's purse.

"You're missing out, Fang!"

"On what?" asked Fang. "Bouncing around in the dark? How do you know I'm not doing that right now?"

"No wonder you think it's dumb, if you do it alone," said Marisa.

"Anything that can't be done alone is not worth doing," said Fang. "And yes, I thought about the obvious sexual implications of that sentence as soon as I said it out loud. Shut up."

Marisa laughed. "Hooray for Fang! It's like talking to the real you again!"

"Because the real me is inside that shell you tried to pull me out of," said Fang. "I like my shell. It has free Wi-Fi."

"C-Gull's going to be stuck in that line," said Anja. "Should we maybe just go out and find him?"

"He said he'd contact us," said Jaya. "We have no idea what he looks like, and he doesn't know us—just this table."

"Speaking of which," said Anja, and leaned across the table toward the couple kissing passionately on the other side. "Excuse me! Hey, excuse me!"

They pulled their lips apart and looked at her, obviously annoyed.

"Sorry to interrupt," said Anja. "This is my first time here: What do you recommend from the bar?"

The couple glared at her, then stood up to leave. Anja laughed and moved around to take their bench. She and Jaya ordered drinks, and they sat back to wait.

They waited a very long time.

"You know," said Sahara, nearly an hour later, "I'm starting to worry that C-Gull won't be able to get in this place at all. I mean, not everybody can. If he was planning on a crappy bar like Lowball, he might not even meet the dress code for Daze." Cameron and Camilla weren't around to overhear them; Sahara had sent them back to the dance floor to get some party footage.

"I called and left another message," said Fang. "He knows you're waiting there . . . or at least he'll know if he checks his private arms dealer phone. Which he doesn't carry around with him, so, blah."

"You suck at good news," said Anja.

"You suck at finding arms dealers in dance clubs," said Fang.

"That's true enough," said Marisa, looking around for the hundredth time. "Should we maybe leave and go over to Lowball?"

"Dressed like this?" asked Sahara. "We'd get mugged by the first person we saw, and then probably the second and third as well."

"The fourth would grope us," said Anja. "And then throw up on himself."

"Don't be mean to the fourth guy," said Fang. "Maybe he's a gentleman, you don't know."

"Oh my gosh," said Jaya, coming back to the table for the tenth time. It seemed like every guy in the place was trying to dance with her. "Still nothing?"

"Still nothing," said Marisa. "Two minutes."

"What?" asked Jaya.

"Ninety seconds," said Anja.

"You're way overshooting it," said Sahara. "Thirty seconds, max."

"What are you talking about?" asked Jaya.

"They're betting on how long it'll be before another guy asks you to dance," said Fang.

"Excuse me," said a voice, and they all looked up at a tall Mexican man with a trimmed mustache and his shirt collar open to the third button, showing off a shaved, muscular chest.

"C-Gull?" asked Anja.

"Seagull?" asked the man. "I just want to ask this muchacha to dance."

"Pay up," said Sahara.

After another hour, they were starting to get really worried.

"What do we do if he doesn't show up?" asked Marisa. "He's our only shot at this. Even with a back door into the Sigan system, we can't get Alain out on our own. He said the trick was to get him out of his cell, and with the access I found I can totally send a fake order get Mr. Park to move him, but then what?"

"I don't think he's coming," said Anja. "Maybe he forgot? Maybe we can set up another meeting for tomorrow?"

"It took us three days to get this meeting," said Sahara. "In three more days the tournament will be over, and who knows where Alain will be."

Marisa looked at Anja. "Have you tried the hoodie again?"

"She hasn't put it on again," said Anja. "I can find Renata, but I can't get into anything."

"Wait," said Fang, "I think I see him."

"You're not even here," said Marisa.

"I'm watching Sahara's vidcast," said Fang. "There's a guy by the side wall who looks like a salty old fisherman. Not exactly your typical Daze customer."

"Which wall?" asked Marisa. The girls looked around but couldn't see through the crowd and lights.

"I have no idea," said Fang. "One with . . . stupid light balls all over it?"

"Ah," said Anja. They were surrounded by walls that fit that description. "That narrows it down."

"I think I see him," said Sahara. "Yep, I got him. Salty old sea dog is right, holy crap. Over Marisa's right shoulder—don't look. He's watching us."

"Trying to see if we're being followed?" asked Jaya.

"Trying to decide if you're his contacts," said Fang. "I guarantee you don't look like whatever he was expecting to find for a secret arms deal."

"Just be patient," said Sahara. "He'll come over eventually. Fang, let us know if he slips out, and we'll go after him."

"Gotcha," said Fang.

They waited almost ten more minutes before the man finally approached the table.

"Finally," muttered Anja.

"Excuse me, young ladies," said the man. He looked about sixty years old, though it was hard to guess ages after forty-five, when so many people started buying antiaging implants. He wore a wrinkled black suit with a poorly tied tie, neither of which looked like they fit him. Even in the suit, his scraggly beard and weathered face marked him as some kind of seaman, perhaps a smuggler. He cleared his throat. "I hate to ask you this, but I need this table."

"Sit down," said Sahara, scooting over to make room, "we've been waiting all night."

"No," said the man, "I'm meeting someone, and I need this table without you in it."

"We're the ones you're meeting," said Fang. "You're C-Gull, right?"

"Your purse is talking," said the man.

"Daze," said Marisa, "Wednesday, third booth on the left. This is us. We contacted you about Alain being captured, and you said to meet us here to talk about getting him out again."

The man stared at them for a moment, then turned to walk away. "I can't believe this."

"Wait!" shouted Sahara, jumping up. The club was so loud and crowded that no one seemed to pay them any attention. She grabbed his arm and stopped him. The shape-shifting pillar undulated brightly behind them. "You said you'd meet us—we've been waiting all night."

"You didn't tell me you were . . . little girls," said C-Gull. "What are you . . . what am I even supposed to do with you? I'm a businessman, not a babysitter."

"You heard about Bluescreen?" asked Marisa. C-Gull looked at her, saying nothing, but the word at least had gotten his attention. Marisa nodded. "We took that whole operation down."

C-Gull raised an eyebrow.

"That's right," said Sahara. "And if you know Bluescreen, I assume you know the Softball virus?"

"Or the Deadman exploit?" asked Anja. "Trust us, we're the real deal."

Marisa watched the man's face, hoping what they said had convinced him. Aside from Bluescreen, their other hacks weren't exactly impressive enough to sway an actual criminal.

"I'll give you ten minutes," said C-Gull. "And then I'm going to kill Alain for sending me his little gaggle of . . . flibbertigibbets."

"You won't regret it," said Sahara, leading him back to the table. They made room for him and he sat down, pulling at his collar.

"I should have known this was bad when you changed the meeting place," he said. "I said yes because I owe Alain, but come on. How long do I have to keep this stupid tie on?"

"Take it off," said Anja. "No one's wearing one anyway."

"They wouldn't let me in without it," he grumbled, taking it off. "I had to go pull my buddy out of bed and borrow his suit just to get in this stupid place."

"That's why you were late?" asked Fang.

"Why is the purse still talking?" asked C-Gull.

"That's our mission coordinator," said Sahara. "Now: Alain has been captured by the megacorp he was trying to sabotage, KT Sigan. He was able to get one message out to us, and said you could break him out."

"Impossible," said C-Gull. "Prison, easy, but a megacorp? They have way more money, and that means better security, better everything. Way harder to suborn."

"What can you do, then?" asked Marisa.

"I can sell you weapons," said C-Gull. "You want to blast your way in? It's a terrible plan, but I'm your man. Now, if you could figure out when they're moving him from one building to the next, I could sell you some explosives to—"

"No bombs," said Sahara. "We don't want to hurt anyone, or land ourselves in jail."

"Typical," said C-Gull, but shook his head. "It doesn't have to be a bomb, though—I've got a whole line of TEDs that'll take out a car without any collateral damage at all."

"TED?" asked Jaya.

"A transient electromagnetic device," said C-Gull. "Instead of a big-boom explosion you just get a pulse wave that takes out electronics—they can shut down cars, djinnis, cameras—"

"And overclocked security guards," said Marisa, nodding. "It's like the teddy bear we used on Mr. Park. Alain must have gotten it from you."

"You put one of my TEDs in a stuffed bear?" asked C-Gull. "I knew this was a bad idea."

"A TED would be perfect," said Sahara. "Mr. Park's still there, so we're going to need one of those to get past him."

C-Gull nodded. "How big?"

"The size you sold to Alain before was pretty good," said Marisa. "It was easy enough to hide, and it took out their best overclocked security guard for a good two or three minutes."

"I have a shipment coming in two weeks," said C-Gull. "One thousand yuan apiece, as many as you want."

"Whoa," said Anja. "We need them way sooner than that."

"How much sooner?"

"Tonight?" said Sahara. "Saturday at the absolute latest."

"We'd have to be in the final match for that to work," said Marisa.

"Final match?" asked C-Gull. "I thought you needed these for a rescue mission."

"The rescue mission has to take place during an Overworld tournament," said Sahara. "It's our only window of access to the Sigan servers."

"Is this one of those hidden camera shows?" asked C-Gull. He glanced around the club, as if expecting to see a camera crew hiding behind a bench. "You can't be police, you're not remotely their style. Maybe in the talking purse?" He grabbed it and opened it up, pulling out a pack of breath mints and a couple of tampons. "Oops, sorry. Whose is this?"

"We need something by Saturday," said Marisa, yanking the purse away from him. "What can you get us by then?"

C-Gull blushed, then put his hand on his chin to think. He blinked, checking some kind of inventory list in his djinni, then shrugged. "Well, I can get you some TEDs, but they're not big enough to take out an overclocked djinni. Especially not if it's shielded."

"How big?" asked Jaya.

"This big," said C-Gull, and reached into his hip pocket, leaning practically into Marisa's lap to open the pocket wide enough for his hand. Finally he pulled something out and slapped it down on the table: a small disk, a little wider than a quarter, and a little thicker than three quarters stacked together.

"That's tiny," said Anja.

"That's the point," said C-Gull. "They're easy to carry and easy to hide. I always have a couple on me in case I need to kill a security camera or something."

"How do you trigger them?" asked Fang.

"Well, talking purse, they're fully programmable, with a little RF sensor that you can trigger pretty much any way you want. You can set them as time bombs, to go off at certain time, or after a certain amount of time has passed; they even have their own unique IDs, so you can trigger them remotely."

Marisa picked up the tiny TED, turning it over in her fingers. An idea was starting to form in her mind. "What about proximity triggers?" she asked. "Like, if a certain djinni ID gets too close?"

"Sure. But they're not strong enough to take out a djinni by themselves. Maybe a whole bunch of them together, but then you lose the benefit of the small size."

"That's okay," said Marisa, "we can work with that."

"Mari's got a plan," said Anja, grinning wildly.

Marisa smiled back, then looked at C-Gull. "How many can you get us by Saturday?"

"A hundred," said C-Gull. "Maybe one-twenty. A hundred yuan each."

"We'll take as many as you can get," said Anja. "How do we pay you?"

"Cash only," said C-Gull.

"And where do we . . ." Anja paused, wincing. "Cash only?"

"You think I want a digital record of my illegal weapons deals?" C-Gull threw his hands in the air. "Why am I even here? I'm leaving—this is stupid."

"Wait," said Sahara, grabbing his arm. "We can pay." She looked at Anja. "Right?"

Anja grimaced. "I can do twelve thousand yuan, but not in cash. That's the kind of thing my dad will definitely notice."

"Good-bye," said C-Gull, and stood up.

"Fifteen thousand," said Marisa. C-Gull stopped, and Marisa clenched her teeth. This was it. They needed those TEDs, or everything came crashing down. She nodded, and spoke as firmly as she could. "In cash. You tell us where."

C-Gull turned around. "You'll forgive me if I'm not convinced."

"We can get it," she said. "We can get it *early* if we have to, just . . . we need those TEDs."

C-Gull thought for a moment, then slid back down onto the bench. "You pay up front. I'll send drop-off coordinates for a neutral location, you take the money there, and then I'll send another set of coordinates for the pickup. Say the word, and I can have the TEDs ready to go in forty-eight hours."

"No earlier than that?" asked Sahara.

"No."

Sahara stared at him, then let out a slow breath. "Do it," she said. "That's Friday night. But you better not be late, because we have zero wiggle room in our timeline."

"You insult me," said C-Gull. "I'm the damn professional here; of course I'll be on time." He stood up, then looked at them and sighed. "Are you going to be dressed like fairy princesses when we make the exchange?"

"No," said Sahara.

"I might be," said Anja.

Sahara stood up to shake his hand. "Thank you for your time, C-Gull. It's a pleasure doing business with you."

"Whatever," said C-Gull, and shoved his tie into his pocket. "I'm getting out of this Barbie Dream House before I go insane." He walked away, and Sahara sat back down.

"So," said Sahara, fixing Marisa with her eyes. "You have a plan?"

"I think so," she said. "At least the beginnings of one. First of all, with this timeline, we have to make it to the final match—we don't have to win, but we have to be in the game. It's the only way to access the company database."

"Screw second place," said Sahara. "If we get that far, we're going all the way."

"Yesssssssss," said Anja.

"And then what?" asked Jaya. "How do we rescue Alain?"

"We don't just rescue Alain," said Marisa. "We rescue him, and get the financial data, and find Grendel, and destroy Sigan—the whole frakking deal. And, apparently, we win the tournament while we're at it, because why not?"

"Awesome," said Sahara. "But *how* do we make all this happen?"

"Easy," said Marisa, and smiled. "We start with salad dressing."

"And the money?" asked Anja. "Fifteen thousand yuan in untraceable cash is not something we can just pull out of our asses."

"Depends on which one," said Marisa. "Who's the biggest ass you know?"

The girls stared at her for a moment, trying to figure out what she meant, and then suddenly Anja's jaw dropped open. "No."

"It's the only way," said Marisa. "We've come too far, and this is too important to back down now."

"What's going on?" asked Fang. "Where are we getting the money?"

Marisa shook her head, and forced herself to say it: "Omar Maldonado."

TWENTY-THREE

That night, Marisa couldn't sleep. Even if Omar helped them—and they wouldn't know for sure until they asked him in the morning—their plan still had so many holes in it. How did it end? Pitting Sigan against Johara was great in the long term, but how did it help them escape the building? The first rule of getting in somewhere, Alain had said, was knowing how to get back out again. They could get Alain out of the building, sure, but then Sigan would just chase him down and catch him again, and Johara couldn't help with that. They needed something better. And what about the data? Their plan to use Johara didn't work unless they revealed what they stole, but as soon as they did they'd be admitting to the crime. So either Sigan got them, and they were never seen again, or the police got them and they spent the rest of their lives in prison. Was stopping Sigan really worth all of that? Even if Sigan turned Mirador into a slum, at least she'd be in a slum with her family. They could stay together and protect each other. But then . . . her family wasn't the only one being ruined by Sigan. How many other people in Mirador would lose their jobs or their homes? How many other neighborhoods around the world would get ground down in the relentless search for profit?

She shook her head. The world already belonged to the megacorps. Stop one, and a hundred more would move in, just as heartless and relentless as Sigan.

She sighed, and shook her head again. She couldn't think like that—like the villains of the world had already won. She had to do something. She had to matter.

She rolled over in her bed, trying to fall asleep, but her mind was racing and her pillow was scorching and her blankets seemed to twist and wrap around her, and finally she threw them off and sat up. Her djinni sensed the change in position, deduced that she was waking up, and showed her the time: two thirty in the morning. She ground her teeth but didn't lie down again. The summer heat was oppressive, even in the middle of the night, and her sweaty tank top was sticking to her chest.

"I need a drink," she mumbled, and stood up. "And what the hell, I'm going to eat some cookies, too." She pulled on a pair of shorts, unlocked her door, and slipped quietly into the hall and down the stairs to the kitchen.

The light was on. She frowned, and peeked around the corner of the kitchen doorway. Her father was sitting at the table, staring at the wall. A half-full glass of milk stood on the table in front of him.

She froze for a minute, not certain if she should say anything. Finally she just said, "Hey."

Carlo Magno looked up. "Hey." He held up a cookie with a big round bite taken out of the side. "Couldn't sleep."

Marisa walked in and sat down, reaching across the table for the box of cookies. "Tell me about it."

"You realize," said Carlo Magno, pushing the box into her hand, "that these are the last cookies we can afford. We're down to subsistence-level shopping: only what we need to survive."

Marisa stared at the box in her hand, trying to decide if it was worth it to eat one. She hesitated, then dumped out the entire contents on the table. Her father raised an eyebrow, and she started counting the cookies into five piles. "Pati, Gabi, Sandro, Mami, Abue." She separated the best ones, two to a pile.

"You forgot yours," said Carlo Magno.

"We get the rest," she said, and swept the broken bits and crumbs into another pile. "That looks like, what, three cookies' worth? Split it half and half."

"I'm good," he said, and held up his cookie again. He sighed. "I wish there were more people like you, Marisita."

Marisa blushed, and kept her eyes on the table. "I'm only trying to be like you."

"Too much, sometimes," said her father. "Being like me is not always a great thing."

Marisa sat in silence, then asked the same old question she couldn't help but ask: "When are you going to tell me about that car crash?"

"Never," said Carlo Magno. The answer came so quickly, like he didn't even think about it. It had been set in stone for years.

"Why not?"

"Because you're better off not knowing."

"Not knowing how I lost my own arm?" she said. "Not knowing why I was in a mobster's car? Was she kidnapping me? Is she my real mother? Why won't you tell me?"

"Guadalupe is definitely your real mother," said Carlo Magno. "You have to trust me—if it would help you to know it, I'd tell you."

"That's not a decision you get to make for me."

"And yet here I am, making it."

Marisa stared at him, trying to summon her anger, but he looked so sad and defeated, like a slowly deflating balloon. "I'm going to find out eventually," she said softly.

"Please don't."

She said nothing, and ate another fragment of cookie. Just a few more days, and she'd finally have the means to track Grendel down. . . .

"I've made a decision," said Carlo Magno.

Marisa chewed her cookie. "You're getting your ears pierced."

"Hoo, not again," said Carlo Magno.

Marisa laughed. "You did *not* have pierced ears."

"Not while you were alive," he said. "When I was a teenager I had a stud in each ear—little silver skulls."

"Gang signs?"

"Nothing like that, just some tontería from my wayward youth. I took them out the day I met your mother."

"Skulls, huh?" asked Marisa. She cocked her head to the side, studying him. "I can see you as a goth. Black hair, maybe a black choker necklace."

"Don't forget the black fishnet T-shirt," said Carlo Magno, and Marisa spat out her cookie, nearly choking on it. He laughed, and leaned across the table to slap her back, helping her clear her throat. She sat back, gasping and crying.

"Don't tell me things like that while I'm swallowing, Papi, you'll kill me."

"You think telling you will kill you, wait'll I pull out the photos."

"Please tell me you have photos," said Marisa. "Goth Carlo Magno *has* to exist, and I'm way too busy to fake the photos myself."

"I've decided to close San Juanito for the week," said Carlo Magno. "I'm going to spend the rest of the week at a protest downtown." He took another bite of his cookie, and Marisa stared at him in shock.

"You're . . . you're not going to open tomorrow?"

He swallowed and spoke. "Yesterday we had two customers. We spent more just turning the lights and AC on than we earned." He shook his head. "We can't keep going anymore. I've already canceled everyone's service—you'll keep your djinnis, because they're already paid for, but they'll be Wi-Fi-only starting tomorrow. And it'll have to be somebody else's Wi-Fi."

Marisa tried to speak, but there was nothing to say.

"Someone's organized a protest downtown at the Sigan building," Carlo Magno continued. "Trying to get them to put the prices back where they were. It won't get our service turned back on, but it might give our customers enough spare money to come in for a taco every now and then. Maybe just enough to keep us afloat."

Marisa finally found her voice. "What can I do? I can pull some extra shifts, or . . . I don't know, stand on the corner with a bunch of flyers?"

"We can't afford to print out flyers," said Carlo Magno. "The best thing you can do, honestly, is just stay in school. Get good grades. You're good enough with computers you can get a real job—not something a nuli will take over a few months later, but a real job for a real human." He glanced at her from the side of his eye. "And it better be a good one, because Lupe and I are going to be living with you."

Marisa chuckled. "I'll see what I can do. Though I honestly think I'd be better off hanging out with Anja's neighbors, trying to land a rich husband and let him pay for everything."

"Don't think I haven't thought of that," said Carlo Magno.

"We might win this tournament, you know," she said suddenly.

"That's . . . great," said Carlo Magno. "I'm proud of you."

"The prize money is ten thousand yuan to the cause of our choice. The team already decided that San Juanito is our cause of choice."

He said nothing.

"Papi?" She looked closer, and saw that he was crying. She jumped up and walked around to his side of the table, hugging his shoulders tightly. "I love you, Papi."

"I love you too, mija." He clutched her arms, then wiped the tears from his cheek. "I'm sorry I won't be able to see you play. I'll be right outside, though, chanting and holding signs and . . . whatever other useless gestures I can make."

"It's okay," she said. "I'm sorry I won't be there with you."

He nodded. "Just promise me you won't jump off the building while I'm standing there, okay? The videos were bad enough—I don't know if my heart can take it live."

"You know I'm not going to jump off any more buildings," she said.

"And you know I'll kill you if you do."

She kissed him on the cheek. "I love you." She stayed there for a moment, comforted by his presence. Then a thought leaped into her mind, and she stood up abruptly. "You said videos. Plural."

Carlo Magno frowned, confused. "Yeah, there's like ten. Every building in the area caught it on their security cameras, and two or three police nulis did too."

"Because this is LA," said Marisa, "and there are cameras everywhere." A light went off in her mind. She walked slowly across the room, pacing as she thought. "You said someone was organizing a protest. Do you know how big it's going to be? Like, how many people?"

"Hundreds, if we do it right," said Carlo Magno. "Maybe not tomorrow, but by Saturday, sure."

"Perfect," said Marisa. "We need them there Saturday. And reporters, and cameras, and police nulis, and maybe even some actual police."

Carlo Magno nodded. "The more publicity the better." He

shrugged. "Maybe we *do* want you to jump off the building."

"Anything for eyeballs," said Marisa.

"I was kidding," said Carlo Magno quickly.

"So was I," she said, "don't worry. But we do need eyeballs. We need everyone in the whole world watching that front plaza."

"Why?"

"Because the first rule of getting in somewhere is knowing how to get back out again," she said, and smiled with the first real joy she'd felt all night. "And I just found a way out."

She went back to her room, found her djinni's notepad app, and pulled up a number: C-Gull's contact phone. She took a breath, asking herself if this was really the best idea. She gritted her teeth and dialed. It went straight to voicemail—no message, just a beep.

"Hi," said Marisa, "this is . . . one of the girls from the other night. Alain's friends. We want to add something to our order, if we still can."

She hesitated again, then said it.

"We want a real bomb."

TWENTY-FOUR

"Our game today's not until the afternoon," said Sahara. "That gives us a chance to visit Omar and . . ." She trailed off.

"Desperately beg him for money," said Marisa.

"I couldn't bring myself to say it," said Sahara.

"We can't trust him," said Anja. The other girls were dressing up in their best "impress the rich guy" clothes, but Anja refused, and was attending the meeting in ripped jeans, a threadbare T-shirt, and an old brown work coat that looked like she'd fished it out of a garbage can. "You know what he did to us last time."

"He screwed us over," said Marisa. "You more than anyone. But then he helped us fix it."

"You think that makes it okay?" asked Anja.

"Omar's an opportunist," said Sahara. "And we're an opportunity he can't pass up, no matter how much we hate the situation."

Marisa looked at herself in Sahara's mirror. She had almost

worn her blue dress again, but she wore that every week to church, and she couldn't stand the thought of Omar's sister, La Princesa, seeing her in it again. She'd gone with a slim jacket and harem pants instead: black and elegant, with faux leather heels to jazz it up a little. She looked professional and competent.

And terrified.

"This is all I brought," said Fang. Marisa looked over at her, wondering what amazing thing she'd pulled out of that tiny bag, but all she wore was another version of the only thing they'd ever seen her in: black shoes, black pants, and a baggy hoodie. This hoodie was dark green instead of dark blue, but that was the outfit's only distinguishing feature.

"You've got to have something better," said Sahara.

Fang disappeared back into the other room, and Marisa frowned at Sahara. "Now you've offended her."

"This is a big deal!" said Sahara. She wore a fitted suit coat with black-and-white vertical stripes over a short black skirt and leggings. "We're going to ask them for fifteen thousand yuan—we need to look like we're worth it."

"If he says one word about what I'm wearing," said Anja, "one word, I will rip his ears off."

"Don't rip anyone's ears off," said Sahara. "Okay, listen: team meeting. This is important. Omar, and his entire family, are inhuman monsters incapable of positive emotion. They're criminals, they're bastards, they're walking tire fires that we have every reason to hate." She paused while everyone nodded, then continued. "They're also our only shot at getting back into this tournament. I'm sorry I'm being a little curt with everyone, but: We will not offend them. We will not insult them. We will make our case and we will be friendly and attractive and whatever else we need to be to get them on our side. Nothing less, but I promise nothing more."

"Fine," said Anja. "Let's go get this over with."

The Maldonados didn't live in a house so much as a complex, about a mile away from San Juanito in the heart of Mirador's most well-kept area. The girls walked the entire way, and Marisa waved at the people they passed; she knew most of them, and she knew their stories. Many were losing their jobs, or even their homes, and she wondered how much longer they'd be here. So many had already gone to Mexico to look for work—how long before the rest of her neighbors followed?

"Is this it?" asked Jaya. They stopped in front of a high wall with a tall iron gate. A grizzled Mexican man in a black suit leaned against the wall, drinking something from a small box with a straw.

"This is it," said Anja. "Brace yourself. From here, things are going to get . . . weird."

The man with the juice box sucked the last bit up with a loud squelch. "Can I help you?"

"We're here to see Omar," said Sahara. "He's not expecting us."

The man stared at them, not leering but simply sizing them up. Marisa expected him to ask what they wanted, but he simply blinked a message inside. Apparently random groups of young women showing up out of the blue for Omar was a frequent enough occurrence not to warrant further investigation.

I hate him, sent Anja.

Juice Box blinked again, reading something on his djinni, then took another sip and spoke to them. "Síganme." He opened the gate, and led them inside.

The brick wall turned out to be reinforced with heavy sheets of plascrete armor, carefully hidden by an artificial rain forest of trees and ferns and flowers that filled the inner courtyard. It was a shocking change from the desolate LA summer out on the street. Even the air was different: cool and soft and pleasantly humid. Juice Box handed them off to another large thug, who locked the gate behind them and then led them along a wide, clean driveway, past lush trees and a small fleet of meticulously washed autocars. Someone was in a nearby garage, the door open, washing another car, though that one looked ancient. Marisa craned her neck to look . . . yes. It had a steering wheel. She looked away, trying not to think of the sheer wealth that was on display. And they hadn't even gotten inside yet.

The complex consisted of at least four buildings: the main house, the garage, a pool house Marisa glimpsed through the trees, and another building she couldn't immediately identify. Another house? The guard led them to the main entrance and ushered them into a posh receiving room, where they sat primly on overstuffed couches and shivered in the air-conditioning while they waited for Omar.

Marisa sent a message to Anja: **This place looks more expensive than your house.**

You have no idea, Anja sent back.

This is the life, sent Sahara.

"Well," said Omar's voice. "Look who's here."

Marisa and the other girls glanced up, looking for him, and he stepped out from a nearby hallway, grinning impishly. He wore a loose collared shirt, the sleeves rolled up and his chest showing through behind the top two open buttons. He hadn't shaved in a day or two, and his chin bore just enough stubble to look rakishly handsome. The entire look was one of calculated nonchalance, and Marisa wondered if he'd changed his clothes on purpose when he'd found out they were there. He beckoned them forward, gesturing at the room behind him. "Come on in. I have to admit that I am absolutely dying to find out what brings you lovely ladies here today."

"I was really excited there for a second," said Anja, standing up, "but then you kept saying more words after 'dying.'"

Omar grinned. "Hello, Anja. It's been a while."

"Don't remind me," she said. "I'm going to have to reset my 'one hundred and seven days without a jagweed' sign."

"You're counting," said Omar. "That's so sweet."

Sahara stood. "We wouldn't come if it weren't important—"

"Please," said Omar, "come into the other room. This one's terrible."

Marisa sighed, but they followed him into the next room, which to his credit looked far more livable: still perversely expensive, but at least it had the kind of couches you could sit on instead of just worry about getting dirty. A massive screen filled one wall, currently set to HD footage of a coral reef—probably a real-time feed, Marisa thought—and the far corner of the room was taken up with a cluster of VR chairs. Another wall held a polished wooden bar, and Omar stepped behind it.

"Can I get you a drink?"

"What, no bartender?" asked Anja.

"Anja . . . ," growled Sahara.

"What gives?" Anja continued. "The chosen son of the Maldonado clan has to pour his own drinks? Were the shakedowns not as successful this week?"

"We're not here to start a fight," said Marisa, standing near the bar. "She's angry, just ignore her."

"How can I possibly pay attention to anyone but you?" asked Omar. He grinned at her hungrily, and she suppressed a shudder.

"I'll take a Lift, if you have it," said Marisa. "Fang, you want anything?"

"Lychee Ramune," said Fang.

"I don't think there's any way he has Ramune," said Jaya.

Fang smiled, just the barest, tiniest hint of one, and Marisa laughed out loud.

"You okay?" asked Omar, placing a bottle of ice-cold Lift on a coaster in front of her.

"I just . . ." She smothered her grin, unreasonably happy at hearing Fang make a joke. "I'm fine. Thanks for the drink."

"Lift is great for everyone," said Sahara. She walked slowly around the wide couch, surveying the room. "I've never been inside before. Nice place."

"Believe it or not," said Omar, gesturing at the room, "most of this was gifts." He popped the cap off another bottle of Lift and set it on the bar for Sahara, then went to work on more bottles for the others. "One of the things I've learned working for my father is that money's primary purpose is not to be spent; it's to be given away. You donate to this group, you donate to that group, you grease wheels and palms and everything else you can find, and things just start working out for you. Most businesses deal in goods or services; my father deals in favors."

He's setting the expectations, thought Marisa. *He knows we're here to ask for something, and he's letting us know that it's not going to be free.*

Omar set out a bottle of Lift for Anja, and another for Jaya, then a smaller, oddly shaped bottle for Fang. "Ramune," he said, and winked at her. "One of our more recent favors was done for a Japanese shipping company. I love the stuff, but I hate the little marble."

"Donations," said Sahara, "are exactly what we're here to talk about."

"Only if your cookies are gluten free," said Omar. "Some of our staff are kind of sensitive. And I'll admit I'm a bit upset you're not wearing the little uniforms."

Sahara clenched her teeth into a forced smile. "It's actually for a—"

"Ay, no me vengan," said a woman's voice. Marisa looked to the far end of the room and saw La Princesa, wearing nothing but skintight leggings and a sports bra. She eyed the five girls with obvious disgust. "These are a little younger than your normal girls, Omar—oh, disculpe, I didn't recognize you. It's Beef Jerky." She glared at Marisa disdainfully, and minced back behind the bar.

"Hello, Franca," said Marisa. "Late night?"

A message popped up from Sahara: **Please don't antagonize them.**

La Princesa stared daggers at her. "Who goes out on a weeknight?"

"Sorry," said Marisa. "I was just trying to cover for you." She dropped her voice to a stage whisper. "You forgot to get dressed."

La Princesa fumed, but Omar threw his head back and laughed. "Flaca likes to give the guards a show when she does her yoga," he said, still chuckling. "It's her own form of charitable donation."

"Cállate," said La Princesa.

"Vete," Omar shot back. "I'm trying to have a civilized conversation here. Go." He shooed her away, and she sneered as she grabbed a drink of her own and left.

"Are you sure this is a good time?" asked Sahara.

"It's as good a time as any," said Omar. "My father's busy, and the guards are too good at their jobs to come barging in like that. With Flaca gone we're practically alone."

"What about Jacinto?" asked Marisa. "I haven't seen him in years."

"And you won't," said Omar. "He's probably listening, but ever since the accident he doesn't do 'public' anymore."

"He's listening?" asked Jaya.

"Hello, Jacinto," Anja called out. The giant wall screen flickered, the blue water and brightly colored fish were replaced for just a half a second with a scene of destruction: red skies and shattered buildings and mushroom clouds boiling through the air, and then just as suddenly it was back to the fish, drifting tranquilly through the water. Anja grinned. "See?"

"Holy balls," said Sahara, her eyes wide. "Does he do that often?"

"Only if he wants our attention," said Omar. "Honestly, I barely ever see him myself."

Sahara grimaced. "It's like living in a haunted house."

Marisa looked around the room, wondering where the camera was hidden, or maybe cameras plural. She did her best to smile comfortingly, just in case Jacinto could see her, and realized she was holding her metal arm to her chest. She didn't know exactly what Jacinto had lost in that car crash, but it was way more than just an arm.

A thought occurred to her: Jacinto had been ten years old in the accident. Did he know the truth? Could she even find a way to ask him?

"So," said Sahara. "I know that we haven't always been on the best of terms in the past—"

"You say that like it's our fault," shouted Anja. "He put a virus in my head and controlled my mind!"

"Anja!" shouted Sahara. "Will you please let me finish!"

Remember why we're doing this, Marisa sent to her. Anja closed her eyes and nodded.

Sahara looked back at Omar. "We need fifteen thousand yuan."

His eyes went wide, but he recovered quickly. "That's what I like about you girls: you are endlessly surprising."

"We know it's a lot—" started Marisa, but Omar waved her quiet with his hand.

"The amount isn't an issue," he said. "*If* I like what you're going to do with it."

Sahara nodded, glanced at the other girls, and then looked back at Omar with her most professional demeanor. "Mirador is dying," she said.

Omar shrugged. "Tell me something I don't know."

"Most people can barely afford to live—"

"You need rent money?" asked Omar.

"No," said Sahara.

"You want to save the restaurant?" he asked. "Done. I'll give you thirty thousand if you need it."

"You know Carlo Magno would never accept it," said Sahara. "We're here for more of a . . . business deal. The high price of telecom service is bleeding this city dry, and neighborhoods like Mirador are being squeezed even harder than most—"

"We want to take down KT Sigan," said Marisa. Omar didn't want to hear all this background stuff; he wanted the juicy details. "We've hacked them, and we've found a way to crush them, but we need your help. Fifteen thousand yuan, and Sigan goes away—not from everywhere, but at least from here. Out of LA, maybe out of the US entirely."

Omar stared at them, so silent they could hear the sound of a distant hose from the man washing cars in the garage. After a moment Omar laughed. "And here I thought you surprised me before. You've just moved past 'shocking' and all the way to 'flabbergasting.'"

"There's no way that's a real word," said Anja.

"How can you bring down KT Sigan with fifteen thousand yuan?" he asked.

Marisa nodded. "We've found financial information that—"

"Our methods are our own," said Sahara. "You either trust us or you don't; the plan is beside the point."

"Fair enough," said Omar. "And I've certainly seen your skills up close and personal, so I have no reason to doubt you." Marisa started to thank him, but he cut her off with a look. "But lack of doubt is not the same as active trust."

"Cut the Scheiße and pay us," said Anja.

"If Mirador falls," said Marisa, "so do the Maldonados. You run this neighborhood like feudal lords—like it's your kingdom. But a king without a kingdom is just another homeless guy."

"Sigan is destroying Mirador," said Omar. "If you've noticed it, I promise you that my father and I have noticed the same. If people can't afford a basic utility, they start not paying for luxuries, and then the shops and the restaurants start going out of business, and people start moving out, and crime goes up and the utility companies charge more to cover for the lost customers and it's a vicious spiral that destroys neighborhoods. This year alone Mirador's had more Red Drinking Days than the previous two years combined, and it's only July. Get rid of Sigan's predatory pricing and the situation starts to normalize again. We're doing what we can—I know you think we're monsters, but at least give us credit as monsters who love our city. But there's only so much we can do. And we definitely can't destroy an international megacorp. No one can."

"Except another international megacorp," said Jaya.

Omar stared at them, appraising them like a jeweler with a tray full of stones. Would he see diamonds, or zinc?

"Fifteen thousand yuan," he said at last. He paused again, then smiled wickedly. "Even if you fail, just the privilege of watching is the bargain of the century."

"Then watch the final match of Forward Motion," said Marisa. "It'll be a doozy."

Omar grinned. "I never miss a Cherry Dogs game."

"So you'll help us?" asked Sahara.

"I'd be a fool not to."

"Don't you need to talk to your father?" asked Marisa. "I thought that we'd convince you, and then you'd convince him."

"I can speak for my father," said Omar. "It's part of my role in the business."

"Wait," said Anja. "One last time, just for the hell of it, let's ask ourselves if this is really worth it. We *know* him. Can we really trust him?"

The coral reef disappeared again, though this time it was replaced by a small grassy hill covered with little white rabbits.

"What does that mean?" asked Jaya.

"It means this house is creepy," said Sahara.

"It's fluffy bunnies," said Omar. "What's creepy about that?" He looked at Sahara a moment, but she looked back without speaking. "He's saying you should trust us."

The bunnies disappeared, but nothing replaced them.

The girls looked at each other. Sahara caught Anja's gaze and held it. "I know you don't trust Omar," she said. "Do you trust me?"

It felt like forever before Anja answered. "Yes."

"Done, then," said Omar. "I hope cash is okay?"

"Perfect," said Sahara.

"Where should I have it delivered?" he asked. "Sahara's place?"

"To this address," said Marisa, and blinked to send him the drop location C-Gull had arranged for the payment. She felt grateful and wary at the same time. "What do we owe you?"

"Didn't I make that clear when we started?" said Omar. "You owe me a favor."

TWENTY-FIVE

"All right," said Sahara. "This is it: round two. The quarterfinal." She bounced on her toes behind the curtain, shaking her nervousness out through her fingers. "We're ready for this."

"Ready," said Marisa. Fang, Anja, and Jaya echoed her: "Ready."

Earlier that morning, Pixel Pwnies had won in a bye, and World2gether had won their match against the Glitches, with no small amount of "lucky" lag spikes helping them along. Marisa felt guilty cheering for Sigan's team, but she couldn't help herself: if Chaewon's team was eliminated early, she might close the server exploit she was using to cheat, and Marisa needed that exploit open on Saturday.

But first, she thought, *we need to make it to Saturday.*

"Next up," said Su-Yun, "coming back from their stunning victory yesterday, the Cherry Dogs!" Marisa and her friends ran through the curtain, cheering and waving at the audience. Su-Yun smiled at them, then turned back to the audience. "Facing them today, on behalf of Eaql Communications, the Turkish national champions and Mediterranean regional champions: Canavar!" The Turkish team ran out to stand beside the Cherry Dogs, looking smug and superior. They were one of the best teams in the tournament. Marisa did her best to think positive thoughts: *Of course we can beat the Mediterranean regional champs.*

No sweat.

The Canavar Sniper, one of the two boys on the team, turned toward Marisa and discreetly flipped her off, carefully hidden from the cameras. Marisa ignored him.

When they finished their game, Your Mom would be playing Get Rekt Nerd, and the Cherry Dogs would play the winner on Friday in the semifinal. Marisa wondered which team they'd have a better chance against, but then shook her head and forced the thought out of her mind. They had to focus on this match first, or none of the rest of them mattered.

And Alain would disappear forever.

"Huddle up," said Sahara, and gathered the team in a tight circle. "We can do this: it's going to be hard, but we can do this. Our first win was pure luck, but that's going to help us here, and you know why? Because Canavar's going to underestimate us. You saw their faces—they could barely be bothered to wake up this morning. They think they've got it in the bag already. Stay sharp, listen to my calls, and back each other up. Hands together."

The put their hands in the middle of the circle, and shouted in unison: "Cherry Dogs forever!"

They sat down and plugged in, and moments later were standing in their private lobby. Marisa had chosen her favorite avatar, which was basically herself in a black stealth suit with red piping on the edges. Sahara wore her classic red dress, Fang wore her ragged shadow assassin costume, and Jaya was in one of her countless flowing, ethereal fantasy dresses. Anja, of course, was the odd one out: her avatar was dressed in a tutu, woolly rainbow socks, and a bulky blue sweater, with drooping fairy wings and a plastic magic wand.

"You look like a four-year-old playing dress-up," said Sahara.

"You look like a seventeen-year-old playing dress-up," said Anja.

Sahara raised an eyebrow but said nothing and turned to the group. "I want to do something flashy. We've got two viral videos under our belt so far, so let's go for another one. Just because we've got other things to play for doesn't mean we can't win a few more fans along the way."

"Play crazy!" said Anja.

Sahara nodded. "Keep your powersets basic: good all-around powers; good damage, defense, the whole thing. We don't know what Canavar's going to throw at us, so we need to be ready for anything. But here's the fun part: part of being ready for anything is staying mobile. I want everyone to play Flankers."

"Ooh," said Jaya. "I like it."

"That'll help us move around the map better and adapt to whatever they throw at us," said Sahara. "It also means no ranged powersets, though, so stock up on melee, buffs, and debuffs. Heartbeat and Quicksand, grab some crowd control to help manage the fights. Anja, we'll hold you back for wave-two picks."

"We're in the game now," said Anja, and waved her toy wand dramatically. "Call signs only!"

"Fine," said Sahara. "HappyFluffySparkleTime, we'll hold you back for wave-two picks. Let Heartbeat protect you, go high damage, and pick an element that targets their weaknesses."

"Jawohl," said Anja, and then the timer ended and they were thrown into the powerset selection screen. The four of them locked in their powers, and they waited to see what Canavar had chosen. The timer ended, and the game posted the first-wave picks. The Cherry Dogs studied them eagerly.

"Lots of defense," said Marisa.

"They're going tanky," said Jaya.

"Not just tanky," said Fang, "they're going for late game. Look at those powersets: Earth Melee? Magic Defense? Every one of those powersets is slow and steady, ramping up to a killer finale. By the time we hit the forty-five-minute mark they'll be unbeatable."

"I've seen this team build before," said Sahara. "Watch: they held back their General for wave two, but I guarantee she's going to go Defender with Light-Based Buff and Ranged. It's the best late-game combo in the catalog. So, Anja, go . . . Dark Melee?"

"No," said Anja.

"There's no time to argue about the call sign," said Sahara, looking at the timer. "Pick now, or you'll forfeit your slot."

"Not that," said Anja. "We have an opportunity to absolutely roll them. You want to play crazy?" She pointed at the display of Canavar's loadouts. "This is the best chance we're ever going to get."

"Thirty seconds," said Marisa.

"They *expect* me to pick Dark Melee," said Anja. "They're already specced against it with their other players. But if I go Tech Defense instead, their elements will be weak against me until they've leveled way up. They might be unstoppable at forty-five minutes, but they won't be able to touch us for the first thirty." She punched one hand into the other. "So we blitz them and win in twenty-nine."

"Nobody plays positions," said Fang, nodding in approval. "We ignore basic defense, we hammer the turrets, and they can't do anything to stop us."

"Fifteen seconds," said Marisa.

"This is insane," said Sahara.

"Only against any other team build in the world, yes," said Anja. She selected the powersets, and held her hand over the big red button that would lock them in. "Against this team, we'll destroy them."

"Ten seconds," said Marisa. "Come on."

"Do it," said Jaya.

"Seven seconds!" said Marisa.

Sahara sighed. "Play crazy."

Anja reached for the button . . .

. . . and the game froze.

Marisa's stomach seemed to plummet into a bottomless hole.

A lag spike.

They were going to lose Anja, forfeiting her spot because she hadn't locked in her powers by the end of the allotted time. Had Chaewon done this? Was she, or her lackey, watching with her finger on a button, laughing?

The game wasn't unfreezing. Why wasn't it unfreezing? How long would they have to wait? The timer had run out ages ago—

And then the game moved again, and Anja slammed her hand on the button over and over again, desperate to make it count: "Come on come on come on!"

One second left. The timer finished, and Anja was in.

"That almost gave me a heart attack," said Sahara.

"Keep moving," said Fang. "We can't risk that again."

They looked at the second-wave picks: the Canavar General chose exactly the powers Sahara was expecting. The power selection room disappeared, and the girls found themselves standing next to a vault in a dank European castle. The final timer was counting down, ready to start the game in ten seconds.

"I love this map," said Marisa, trying to lighten the mood. "All the drones are dragons."

"Okay," said Sahara. "There's only one way this is going to work: feed and starve. They get experience based on the level of the agent they kill, so don't let them kill anyone high level. Heartbeat, you're the designated corpse: drop your blind on whoever's the most dangerous, then sacrifice yourself to take as much of their damage as you can. You'll probably die twenty or thirty times in this match, and I don't want you to level at all."

"I . . . guess I can do that," said Marisa.

The timer finished, and a loud, sonorous cathedral bell rang out, starting the match. Sahara started running behind the first wave of minions—mail-clad knights with swords and shields—and the rest of the team fanned out to their starting spots.

"Yīnyǐng has the best high-level powersets," Sahara continued, her voice carried through the team comm channel, "so she's the one we feed: let her get the killing blow on everything you possibly can. She'll be a raging damage monster, Heartbeat will be a zombie, and the other team won't know what's going on."

"Can you imagine what they're even saying out there?" asked Jaya. "An all-Flanker team, with a Sniper playing defense and debuff. They must be going *nuts*!"

Sahara laughed. "Isn't it great?"

"Cherry Dogs!" shouted Marisa.

"Start normal," said Sahara. "Kill some dragons, get some XP, do your standard early-game stuff. They won't suspect anything yet. Yīnyǐng, call the signal when you're ready for the first ambush."

Marisa and Anja reached the roof—an uneven layer of medieval rooftops, made of stone and thatch—and started fighting the weaker dragons, running from group to group as quickly as they could. Marisa let Anja get all the XP, and kept her eyes on the enemy, wary of attacks, but nobody came after them. Canavar was playing textbook early-game tactics—hanging back, farming for gold and experience where they could, and using the minions to weaken the towers. Exactly what the Cherry Dogs were pretending to do. Marisa smiled: they didn't even know what was about to hit them.

"Ready for an ambush," said Fang. "Center turret in fifteen seconds."

Marisa and Anja sprinted to the nearest staircase, plunging down through a church steeple toward the city below. They reached it with perfect timing, and suddenly the enemy General found herself outnumbered five to two. Jaya rooted her in place with some vines, and the team dropped her before she could escape; the Canavar Guard did a fair amount of damage before running away, but Marisa didn't even have to sacrifice herself to save anyone. They beat on the turret for a while, then Sahara led them down a hole to the sewers to kill the Canavar Jungler. It was all over from there. The Cherry Dogs ignored their own defenses, their own minions, even their own vault—Canavar stole thousands of gold from them—but it didn't matter. Fang racked up kill after kill, and the enemy wasn't able to take out any agents except Marisa, who very studiously avoided killing anything and was thus barely worth any experience at all. The Cherry Dogs retreated each time she died, finding more minions or dragons or loners to fight, and then when Heartbeat respawned they dove back into the fray—and because Heartbeat was so low level, she was never dead for long. First one turret fell, then the next, and barely fifteen minutes into the game they were already beating down the defenses of the enemy vault.

The Canavar Sniper attacked Marisa from behind, and she died again. Nine times so far, according to her stat line. She looked at her respawn timer, and it occurred to her: she'd never checked to see how long she would actually have to get into Sigan's system, assuming they made it to the final. She thought about blinking out to check the back door again, but she didn't have time. At such a low level, she was respawning too quickly. She reappeared at the vault, and ran out to join the others.

"I'm really starting to hate this Sniper," said Anja. "Just

because he kills Heartbeat all the time doesn't mean he needs to teabag the corpse."

"His name's Abouti Sahin," said Fang. "Most of this team's actually pretty cool, but Abouti's a wángbādàn."

"Somebody murder him, then," said Marisa.

"Five times so far," said Fang.

Fang had nearly double the levels of any Canavar player, and even Sahara and Jaya had outleveled their top player. Anja's all-out blitz strategy would have crashed and burned against any other team, but Canavar's late-game strategy was simply too weak in the early game to stop them, and even the constant lag spikes weren't enough to slow their momentum. The Canavar players did their best, and were actually starting to rally as their strategy finally got rolling, but the Cherry Dogs didn't win in twenty-nine minutes.

They won in twenty-seven.

The Canavar vault went down, the minions started dancing, and Marisa blinked out of the game as fast as she could, turning off the VR and waking up to the auditorium going wild.

"That's becoming one of my favorite sounds," said Sahara. She was grinning so widely she looked ready to burst.

Marisa stood up, basking in the applause, and then jerked her head toward the shell-shocked Canavar team. "Let's go say hi."

"Yup," said Sahara. They walked to the other team, the other girls following behind, and started smiling and shaking hands. "Good game," said Sahara, treating each opponent like they were her best friend. "You did a great job. We're going to steal that Jungler build one day—it was amazing. Good game."

"You think you can make it to the final?" asked Abouti. He

stood in front of Marisa with his legs planted firmly, his hands on his hips. His face was an angry sneer.

"I hope so," said Marisa, and stuck out her hand. "Good game."

"You can't make it," said Abouti, ignoring her hand. "You got lucky twice, and that's not going to happen a third time. Get Rekt Nerd will wreck you."

"Hence the name, I guess," said Marisa. She wanted to smack him, but they were surrounded by cameras. She hesitated a moment, then got a wicked idea. She cocked her head to the side: "But you're assuming Get Rekt Nerd will win their game today. You don't think Your Mom can win?"

Abouti sniffed. "Of course not."

"Probably not," Marisa agreed. "I actually don't think Your Mom can win anything. Your Mom sucks."

"Then that's one thing we agree on," said Abouti, and his eyes narrowed. "But it's the only thing."

Marisa smiled. "Good talking to you."

Abouti fumed a moment longer but walked away, and Jaya sidled up next to Marisa. "Don't worry, I got that whole thing on video."

"That makes up for every time he killed me."

"Did you have a chance to . . ." Jaya trailed off, and sent the rest of her question in a private message: **Did you have a chance to check on the back door?**

No, sent Marisa. **I was respawning too quickly. But I'm worried: even if I wrote a script that could search the database for me, I don't think I'd have time to blink out, crack**

the security, activate the script, and get back in before respawning, even if I were higher level. There'd be obvious dead time where my avatar just stood there doing nothing, and someone would start to notice.

Which we can't risk, sent Jaya. **Sigan's already suspicious of us—they're probably watching every move we make in here.**

We have to think of something, sent Marisa. **Or this whole plan is going to fail.**

TWENTY-SIX

"I think I've figured out how to do it," said Jaya. All of the Cherry Dogs but Anja—she was at home, playing the dutiful daughter to their corporate sponsor—were sitting in Sahara's tiny living room, stretched out on floors and couches while a little plastic fan tried valiantly to create a cooling cross breeze between two open windows. It wasn't working. The sound of cars and distant, drunken singing drifted in through the screens.

The sounds of home, thought Marisa.

"It has to be fast," said Sahara. "There's no way we can let Mari be gone for more than a few seconds."

"But what if we can let her be gone for minutes?" asked Jaya, eyes wide. "Maybe even the whole match?"

"Aha," said Sahara. "You want to run her as a bot."

"Bots are illegal," said Marisa. "You don't think they've got measures in place to keep us from using them?"

"Hacking into megacorp databases is also illegal," said Jaya, "and to a much higher authority."

"I just don't think we can get away with it," said Marisa.

"I like the idea in theory," said Sahara. "Spotter is already a support position, so if we spec her for pure support—heals and buffs, all targeting Anja—we could run her as a bot and her behavior won't look out of place to anyone watching. Her connection might look wonky to whoever's monitoring the game servers, though, and that's where we run into trouble."

"All their anti-bot stuff is designed for doubled signals," said Fang. "People running a buffbot through their own djinni, or on a second computer through a single ID. Stuff like that. But no one's tried to run an automated player script out of their own head, instead of playing themselves. It might work."

Marisa stared at the open window. "It might, but only if I'm out of the game completely. As soon as I turn on the bot script and let it take over, even if I blink out immediately, there'll be a little window when the game is registering two separate controllers behind my avatar, and that's exactly what a referee program would be looking for. We'd have to initiate the bot before the game even starts—which means it would have to do more than just play, it'd have to pick its own costume and powers."

"That will be tricky," said Jaya.

"The game starts even earlier than that," said Fang. "You'd have to get out before the server even authenticates your ID—pretty much as soon as you plug in to the VR chair. The bot would have to be in charge the whole time, with you as a passenger, instead of the other way around."

"That's creepy," said Marisa.

"And dangerous," said Sahara. "What if something went wrong? What if the bot glitched and started running into walls, or something else that's obviously scripted? We can't risk Marisa's avatar going completely off the rails without some way of regaining control."

"Do you have any better ideas?" asked Jaya.

"I'm not nixing the bot idea," said Sahara. "I'm just saying we need to find a way of hiding the switch between one controller and the other." She thought for a moment. "How about the lag spikes?"

Marisa frowned. "What do you mean?"

Sahara leaned forward. "The lag spikes are already a jumble of data, where the servers lose information from everyone connected, and have to invent data to make up for it. Double connections will just appear to be part of the mess. And we know there's going to be lag over the course of the match. So we set up the bot script to trigger when the lag hits: on the first spike, Mari pops out and lets the bot take over, and on the next one, she pops back in. Back and forth, all through the match."

"That's not going to be easy," said Jaya. "The timing would have to be perfect."

"Which means the switch would have to be involuntary," said Sahara. "If you take the time to decide whether you want to switch or not, you're adding seconds to a process that's only measured in milliseconds. That might be too chaotic."

"I can handle it," said Marisa. "If I bring another program or two, like my Goblins, then they can do the search for me—when

I'm in the database the bot can play the game, and when I'm in the game the Goblins can search the database. I'll just bounce back and forth and maintain them both."

"Can you do it fast enough?" asked Sahara. "You said at the gala you needed hours to download everything, and there's no way we can drag this match out longer than an hour. Ninety minutes at most."

"And assuming World2gether makes the final, Zi's going to be gunning for us," said Fang. "This will be a revenge match, for both her and Chaewon. It won't be easy to stall if they're playing aggressively."

"I know what I need to find this time," said Marisa, "and I know more or less where it is. I'll code up some Goblins who can get it all in an hour, easy." She grimaced. "I hope?"

"And meanwhile," said Fang, "we still have to win our semifinal match tomorrow."

"Against Your Mom?" asked Sahara, in mock horror. "You want us to beat Your Mom?"

"I can't believe Your Mom beat Get Rekt Nerd," said Fang.

"I can't believe you're all *still* making Your Mom jokes," said Jaya. "That got old days ago."

"It's literally my new favorite thing in the world," said Marisa. "I'm, like, that team's biggest fan now."

"You're going to have to get over it, then," said Sahara. "And I don't know how we're going to get past them. We can't rely on luck three games in a row."

"The first game was luck," said Marisa. "The second one was brilliant skill and metagaming."

"Made possible by luck," said Sahara. "How would that game have gone if Canavar's powerset picks hadn't gone exactly down that one specific line, and we didn't have an immediate counter? We were smart enough to recognize our good luck, and we played well enough to take advantage of it, but it was still luck. These teams are pros. All Your Mom has to do tomorrow is build a normal team, and not get greedy in a vault raid, and they nullify every advantage we've had this whole tournament. We have to raise our game."

"And program a bot script," said Jaya. "And hack a corporate database, and plant a bunch of TEDs, and infiltrate a skyscraper, and break out a prisoner, and escape from a cybernetic super thug, and, what am I forgetting—cause a riot?"

"I hope not," said Marisa. "My family's going to be there."

"You forgot one more thing," said Sahara. "We've figured out how to get and find the data, but we still need to get that data back out again."

Fang frowned. "That's called 'downloading.' It's like the easiest part of this whole thing."

"I'm even on a hard-line connection," said Marisa, "so it'll be a super-fast download once we find what we're after."

"But it'll also be traceable," said Sahara. "Part of your brilliant plan is to leave no fingerprints, right? So they can't ever trace it back to us. So what happens when the data goes public, and they check their server logs and see that that exact data was transferred into your djinni? You can't download it directly—the only option is to download it onto the Overworld server."

"That's not going to be easy, unless we can disguise it as

something." Jaya scrunched up her mouth, thinking. "And then we still have to be able to pull it down ourselves at some point."

Marisa's jaw dropped. "Oh baby." She raised her arms, striking a series of poses. "Bow down to me, I just figured it out."

"You're amazing," said Sahara. "What is it?"

"The costume creator," said Marisa, pointing at her. "That's the hole in the armor—they've allowed us to link our personal game accounts to the tournament servers, so that everyone could use their own avatars and costumes, and that includes the costume creator."

"How does that help us?" asked Sahara.

"Because the costume creator lets you upload your own images and textures," said Marisa. "It stores them in a central database, and calls them up when you load an avatar that uses them. So we download the files into that database, and link them to one of my costumes as image files. They won't actually render as images, but I can still link them, and they'll be loaded into my own game account. Then all I have to do is pull them out later, whenever I want."

"Zhēn bàng," said Fang.

"I've played with the costume creator a lot," said Jaya. "It won't link image files unless the costume is in active memory—like, in the creator interface. Even if you can figure out how to do it outside of that interface—"

"That shouldn't be hard," said Marisa.

"—you'll still need to use a costume in active memory," said Jaya.

"So you'll have to be wearing it at the time," said Sahara.

"Which means you need a costume with a blank layer, that you can add a new image to in the middle of play."

"Maybe a cloud effect?" asked Fang. "You can even make those transparent."

"They're not big enough," said Marisa. "This is going to be a ton of data, so we'll need to spread out across a lot of little spaces. And if they can be hidden, that's ideal."

Sahara pursed her lips. "So. What kind of a costume has a whole ton of hidden layers?"

"And when will you have time to design it?" asked Jaya.

"I won't," said Marisa. "Which is why it's super handy to have a friend who makes Overworld costumes for a living."

Sahara smiled. "Time to call WinterFox."

TWENTY-SEVEN

With only two matches to play on Friday, the tournament staged them one at a time, so that everyone who wanted to could watch both of them live. The Cherry Dogs and Your Mom would play first; World2gether had gone first during the other rounds, but Marisa suspected Chaewon was probably sick of losing the spotlight to the Cherry Dogs' out-of-nowhere wins and ridiculous upsets. She wanted to go last today, so that her performance would be at the top of everyone's mind going into the final.

"Your Mom will be expecting us to do something crazy," said Sahara, discussing strategy as they rode the train to the event. Anja was taking her father's car, and was patched in through a voice call. "They'll go for high speed and mobility, like we did yesterday, so they can respond to whatever weird thing we do. Our best bet to counter it is to play as safe as we can—nothing flashy, nothing risky, just a clean, efficient, well-played game of

Overworld. No wasted steps, no wasted shots."

"Sounds boring," said Anja.

"It sounds smart," said Sahara. "I've gone along with your plans all week—this time trust me, and follow mine. We'll undercut their mobility by not giving them anything crazy to respond to, and if they decide to blitz us with team fights, we'll be ready for that, too."

"I trust you," said Marisa. She looked at the others. "We know we can win this on skill instead of gimmicks—let's show everyone else."

"Take powersets you know," said Sahara. "The ones you know backward and forward—the ranges down to the centimeter, the timings down to the second."

"You got it," said Fang. "I know the Decay Melee set so well I could count the timers in my sleep."

"That's insane," said Anja.

"That's how you win," said Fang.

"That's what I like to hear," said Jaya. She looked at the group. "Let's do it." She put out her hand, and Marisa and Sahara put theirs on top of it. Fang looked at them from across the aisle of the train car, and glanced uncomfortably at the rest of the passengers.

"Come on, Fang," said Marisa.

"Cherry Dogs forever," Sahara prompted.

"What's going on?" asked Anja's voice. "Are you doing a team hand thing? You can't do a team hand thing without me."

"Yeah," said Fang. She folded her arms.

Sahara glared, but then took her hand back. "Fine," she said. "Cherry Dogs *eventually*."

The five Your Mom players were waiting for them backstage at the convention center.

"I can't believe you made it this far," said Diamante. Marisa had looked their team up, and even watched a few replays of their old games. They were just as unpredictable as the Cherry Dogs, which was going to make this an interesting match.

"I believe it," said Moreno. He turned to Marisa. "You guys have a good team."

"Your Mom has a good team," said the girl, Nomura.

Marisa stared at her, then shook her head. "That's . . . really not as much fun when other people do it."

"Your Mom's not as much fun when other people do—"

"Whoa," said Sproatagonist. He stepped in quickly, interrupting the girl and holding out his hand. "Hi, sorry about that. We met the other night but we didn't really get a chance to introduce ourselves. I'm Ethan Sproat, and this is our Sniper, Maija-Liisa Nomura."

"I'm Marisa Carneseca," said Marisa. The girl was still staring at her, so she said the first nice thing she could think of. "I love your name. Where's it from?"

"Where's Your Mom from?" asked Nomura.

"Is that . . ." Marisa looked at the other players. ". . . seriously all she says?"

"Mostly," said Moreno.

"Her name is Finnish-Japanese," said Diamante.

"I didn't know that was a thing," said Marisa.

"I didn't know Your Mom was a thing," said Nomura.

"That doesn't even make sense," snapped Marisa. "That's

more of an insult on your team than it is on me—"

"Next up!" Su-Yun Kho's voice boomed through the loudspeaker. "The Cherry Dogs!"

Marisa hesitated, staring at the girl, then ran out through the curtain with the rest of her team. She could hear the Your Mom players laughing behind her.

"They're just trying to get under your skin," Sahara whispered. "Ignore them. You're a Zen master. This is going to be the best game of Overworld you've ever played."

"I'm a Zen master," whispered Marisa. She wondered if she said it enough, she'd actually believe it.

They plugged in to their chairs and chose their powersets, keeping it simple and safe. Your Mom's first-wave picks were, as expected, heavy on mobility, but since the Cherry Dogs weren't skewed toward one single strategy, that mobility would mostly be wasted. Anja used her second-wave pick to target the opposing Sniper and Spotter, and they started the game.

It was the most grueling game of Overworld they'd ever played.

Sahara's plan was sound, but carrying it out was exhausting. "Play flawlessly" wasn't exactly a revolutionary strategy, and the two teams settled down into a fast-paced game of wits and reflexes, each trying to play as smoothly as possible, hoping the other team would blink and screw up first. Marisa felt like her brain was working overtime, laser-focused on each use of her powers, each shot from her weapons. Was she timing it right? Was she aiming it right? Was she even in the right part of the map? The game arena was an African jungle, loosely modeled on the

Ngorongoro Crater, and she stalked through the trees with Anja, intense and ready to snap.

"You need to loosen up," said Anja.

"We have to be perfect—if we lose, we lose so much more than just a match."

"You'll be more perfect if you're loose."

Five minutes later, after both sides retreated from a skirmish, Sahara broadcast to the team while they set up for another wave of minions. "This is good. You saw the way they fought? The way they backed out when it started to go against them? They're trying to wear down our defenses, but we're specced for stamina. That's already giving us an edge."

Two minutes later the first lag spike hit, right in the middle of the first major team fight. Marisa was dodging an attack from Diamante—whose call sign, in a rare move, was Diamante—when suddenly the game froze, his sword hanging above her head, and all she could do was dodge, activate her nanobot armor, and hope that the hit didn't register. When the game snapped back a few seconds later, she was at full health and Diamante was almost dead, hit from behind by an attack from Fang. Marisa moved smoothly from dodging to attacking, and she and Fang finished him off while the rest of his team retreated.

"That lag spike came in one of the few skirmishes we've had all game," said Sahara, her breathing heavy from the fight. "It's got to be Chaewon. She's trying to get one of us killed and tip the scales."

"She tipped them the wrong way," said Anja. "This match is too close for her to risk any more of those—we're going to get a lot less lag the rest of the game, just watch."

Marisa wanted to try the bot script, to make sure their code was ready for the big day, but they couldn't afford the risk. If the code was bad, and she was locked out while her bot script did something stupid, they'd lose for sure. They couldn't afford a single mistake.

As the game wore on, they realized Anja was right. The game had less lag than they'd ever experienced before in the tournament; this made it more predictable, and each side pressed their advantages when they could. The Cherry Dogs won another team fight, dropping Sproatagonist and Sinister Ditz—Nomura's avatar—and used that victory to push hard against a turret, though they didn't quite drop it before Your Mom came back to defend it, killing Jaya in the process. The match stayed painfully even, seesawing back and forth as one team and then the other claimed a brief upper hand, but ever so slowly, bit by bit and shot by shot, the Cherry Dogs pulled ahead. They didn't do anything flashy, they didn't do anything crazy. They just played as well as they possibly could, maximizing their efforts, and the statistics added up. At one hour and three minutes, the Your Mom vault exploded. Marisa collapsed in the loam of the jungle floor, as exhausted as if she'd just run a marathon.

"How can virtual reality be this tiring?" asked Anja.

"You're only virtually tired," said Sahara. "Your actual muscles are fine. Jack out."

Marisa blinked, leaving the game and sitting up in the real world. Her body felt fine, but her mind felt like pancake batter. She swung her legs off the chair, only peripherally aware of the cheering crowd, and stared at the floor. She pulled the plug from the back of her neck, but that was about all she could muster.

"Get up," said Jaya. "We need to 'good game' them."

"Coming," said Marisa. She stood up, ready to follow her friends to Your Mom's side and congratulate them, but when she looked up she realized that Your Mom was already on their side, smiling and shaking their hands.

"Good game," said Diamante. "Juegas bien."

"Gracias," said Marisa, "tú también."

"Not as good as you," he said, "at least not today. I've never seen anyone play like that."

"Thank you," said Marisa again. "You're very kind."

"I thought your team was a gimmick," said a voice behind her. Marisa turned, and her jaw dropped when she saw Su-Yun Kho. The older player smiled, and bowed slightly. "No one can say that after today."

Marisa bowed back, struggling to remember the proper Korean etiquette from her classes at school. "Thank you."

"You've made it to the final," said Su-Yun. "No matter what happens tomorrow against World2gether, remember today."

Marisa frowned, confused. "I thought they hadn't played yet."

Su-Yun's face hardened. "Do you honestly think there's any chance they'll lose?" She didn't say anything else, but the scorn was obvious on her face.

Marisa was suddenly conscious of the cameras watching them, and did her best to smile. "They're a great team, and I look forward to playing against whoever wins the semifinal."

Su-Yun put her hand on Marisa's shoulder, held it there for a moment, then moved on to congratulate Sahara.

"Never wash that shoulder again," said Diamante. "Actually: Can I buy that shirt?"

"Touch it," said Marisa. He put his hand reverently where Su-Yun's had been. "Feel the power."

"Beat them tomorrow," said Diamante, pulling his hand away. "Beat them like a broken drum."

"We'll do our best," said Marisa.

A message popped up in her djinni display, bright red and bouncing in agitation. She saw that it was from Fang, and looked up to find her; she was on the other side of the crowd, looking back with wide, nervous eyes. Marisa frowned and blinked on the message:

C-Gull sent me the drop-off coordinates. He'll meet us with the shipment at ten p.m.

"We're going to be so tired tomorrow," said Bao.

"Sorry," said Marisa.

"Don't worry about it," he said, looking up at the stars. "If you hadn't brought me out here at three in the morning, I never would have known that LA can get chilly."

"Thank you for coming," said Sahara. "All of you. This is important, and we need all the help we can get."

The group of friends were clustered together in an alley downtown: Bao, Marisa, Sahara, Anja, Jaya, Fang, Jin, Jun, and their old friend Jennifer Stashwick—WinterFox. Even Marisa's older brother Chuy was there.

"Thanks again for being here," Marisa whispered, leaning

close to Chuy's side. He was a head taller than she was, and covered with tattoos. Given what they were doing tonight, no one would have made her feel safer. "I hope it didn't cause any problems."

"I figure my hermanita deserves at least a couple of hours," said Chuy with a smile. "Three a.m. just means it's easier to get away without bothering the kid."

The highway was a distant rumble, and other parts of the city were alive with activity, but they were in the business district, just a few blocks from KT Sigan, and the world was dark and empty.

"You all know the plan," said Sahara. Her camera nulis were at home, silently watching two beds and couch that had been carefully made up to look like Sahara, Jaya, and Fang were sleeping in them. Marisa had asked if that was really necessary, and Sahara had replied that it wasn't just about deception: she averaged three thousand viewers while she was sleeping, and she couldn't afford to lose the numbers. Marisa shuddered again at the thought, and Sahara continued her speech. "We've made it to the finals, we've picked up the TEDs from our arms dealer—"

"I *love* saying that," said Anja. "'*Our arms dealer.*'"

"—and tomorrow's the big day," Sahara finished. "All we have to do now is get the last little pieces in place. You know your roles. Any questions?"

"Is the costume finished?" asked Fang.

Jennifer smiled. "Down to the last pretty bow."

"Ooh," said Jaya, "Mari gets to wear pretty bows? What does the costume look like?"

"You'll see," said Jennifer.

"I still can't believe you got it done so fast," said Marisa.

"I already had a perfect one in my catalog," said Jennifer. "All I had to do was go in and pull out the interior image files."

Sahara nodded. "And it has enough storage space for the data we're dealing with?"

"Trust me," said Jennifer. "This has enough storage space for the entire Sigan database. I even preloaded it, like you asked—three of the image fields have your Goblins, stored as compressed files. Another one has the decompression program. Once you get into their system, you'll have access to everything you need."

"Here you go, then," said Sahara, and handed her a black bag. "You and Fang take Jejune—it's two blocks north."

"Got it on GPS," said Fang.

The two girls turned and ran off, and Sahara handed out more bags. "Jin and Jun, you do the Carrot Cafe. Anja and Jaya, you take The Crèche. Mari and Chuy, you have Solipsis." The others ran off, but Chuy hung back, and Marisa stayed to hear his question.

"And you're sure this is going to work?" he asked. "I mean, breaking into a megacorp I understand, but a fast food place?"

"We're breaking into the fast food places to help us break into the megacorp," said Marisa.

"With the four cafes we're hitting," said Sahara, "we should have the whole office building pretty well covered. It took Jaya and me a full day of hacking to get access to the ordering histories, but these are definitely the right cafes."

"So the employees order lunch from these places," said Chuy. "I get that. But how does that help *you* get in—what are you going to do, hide yourself in the delivery nulis?"

"No," said Bao, "we're hiding bombs in the nulis."

Chuy smirked in disbelief. "What?"

"Only two," said Sahara, hefting a larger black sack bulkier than the others. "And they're not delivery nulis, they're gardeners. That's what Bao and I are off to do." She looked at Bao. "You have the rest of the stuff?"

"A clean phone and a gun," said Bao, holding up the two items.

"You're serious?" asked Chuy. "What, are you going to shoot somebody?"

"Of course not," said Bao, and tapped the gun on his head. "It's a plastic prop—Sahara printed it out this afternoon." He tucked the items away, and glanced at Marisa. "Didn't you tell him the plan?"

"I didn't have time," said Marisa.

"Then explain it on the way," said Sahara.

"Here's your end of the phone line," said Bao, and handed her a small dermal patch. "It's Eaql brand, believe it or not. They had the best match for your skin tone."

"I'll remember to thank Canavar," said Marisa, taking it from him and turning it over in her hand. "How'd you match my skin so well?"

"Just a good memory," said Bao, and looked at Sahara. "Ready?"

"Let's go hack a gardener," said Sahara. She slung the bag of explosives over her shoulder. "See you tomorrow, Mari. Call me if something goes wrong."

"Cherry Dogs forever," said Marisa.

"Cherry Dogs forever," said Sahara. She and Bao turned and ran off into the darkness.

"Our job is Solipsis," said Marisa, dropping the dermal phone in her pocket. "Follow me."

Chuy pointed at the pocket. "Aren't you going to put it on?"

"That's for tomorrow. Tonight we're on our own." She jogged to the end of the alley, Chuy close behind, but they slowed at the corner and peered out carefully for any sign of police nulis. Some of the protesters were sleeping in the plaza in front of the Sigan building, and the whole area was under even more scrutiny than it usually was. She saw nothing, and blinked to switch her vision to infrared. Still no nulis.

"Wait," whispered Chuy, holding her back with his hand when she tried to run out. "Over there." He pointed to the far side of the street, high on the right, and when Marisa stared at it long enough a faint red signal lit up her vision. "Security nuli."

"I didn't even see it," Marisa whispered. "This infrared sucks."

"Because you're using a free app," said Chuy, and tapped the side of his head. "La Sesenta bought me the real stuff."

"So you can be lookout for all your little gang crimes?"

"You're the one breaking into a damn restaurant," said Chuy.

"Touché," said Marisa. The police nuli moved, turning a corner to patrol the next street. "Go."

They ran across the street and into another alley, making their way around the base of a massive skyscraper. Marisa carefully threw a miniature TED at each wall-mounted camera they passed, cutting the signal just long enough to get by. At the end of the alley stood a tall bay door, where delivery nulis could come and go in flocks during the lunch-hour rush. Marisa turned around, looking back the way they'd come, while Chuy used a pistol-shaped device to pick the lock.

"Got it," he said. He turned around and took his turn as lookout, while Marisa faced the door and blinked at it, opening her mapping program. A green grid overlaid the entire alleyway, outlining the wall in one-inch increments.

"Seven inches from the left edge," she murmured, remembering the numbers she'd found in her research. "Five feet up." She marked the spot with another blink, fixing a red dot to the exact coordinate, and then walked toward it. The dot stayed firm, and she placed a miniature TED directly on top of it. Then she triggered the electromagnetic pulse, and heard a faint pop from the other side of the room. "That's it, let's go."

Chuy grabbed the door and rolled it open about ten inches. Marisa slithered through the gap, and Chuy followed; they closed the door just before the police nuli came back.

Marisa held her breath, but it didn't seem to have noticed them.

Chuy stood up, brushing himself off. They were in the kitchen of the Solipsis Cafe, dark and quiet. The ceiling was covered with delivery nulis, hanging from charging stations like bats in a cave. A small metal box on the wall was smoking—a single, slender tendril of smoke rose up from a gap in its side. Chuy tapped it.

"Interior security system," he said. "Right where you said it would be."

Marisa stood up next to him. "I'm amazing."

"Those little TED things are awesome," he said. "Who's your

hookup again? I need to get some."

"You know I don't want to help your gang," said Marisa.

"But you don't mind taking help when you need it."

"My crime isn't going to get anybody killed," said Marisa. "La Sesenta is not worth it."

"La Sesenta is the only reason I even have a house," said Chuy. "They take care of me—and my family."

"And they make you pay for it by risking serious jail time."

"Are you really one to talk right now?"

Marisa sighed, and closed her eyes. "I'm sorry," she said. "I didn't bring you here to argue."

Chuy folded his arms sternly. "You're not exactly telling me your plan, either."

"You want to know the plan?" She walked to the preparation table in the center of the room. "First, we hide all of these." She dumped out the black bag Sahara had given her, making a pile of forty or so TEDs on the table.

"That's . . . a lot," said Chuy. "Where do we hide them?"

Marisa smiled. "Where do you think?" She opened the tall metal fridge, and pulled out a tray covered with dozens of small plastic cups, each topped with a snap-on plastic lid. "We hide them in the best salad dressing you've ever tasted."

TWENTY-EIGHT

"Ladies and gentlemen!" Su-Yun Kho's voice echoed through the convention center, booming from the massive speakers over the enthusiastic crowd. "Welcome to the final match of the Forward Motion charity tournament!"

"Hold still," said the makeup artists, dabbing at Marisa's face with a brush. "You have plenty of time."

Marisa looked away from the stage door, trying to stay motionless. "Sorry. I'm just nervous."

"We'll be fine," said Jaya. It was almost noon, and time for the final to begin.

Zi called over from her own makeup chair, on the other side of the room. "Don't worry, we'll make it quick."

Sahara smirked, and glanced at Marisa from the side of her eye. "That's the same thing she tells all the boys she tries to kiss."

"I just want to say how happy I am to be playing in this match with you," said Chaewon. Her angry scowl was gone, and she was back in pretty princess mode, smiling beatifically at everyone in the room. "We've had our differences in the past, but today we can put that all behind us, come together as athletes, and help make the world a better place."

"And that," said Anja, "is what *she* says to all the boys *she* tries to kiss."

Chaewon continued smiling, shaking her head in that special, condescending way she had.

"And this," said Bubba, carefully adjusting her trucker hat, "is what I say when I kiss a boy." She stood up, planted her feet, and held her hands out to the side, as if inviting them to fight her. "You are not remotely ready for this."

"You're supposed to say 'try to kiss,'" said Jaya. "You messed up the whole pattern."

"Kiss or kiss not," said Bubba. "There is no try."

"I take issue with your concept of consent," said Sahara.

"I take issue with your face," hissed Bubba.

"Your Mom takes issue with your face," said Marisa. "At least, I assume they do; everyone else does."

"Can you even afford to import your jokes like that?" asked Zi. "That feels a little out of your price range."

"Said the paid escort," murmured Fang.

"Shut up, Fang," said Zi. Fang looked back down at the floor.

"Sorry," said Sahara, anger seething under her voice. "Not all of us have lucrative jobs cheating at Overworld as a paid best friend."

Zi smiled, though there was no humor behind it. "Who said

anything about cheating?"

"I'm sorry," said Anja. "Are we pretending you didn't cheat your way through this whole tournament? What's the cover story, then? I can't even think of a plausible one."

Marisa glanced up at Cameron and Camilla, dutifully streaming the entire scene to Sahara's viewers. They'd been so careful throughout their planning to keep any hints of their criminal activities off camera. Was it wise to bring up the cheating so brazenly? What if someone involved with the tournament was watching, and decided to take a closer look at what was happening during the lag spikes? This was already going to be tough enough as it was.

"Of course we've been cheating." The smile on Zi's face was now downright evil. "Chaewon's been manipulating the lag spikes since the very first game."

Marisa's eyes went wide, and she kept her face forward, not daring to look at the cameras. Instead she looked at Chaewon, whose face had fallen—she didn't look sad, or angry, or disappointed, just blank. The same broken-doll face she'd made when Anja had insulted her at the party.

None of the other girls said anything, too shocked that Zi had brought it out so abruptly into the open. Even the makeup techs looked stunned. Bubba glanced up the cameras, more pale than Marisa had ever seen her.

"But now," said Zi, standing up slowly from her makeup chair, "I'm delighted to report that the cheating is over. I've figured out who Chaewon was paying off in the tournament server room, and let's just say he won't be responding to her messages anymore." She raised herself to her full height, and stared at them with hate-filled superiority. "When I beat you today, you won't have any excuses."

"Dagchyeo!" growled one of the girls behind Chaewon.

Marisa was already shocked; now she was almost paralyzed with a sudden burst of fear and indecision. Did this mean the lag spikes would be random—as the tournament originally intended—or that there would be no lag spikes at all? They needed those lag spikes—their entire plan depended on it. How else was she going to flip in and out of the game and trigger the bot script? She had to think of something. . . .

One of the red-jacketed stage managers poked her head through the doorway, Su-Yun's voice still booming in the background. "Sixty seconds. We need everyone onstage now."

The two teams stood up, filing into lines. Sahara gestured for World2gether to go first, but Zi shook her head.

"Ladies first," said Zi.

"Who goes second?" asked Sahara.

Zi smirked. "Goddesses."

Sahara raised an eyebrow but jerked her head toward the door, and the Cherry Dogs walked out first.

Marisa sent a message to the group as they lined up behind the curtain: **What do we do?**

You're sure the bot script works? sent Sahara.

More or less, sent Jaya. **We couldn't test it on a real Overworld server, because it's designed specifically for this closed network.**

If I time it right, said Marisa, **I should be able to activate the script and blink out right at the end of the powerset**

selection screen. Right as the game starts. But I won't be able to get back in without triggering the anti-cheating software.

If you're in Sigan's system, sent Fang, **you might be able to get into the game servers and initiate a lag spike yourself.**

You want us to cheat? asked Anja.

Fang's answer was simple: **What else are we going to do?**

Marisa sighed, and sent a message to Bao. **Ready?**

His answer took several seconds—he couldn't just think a message like a normal person, but had to take out his phone, read the text, and type a message back with his fingers. **Ready,** he answered. **You've got that dermal phone?**

Marisa nodded, touching the derm lightly in the space behind her ear, hidden even from the makeup artist. It was like a tiny bandage, but it could pick up her subvocal vibrations and make a voice call just like a djinni. She activated it, and heard Bao's voice in her ear.

"Hey," he said. "Welcome to KT Sigan's finest custodial closet."

"They have human janitors?" she asked. The question was inaudible to anyone standing next to her, but crystal clear to Bao on the other end of the line.

"Just nulis," he said. "So I'm dressed as a nuli maintenance guy."

"And now," said the amplified voice of Su-Yun Kho, "the wait is over. Let's bring out our players! First up: the one, the only, the Cinderella story of the Forward Motion tournament . . . the Cherry Dogs!"

"Talk to you soon," said Marisa, and followed her friends as they ran through the curtain and onto the stage. The lights were bright, and the audience was cheering, but Marisa was too nervous to enjoy it. Sahara stepped forward, reveling in it, tanking the social aggro so the rest of them could get a moment to breathe. Marisa planned her moves, trying to work out from memory where in the database the Overworld tournament server settings would be, and thus where the lag spike program might be hidden. If the script went wrong, and she had no way to get back in, everything would collapse—not just the game and tournament, but the mission as well. They'd know she'd been doing something else instead of playing, and when the hacked information was revealed, it would be obvious that she had been behind it. The only way this plan didn't land her in jail—or worse—was if they never linked it back to her. She shook her feet and her one human hand, so nervous her non-prosthetic extremities were numb. This is what it came down to—this is what it all depended on.

An untested healbot in a video game.

Su-Yun finished her intro, and the players jogged to their VR chairs. Marisa lay down and plugged in, feeling a sudden relief of tension as her nerve-wracked physical body was suddenly replaced with a virtual one, pristine and perfect. She took a moment to breathe deeply, centering herself, and then chose her costume: the WinterFox special, deposited late last night in her account.

It was a rococo dress, almost as wide as it was tall, with a wine-colored corset above the waist and endless folds of dark, rippling moiré taffeta below it. The neckline descended just to the top of her breasts, accentuated by a line of lace; below that was a triangle of patterned duchess satin. Her sleeves were tight from shoulder to elbow, where they suddenly exploded in a burst of organza flounces. Small black-and-cream-colored ribbons adorned the dress in lines, tied into tiny bows, and there was even one on her throat, like a choker necklace. In the real world it would have been all but impossible to move in, but in virtual reality it was just a construct of ones and zeroes, conforming to the rules WinterFox had programmed into it. Marisa moved around a bit, testing it out: spinning, kicking, jumping, and even rolling across the floor. It was every bit as mobile as her stealth suit, and for her current needs it was far superior: the dozens of layers underneath it, the train and the bustle and the bloomers and the petticoats stacked seven deep, were completely empty of image and texture. When she found the files she needed, that's how she'd smuggle them out.

"Salad dressing and French underwear," she muttered. "This is how we change the world."

She blinked into the team lobby, and Jaya could barely contain her excitement over the dress. She was wearing a similarly historical gown, though hers was Indian, with oranges and blues so vibrant they almost seemed to glow.

"WinterFox told me to go historical," said Jaya. "I think it's a great theme."

"Me too," said Anja, and spun around to show off her own costume. She looked straight out of Oktoberfest, complete with pigtails.

"You're a barmaid?" asked Fang.

"It's called a dirndl," said Anja. "Minus ten cultural sensitivity points for you."

"I don't get yours," said Jaya, looking at Fang. "You're a . . . soldier?"

"US Navy SEAL," said Fang, looking down at her costume. "Black-and-blue camouflage, pre-cybernetic helmet optics, and more pockets than any reasonable person should ever need."

"You're supposed to be historical, though," said Jaya.

"It's turn-of-the-century," said Fang. "Fifty years ago; that counts."

"It's better than Sahara," said Anja. They looked up, and Sahara walked up to them in her classic red evening gown.

"I make my own history," said Sahara. "Everyone clear on the plan?" They couldn't talk about it in detail, on the assumption that Sigan could listen in on anything they said while connected to the server.

"Ready," said Marisa. The rest nodded, and they blinked into the powerset selection screen. Marisa chose Water Buff and Nature Defense, the two powersets they'd programmed the bot to use, and watched the timer count down. She didn't even pay attention to the second-wave picks, just waited for the perfect moment to activate the bot, praying the whole time that she could do it without raising suspicion.

"Good luck," said Sahara.

"You too," said Marisa. She held her breath, eyes glued to the timer. It hit zero, and she blinked out of the game.

She was floating in a formless space, still in her dress,

peripherally aware of the roaring crowd—not through the VR, but through her real ears. She wasn't really inside of virtual reality anymore, but her djinni still was, and the effect was disconcerting—her djinni was trying to interpret the sudden lack of data as if it was a VR program, and her senses were wildly disoriented as she tried to make sense of it all. It was even more strange, she thought, to realize that this was a side effect, and that she was only experiencing a small portion of her own consciousness. It was like the bot was in charge, and she was just a passenger, using extra bandwidth for a weird little side project inside of her own brain. She murmured "Hello," and got an answer back from Bao.

"Hello again," he said. "I'm in position; just give me the word."

"Give me twenty minutes," she said, and blinked open the interface that let her prowl the game's database. It appeared around her like a cascade of data, slowly coalescing into a branching web of links and nodes, like the visual representation of a flowchart. "Exploring a database in virtual reality is weird."

"Anything in virtual reality is weird," said Bao. "Actual reality is weird enough for me."

"Says the guy dressed up as an imaginary maintenance guy."

"That's what I mean," said Bao. "Weird enough already."

Marisa grinned, and got to work. She had to rescue Alain, but there were a few pieces to put in place first, starting with her access to the airgapped server. She followed the nearest path of data to its source, which turned out to be one of the tournament's main servers, and once there she searched for the back door Chaewon had built into the code. She found it, summoned her courage, and went in.

Inside of the private network she felt a little more comfortable, though she didn't know if that was because she was already familiar with the layout, or if she was finally getting accustomed to the strange VR effect. She blinked to search her dress for the three Goblin programs WinterFox had hidden there, and was briefly disappointed when they didn't jump out and snarl like actual little goblins. She simply unpacked them with a blink, and they appeared in her sight as more lines of code that merged into the constant flow of data around her. One of them was her old standby—the one she used to hide her presence from the user logs—but the other two were new ones she'd designed specifically for this mission. The first ran off to search for the financial data she needed, and the second went in search of the client database, and the personal info about Grendel.

Grendel. She was so close now, she could practically feel it. Another hour, at the most, and she'd know exactly where to find him—and with him, all the secrets from her past. She smiled, and let the Goblins go to work.

Now it was time to free Alain.

Their plan was simple: figure out exactly where he was, and then send Mr. Park a faked order to move him to a new location off-site. And it had to be Mr. Park, because that was the only way to control where Park was when the TEDs started going off. Marisa started searching for records of Alain.

The more she explored the database, the easier it became to navigate it—after all, she wasn't actually inside of it, just lying in a VR chair looking at code. She learned how to move quickly, how to jump from one folder to another, how to follow the branching tree of the file directory. But at the same time, the VR representation seemed to reveal more info than she was used to—data, for example, didn't just appear, but actually came from somewhere, and the more she watched it the more she thought she could tell where and how those streams were flowing. She followed the nested folders of the database until she found the secret folder that contained all mentions of Alain. She opened one of the files, trying to make sense of the data, when suddenly the file next to it disappeared.

Someone was deleting them.

Her first thought was one of terror—*they can see me, they'll catch me*—but no. *I'm not really here,* she reminded herself, *I'm just accessing this from a VR chair.* The only actual evidence that she was looking through this archive was buried in a user log somewhere, and her Goblin was making sure nobody found that. By the same logic, then, she had no idea who was deleting the files in this archive, or where that person was located in the real world. All she could do was look at the data and try to figure out what it meant.

The rest of the files disappeared, and Marisa looked at the one in her hand—the only one left. They couldn't delete it, because she was accessing it. That meant she'd saved the data, but it also meant that whoever was deleting the files now knew someone was hacking around in the network. She kept the file open and checked on her Goblins: they were all working perfectly. There shouldn't be any way for anyone to find her.

Then a message appeared in the code, exactly like it had when she'd first encountered Alain during a hack:

Is that you, Heartbeat?

Marisa's jaw fell open. She wondered if it was open in real life as well, or just in here.

She didn't respond. She didn't dare. She watched, waiting to see if another message appeared. She got three.

Heartbeat?

Marisa?

Parkslayer?

It was Renata.

TWENTY-NINE

What was Renata doing here? She couldn't have been sabotaging Sigan—she'd betrayed Alain to Chaewon for doing that exact thing. Marisa didn't even know what she could be thinking, messing around in their network—Renata was a hired gun, not a coder. There was no way she could even get into such a protected system.

Unless . . .

Chaewon. Renata was still working for her. When Chaewon had found out that Zi had ruined her plan to rig the match, she'd needed someone to go in and fix it. Someone who wasn't afraid to break the law, and whose loyalty could be assured—or at least purchased. In the few minutes before the match started, Chaewon must have contacted Renata and sent her whatever permissions and security keys she needed to get full access to the building and the system, as well as rough instructions for messing with the lag spikes. She had the full run of the network. And she'd known

Marisa's tricks well enough to find her.

You didn't think I knew about your little trick, did you? The message appeared beside the others. **But Alain told me everything.**

Marisa said nothing. Was Renata going to turn her in? Was she going to attack her? Marisa held her breath, waiting, and then shook her head and got back to work. She had to find the email server, and fake an order with enough authority to get Mr. Park moving. Who was his direct superior? Kwon Dae himself, the CEO?

I thought that was pretty classy of you, by the way, abandoning him to Sigan like that, wrote Renata. **You never tried to reach him, and after that first night you never tried to contact me again. Real love-'em-and-leave-'em type, aren't you?**

Marisa found the email server, and searched desperately for Kwon Dae's account.

It's a shame, really, wrote Renata. **Your team actually isn't playing so badly. Too bad I'm about to screw them.**

Wait, thought Marisa. What was she doing?

Nos vemos in hell, wrote Renata, and suddenly Marisa was bombarded with light and color and sound so jarring it seemed to explode inside of her skull. She clutched at her head, screaming in pain, and dropped to the ground. It was solid, impacting her hands and knees with a force she couldn't possibly have felt inside of the ghostlike database. Where was she? She forced her eyes open and saw that a fight whirled around her, each shout and scream and gunshot assaulting her ears like a hammer. She dropped flatter to the ground, trying to figure out what was going on, when suddenly a train roared past, and she looked up in shock. The Red Line. She was in downtown LA, right in front of the Sigan building.

And the world had gone mad.

All around her crowds of people were running and screaming, and gunfire shattered the air in vicious bursts. Marisa scrambled to the side, looking for better cover behind a solid wall, only to stumble as an explosion rocked a nearby building. She threw herself down again and crawled the last few feet to cover.

"What's going on!" she yelled. "What happened?"

"Heartbeat's in trouble," said Sahara's voice. "Somebody grab her!"

"That was epic lag," said Fang.

"This is the game?" cried Marisa. But this was the real world—

"I've got you, Heartbeat," said Jaya, and suddenly the shimmery pink haze of a magic shield rose up around her. Jaya grabbed her by the arm, dressed in her historical Overworld costume, and hauled her to her feet. She handed her a gun—a Drachen 67 assault rifle—and pulled her toward a storefront by the edge of the plaza. "You dropped this. Now run!" Marisa followed her, pelting fire across the embattled square, and they dropped to cover again in the ruins of a battered cafe. Solipsis.

"That was the worst lag spike we've ever had," said Jaya. "You're just disoriented because we've never played on this map before."

"But . . . ," said Marisa. "I was—"

"You're disoriented," said Jaya again, more firmly this time. "This map is an exact replica of downtown LA, and it's throwing you off. Just be calm." The meaning behind her look was clear: *don't say anything incriminating, because everyone watching the match can hear us.*

Marisa breathed deeply, regaining her bearings. Renata had caused a lag spike, and it had thrown Marisa back into the Overworld match to replace the bot. Exactly what they'd programmed the bot to do. "Sorry," she said. "This is still kind of freaking me out."

"Pretty talky all of a sudden," said Sahara's voice on the comm. Marisa got the hint: the bot didn't talk, so Marisa needed to say as little as possible to help keep up the illusion.

"We lost HappyFluffy in that last skirmish," said Jaya, "but they lost Chaewon."

"I tell you one thing," said Sahara, "killing her never gets old."

Marisa was stuck in the game—and Alain was still stuck in his cell—until another lag spike triggered the bot program again and sent her back into the database. She wanted to update her friends on the status of the hack, but she had to keep it vague.

"Sorry I slipped up," she said over the comm. "Everything's good, though."

"Someday you'll have to tell me all about it," said Sahara. "For now, regroup with Happy at the vault."

Marisa nodded. She turned and ran west, calling up the wireframe map display to show her where the vault was. The map was completely different than any she'd ever played in—all the other

Overworld arenas were copies of each other, completely identical except for the theme draped over the top, but this one was new. Completely original, probably built just for this tournament. It was a fun idea, but they'd spent hundreds of hours practicing on the old layout. Playing in here was like playing football on a baseball diamond—it kind of worked, but nothing was where you expected. She rounded the corner and saw the vault turrets, looking like giant police drones bristling with weapons. Anja was behind them, beckoning her forward.

"I just respawned," said Anja. "I see your plan worked."

"For certain definitions of 'worked,'" said Marisa. Flipping between realities was a lot more painful than she'd expected, but at least it was possible. "What next?"

"Hell if I know," said Anja, choosing her words carefully. "We're losing hardcore. This stupid map has a roof, sort of, but it has terrible sniper lines."

"I know," said Marisa, pretending to know what she was talking about. "It's the worst. You lead the way."

Anja nodded, and led her through the crowd. The people were all fake, of course, just NPCs controlled by the server. They ignored the girls completely, going about their own meaningless business. It made Marisa wordlessly uncomfortable to see them, and she tried to focus on the map instead.

Half a block later they arrived at an alley—the same alley, Marisa noted, that they'd hidden in after jumping off the building. Funny. Now there were attack nulis in it, standing in for the typical creeps that swarmed the other maps. Anja attacked one, and Marisa went into action buffing and healing her, when suddenly another lag spike hit—

And she found herself back in the database.

The sudden shift was less painful going in this direction, but no less jarring; instead of being assaulted by light and noise, she felt suddenly deaf, almost blind, and eerily disembodied. The rules of this network world weren't defined for VR, and trying to interact with it that way felt wrong in a way she couldn't put words to. It was like being a ghost, but in reverse—she was real, and the world itself was dead and ethereal. She shook the folds of her massive dress, so eager for anything familiar that even a sound would be enough. The dress, just as virtual as the rest of it, was silent.

She closed her eyes, imagining she was somewhere real instead of this ghostly non-place. "I'm real," she said out loud.

"Me too," said Bao. "Cool coincidence."

Marisa felt a sudden rush of embarrassment. "Sorry, I'm just kind of freaking out."

"You were quiet for a long time," said Bao. "Everything okay?"

"Perfect," said Marisa. "The Goblins are finding the data. The bot script is working as planned, though it's more disorienting than I'd expected." She opened her eyes. "I don't know how long I have before the next lag spike throws me back into Overworld, so let's get this party started." She swam through the network until she found the email system again, then pulled up the address for Mr. Park and wrote him a fake email, using the secure database to make it look like the email came from Chaewon's father, the Sigan CEO:

This building is no longer a safe place to hold the prisoner. Move him to our off-site location immediately.

Marisa didn't know what the off-site location might be, but it seemed like a good bet that they had one. It didn't matter anyway; they just had to move him, and if the plan went the way it was supposed to, they'd never get wherever it was they were going. She hesitated a moment—they'd only get one shot at this, and if it didn't all go to plan, she didn't know when she'd see Alain again. But they had no other option. She blinked, and sent the message.

"Email away," she said. "Time to rescue Alain."

THIRTY

The file Marisa had left open was the location of Alain's cell. Marisa found the link to the security camera network, and watched him.

Alain Bensoussan sat on the edge of a small cot, which was bolted to the floor. It disturbed Marisa to think that a megacorp would even have a holding cell, let alone a prisoner currently locked up in one, but that was the whole problem, wasn't it? Megacorps were above the law. Alain looked like he'd been beaten pretty severely, but the fact that he was alive said that he hadn't given up any info yet.

The lock on the door clicked open, and Alain's eyes flicked over to watch as someone entered. That was the other benefit these cameras had over the hoodie: sound.

"GetUpYou'reBeingTransferred," said Park.

Alain narrowed his eyes, suspicious. "To where?"

"YouWillNotBeConsciousForTheJourney," said Park. "StandUpAndMakeThisEasyOnYourself."

Alain stood, wincing just enough to make Marisa wonder if he had a broken rib. That would make it hard for him to run. He was wearing a set of three-armed manacles, one for each wrist and the third connecting him to the floor; Mr. Park unlocked this third ring and marched him toward the door. Marisa flipped to another camera and watched them walk through the hall toward the elevators. They waited, and when it came Alain hesitated a moment before stepping in. Was he expecting an ambush? Planning an escape?

"Just hang on a minute," she whispered. "We've got you."

"What?" asked Bao.

"Nothing," said Marisa. "He's on his way to you. Elevator number two."

Mr. Park stepped in after him, said "ThirdFloor," and the doors closed.

"Third floor?" asked Alain. "That's not much of a transfer."

"We'reGoingOff-Site," said Park. "That'sTheTransferPointToTheParkingGarageElevators."

"I'm in position," said Bao.

Marisa flipped over to a camera in his hallway, and saw him waiting outside the elevator, wearing a nuli maintenance uniform and pushing a small cart. He held the burner phone in his hand, his thumb hovering over a small black button on the screen.

"Three," Marisa counted, "two, one."

The elevator opened, Mr. Park stepped out, and dropped like a sack of rocks when Bao pushed the button on his phone. His fall yanked on the chain connected to Alain, but he'd already braced himself—almost as if he'd been expecting it.

"Bao?" asked Alain.

Bao looked up, surprised. "How did you know it was me?"

"Because it's exactly how I'd break someone out," said Alain. "This is the weak point in their security—you couldn't get me any higher up, because then there's no way out of the building, and you couldn't get me any farther down because there's probably a whole security team waiting in the parking garage."

"Wow," said Marisa.

"I . . . okay," said Bao. "You just saved me the introduction, so we'll jump to the next part—and please answer quickly, because even the twenty TEDs in this bag aren't going to keep Park down for long." The overclocked security officer was already starting to stir. Bao stepped closer. "Before I give you anything else—before you take one more step toward the front door—I need you to answer a question."

Marisa frowned. This wasn't part of the plan.

Mr. Park twitched, slowly coming back online.

"Ask it," said Alain.

Bao looked at him solemnly. "Are you for real?"

"What do you mean?" asked Bao.

"My best friend in the world is putting her neck on the line for you," said Bao, "and I'm not saving you until I know: Are you for real? Are you really, honestly, the noble warrior you claim to be, or are you gonna ruin her life?"

Alain studied him for a moment before answering. "I won't claim to be noble," he said at last, "but I promise that I'm sincere.

I would never betray anyone who helped me, but Marisa least of all. She's . . . . I'd do anything for her."

Marisa felt her heart flip over in her chest.

Bao rolled his eyes. "Even if it means prison?"

Alain lifted his shirt to show the bloody bandages underneath. "A government prison will be a welcome relief from Sigan."

Bao scowled at the bandages. "Damn. Can you run? The next part of the plan involves a lot of running."

Mr. Park moved his arms, trying to lift himself off the floor.

"I'll do my best," said Alain, and raised his manacled wrists. "Do you have a key for these cuffs?"

"No, you're gonna need those," said Bao. "So: here's the plan. In just a minute you're going to run down that hall, turn left, and head for the stairs. Stay close to the cubicles as you run."

Alain frowned. "What's our exit point?"

"The front door," said Bao, and handed him the burner phone. "This phone is shielded from electromagnetic attacks—cost Anja a fortune. Say hi."

Alain put the phone to his ear. "Hello?"

"Hey," said Marisa. "Good to hear your voice."

"Yours as well," said Alain. "Is this whole thing your plan?"

"Only if it works," said Marisa. "If you end up caught or dead or something, it was totally someone else's."

"And I'm supposed to just . . . go through the front door?" asked Alain.

"Trust me," said Marisa. "And keep the phone on you. Your djinni's broken, so the phone's programmed to emit an RF signal and trigger a bunch of proximity sensors. That will help keep Mr. Park away from you."

"Shouldn't I just start running now?"

"Bao told you to wait," said Marisa. "I'm watching the security cameras, and there's a team coming straight for you."

Alain looked up urgently. "Isn't that a reason to *not* wait?"

"We need them to see us," said Bao. He dropped his bag and held up his fake plastic gun. It was exactly the kind Sigan's security staff used, and when he tapped a button on his technician's uniform, the color and insignias shifted until his jacket and hat also looked like that of the security staff. He leveled the weapon at Alain, and in that moment a team of three security guards came around the corner behind him. "He's getting away!" shouted Bao. "Catch him!"

Park lurched to his feet, and the guards shouted in alarm. Alain turned and ran.

Pablo Nakamoto worked on the third floor of the KT Sigan building, answering customer calls for tech support questions, though right now he was on his lunch break. Marisa watched on the security cameras as he and his cubicle partner, a woman named Kendra Billman, streamed the Forward Motion final on Pablo's computer screen. If Marisa squinted just right, she could almost see the stats in the corner.

"I know we're supposed to cheer for World2gether," said Kendra, "but I love this other team. Have you been watching?"

"They're amazing," said Pablo. He picked up the plastic

container with his lunch—a roast pepper salad from Solipsis Cafe—and opened it. "I love how they always do something you don't expect."

"Except today," said Kendra. "They're playing pretty standard tactics."

"I know," said Pablo. He picked up the little cup of salad dressing and popped off the lid. "I guess we're not going to get any surprises." He poured the dressing over his salad, and stared wide-eyed at the slim, round disk that plopped out onto the peppers.

Marisa smiled.

Kendra frowned at it. "What's that?"

"I . . . have no idea," said Pablo. He poked it with his plastic fork. "It's not food."

"It looks like ceramic," said Kendra. "Or . . . resin. Like a little poker chip or something."

"Why would there be a poker chip in my salad dressing?"

"I have no idea."

The woman in the next cubicle over stuck her head around the divider. "Hey, did you get something weird in your salad dressing?" She held up a disk exactly like Pablo's.

"Yeah," said Pablo. "Do you know what it is?"

"No idea."

"I got one, too," shouted another voice, followed by a chorus of "Me toos" from a dozen or so other people in the call center. Pablo looked at Kendra, who simply shrugged.

Pablo looked at his salad. "What should we do about—"

"Coming through!" shouted Alain, followed almost immediately by the sound of pounding feet and shouts of alarm. Pablo looked up just as Alain came charging around the corner, his hands chained together, his face twisted in pain. Mr. Park was close behind him, followed several steps later by a pack of security guards, but as they ran the burner phone in Alain's hand triggered each of the tiny TEDs, and the office went berserk—lights and lamps exploded, computer screens went black, and workers fell back, untouched but clutching their heads as their djinnis shivered and fizzed from the electromagnetic pulse. Mr. Park staggered wildly at each new invisible attack, barely staying on his feet as he reeled from the endless series of explosive technical glitches. Alain raced past Pablo's cubicle, the slim black phone clutched in his hand, and the disk in Pablo's salad made a tiny popping sound. Pablo staggered back, Mr. Park stumbled to one knee, and Alain ran toward the stairwell at the end of the row.

"I'll guide you through the next floor," said Marisa, but a sudden explosion of light and sound battered her senses.

She was back in Overworld.

THIRTY-ONE

"Protect her!" shouted Sahara. Her voice thundered through Marisa's skull like a stampede of iron hooves, and she screamed in pain. She fell to the ground, scraped by asphalt and assaulted by showers of enemy fire, and died in seconds. The empty blackness of the respawn lobby was a welcome relief.

"You okay?" asked Fang.

Marisa peeked out of one eye to see Fang, also dead, waiting for her own respawn.

"I have to get back," she said.

"I know," said Fang. She looked at Marisa with wide, insistent eyes, as if begging her to stay quiet. Marisa remembered not to say anything incriminating, and nodded. Fang nodded in acknowledgment. "We're going to lose," she said.

Marisa thought about Alain, injured and alone, surrounded

by guards closing in from every side. "We always knew we would," she said.

"That doesn't mean we give up," said Fang. "You've got to keep fighting, to the last, dead second."

"I can't do anything from here," said Marisa.

"I'll go after Chaewon," said Fang with a smile. "Nothing brings on a *purely random* lag spike like taking her health down into the red."

"Thanks," said Marisa.

"Cherry Dogs forever," said Fang, and disappeared as her respawn timer hit zero. Marisa waited, watching her own timer: four, three, two, one. She was catapulted back into the map, finding herself in a vault filled with cowering people and heavy gunfire.

"Focus fire on Nightmare!" shouted Sahara. "Quicksand, cover me!"

Jaya cast a bright magic shield around Sahara, and Marisa searched frantically for Anja to try to support her as well. They were going to lose, but they couldn't afford to lose yet—she had to get back into the file system and get the data from her Goblins, or this whole plan would be for nothing.

"Anja's dead," said Jaya, snarling through clenched teeth. "Fang ran off after Chaewon, so it's four of them against three of us. Hit Nightmare or we'll lose the vault!"

"I don't have any attack powers!"

"Protect me, then!" shouted Jaya, and dove into the battle. Marisa blasted her with a healing spell first, shielding her from the initial burst of damage from Nightmare's gun, then sent a swarm of protective nulis to surround her, increasing her accuracy and damage. Jaya twisted and spun through the enemy agents like a wraith, almost dancing as she dodged their strikes and lashed out with her own slim, sharp sword. Sahara crouched in her magic shield and fired round after round of heavy ammo from her machine gun, screaming in defiance. Marisa poured healing magic into Jaya as fast as she could, and when Anja respawned, the tide slowly started to turn against the World2gether attack. The enemy agents retreated, the Cherry Dog vault already half destroyed.

"We can't take another attack like that," said Sahara, gasping for breath. "We have to blitz them first—an all-out attack. Where's Fang?"

"Hunting Chaewon," said Marisa.

"She can't take Chaewon by herself," said Jaya.

"She might," said Sahara. "If she does we have them, five against four; if not, I don't know—we still have to attack, even if we're outnumbered."

"We can't lose yet," said Marisa.

"I'm not planning to lose!" shouted Sahara. "A blitz is our only chance!"

"We need time," said Marisa.

"We need—" started Sahara, but then suddenly Marisa was thrown back out of the match and into the private network. She closed her eyes again as her mind adjusted to the ghostly unreality of the VR database. When she opened them, she did it slowly, looking down at her massive rococo dress that seemed to float in a vast nothingness.

"Alain?" she whispered.

"Where have you been?" he whispered frantically. "I had to hide."

"Where are you?"

"In a supply closet somewhere," he said. "My djinni's been completely fried by those TEDs you used, so the building's sensors aren't picking me up. I'm safe for now."

"But for how much longer?" asked Marisa. "They have to check the supply closet eventually."

"Can you tell me what's outside?"

"Let me see if I can find you." She flew through the database, bits and bytes and endless files streaming past her, looking for the security camera feeds, when she realized that one of her Goblins was trying to get her attention. It was the one that kept her hidden. She blinked on the alert, calling up the log, and looked with horror at a message from Renata.

You didn't think I'd find the little program you use to hide yourself? wrote Renata. **You've already used this trick on us before, Marisa; how stupid do you think I am?**

Marisa's stomach sank into a deep, sickening pit. If Renata had found her, she could have alerted the sysadmins. The entire mission could be dead. She blinked back toward a broader view of the database, searching for signs of activity, and grimaced when she saw it—slowly, folder by folder, someone was locking down the network. If they found the files she needed, or the hole she'd gotten in through, she'd lose everything.

Think, Marisa told herself. *They haven't found you yet. You can still do something.* She didn't have much time, though—the Goblin that kept her hidden was useless now that Renata had exposed it. All it did was redirect other users to a false copy of the user list; if Renata had shown them how to get around it and see the real user list, they'd see Marisa as clear as day. It was only a matter of time until they hunted her down.

But what if she gave them something else to hunt?

Marisa checked on her first two Goblins, making sure they were still searching for the data they needed. They'd collected almost all of it. She flew to the third and found it still dutifully redirecting data, just like it was programmed to do. She blinked into its inner programming and changed some lines of code, altering its function and feeding it Renata's ID. When she finished she blinked again, recompiling the program and setting it loose in the network. It started combing through usage logs, finding everything Marisa had done and attributing it to Renata instead. The fake email she'd sent to Mr. Park—now it looked like Renata had sent it. The unauthorized access of the camera feeds now had Renata's digital fingerprints all over them. Everything Marisa had worked to keep hidden was now right out in the open, and Renata was getting blamed for it. Even Marisa's own presence in the system was tagged with Renata's ID.

She found the security feeds and looked at the seventy-second-floor workstation where Renata was working. She was still plugged in and working madly, probing the system for Marisa, but now the sysadmin beside her stood up, looking at her and then back at his own display. He typed out a discreet call for security, but Renata noticed it, unplugged, and ran. Marisa grinned.

That was one problem off her back.

"Marisa," said Alain. "You still there?"

"Yes," she said quickly, looking back at the security feeds. She found the only supply closet on the second floor, and whistled lowly when she saw it.

"That doesn't sound good," said Alain.

"It's not," said Marisa. "You have a whole team of security right outside your door. Give them a chance to walk away, and then go out and to the right. The second door leads to the mezzanine, and then you just have to make it to the front entrance."

"And then what?"

"Then you stay away from planter boxes," said Marisa. She glanced back at the network, and swore sharply. "Mierda! They're still closing the system! I don't have the data yet!"

"What data?"

She flew to her Goblins—they were almost done. Each one would take about ten seconds to upload back into the dress.

"I can pull what they have so far, but—no!" The Sigan sysadmins were moving even faster now, locking down the files and slamming closed all the exits. It was a full-security response; they'd realized by now that someone was targeting their data, and they were pulling out all the stops to protect it. She had fifteen seconds left, at best. "I don't have time to take them both!"

"Both?"

"I have one Goblin grabbing your financials," she said frantically, "and one searching the client list for Grendel. I can't lose him!"

"Marisa—"

"I can't!" she shouted. "I've searched too long and I've lost too much—I need to know what he knows about my family!" She was crying now. "He knows who I am!"

"That's the thing about people," said Alain softly. "You always get to choose who you are."

Still sobbing, Marisa blinked on one of the Goblins, compressing all the data into the folds of her virtual dress. It seemed to take an eternity for the progress bar to creep across her vision, using every available bit of bandwidth her djinni connection could muster. The sysadmins crept closer, closing files and sealing exits. She didn't have any more time—she stopped the upload at 93 percent, left the other Goblin behind, and blinked out of the database milliseconds before they caught her.

She felt herself crying again, tiny tears tracing wet, cold paths down her cheeks, somewhere far away in the real world.

"Which files did you get?" he asked softly.

"The financials," she whispered. She pulled the data from the Overworld costume creator into her own djinni, and then transferred a copy to the burner phone. "KT Sigan's going down."

"You did the right thing," he said, and she heard him wince in pain as he stood up from his hiding place in the closet. "Now I'm going to do the same."

"Buena suerte," she whispered.

She heard him open the door, followed by a muffled shout: "There he is!"

She wanted to look at the security cameras, but outside of the network she couldn't access them, and without Renata to run the lag spikes she couldn't get back into Overworld, either. She blinked into one of the many vidcasts and saw the final seconds of Sahara's failed blitz: all five Cherry Dogs attacking the enemy vault, dying one by one. They killed most of Chaewon's team, but it wasn't enough. Nightmare was still there, cutting down one player after another in a flurry of deadly skill—Jaya, Anja, Marisa's bot, and Sahara. Only Fang was left, and Nightmare shot her with a bolt of dark energy.

Fang dodged, and kept hitting the vault.

"Come on, Fang," Marisa whispered. "Get out of there."

Fang dodged another attack, and continued laying into the vault with everything she had. She was using Decay Melee, and every dagger strike left a trail of corrosive green acid. Nightmare closed the distance, slashing at her with claws of pure shadow, but Fang triggered her short-range teleport—an escape power, but instead of escaping she simply reappeared on the other side of the vault, and kept attacking it.

"Come on, Fang," Marisa repeated. "This is the same mistake the Thunderbolts made. Don't focus on the vault when there's still an enemy trying to kill you!" But Fang kept moving and attacking, and Marisa realized she was counting her timers flawlessly, triggering each power the instant it was available again, and planning her steps to stay exactly out of range of Nightmare's claws.

Nightmare shot her with another blast of dark energy, but Fang was already dodging, and Marisa realized with a shock that Fang was counting Nightmare's timers as well, juggling it all in her head while she attacked the vault.

Did they actually have a chance?

Chaewon respawned and came out firing, but Fang was already on the move, dodging most of the damage and dropping a pool of acid in the space she'd just left. Nightmare stepped to the edge of it and reached across with her claws, slashing viciously, but Fang had gone just far enough to avoid the attack and unleash a flurry of blows against the vault. Bubba respawned a moment later, and now Fang was dancing in and out of all three enemies, counting ranges and timers and respawns with flawless accuracy.

It was almost enough.

No matter how precise, no one could stand up to three enemies forever, and Fang started taking more and more damage. She hacked at the vault with everything she had, but when the fourth World2gether agent respawned and joined the fray, it was too much. Fang dropped her final acid pool, and Nightmare cut her down.

"I got you!" screamed Nightmare. She bent down over Fang's corpse and shouted in her face. "You were never any good, and I got you! Bái mù xiǎo tùzǎizi!"

And then the acid pool finished its last few ticks of damage, and the vault crumbled to pieces.

"Cherry Dogs win!" shouted Su-Yun Kho. "Cherry Dogs win!"

THIRTY-TWO

Pati Carneseca held her arms straight up in the air. "Yes! They won!" She looked at her father, standing beside her with a large anti-Sigan sign. "Mari won! They won!"

Carlo Magno glanced down, stopping his chant. "They won their game?"

"They won the whole tournament, Papi! The Cherry Dogs won!"

Carlo Magno smiled. "Bien bien, mija." He hoisted his sign back up. "At least one of us beat this triste megacorp today. Take back the net! Take back the net!"

Pati wrote Marisa a quick message, with more exclamation points than letters, and sent it. She blinked and replayed the final moments of the game, then clipped the section off and sent it to her father. "Here, you can watch it."

"This is . . ." He frowned. "Mija, Mari's not even in this."

"I know," said Pati, "but Fang won anyway. Isn't that amazing?"

"Pati, I don't have time for th—what's that?"

Pati looked at him, then followed his sight line to the front doors of the Sigan building. The protesters were being held about thirty meters back, with a row of police in front of them and another row of KT Sigan security guards in front of the building. Between them were a dozen reporters, a giant swarm of camera nulis, and two gardening nulis, unobtrusively watering the plants. It was the same view Pati had had since they'd arrived that morning, but now the line of security guards was in chaos as some kind of scuffle took place by the doors—not someone trying to get in, but someone trying to get out. She saw a figure in the middle of the security guards, barely visible but with dark skin and hair, trying to get past them. Was that . . . ?

"Alain?" she said out loud.

More guards poured out of the building, trying to apprehend him, including a man at least a head taller than the others, with a metal sensor plate covering most of his face. The tall man attacked Alain, knocking him to the ground, when suddenly the gardening nulis in the plaza exploded. The massive crowd of reporters and protesters and bystanders screamed and fell back, and Alain broke free of the shocked guards and sprinted toward the street. The police recovered and stopped him, surrounding him with weapons drawn, and Pati pressed forward close enough to hear.

"They were holding me prisoner," said Alain. He knelt and held his hands over his head. One of his hands was clutching an old, black, handheld phone. "My name is Alain Bensoussan, and

I've been held captive by KT Sigan for seven days."

"ThisManIsOurPrisoner," said the tall security guard. "ReturnHimToUsAtOnceUnderTheProvisionsOfShared-MegacorpJurisdiction—"

"This phone contains evidence that KT Sigan has been defrauding the US government out of billions of dollars," said Alain. "That bypasses Shared Megacorp Jurisdiction and makes my capture a federal matter." He looked at the reporters. "The phone is also programmed with all of your IDs, and the upload is being mirrored to your djinnis. You have all the evidence you need to take this story public."

"WeDemandThatYouReturnThisManToUs—" said the tall security guard with the faceplate, but the ranking police officer shook her head.

"If what he says is correct," said the officer, "we need to take him with us. If his story doesn't check out, you can have him back."

"ThatDataWasIllegallyObtained," said the tall man. "ItIsIn-admissibleInYourCourts—"

"And if it contains what he says it contains," said the police officer, "a legal loophole is not going to save you. You and I both know the government's not the real threat here. Now step back or I'll arrest you, too."

The tall man grimaced but stepped back. The police officer took Alain's phone, and a reporter pressed close, a camera nuli flying in for a close-up. "You realize that if any of your story is true," the reporter said, "you've just confessed to half a dozen counts of federal cybercrime. Not to mention the two bombs you just set off, which probably makes you a terrorist."

"I'm not a terrorist," said Alain. "I'm a freedom fighter."

"Whatever," said the police officer. She pocketed the phone, and nodded to some nearby police. "Take him away."

"No!" shouted Pati. "He's innocent! Alain!" But her voice was drowned out by the rest of the crowd, some clamoring for more information, others screaming for his head. Carlo Magno pulled Pati back into the heart of the protesters, where she wouldn't be noticed, and hushed her angrily.

"Stop saying you know him," Carlo Magno hissed. "Do you want to get us both arrested, too?"

"But it's not supposed to end with him arrested," Pati cried. "Why did he have to get arrested?"

"It's simple," said a voice by Pati's side, and she looked up to see Bao standing over her. He was dressed like a Sigan security guard, but he pushed a button on his jacket and it changed color, becoming a plain old jacket. He took off his ball cap and stuffed it in his pocket, and suddenly he looked exactly like every other protester in the crowd. "When you try to get in somewhere, the first thing you do is plan how you're going to get back out again. The only way to get Alain out of Sigan was to send him to prison."

"Are you a part of this?" asked Carlo Magno.

"Good to see you," said Bao. "Tell Mari congratulations."

"But then how are you going to get him out of prison?" asked Pati.

"Getting out of prison's easy." He smiled and slipped into the crowd. "Just ask the seagull."

"Wait!" shouted Carlo Magno. "What's going on?"

But Bao was gone. Carlo Magno held Pati tightly, and the police put Alain into one of their cruisers.

In the middle of the plaza, the reporters looked earnestly into their camera nulis and shared the story with the world.

"I hate this part," said Jaya. "Saying good-bye is the worst."

Marisa pulled the last suitcase clear of the autocab, and it closed its doors and drove away. Anja grabbed Fang's roller bag and the five girls headed into the airport, with Jaya's little suitcase nuli following like an eager puppy.

"Look on the bright side," said Sahara. "Which is literally every other side. We won the tournament, we gave the prize money to Mari's family, and we friggin' decimated KT Sigan. It hasn't even been twenty-four hours and Johara's already buying up their stock. It's a classic hostile takeover."

"It doesn't sound very sexy," said Anja, "but it's going to destroy them. Or their American branch at least."

"Plus we saved the restaurant," said Jaya. "Ten thousand yuan isn't a ton, but it'll keep you going until the rest of Mirador gets back on its feet."

"Not all the sides are bright sides," said Marisa. "We lost Grendel—and if Sigan goes down, we've lost pretty much any chance we had of finding him again."

"Don't worry," said Anja. "We'll get him back."

"How?"

"However we can," said Jaya. "No one can disappear forever."

"Thanks," said Marisa. "Grendel doesn't even affect you, so . . . that means a lot."

"Of course we'll help you," said Fang. "What are friends for?"

Sahara smiled. "And can we please take yet another moment to bask in the stunning victory of Wong Fang and her Cherry Dogs? One of the most astounding victories this sport has ever seen?"

The girls cheered, for what felt like the thousandth time that weekend. The other travelers paid just barely enough attention to glare as they moved around them.

"That's the great thing about fame," said Marisa, watching the crowd ignore them. "We just did something amazing—and part of it was even public and legal, which is kind of new for us—and yet none of these people have any idea. The world goes on."

"But *we* know," said Jaya.

"And the Overworld fans know," said Sahara. "We've already been invited to a real league—three different invitations to real leagues." She grinned from ear to ear. "We did it."

"Time to get a coach," said Fang.

"Probably," said Sahara. "Doesn't hurt to look around, at least."

"Heads up," said Marisa, watching as the doors opened and another group of travelers walked in. "Psycho hose beast at six o'clock."

They turned and saw Nightmare walking toward them, a purse in her hand and a very expensive suitcase following close behind. She walked toward them solemnly, and stopped a few feet away.

"Congratulations again," she said, and looked at Fang. "Zhùhè."

"Xiè xie," said Fang.

"Now that you've had a taste of the big leagues," said Zi, still looking at Fang, "have you thought about joining a real team?"

"She's on a real team," said Sahara.

"She's on a very good up-and-coming team," said Zi. "One that's definitely going to be a real team *someday*." She looked at Sahara. "I mean that." She looked back at Fang. "But it's going to take a while, and you're ready now. I'm offering you a place on Wu Squad, if you want it. Our Jungler is retiring at the end of the season."

Fang looked shocked. "I . . ."

"You're too good for the Cherry Dogs," said Nightmare. "Believe me. You're probably fighting with Sahara constantly over strategy, right?"

Fang and Sahara looked at each other, guilty grimaces creeping across their faces.

"I can give you something they can't," said Zi. "A major-league team, with a coach and sponsors and living expenses and the whole thing. Endorsement deals and top-level play. That's the world you belong in, Fang."

Fang looked at her a moment, then at the other girls in the group. Her gaze fell on Marisa last of all, and she stared at her a moment before turning back to Zi.

"I already have something you can never give anyone," said Fang, and smiled. "The best friends in the world." She put her arms around Marisa and Sahara, the two girls standing closest to her; it was the first time she'd voluntarily touched anyone since she'd arrived. "I'm pretty sure I'm *exactly* where I belong."

Zi stared at them a moment, then rolled her eyes and walked away. Anja and Jaya gathered in from the sides, and Fang stuck her hand into the middle of the circle.

"Team hand thing?" asked Fang.

"See?" said Anja, putting her hand on top of Fang's. "This is the perfect time for a hand thing—not in the cab when I'm not there."

Jaya and Sahara put their hands on the stack, and Marisa put her hand on top. "I love you guys," she said.

Sahara smiled. "Cherry Dogs forever."

ACKNOWLEDGMENTS

Can I thank the entire video games industry? And everyone who ever made a sports movie. And a heist movie. And a sports movie that was also a heist movie. Do they make those? I don't think they make those. A hearty thank you, then, to Jules Dassin, who created what is arguably the first heist movie in 1955, called *Rififi*, and thus kicked off my favorite little subgenre of fiction. I'm delighted to have finally joined that subgenre with *Ones and Zeroes*.

I must also thank my editor, Jordan Brown; my agent, Sara Crowe; and everyone who works with them behind the scenes. My assistant, Kenna Blaylock, is invaluable. My friends and early readers are indispensable: Allison Hill, Mary Robinette Kowal, Gama Martinez, Brandon Sanderson, Howard Tayler, Larry Van Lent, Audrey Wells, Dawn Wells, Robison Wells, Natalie Whipple, and more. And, of course, I can't forget my second-favorite Overworld team, the illustrious Your Mom: John Brown, Steve Diamond, Javier Mixco, Maija-Liisa Phipps, and Ethan Sproat. I couldn't have written this book without Your Mom. Your Mom was really useful in those long, hard, late-night sessions.

I am not exactly good at video games myself, but I do love to play them, and I have a Cherry Dogs team in both League of Legends and Overwatch. If you've played with me online, thanks for inspiring me; if not, look me up, and let's have a game.

Turn the page to read an excerpt from
the next book in the Mirador series

ACTIVE MEMORY

Marisa looked at the crowd; it seemed like everyone in Mirador was at the high school science fair, but finding Sandro would be easy—he had a djinni. She blinked on her guidance app, and a blue line appeared in front of her, leading her through the crowd. She followed it with a smile. Other kids on every side were hawking their projects like vendors in a street market: this girl had a nuli that cleaned pollution from solar trees, improving their energy transfer rate; that boy had a small-scale factory robot with a new kind of joint that required less maintenance. Marisa stopped by one of the tables and read through her friend Rosa's new code for a ranger nuli—the kind that followed endangered species around and protected them from poachers. Rosa Sanchez, eighteen years old and living in the barrio, had modified the AI to start actively hunting the poachers instead of just passively shocking them anytime they got too close. It had the potential to change the entire balance of power between poachers and rangers.

Everything in the room was amazing, and Marisa felt a swell of pride for her friends and neighbors. This was the future, right here and now. A hundred kids with big ideas, and a room full of people telling them yes instead of no. It was the greatest thing Marisa had ever seen.

She found her brother Sandro by the back wall, telling the crowd about his forestry nuli. He had a poster, because of course he did.

"Just like animals, plants can get sick," Sandro was saying, "and when they do, it can spread through an ecosystem like wildfire. A single parasite, like the blight you see in this image, can destroy an entire orchard or forest in weeks." He held up a screen with a picture of a tree; massive patches of the leaves were shriveled and black, almost like they'd been burned. "This is called fire blight, and it's caused by a bacterium called *Erwinia amylovora*, which targets fruit trees. We can spray for it, but the spray is poisonous and gets on everything—the sick leaves, the healthy leaves, and even the fruit. My nuli can sense this bacteria and dozens of other plagues and parasites, and spray for them precisely—with no collateral damage. It patrols its area 24/7, and the precision also means it uses less chemicals than traditional methods, so it's cheaper."

The small crowd applauded, and Marisa whooped more loudly than anyone: "Ándale, Sandro! Lechuga!"

"You know he hates that nickname," said Bao, suddenly standing next to her. Marisa hadn't even seen him approach.

"Why do you think I use it?" she asked, and then started chanting the name loudly: "Le-chu-ga! Le-chu-ga!"

Sandro looked at her as the crowd moved on to another project. She wanted him to sneer or roll his eyes, but instead he simply raised his eyebrow; he was one year her junior, but always treated her like the younger one.

"Thanks for coming," he said.

"Claro que si, hermanito. Your presentation was perfect."

"You think?"

"It was great," said Bao. "Do you have a video to show it in action?"

"It's on the tablet," he said, gesturing with the screen in his hands. "I'm keeping the presentation short for now, but I'll show it to the judges."

"Pop quiz," said Bao, glancing at Marisa. "What do you call a reptilian ferret with wings?"

"Those are called MyDragons," said Marisa. "There's ads for them all over the city. Why do you ask?"

"Correct," said Bao. "If you've ever wanted to see one in person, La Princesa has one right over there." He pointed, and Marisa's mouth fell open as she looked. There she was: Francisca Maldonado, La Princesa de Mirador, with a bright purple MyDragon perched on her shoulder.

"They're here?" asked Marisa. It wasn't just La Princesa, it was the whole Maldonado family: Omar, Sergio, and in the middle of the group was Don Maldonado himself. The richest man in Mirador; the head of a massive crime family that ran the neighborhood like a personal kingdom. Don Maldonado and Marisa's father hated each other with an old but ever-burning passion, and that feud had shaped much of Marisa's life. Worst of all, they refused to even tell her how the feud began.

Hey, Mari. It was a new message, bouncing at the edge of Marisa's vision in a window she never closed: a private conversation with her best friend, Sahara. **Don't look now, but your favorite people are here.**

Just saw them, Marisa sent back. **And with a frakking MyDragon. Just to let us know how much richer they are than the rest of us.**

I'm wearing a bouquet of flowers on my shoulder, sent Sahara. **Franca's wearing a gengineered custom pet.**

I drove here in a taxi so old it still had a steering wheel, sent Marisa. **They look like they were carried here on a palanquin while someone waved palm fronds over their heads.**

"Earth to Marisa," said Bao. "Are you volleying insults with Sahara again?"

"I applied my own makeup in under five minutes," said Marisa out loud. "She looks like she has a closet full of 3D-printed faces, and just swaps them out whenever she goes somewhere."

"Don't compare yourself to them," said Sandro. "You'll just make yourself feel bad."

Why are they even here? sent Sahara.

Pati and Carlo Magno walked toward them through the crowd, with Triste Chango following behind like a box-shaped puppy.

"I couldn't find Bao but I found Papi—" yelled Pati, and then stopped instantly when she saw that Bao was already there. "Hi, Bao! Good to see you! Did you see Sandro's nuli? Isn't it awesome?"

Marisa smiled. At least Pati wasn't shy.

"I saw it," said Bao. "It's the best one here by a mile and a half."

"For all the good it's going to do him," said Carlo Magno, angrily shaking his cane toward the knot of people that had formed around the Maldonados. "Do you know why that chundo's here?"

"I was just wondering that," said Marisa, but she felt her stomach sink as she realized there was only one possible answer.

"He's the judge," said Carlo Magno, confirming her fears. "Don Francisco Maldonado is picking the winner of the science fair, and handing out the check with his own filthy hands, and do you think he's ever going to pick a Carneseca?"

"I think he'll let the work decide," said Sandro, but their father cut him off with a loud *bah*.

"You're a fool," said Carlo Magno. "A genius, but a fool as well. He hates us, and he always has, and no science project is ever going to change that. No matter how brilliant."

Marisa realized that she was clutching her metal arm with her human one. She'd lost the arm in a car accident when she was two years old, and the mysteries that surrounded that one event seemed to permeate every aspect of her life. The basic details were well known to everybody in Mirador: Don Francisco's wife, Zenaida, went for a drive—actually driving it herself, like people used to do before self-driving cars were the norm—and got into an accident. Nobody knew where she'd been going, or why, and since she'd been thrown from the car and died on impact, no one had ever been able to ask her.

But that's where things got weird. The first people to arrive on the scene had found three children in the car with her: Jacinto Maldonado, their second child, very nearly dead as well; Omar Maldonado, their fourth and youngest child, completely unharmed—and Marisa Carneseca, who had absolutely no reason to be there whatsoever. Her arm had been severed just below the shoulder.

Why had Marisa been in that car? Why had Zenaida been driving it manually? And why did any of that cause Don Maldonado and Marisa's father to hate each other so intensely?

Great. Holy. Handgrenades, sent Sahara. **That's not just**

the purple MyDragon, it's the iridescent purple MyDragon. They only made three of them!

Yeah, sent Marisa, and closed the chat window. She didn't feel like gossiping anymore.

"Good evening, Mr. Carneseca," said Bao, trying valiantly to cut the tension that had silenced the group. He reached out to shake his hand, and Carlo Magno absentmindedly shook back. "It's good to see you up and moving around."

"I'm doing my best," said Carlo Magno. "Well enough I don't need this stupid thing." He kicked feebly at Triste Chango, and it beeped cheerfully in response.

"We couldn't afford one of the really good livers," Marisa explained, "or even a midrange one. The cheapest ones come with a ten-week nuli rental to make sure nothing goes wrong. Hospital subsidy to help prevent lawsuits."

"Way to clip the coupons," said Bao.

Carlo Magno sneered at the Maldonados. "My wife couldn't even be here tonight because we can't afford to close the restaurant, and he brings his entire family."

Bao smiled. "I always forget how much like Marisa you are."

Carlo Magno and Marisa looked at each other, neither one certain if they liked that comparison.

"Not the whole family," said Pati. "Not Jacinto."

"Jacinto hasn't left home since the . . ." Carlo Magno looked at Marisa again, then gave another loud *bah*.

"Here comes another group," said Sandro. "Give me some room, I'm going to do my presentation again."

They moved to the side, away from the Maldonados, and

Marisa found her father a bench to sit down on. Triste Chango scooted in close. "Your heart rate is approaching the upper limits specified by your doctor. Please take deep breaths as follows: in, out. In, out."

Carlo Magno hit it with his cane.

Another message popped up from Sahara, and Marisa leaned her forehead against the wall. Why wasn't anything ever easy? Sahara sent a second message, and then a third, and the icon started glowing faintly red. Marisa blinked on it, and the messages exploded across her vision.

Ohmigosh.

Are you seeing this?

MARI, ARE YOU SEEING THIS?

Marisa frowned, confused, and sent a response. **Seeing what?**

Look at Don Francisco!

Marisa snapped her head around, searching through the crowd, but there were too many people. She craned her neck in various directions, trying to get a look at whatever Sahara was freaking about, and finally just stood on the bench next to her father. A space had cleared around the Maldonados, and a woman was talking to Francisco.

A woman holding a badge.

"What's wrong with you?" asked Carlo Magno. "Get down from there before a teacher sees you."

"It's a cop," said Marisa, still wondering what exactly was going on. "Don Francisco's talking to a cop."

"He talks to cops all the time," said Carlo Magno, "they're

practically his own private army. His son's the captain of the local precinct!"

"But that's not a Mirador cop," said Marisa. "I know all the locals. She's not in uniform, either. And she's not happy."

"Off duty?" asked Bao.

"She's showing him her badge," said Marisa.

Found her, sent Sahara. **I ran an image search through the LAPD database—her name's Kiki Hendel, and she's a homicide detective from downtown.**

Why is she here? sent Marisa.

How am I supposed to know?

"Maybe they finally got him," said Carlo Magno. "Maybe they finally caught him on some charge, and he's going to prison—taxes, maybe. That's how they got Al Capone."

"Who?" asked Pati.

"Tā mā de," whispered Bao, standing on the other side of the bench. "She's taking him away."

"What?" asked Carlo Magno. He stood up so fast that the bench unbalanced, and Bao and Marisa had to jump clear to keep from falling. The bench clattered to the ground, and Carlo Magno raised himself to his full height. "Are they arresting him?"

"It didn't look like it," said Bao, trying to stand the bench back up again. "Just . . . leading him outside."

What the what? sent Sahara.

I know! sent Marisa.

I'll see if I can get Cameron outside after him, sent Sahara, and across the room Marisa saw one of Sahara's small camera nulis rise up above the crowd and race toward the door.

"Look online," said Marisa, blinking on her djinni. "All of you—look for everything you can. What's in the news, what's going on here or downtown or at their estate in Mirador, what's going on with any of their investments or their enforcers or anything at all." She started running searches on the internet, going through all the local news blogs.

Hold up, sent Sahara. **What was his wife's name again?**

Zenaida, said Marisa, **but you're not going to turn up anything on her, she's been dead for fifteen years—**

Are you sure about that?

Marisa froze.

The LAPD found her . . . hand, sent Sahara. **At a crime scene in South Central. Her left hand, severed at the wrist, lying on the ground.**

Marisa couldn't move. She could barely comprehend the words in Sahara's next message:

I don't know what happened fifteen years ago, said Sahara, **but Zenaida was alive last night.**

ALSO BY
DAN WELLS

HUMANITY IS MAKING ITS LAST STAND

"One of the most compelling and frightening visions of Earth's future I've seen yet. I couldn't put it down."

—Pittacus Lore, #1 *New York Times* bestselling author of *I Am Number Four*

BALZER + BRAY
An Imprint of HarperCollinsPublishers

www.epicreads.com